# THE STORY OF VERONICA

*'Nobody goes so deeply down into a woman's heart or understands human passions so well.'*

In 1939 war clouds were gathering. Veronica Hallard, who had been happily married and living in Lagos with her husband Charles, was sent home alone. The ship in which Charles followed was torpedoed, and his loss was so great Veronica broke her heart. She suffered a complete nervous collapse, and her only consolation was the friendship of Boyd Mansell, who she had met on the voyage home. Two years later she had recovered enough to face normal life again, married again and had a son – then Charles returned from the dead!

# THE STORY OF VERONICA

FOR IRIS WHEATLEY

# The Story of Veronica

*by*

Denise Robins

**Dales Large Print Books**
Long Preston, North Yorkshire,
BD23 4ND, England.

British Library Cataloguing in [Publication Data]

Robins, Denise
    The story of Veronica.

    A catalogue record of thi[s book is]
    available from the Britis[h Library]

    ISBN   978-1-84262-724-2 pbk

First published in Great Britain in 1946

Published in Large Print 2010 by arrangement with
Patricia Clark for Executors of Denise Robins' Estate

Dales Large Print is an imprint of Library Magna Books Ltd.

Printed and bound in Great Britain by
T.J. (International) Ltd., Cornwall, PL28 8RW

# PART I

## 1

It was the chirping of the crickets all night long that had got so badly on Veronica's nerves.

When she first came out to West Africa with Charles nearly twelve months ago, she found it difficult to sleep because of the sticky heat. She had grown used to the heat, even though it devitalised her and reduced her normally abundant energy to a minimum. She could stand the heat. The fiercest sunshine failed to bring her to the state of sighing (or cursing) which was the ultimate condition of the average woman who came out to the West Coast. Even while she flagged, physically, she adored the sun. She found that she could bear the noonday heat better than the humid, breathless nights. But the incessant noise of the crickets seemed to penetrate her consciousness even when she was deadly tired. And finally it attacked her nerves. Eventually, without a sedative of some kind, she hardly slept at all.

'If only they would be quiet … just for an *hour*…' she would say to Charles, her husband, as they lay side by side on the two narrow beds under the mosquito-netting, and Charles would take her hand, kiss it, try to soothe her, and fall asleep himself almost at once; waking later to remorse and fresh tenderness for her when he found her still awake, smoke-grey eyes wide open, staring at the unearthly brilliance of the African moonlight.

And the crickets went on creating their incredibly persistent din ... making Veronica's head feel that it would split with pain and irritation. She fell asleep only when peace and quiet descended suddenly with the sunrise.

It was just before the rains came that Charles said that he had decided to send her home.

'You can't possibly go on like this, darling,' he had declared a week ago, after a sudden bout of fever had laid Veronica really low and taken away her last shred of humour. 'You've been cross for days. You're never cross in England. I'm not going to let this damned climate get you down. You've got to go back to England...'

Veronica Hallard remembered those words and the feeling of panic which had gripped her the moment Charles spoke. To leave Charles ... go home alone ... live without him. Oh, it was unthinkable. She said so, sitting up in bed in a fresh diaphanous nightgown (one of her trousseau) which was the third she had put on in the last hour. Her body would not keep dry. She was always drenched with perspiration which made her hair lank and lifeless and make-up a farce. She had held on to his coat with small, frightened hands and said: 'Charles, I can't ... I can't leave you. I'd die ... you know I would!'

They had only been married eleven months. They had come out to Lagos immediately after their wedding. They were still desperately in love. In love in a way which they both firmly believed was only given to a chosen few in this world. They had everything in common, mentally and physically. It seemed to them now, after the trying months out here together, just as it had seemed when they first met ... that they had been born for each other. It was a miracle, and to separate even for a little while would be a calamity.

Charles had taken her in his arms, smoothed back the damp dark hair which in England had looked so crisp and richly brown and had grown so dull out here; had closed her eyelids with his sensitive musician's fingers, and said:

'Don't look at me like that, Nic darling. Don't ... I can't bear it.'

'Then don't send me home,' she had said, breathing hard and fast, and her small perfect body, which he worshipped and which had grown so much too thin, was convulsed with weeping.

After that he said no more about her going home. If she could stand the infernal climate and country a bit longer, he'd try to get home with her himself, later in the year, he said. He didn't want her to be unhappy, God knew. And without her he'd be sunk himself. The bungalow would be hellishly lonely; the whole place intolerable.

So no more had been said. But Charles went about looking worried and Veronica recovered slowly from her fever, and although she tried to deceive him that she was sleeping better and feeling better, her face grew small and white and her eyes enormous.

If only she could *sleep...*

Veronica lay on her bed this afternoon on what seemed one of the hottest, most breathless days she had experienced here and looked out at a sky of burning blue; at the brilliant hues of the flowers twined in the creeper round the balustrade of the white verandah; at the glossy green of the tall giant palms; and she dreaded the night. She hated those baleful, winged insects of which she had not so far learned the names. They came in their dozens and flew round the bungalow as soon as darkness fell and the boy switched on the lights. She disliked the harsh chatter of the monkey which lived up in one of the nearby trees; and most of all the crickets. Chirrup ... chirrup ... chirrup ... all night long with a persistent monotony that drove one crazy.

Wearily she put a hand up to her head and thought:

'I must try to conquer this ... to sleep as Charles does. I *must* stay with him. If I break down he'll *have* to send me away ... and I couldn't bear it.'

She loved him so much. It was terrible, really, to love a human being quite as much as she loved Charles. Terrible and yet wonderful when that person loved you in the same way. Only it was never *quite* the same for a man as for a woman. Charles had his work. The plantation which had become his new concern. The production of *cacao*. Veronica would have been interested in the cocoa plantation if she had not felt so listless and nervy ever since she arrived in Lagos. It was such a shame. Charles had been so wonderful about it ... thrown himself into the job with such enthusiasm, and everyone said out here that he was doing marvellously. The District Commissioner had told her at dinner the other night that Charles might be a musician at heart but that he had a very good sense of 'business' as well, and an extraordinary aptitude for learning a new trade. Veronica, who always loved to hear

11

her husband praised, had said proudly:

'Oh, Charles is good at anything he does.'

The D.C. laughed and grimaced at his wife.

'Hear that, Letty? That's how I like to hear a woman speak of her better half. Take a lesson.'

Letty Chaddon, a small, insignificant-looking woman nearing forty (she had a strong constitution which Veronica envied her, and had been out in Lagos for two years with only one short break – a trip to Kenya), had grimaced back at her husband and snapped:

'Maybe that's how I would speak of you if you were as attractive as Mr Hallard…'

Charles had looked uncomfortable, but the D.C. laughed. He seemed accustomed to being sneered at by his Letty. People said they were really quite happily married. But Veronica could never bear a married couple being derogatory about each other in public … even in fun. It was such poor taste. And it couldn't be a sign of real love. Not the whole-hearted, overwhelming sort of love she and Charles felt for each other.

Women like Letty Chaddon, Veronica decided, could never have been in love *that* way. She was so cold and hard and prosaic. Mrs Chaddon had admitted it when they talked together while the men lingered over their drinks and cheroots in the dining-

12

room. She looked with curious, prying eyes at Veronica's exquisite black chiffon dinner-dress and gold and ruby clips, and said:

'Lord knows why you bother to get yourself up like that with only old Tom and me coming to dinner. You needn't bother in future. Just put on an old cotton frock, like me.'

Veronica had exclaimed:

'Oh, but I always dress like this … for Charles.'

Letty Chaddon, a cigarette sticking to her lower lip, laughed good-naturedly but with genuine amazement.

'You are a scream!' she said. 'I've never come across such a romantic girl. Properly keen on your husband, aren't you?'

Veronica remembered that later in the evening. Letty and Tom Chaddon had had a somewhat acrimonious discussion about finance … and she had ended by saying, 'Oh, shut up, you old idiot! You bore me stiff!'

Veronica supposed Tom Chaddon liked it. He laughed a lot. He was fat and amiable and unconcerned. But Veronica thought it dreadful. That wasn't what marriage had been intended for. Bickering … arguing … disparaging each other. Did the Chaddons still sleep together? Presumably. How awful … two such people who scoffed at romance. Veronica had mentioned it to Charles after

13

the Chaddons left.

'I'm glad we're not like that, darling,' she said.

Charles was switching on the radio – trying to tune into a station which was playing good music. He gave her that slow, sweet, lazy smile which made his faun's mouth go up at the corners and his dark, thoughtful eyes look warm and tender ... and said:

'Ah, but we're unique, darling ... we can't compare ourselves with other couples. I dare say old Chaddy and that ghastly memsahib of his are devoted in their own way. It just isn't *our* way...'

She had walked into his arms. He had put down the cheroot he had been smoking and holding her close, ran his lips down her cheek to her throat, shut his eyes and murmured:

'You smell so heavenly, darling...'

He was much taller than she was. She had to stand on tip-toe to touch his chin with her lips. He teased her about her smallness and always seemed amused by the special sandal shoes she wore with wedge-heels, coloured 'Joyce' shoes, sized two and a half. She raised her lips for his kiss, and then he lifted her and carried her into their bedroom. She had thought, with fast-beating heart: 'Oh, how lucky I am not to be a Letty Chaddon ... or one of her kind.'

Charles was an irresistible lover.

14

She had not tried to resist him … from the start. She lay on her bed this afternoon and went back in her mind over the last year of her life. It had been such a wonderful year.

She and Charles had met in London at a cocktail party given by their mutual friend, Iris Williams, at her flat in Sloane Street. Veronica and Iris were old school friends. Iris was married to Mervyn Williams, who was a regular officer in the Royal Artillery. They had just come back from Egypt, where they had been stationed for the last four years. This was the celebration of their return home. Iris, as small and attractive in her way as Veronica, was one of the 'chosen few' who, in Veronica's estimation, had married the right man. So crazy about her good-looking, amusing soldier husband. For no other man in the world, as she had often written to Veronica, would she have 'sacrificed herself' to an Army career. She hated having no settled home and being badgered from pillar to post, as is the fate of Army officers and their wives. But for Mervyn she managed it and 'coped' extremely well with all the vagaries of the unsettled existence.

This was her reward, she said… Mervyn had been sent to a special job at 'The Shop'. This Sloane Street flat was the first home she had been able to get together with their own furniture. At the housewarming, Veronica met Charles.

15

## 2

Veronica at twenty-four was leading rather a tiresome existence in Buckinghamshire with her parents, Sir Giles and Lady Lowring. She could not have said that she had had an unhappy childhood because she had always been devoted to her parents and they to her, their only offspring. Whitelands Hall, which had been her home since infancy, was a Georgian place of incomparable beauty, and Veronica was reared in luxury and sent to the best schools, finishing off in Paris. The conventional upbringing had been rounded off by her 'coming out'; her presentation at Court and a London 'season'.

She had a host of friends and a great many admirers. She had been, in fact, considered one of the 'catches' among the debutantes of her year, but she was ever conscious of the fact that she had been a great disappointment to her mother. Her father was very fond of her but did not attempt to understand her. He considered all women incomprehensible, anyhow.

Lady Lowring was an ambitious and determined woman. Having produced a beautiful daughter with a decided gift for music (Veronica played and sang with more than average talent), she had set her heart upon her making a brilliant marriage. Sir Giles, whom Veronica remembered always as being a vague, gentle person much older than her mother, and an ardent genealogist – steeped in heraldic art and literature – took little interest in his daughter's prospective marriage, or, indeed, in anything but his hobby. He let his wife do what she wanted. And what Beatrice Lowring wanted was for Veronica to marry money. Her own husband was a baronet, but more or less an impecunious one, and their limited income necessitated a persistent struggle to 'keep up appearances'. (It was of vital importance to Lady Lowring, who was an undiluted snob.) So she hoped ardently that her one and only daughter would make a sensible match and remember the importance of pounds, shillings and pence.

Perhaps it was because Veronica from her earliest childhood had listened to her mother talking 'money' and titles as well as her father stressing the significance of the 'family tree' that she had now a profound dislike of the whole thing. She was totally different from her mother. She had inherited her father's retiring qualities. And her chief passions in life were books and music.

Lady Lowring found it a well-nigh impossible task trying to make Veronica interested in anybody just because they

17

were 'well born' or 'very rich'. There were constant scenes at home because Veronica used to gather round her friends with little to boast about so far as either of these attributes went. Veronica liked people for themselves and not for what they were. People who could achieve things – who were artists, or musicians or writers – interested her most.

The results of her London season were bitterly disappointing to her mother, who never really forgave Veronica for turning down the proposals of two men whom she, Beatrice Lowring, considered most eligible bachelors. One was young Viscount Blentford (Lady Lowring wept with chagrin at the thought that her Veronica flung away the chance of being a future countess), and the other, a wealthy widower who had recently bought big estates near Princes Risborough where the Lowrings lived.

Veronica firmly refused to marry either of these suitors. Dicky Blentford was a chinless, spineless young man who bored her to tears; and the elderly widower was too old and mercenary, and his accumulation of wealth and pretentiousness merely disgusted her.

So time went on … and Veronica remained unmarried, living a somewhat dull life; enduring the social round which was forced upon her at home, using her music (she was still studying her singing) as an escape. Lady Lowring grumbled and cajoled in vain. Veronica was not going to marry until she found the right man.

One day when she was sitting at her piano, trying out a new song, her mother had come in and remarked bitterly that Veronica was 'letting the foolishly romantic tendencies and artistic streak in her ruin her life'.

'You're getting on, dear. You'll be left on the shelf if you are not careful,' Lady Lowring complained.

Veronica had smiled and said:

'Better that than marrying the wrong man, Mummy.'

But Lady Lowring couldn't see it. In her opinion, better the wrong man so long as the cash balance was on the right side. Oh, she wanted to *slap* Veronica for being so obstinate. She looked so small and lovely and gentle... And had such an *iron* will ... the stubborn, foolish girl. Who *would* she marry in the long run?

Sometimes Veronica asked herself the same question. Once she had met a man whom she thought she loved ... for a little while. Mario Cauucchi sang ... he had a fine baritone voice and was a pupil of old Madame Marchelli, who was also coaching Veronica. They had met several times. Mario was an ardent, handsome Italian. He fell madly in love with the small, shy English girl with her big grey, black-lashed eyes and gentle manner. He tried to sweep her off her feet and rush her into marriage. For a short space of time Veronica had thought this might be 'it'. It was her first experience of love... Mario was far from inexpert, and she thrilled to his kisses, his poetic letters and lavish attentions. Until one morning she entered Madame Marchelli's studio and found Mario there passionately embracing a pretty Norwegian blonde who was yet another of Madame's pupils.

That finished Veronica's first encounter with love. She walked out of the studio with a white face and a sick feeling of disillusionment in life and men in general. Nothing that the handsome Italian could say persuaded her to reopen the affair. Veronica firmly believed that love between a man and a woman must be based on trust. Without it, love could not survive. Her passion for Mario died.

She was hurt ... but not mortally. And she had recovered entirely from the pangs by the time she went to Iris Williams' party and met Charles Hallard.

She had heard about Charles from Iris, who telephoned one day to Princes Risborough and persuaded Veronica to come up to town for her party.

'We'll put you up, darling,' she said. 'Come for the night. It will do you good to

20

get away. And I've got a marvellous young man coming I'm sure you'll fall for. Charles Hallard is his name.'

'I don't want to fall for anybody,' Veronica had said, still just a shade embittered. 'I don't believe in love.'

'Don't be silly, darling,' Iris had laughed back. 'You know that's not true. Mervyn and I are still crazy about each other and you'll meet the right person soon. It might even be Charles...'

It was. Right from the start. Veronica, hands laced behind her head, lay on her bed in the intense sticky heat of the West African afternoon and recalled, dreamily, luxuriously, that first meeting with Charles and all that had followed. She could remember every detail of it. It meant so much.

She had gone to that party feeling no particular interest in the prospect of meeting Charles, although Iris had stressed his good looks, his charm and his love of music ... all of which Iris had imagined would appeal to her friend. Dear little Iris! With affection Veronica thought of her ... how worried she used to be because she thought it time Veronica got away from the home circle and her mother's influence and indulged, not in a schoolgirl romance such as she had had with Mario, but in a full-blooded, hundred-per-cent love-affair. She needed it, Iris said ... to wake her up ...

21

change the face of the world for her. She was young and lovely and she was wasting her gifts stuck away down there in the country.

Well, Charles had changed the face of the world for Veronica, sure enough.

She remembered going into the small green-painted drawing-room of the Williamses new flat overlooking Sloane Street; seeing nobody, for the moment, that she knew amongst this crowd. It was a real 'crush'. Iris and Mervyn had gathered together everybody they knew for their house-warming. It was a perfect June day. London was bathed in sunlight and Veronica wore a new linen dress and short coat perfectly cut. Lady Lowring made herself responsible for her daughter's clothes even then when she was adult. And she saw to it (with ulterior motives, of course) that Veronica was always beautifully dressed. Veronica was thankful later that day that she had put on the new linen, and the tiny blue straw hat with the palest of pale pink veils tied in Victorian fashion under her small round chin. Later, Charles told her that he watched her come into the room, took one look at the small slender figure and the enchanting face with the enormous smoke-grey eyes, and said to an old friend to whom he was talking at the moment: 'That's the girl I'm going to marry ... or I'll

22

never marry at all.'

Iris and Mervyn came forward to greet Veronica. Iris squeezed her friend's hand and whispered, enviously:

'You look a *knock-out,* darling ... you always do. You can sell me that divine suit when you're sick of it...'

Then without wasting time she had beckoned to Charles.

'Come and meet Veronica Lowring, who was at school with me and sings like an angel...'

Charles came towards Veronica, a half-finished cocktail in one hand, a cigarette in the other. The cigarette he hastily put on the nearest ash-tray. The drink he set down. He came up to Veronica and bowed in an almost old-fashioned way.

'How do you do?' he said.

She could feel, now, the extraordinary way her heart had missed a beat, and felt the colour surge into her face. He was very tall – and rather slender. He moved gracefully. One always noticed how graceful Charles was in all his movements, despite his six foot two. He wore rather shabby grey flannels which were excellently tailored and an old Etonian tie. His head was a shade darker than hers. Smoothly brushed with the merest suspicion of a wave lifting crisply from a broad, intelligent forehead. With swift perception she had noted that amusing

23

faun's mouth of his; the way his eyes crinkled at the corners when he smiled. Dark, searching hazel eyes. And the next thing she noted were his hands. Long, thin, expressive. He wore an onyx signet ring on the little finger and a gold wrist-watch on a broad white band around his left wrist.

He said, without waiting for Veronica to speak:

'I must get you a drink...'

Veronica murmured a few confused words. Charles went off, fighting his way through the crowd to the table on which the drinks were being poured out. Iris Williams whispered in Veronica's ear:

'Isn't he a knock-out, darling? I told you he was...'

And added a few swift details about him which Veronica only half took in. That he used to be very rich. That he played the piano and composed a little. That he had no parents living and had been brought up by his uncle and everybody had thought he was coming into the uncle's fortune. But the uncle had gambled away his money and died the other day leaving poor Charles a mere pittance. Wasn't it a *shame*! And now Charles had to do some work for the first time in his life...

Iris had no time to tell Veronica any more. Charles was coming back, carefully poising in the air a cocktail for Veronica. She found herself sitting in a corner, talking to him. She said very little, but listened, fascinated by his charming, modulated voice. He had a flair for facile conversation and making one laugh. He said a lot of witty things ... quick, clever criticism of various people in the room ... things which made her giggle delightedly. He had a gaiety of spirit which delighted her. She felt completely at ease with him. Shy, reticent men embarrassed her. She was herself so shy. But with Charles Hallard she just *couldn't* be.

He brought her out of herself ... made her talk to him. And of course they soon discovered their mutual passion for music and had no eyes or ears for anybody else in the room after that. Charles wanted to know all about her singing. She wanted to know what sort of music he composed. He told her that his ambition when he first came down from Oxford, three years ago, had been to write a piano concerto. He had gone to Dresden and Florence and studied in both places. Then he had come back to England to face the financial collapse following his uncle's sudden death. He, who had wanted to devote his life to music and spend the money which he thought he had on further study, found himself with a meagre income of £200 a year. The great concerto had to go to the wall. He must become a 'business man'...

Veronica's great grey eyes looked into his with warm sympathy.

'Oh, how awful for you!' she murmured.

But he smiled in his gay, insouciant fashion and said:

'Oh, it was good for me. I was getting lazy and spoiled. And I was damned lucky. I knew a fellow at Oxford who had business connections in Nigeria. He offered me a job on a cocoa plantation. I've been learning a bit about it and I sail for Lagos in September.'

'Lagos!' echoed Veronica. 'It sounds an awful long way away and a dreadful climate.'

He shrugged his shoulders.

'I don't know. One gets used to it, and this white man's grave theory is exploded, really. They've cleared up the swamps and the mosquitoes and it's much healthier than it used to be.'

Veronica said:

'I think you're awfully brave about it all. It must be grim ... growing cocoa ... when you want to write a marvellous concerto.'

'One day when I've got on top of my job and saved a bit of money I'll start composing again,' he smiled.

'I would like to see something you've written,' she said.

'And I'd like to hear you sing.'

'You must come down to my home, which is near Princes Risborough, and we'll have some music,' she added.

Eagerly he said:

'May I really? Do you mean that?'

Of course she had meant it. And long after all the guests had drifted away and the Williams' green drawing-room was empty and cooler, Veronica and Charles were still 'talking music'; recommending gramophone records to each other, exchanging views on the classics. Lagos and the cocoa plantation and Charles's misfortunes were forgotten.

Charles stayed on.

Iris and Mervyn – still in a 'party mood' – suggested that the four of them should go out and dine and dance somewhere.

They went to the Berkeley.

Veronica learned what perfect dancing was ... with Charles Hallard's arm around her. Afterwards, Iris teased Veronica about it all and said:

'Honestly, darling, Mervyn and I watched you two, and anybody would have thought you had both just found heaven ... you looked positively *enraptured.*'

That word really described Veronica's feelings. She *was* enraptured ... by Charles and by life tonight. The boredom of existence down in Buckinghamshire ... that foolish affair with Mario ... were wiped out. Everything that had passed before in her life was wiped out by this meeting with Charles.

It was ecstatic. And Charles appeared to feel the same. They danced every dance ... his bright handsome eyes scarcely leaving her small sweet face. He held her very close ... and once brushed her dark cloudy hair with his lips and whispered, stammering:

'Sweet ... Veronica... Oh, so sweet...'

Iris and Mervyn faded away early, apologizing for being 'tired', they said, and begged Charles and Veronica not to break up the evening but to stay on if they liked. So they stayed. But they didn't dance any more. They sat at their table looking at each other very seriously (surreptitiously holding hands). Charles said:

'Nothing like this has ever happened to me in my life before. I thought myself attracted by various women... I don't pretend I've had no affairs. But you... *God,* Veronica ... you go straight to my head. You intoxicate me.'

She remembered laughing, dizzy with happiness and pride.

'Why should I? ... there's nothing in me... I ... I'm so dull and insignificant and–'

But he would not let her go on with that speech.

'You're the sweetest thing I've ever met. I've never seen such glorious grey eyes. And you're so gentle ... you don't know how I hate hard-boiled young women. Veronica, you've done something to me tonight.'

She drew a deep breath and whispered back:

'You've done something to me, too...'

In the taxi, driving back to Sloane Street in the soft June starlight, he drew her into his arms and they exchanged long, deep kisses which sealed Veronica his ... for always. She had not known or dreamed that life and love could be so passionately sweet.

The next week-end, Charles went down to Whitelands Hall.

Lady Lowring, for all her hard worldliness, had not been able to resist Charles (no woman could, Veronica thought), he had such a way with him. When he sat down at her Steinway and played one of his own compositions, his face pale and serious with feeling, Veronica fell quite insanely in love with him. In return she sang to him Bach's 'Jesu, Joy of Man's Desiring' (he played her accompaniment), and he told her that she had a small sweet voice, as pure and passionless as a choir-boy's, and that he was crazy about it – and her.

That was the second time they met.

On the third occasion he asked her to marry him.

'I've no money. You've been brought up in luxury. And I'm shortly going abroad. What are we going to do?' he said. 'I adore you. You've got to marry me ... yet I ought not to ask you.'

But Veronica had no doubts as to what they were going to do. She had quite made up her own mind. It was this man ... or no other. If he had to go to Lagos, she would go with him. He argued that she couldn't stand the climate. She argued that she must try. She *must* go with him. The argument ended in each other's arms.

Delirious with happiness, they went down to the Hall. Charles approached Veronica's parents. Sir Giles had no particular views on the matter. Mildly he liked the charming young man whom he had heard once or twice playing the piano, and seen at mealtimes or in the garden. And Beatrice Lowring had to swallow her natural inclination to call the whole thing 'ridiculous' and refuse her sanction ... and accepted Charles as a future son-in-law. He was the reverse of the man she wanted for Veronica. No money, poor prospects. But he was undeniably attractive and, as she said to Veronica, a *gentleman*. He had Eton and Oxford behind him. His uncle, old Godfrey Hallard, had been well-known on Lloyd's. Of course, it was more than a pity that he had gone 'broke'. But that was not Charles's fault. No doubt with his intelligence he would 'get on'. She had better marry her impecunious musician, or cocoa-planter, and be done with it.

Once or twice Charles hesitated. He really

felt, he said, that he had no right to take Veronica. But when he so much as breathed such sentiments to her, he saw such a look of terror come into those dewy grey eyes of hers that he had to capitulate.

'Darling ... I'd *die* ... if you left me now,' she said.

'I'd die too if I had to go,' he said. 'We were born for each other and I'll try to make a good thing of my job, and be able to give you what you want ... what you deserve, one day.'

Veronica assured him that *he* was all that she wanted.

So they were married ... three months and a bit after they met. Lady Lowring with a sigh of resignation abandoned all the old ambitions for her daughter, gave her a lovely trousseau and insisted on a big wedding, which neither Veronica nor Charles wanted. They longed to be married very quietly and creep away. But as Veronica said, 'Mummy must have a break, poor dear...' so for her sake it was a 'splash' and photographed for all the papers and society magazines. At least it was a country wedding, which was nice. The reception took place in the glorious, flower-filled gardens of Whitelands Hall. Crowds of people came. Veronica wore white slipper-satin and her grandmother's Limerick veil and a Russian head-dress of pearls and orange blossom, and looked, Charles told her, like a little saint ... something too ethereal and lovely to be true. She carried a sheaf of lilies and stephanotis; around her slender throat a double row of pearls with a sapphire clasp which had belonged to her mother, and a diamond star on her breast which Charles had insisted on buying for her, even though he couldn't really afford it.

They did not go abroad for the honeymoon; they were due so soon to travel to West Africa. (That part of it horrified Lady Lowring, who was convinced that Veronica would never stand the unhealthy climate.) They spent a fortnight in a small, charming hotel on the borders of the New Forest. Charles in his shabby old flannels and Veronica in her exquisite linens lazed away most of the long summer days, touring the countryside in the old shabby two-seater Austin which Charles had managed to buy when he sold his own Rolls-Bentley at the time of the 'crash'. When he said: 'I wish to God I'd known and married you when I had money and a decent car, darling,' Veronica looked at him with her luminous eyes and said, 'I've no ambitions to have Rolls-Royces or money. I've *never* been so happy as I am now.'

It was true. He had never been so happy either. They savoured every hour of those long, golden days and the ecstatic silver nights ... tasting the very essence of life's meaning in one another's arms. Charles was the perfect lover. Veronica swift to respond. They fell more deeply in love with each other than ever.

In the little hotel they found a moderately good piano which nobody used, and when nobody was in Charles played and Veronica sang. It was her Schumann songs that he loved best. And he began to compose again … just a little. A theme for a new concerto which one day he would write. He called it 'Veronica's Concerto'…

She liked to watch him working … his dark hair untidy, ruffled over his eyes … pen moving with incredible swiftness over the sheets of music … slim body taut with concentration. She liked it when he flung the pen aside, drew her into his arms and said: 'I can't work when you're so near. I want to kiss you. Nic, I love you, sweet!'

She thought sometimes how incredibly dreadful it would have been if she had never met Charles, never married him.

On the last day of the honeymoon a telegram recalled Veronica to her old home. Her father had died quite suddenly of heart failure … a 'heart' which nobody had even suspected.

Charles took Veronica back to Whitelands and left her there. He had to get on with his job and he was due to leave London for the Gold Coast in a fortnight's time. He had kit

33

to buy and a lot to do. Veronica thought she ought to stay with her mother. Veronica grieved for her vague, kindly old father but could not be hypocrite enough to feel that his loss made any actual difference to her life. It was for her mother she felt most deeply. Sir Giles died as he had lived, a man of title and estates and little money. Lady Lowring as his widow would have to live even more quietly in the future. Whitelands Hall must eventually pass to Veronica's unmarried cousin, Digby Lowring, who was in the Guards and at the moment abroad. But there was a lovely old cottage on the estate and Beatrice Lowring intended to let the Hall for a year and move into the cottage once Veronica went abroad. It was just as well, she said ... she would not wish to live on in the big house with both husband and daughter gone.

Veronica felt a momentary pang at the thought of leaving her once-ambitious mother to 'come down' in the world, all alone; but Lady Lowring had grit and showed it. She pooh-poohed the idea that Veronica should make a sacrifice and stay with her. She must, of course, go away with her husband when Charles was ready to go.

On the last day of September 1938, Mr and Mrs Charles Hallard sailed for West Africa. A totally new life began for them both.

## 3

Those eleven months had brought great personal happiness to Veronica. Charles, too, she knew, was happy with her. Their voyage to the Gold Coast had been like a second and even more exciting honeymoon. And, upon reaching Lagos, like two gay, excited children they had explored together the mysteries of West Africa ... that strange hot land of harsh colours, fantastic birds and beasts ... slow-moving rivers infested with crocodiles, jungle-land and swamp, of sun-baked native villages, white modernized towns, white sandy beaches on to which rolled incredibly long white breakers which made surf-bathing a sheer delight. Land of exotic flowers and fruits, grinning black servants, colourful shops. Life at the Club. Bridge and race-meetings and tennis when it was not too hot. 'Sun-downers', 'smalls' – 'chop', and lazy evenings sitting on the verandah, doing nothing. An open-air cinema and, on occasions, an open-air dance. Parties at the Residency. A narrow social life. Drinks in somebody else's bungalow or in your own. The daily dose of quinine. The everlasting battle against the mosquitoes and white ants.

Life in Lagos. Far removed from the old

one in Veronica's English country home run by Lady Lowring ... or from Charles's studies at Oxford and on the Continent. An exciting life to begin with; eventually a boring one. No concerts or good plays. Everything weeks old – the papers, the magazines, the books. Clothes rotting with heat, silks eaten away by ants. The same faces ... day after day ... a nostalgia that came upon one very suddenly for England ... Piccadilly Circus ... Bond Street ... grey skies, a cool breeze and green, rain-wet lawns.

Veronica and Charles became simultaneously bitten with this home-sickness. But they were still happy ... until Veronica went down with fever and the nervous exhaustion out of which she could not, somehow, drag herself.

Wearily she stared at the merciless blue of the sky and listened to the harsh screech of a parakeet. She thought of Charles ... darling Charles ... down in his office on the cocoa plantation. He had been so good about it all and he hadn't been able to write a note of music for months. It was wonderful the way he had adapted himself to his new existence. He quite liked Lagos, he said. But she knew that already he longed to go home ... with her...

A knock on the door made her raise herself on one elbow.

'Come in,' she said.

36

Nicholas, their head boy, dressed in fresh white linen, came in, salaaming, showing his teeth in the usual wide grin.

'Massa coming soon?'

'Soon, yes. What is it, Nicholas?'

His grin broadened. He kicked one large bare brown foot bashfully against the other.

'Nicholas want more "dash".'

Veronica concealed a smile. Nicholas and his 'dash' always made her laugh. He meant that he wanted his weekly pay. This was his night out. Jack Jackson, the cook-boy, took his place when Nicholas was out. They were a hard-working pair, but a couple of rogues. Natural thieves, Charles said. Things were missed; asked for sternly by 'Massa' and mysteriously replaced the next morning. Dust could be found in many corners when looked for. Bananas and oranges were brought to Charles and Veronica and sold to them for a penny more than Nicholas ever paid in the market. But they let him have his little joke and gravely paid the penny, which gave him huge delight.

Veronica said:

'Massa come soon. Get bath ready…'

Nicholas, still grinning, nodded and departed.

Veronica got up and stretched her arms and took off the light cotton wrapper which she had been wearing. It was too hot for anything else. Now for a cool plunge and

37

then into one of the pretty dresses which made Letty Chaddon stare.

Veronica wished her head did not ache so badly. She must try not to let Charles see that she had a headache. But he always knew ... he knew every little detail about her ... her darling Charles.

The two boys came in together, carrying a bath-tub full of water, and set it down in the small room adjoining this large bedroom in which Veronica and her husband slept. One of the things she missed most was a proper bathroom and running water. The houses in Lagos had them, of course, but this plantation was twenty miles up-country. There were few amenities here except electric light. They had their own plant and – mercifully – a refrigerator and plenty of ice.

Veronica walked a moment out on to the verandah, and shading her tired eyes with a slender hand, looked across the garden through the tall palm trees ... across the violent wicked red of the 'flame of the forest' which grew out here so plentifully ... watching for her husband. In a moment he would be driving home in the old Ford. He would fling off his wide-brimmed *terai* and leap out of the Ford, up on to the verandah, into the bungalow and call for her, using the pet name which only he ever used.

'Nic ... Nic darling ... where are you?'

He couldn't bear to be home for a

moment without her by his side.

'I must get well,' Veronica thought, with a sudden stab of pain making her shut her eyes. 'I couldn't leave him.'

Charles was late this evening. He was usually home by five. Tonight not until six did Veronica hear the familiar scraping of the old Ford wheels on the gravel drive. She went out on to the verandah to meet her husband. It was hotter outside than in the big, spacious drawing-room where there were electric fans and green rush blinds to keep out the blinding sunlight.

She watched Charles get out of the car, throw off his hat and smooth back his dark roughened hair, just as she had known he would do. Her heart swelled with tremendous love for him… For an instant she forgot the pain in her head, her utter weariness and the fact that already the fresh gossamer lingerie she had put on was sticking to her damp thin young body. This steaming heat was remorseless. She said:

'Charles … *darlingest.*'

He came towards her. She was wearing a favourite *négligée,* filmy georgette as smoke-grey as her eyes, with a wide coral-coloured sash. There were corals in her ears and round her throat, which he had bought her in Lagos a week ago. A sophisticated affair … and she had put blue shadow on her eyelids and a lot of brilliant rouge on her rather wide, curved mouth. Yet along with the sophistication which he so loved was the almost childish simplicity and charm which drew the average man instantly to Veronica's feet.

Charles Hallard adored this small, sweet wife of his. He was ready to die for her, if necessary. This evening he looked at her with deep concern and the most profound feeling of depression because of the news which he must break to her. But first of all he kissed both her hands, then put an arm around her and drew her into the cool, shaded drawing-room.

'Let's have a drink, darling,' he said huskily. 'A nice long orange juice for me. What for you?'

'The same, darling...' She looked at him inquiringly. 'Had a good day?'

'No ... not very,' he said abruptly.

'Why?'

'I'll tell you in a moment,' he said. 'Let's look at you first. You're so lovely ... it's so refreshing to come back from the heat and dust and the din those damned blacks make ... and see you. Like a draught of spring water.'

'Oh, darling,' said Veronica, 'you say such sweet things to me always.'

He mopped face and neck with a handkerchief and flung himself on to the sofa. He wore white shorts and short-sleeved shirt.

He had not browned much out here. Naturally pale, he was still the same pale, slender, artistic-looking man whom Veronica had met at Iris Williams's party, only his skin these days – like Veronica's – had the faintest yellow tinge; result of the anti-malaria dope which the local doctor made them take regularly.

Charles Hallard was standing the climate comparatively well and quite interested in his job, despite his occasional nostalgia for home and his music. But it was Veronica's condition which worried him. Her insomnia … her losing so much weight. He knew that she should have gone home weeks ago. Now fate had taken it out of their hands. She would *have* to go.

Veronica seated herself at his side. He poured out the drinks which Nicholas had put ready on the small table. The room was cream-painted, with green chair-covers and curtains and full of flowers. Veronica adored flowers and arranged them charmingly. They had managed to hire an old and worn-out piano. On it stood a bowl of magnificent orchids and Charles's own leather-framed, full-length photograph of Veronica in her wedding dress.

He took a long drink then set down his glass with a sigh and caught one of Veronica's small hands in his.

'Oh, darling,' he said. 'Damn and blast!'

At once she knew that something was wrong. Charles never came home in a serious or despondent mood, but always with a gay smile ... a jest ... a 'Thank God I can be with you now, my sweet...'

Her large grey eyes instantly registered panic.

'Charles, what's happened, darling?'

Keeping her hand in his, he looked down at it. He had been fascinated the first time he met her by Veronica's absurdly small hands. Like a child's, with fragile wrists. He said:

'Nic, my sweet ... you haven't read the papers lately, have you?'

'Papers?' she echoed vaguely. 'No ... only the old *Times* Mummy sends us... I scarcely ever look at our local rags. But why, Charles darling?'

'We've been away from home a year, Nic. Things have been brewing in Europe. We just haven't taken much notice. But I've read the papers at the Club and talked to fellows who've just come out. One in particular I met last night who was in Germany a month ago. There's a fellow called Hitler out there ... you know all about the Munich crisis just before we left England.'

Veronica's small sweet face looked serious but still vague.

'Yes, darling. But I don't know much. Ought I to?'

42

'Yes, darling. I suppose it would be better for us all if we took more interest in politics abroad – and at home,' said Charles, with a grim look on his face that Veronica had never seen there before. She did not like him to look like that. It aged him. She liked it when he was gay; when the corners of that clean-cut mouth of his turned up; and his brilliant hazel eyes were smiling. She felt definitely alarmed.

'Oh, Charles, what is it?'

'War, darling,' he said, in the same grim voice. 'It looks as though there's going to be war. You do know, don't you, all about the *Anschluss* ... the trouble in Austria – in Czechoslovakia?'

'Yes...' (still rather vague). 'But I'm not very intelligent about these things, Charles darling. I feel I ought to be, but I've *never* taken the slightest interest in European squabbles.'

'This is going to be more than a squabble, sweet. Nazi Germany, run by Mr Hitler, wants war. They may declare war on Poland and we shall be drawn into it.'

Veronica stared at Charles.

'England ... war ... but, *darling!...*'

He dropped her hand and stood up, hands in his pockets, and began to walk restlessly up and down the long room without looking at her.

'Sweet, I'd better come to the point. I've

been talking to Phillips...' (that was Charles's 'chief'), 'and he seems to know a bit more than most of us out here. He has contacts in Berlin. He advises me to send you home ... at once, and I'm going to take his advice.'

Veronica went white under the delicate rouge which she had rubbed into her already pale face. So white was she now that the colour stood out suddenly on the cheekbones which recently had grown so much more defined. Her heart seemed to miss a beat, then jerked unevenly. She looked at her husband aghast.

'*Charles!*' she exclaimed again.

He stopped and looked down at her gloomily.

'I know. It's hellish, sweet. But Phillips is right. If we're going to have a war – you've got to get home before shipping becomes difficult. You are not strong. This climate is killing you by inches. It's rather settled the problem that's been weighing heavily on my mind for some weeks. The problem about you staying in this damp heat out here any longer. Eleven months has been more than enough. They don't generally let the chaps stick it for longer than eighteen months. It wouldn't do for you to be stuck here because of transport. The doc agrees. You've got to go home at once ... and stay with your mother until I can join you, darling.'

There. It was out, and one of the most difficult speeches Charles Hallard had ever had to make in his life. He loathed making it. In so doing he was sending from him the most precious thing in his life. But it was for her sake. It must be done. He hated to see that look of dismay on her face, the sudden pinched look about her lips. He added quickly:

'I'm sure to be able to join you quite soon. I know I will. If there's a war, a lot of things will crack up out here and I may even come home before my time's up. In any case, I'm due for a holiday in England round about Christmas.'

Veronica stood up, swallowing hard. Her lips were quivering.

'I see,' she said, in a small voice. 'You really mean I've got to go now, Charles?'

'Phillips and the doctor both advise it, sweet.'

'Do you ... want me to?'

'Darling!' he said, and caught her close. 'You know damn well how I feel. It's the last thing I want. But I couldn't let you be caught out here in this filthy climate ... should trouble in Europe flare up, as everyone thinks it will do.'

'But we couldn't have another war with Germany. Daddy used to say it was impossible again in our lifetime.'

'I know that's what most people say. But

45

Phillips and that fellow from Berlin think differently.'

Veronica put both arms round him and hugged him close, her cheek pressed to his shoulder.

'Oh, Charles ... if there was war ... and we were *separated!*'

He tried to comfort her by assuring her that the separation would not be for long. He would join her at Christmas at the latest. Maybe even before. She would have time to get well and strong before he saw her again. She would put on weight and get some colour back into those white cheeks. Genuine colour, not Elizabeth Arden; he tried to laugh and make her laugh with him.

'Come on, sweetheart; chin up ... smile at me.'

She shook her head dumbly, burying her face against his neck.

'Oh, Charles!' was all she could say in a muffled voice.

He kissed the top of the dark head on top of which the little curls were pinned in a Victorian bunch, and tied with a coral ribbon. He had so often seen her pin up those curls, taking the greatest pains to look lovely ... for him ... never to let herself grow careless and slovenly and unfashionable ... like Letty Chaddon and her kind. He adored her because she was always so fresh, so fragrant, this small wife of his. It would be more than grim here in the bungalow without her. No Nic in one of her charming trousseau *négligées* or dinner-dresses, waiting on the verandah, watching for his car ... no lovely lazy evenings spent at their piano together ... no sweet choir-boy's voice, pure and high, singing his favourite Bach or Schumann *Dichterliebe*. (Damn those infernal Germans! ... they produced the greatest musical geniuses in the world ... as a nation they were second to none in musical creation ... he had loved every moment of his life as a student in Dresden... Why must they let this bullying martial side lead them into these damned wars...?)

He heard Veronica's muffled voice:

'Let me stay ... please let me stay ... darling...'

'No,' he said rather roughly. 'I can't allow you to risk it, and see you go down in health in front of my very eyes. The spirit is willing, my darling, but the flesh is weak. Lagos doesn't suit you, you must admit. You've fought a grand battle, but you've got to give in now. As a matter of fact, I've booked a cabin for you ... on the Elder Dempster liner – their next available ship ... you've got to pack up and be ready. And you won't be alone. One or two of the fellows in Government jobs out here are sending their wives home.'

Veronica drew away from her husband's

arms. Her heart had sunk to its lowest. She felt numb, it was all so sudden, so frightfully unexpected, she thought. But now that Charles had come right out with facts, she knew where she was. She knew that she had to go. And she was vaguely ashamed because she had been so immersed in her own emotional life, so steeped in personal happiness with Charles that she had not bothered to read the news, to notice that the clouds of a new and terrible war were sweeping across the world's horizon. *Another war.* Why, Charles might be in this war, too. He was young … and strong…

Now a new and very real fear darted into Veronica's sensitive young mind.

She looked at her husband with dilated eyes.

'Charles … will this war … if it comes … affect *you?*'

He looked not at her but at the point of his cigarette.

'I don't know, darling. I haven't thought. I don't imagine it will … of course, it's too early to say … anything much. But let's get over one stile at a time, Nic darling. The first thing is for me to get you safely back to England.'

'You couldn't possibly come with me?'

'Out of the question, darling. I'm needed here and I'm not due for home for another six months. You know that.'

48

'Yes. I only ... hoped...' she said, in a desolate little voice that wrung his heart.

He said:

'Oh, Nic sweetheart ... don't make it too hard for me.'

That made her flush and square her shoulders. She could see that it was her duty to make light of this, if possible. It was futile to fight against his decision to send her home. If she loved him, she would help him. She *must.* It was not easy for her. The soft romantic side of Veronica was and always had been so much uppermost. To go back to England without Charles seemed a major calamity in her life. She shrank from the idea of so much pain and grief. But she accepted what he wanted for her, knowing that it was wise – and inevitable. She said:

'All right, darling. I ... I'll go. I'll be all right. You needn't worry.'

He looked at her with gratitude. He knew his Veronica and how hard this was for her. He himself hated the thought of the parting so much that he was indeed grateful for her co-operation, her show – no matter how small and pitiful – of courage. He said:

'That's wonderful of you, darling.'

She gave him a set little smile.

'We'll have a lot to talk over. Hadn't you better go and have your shower and change now, darling? Dinner will be ready at eight.'

He glanced at his watch.

'Right. I won't be long. Where's that scoundrel Nicholas?'

'He's off tonight, really, but he's hanging about somewhere waiting for more "dash",' said Veronica – maintaining her effort to be normal, even bright.

She watched Charles walk across the long room and through the archway into the hall. She loved the way he moved ... the lithe grace of him. She stood still a moment, staring at the bowl of flowers on the old grand piano, then let her gaze wander slowly round the room. She could not believe that she must leave it all ... perhaps never see it again. It wasn't that she particularly liked Lagos. There was so much about West Africa that depressed her and the climate was definitely making her ill. But this had become her home with Charles. The first home they had shared. She had grown used to it. And she had grown so much *into* him. Spiritually as well as physically, they were one. Leaving him would be almost unbearable.

She fought against the inclination to give way, to burst into tears, to run into the bedroom and beseech Charles to change his mind. It cost her a lot to conquer that wild impulse. She *must* be good about it; she must help him, as he had asked.

## 4

When Charles came back into the sitting-room, he found Veronica sitting at the desk, writing. She looked up and smiled at him. He looked cooler and delightful, she thought ,in the fresh white drill suit which he wore in the evenings with a silk, open-necked shirt. His dark head was brushed and shining, cheeks smoothly shaven. The charm of this man whom she had loved at first sight was a poignant thing tonight, touched with grief because she must go from him. But her smile persisted. She said:

'I've been jotting down all the things I must do tomorrow. I'd better ... take all my clothes, hadn't I, darling?'

He nodded, lighting a cigarette.

'Yes. You won't come back. I'll be coming home to you.'

She looked blindly at the list she had been trying to compile.

'When ... will I go, do you think, Charles?'

'They thought in four or five days there will probably be a boat, and you'll get on it. You may have an uncomfortable journey and have to share a cabin with a few other "wives", darling, but it can't be helped.'

'As soon as four or five days? Oh, Charles!' she said, dismayed. Then without looking at him, added:

'It won't be like the voyage we had coming here, will it?'

'I'm afraid not, darling,' he said gently.

They were silent a moment, both remembering so many details of that wonderful fortnight they had spent at sea on their way out to Lagos ... their real honeymoon, Charles had called it... They had had a state cabin and it had been a smooth trip. They had called in at Madeira. What a lovely time they had had together on shore! He had bought her masses of carnations and filled her cabin with them. He was a wonderful lover, she thought, and her throat ached with remembrance. And he looked at the small brown head bent over the desk and recalled the utter sweetness of his young bride on that voyage; how utterly absorbed she had been in him ... in his forthcoming job ... in their future...

'I'm afraid it will be a rotten trip back for you, sweet,' he spoke again. 'I shall have a dreary one, too, without you.'

'Charles,' she said, without daring to look at him, 'if war does break out ... won't it be dangerous ... travelling? I mean ... there'll be submarines and mines ... awful things ... like there were in the last war.'

'Oh, we'll soon settle Germany,' said Charles Hallard loftily. 'No need to worry your darling head about that.'

She did not question what he said. She was thinking:

'Only four or five days more with him. How *awful*... I can't believe it...'

'Darling,' said Charles, 'I'll try to get off from the office after lunch tomorrow and help you pack.'

Now she turned her head and looked at him with something of the old glow in her grey eyes. He adored that quick responsiveness from Veronica.

'How lovely!' she exclaimed.

'I've got to be there in the morning,' he added. 'We've a fellow coming from the Colonial Office to see us about "swollen shoot".'

She got up and walked to him, and he put an arm around her and kissed the top of her head.

'What on earth's that, darling?' she asked.

'A cocoa pest, my sweet ... and rather a dangerous one. We've got to find a way of stamping it out.'

'Tell me about it,' said Veronica.

They sat down together on the sofa, talking about his work, both deliberately avoiding the subject of her coming departure. They were smiling – and unutterably depressed. They were still smiling to comfort the other when Jack Jackson, their No.2 Boy, came in, grinning, to announce that the evening meal was served.

Much later that night Veronica lay in her small white bed beside Charles – struggling desperately, as had been her habit lately, to sleep. The humidity now was unbearable. It seemed to crush and suffocate her. She felt as though she were enveloped in a hot fog. There was no glass in the windows, they opened on to the verandah; rush blinds keeping out the sunlight. They had been lifted now to let in as much air as possible during the night. The big spacious bedroom was flooded with the brilliant moonlight which unfortunately was a further deterrent to sleep for Veronica. How she envied Charles! He lay sleeping as soundly as a tired child. She could see his face, carven, marble pale in the moonlight; one untidy lock of black hair, Byron-like, tossed across his forehead. He slept, as was the custom of men in this country, with only a towel wrapped about his loins. She could look with adoration at his lithe, pale body with the wide shoulders and narrow hips; the long straight legs. His physical perfection was always a source of delight to the artist in her. And she had begun to deplore the fact that she herself was fast losing so many of the rounded, delicious curves which he admired. She was painfully thin nowadays. Perhaps it was just as well, she reflected, that she was going back to a normal climate. She must, before Charles saw her again, get rid of the hollows in her throat, the sharp outline of shoulder-blades.

She tossed and turned, her chiffon nightgown already damp with perspiration. The crickets were creating their usual maddening din. And in the distance the thunder rolled … a low, warning growl. She hated the violent thunderstorms out here, but had grown almost used to them. They were so continual.

She thought of what lay ahead of her: the hateful parting from her husband, the journey home with all the other 'wives', on a boat which was more than likely to be packed with women and children who were also being sent home. A disagreeable prospect. Far, far rather would she have stayed her and put up with this devastating heat and the insomnia. But as Charles had pointed out this evening, insomnia, if not cured, can soon lead to other evils. She would soon become really ill and have to go into hospital. What use then would she be to Charles?

With passionate intentness she looked at the slumbering man … stared until something in the marble pallor of his limbs, his stillness, frightened her. It was a stillness reminiscent of *death*. Veronica's imagination ran away with her. She began to brood on the possibilities of Charles dying before she saw him again. Dying suddenly of fever …

or snake-bite ... or some strange tropical disease, contracted once he was out here alone with no wife to look after him. Or he might go home in the midst of a new and terrible war ... and be torpedoed... Charles, her lovely vital Charles, drowned and dead ... never to take her in his arms again.

One ghastly fear after another gripped Veronica's over-tired mind until it became too much for her. She sat up, pushing the damp silky hair back from her hot little face, and said, piteously:

'Oh, Charles ... *Charles*...'

At once he was awake, blinking at her, sliding his legs over the side of his bed. He pushed the hair out of his eyes.

'Darling ... what is it?'

She could not speak for a moment. He saw her, face screwed up like an unhappy child's and the gleam of tears on her lashes. Immediately he was lying beside her, drawing her near him, smoothing back her damp, tumbled curls.

'My darling ... my love ... what is it?'

He could not bear to see Veronica in tears. She was not one to cry, nor complain. He knew that she had suffered many physical discomforts since she had been out here and in particular from blinding headaches due to her inability to sleep. But he seldom heard her grumble. She maintained stoutly that she was well and gloriously happy with

56

him. The latter he believed. The former he knew was sheer bravado, because she did not want to worry him.

He could feel the thin young body trembling and the wetness of her tears on his bare shoulder. He was filled with pain for her ... and for himself.

'I know, Nic,' he whispered. 'I know how it is, darling. But you mustn't fret. You must be brave. You've been so marvellous out here. Try not to be too unhappy about our separation. Try, darling ... for me...'

She clung to him in dumb despair. He kissed her tear-drenched eyes and quivering lips, murmuring his love for her, seeking to comfort her ... in need, himself, of comfort. The last thing on earth Charles Hallard desired was to send this small adorable creature whom he had married away from him.

'Darling, darling, be brave,' he kept whispering. 'It won't be for long, I swear it. I'll be home within six months and possibly before, if the war changes things out here.'

She swallowed hard.

'I ... I'm sorry to be such an idiot, darling Charles.'

'You're not an idiot, sweetheart. You're altogether adorable, and I adore you and always will. We've had a glorious year together, Nic.'

'Don't speak as though it's all past. There

must be much more ahead for us.'

'Of course there is, darling.'

She swallowed again, trying to stop crying. 'I ... I'll miss you so awfully.'

'I'll miss you too ... like hell.'

'You will take care of yourself, won't you? You'll make Nicholas and J.J. look after you properly ... air your clothes ... everything...?'

'Yes, everything, darling.'

'Darling, we can write to each other every day, too.'

'Every day,' he soothed her.

She was calmer now, drew away from him to blow her nose, and managed to laugh a little.

'Do you know, you've written very few letters to me, darling. We've never really been separated since we first fell in love.'

He picked up one of her hands and drew it across his lips.

'I know. It was a damned lucky chance meeting you that evening, Nic. I very nearly didn't go to Iris's party. I don't like cocktail parties. But Iris insisted. She said she had an absolute knock-out of a girl for me. And when you walked into the room ... oh, lord! ... I can see you now in that blue linen suit ... that little hat ... the pink veil tied under your little chin... I looked at you and I said to myself, "Charles old boy, you've struck oil..."'

Veronica was laughing in earnest now, hugging her knees with her bare, thin young arms.

'Oh, Charles ... did you really say that?'

'I did, my sweet.'

'But you didn't strike oil, really, darling ... only cocoa.'

They laughed together at the absurdity. Veronica's volatile spirits were rising again. It was so lovely, diving back into the past and remembering that first glorious meeting with Charles. She thought further back still ... of her old life at home ... of Whitelands Hall ... poor Mummy living alone now at Monks Rest. She supposed that she, Veronica, would be going back to live at Monks Rest with Mummy until Charles joined her. It would be lovely down there in Buckinghamshire at this time of year and the cottage was charming; Veronica preferred it, really, to the larger house. It would be wonderful, really, after the damp, sticky heat, the brooding skies, the fierce sunlight, the violent contrasts of life out here in West Africa. And yet ... she would so gladly have stayed here in order to be with *him*. She began to think about leaving her husband again. She heard him say:

'Tomorrow you must cable your mother to expect you home. She'll be pleased. It must have been lonely for her after old Sir Giles went...'

Vaguely Veronica answered:

'Yes, of course.'

'I don't know what she'll say when she sees what a little ghost Lagos has made of you, my darling,' added Charles in a remorseful voice. 'She never did approve of me, and now...'

'Oh, she did ... she adored you, Charles!' Veronica had to interrupt now.

'Me, but not my money or position,' he laughed.

'Oh, she got used to it, darling. In her last letter she said she was very glad that I was married to you because I seemed so ideally happy.'

'Are you?' He was lying back on the pillow, the faun's smile on his clean-cut lips.

A great wave of love engulfed her. She threw herself upon him and his arms caught her close. She said, with her lips against his ear:

'Terribly, terribly happy. I love you so much.'

'Sweetheart,' he said, 'nothing can ever separate us really. You know that. I shall be with you in spirit – wherever you go; whatever you're doing. You'll never really be alone or without me.'

She pressed her cheek to his. He could feel the small slim body trembling. Passion mounted in him ... his lips turned to hers. He said:

'Nic … darling, *darling*… I want you…'
They had never loved each other more passionately or completely than that night.


## 5

The necessity to keep a stiff upper lip during those next few days imposed more of a strain upon Veronica than she had ever imagined it possible to stand without breaking down. But she went through it extraordinarily well, strengthened mainly by the knowledge that if she did give way it would upset Charles. For his sake she must 'keep going'.

It was exactly five days before the Elder Dempster liner called at Lagos and took Veronica away. During that time she was, fortunately for her, perhaps, almost too busy to sit down and grieve. There was so much to be done. So much sorting and packing and letter-writing to be got through.

The cable to Lady Lowring had been sent and Veronica received a joyful reply. *More than delighted. Mummy.* She was touched by that. After all, she was lucky to have a mother and home to go to, and Mummy had been so much alone this last year, she would benefit by this affair, if nobody else did, Veronica thought wryly. And she, Veronica, must now look upon it as her mission in life to cheer poor Mummy up

61

once she was back in England.

To make matters harder for Veronica, Charles was more than ordinarily busy that week. The conference which was being held by representatives of the Nigerian and Gold Coast Agricultural Departments in Tafo happened to take place at this psychological moment, and Charles, much to his disgust, was forced to attend it and leave Veronica alone for two whole days. The loss of two such precious days immediately before her departure was a blow to them both. But Charles had a job to do and his chief particularly wanted him, so he could not get out of it. He was a little astonished by the manner in which Veronica behaved just before he left by 'plane for the meeting. He was hot, overworked, worried about current affairs in Europe, and depressed by the thought that he was so soon to bid farewell to his beloved Nic. He cursed cocoa and its diseases and everything connected with growing it. But Veronica was cheerful and saw him off with a bright smile.

'I shall need two full days without a great man about the house to think of. And I shall probably sleep much better when I'm with the Chaddons. I shan't have you beside me. You're always so exciting, darling,' she said, with a little laugh.

He kissed her gloomily and went off to Tafo. He knew his Nic. Without a doubt, she was just being 'brave'. There were tears behind that smile of hers. But it was a help, he had to admit, to see the smile and feel that she was making the best of a bad job. He was full of admiration of her, and went to the conference with a burning longing to get back to Veronica again.

She, as he had known full well, felt none of the cheerfulness she had exhibited and was sunk in gloom the moment her Charles had gone. Two whole days without him! How awful! Their first parting, even for so short a time, since their marriage. And this was Wednesday, and on Sunday that wretched boat would be in. She would have to leave him for a much longer time. Oh, why had there to be a campaign against cocoa diseases just at this very instant!

She was staying these two nights while Charles was away with the Chaddons. He did not want her to sleep alone at their own bungalow. She was being fetched by Mrs Chaddon in the car at half past four. Charles's 'plane had left Lagos at two. For an hour or so, she could continue with the packing which was still only half done. On Charles's advice she was taking back several cases of linen and some of the wedding presents they had brought out here. If there was to be war ... and the news was bad ... things looked blacker than before ... it might be difficult to get one's possessions

63

back to England. So these must be packed as well as Veronica's personal things.

Letty Chaddon was going back to England by the same boat. Veronica did not care for Mrs Chaddon, nor understand her. But this was a time in which the touch of hardness in the unromantic and practical Letty was a blessing in disguise. Veronica needed the firm hand and sound common sense of the older woman. She was, she knew, far too soft and vulnerable herself. She could not think about war in Europe or dangers abroad or anything but leaving Charles. But Letty was entirely material-istic. She had said, only last night when the Chaddons came for a drink:

'I think it'll do old Tom a world of good managing without me for a bit. Show him how useful a wife is about the place. As for me, if there's a war on when we get back, I'm for a job. I drove an ambulance in the last war and I'm not too old at forty-five to drive one in the next.'

Veronica had looked at her with amaze-ment and awe.

'Oh but surely you'll want to see what happens to Chaddy? I mean, if he got back to England, you'd want to be with him, and if you were away driving—'

Letty Chaddon interrupted with a shout of laughter and grimaced at the D.C.

'Isn't she sweet, Tom? Just a piece of sugar.

Wouldn't you like a wife like that? I bet she'll write to Charles every day when she goes.'

'Certainly I will!' said Veronica.

'Well, Tom'll be lucky if he gets one a week,' announced Mrs Chaddon triumphantly.

The D.C. shrugged his shoulders and grinned.

'Good old Lettice! Don't you listen to her, Veronica. You stick to your romance.'

Veronica fully intended to. But she did recognize the fact that women of Lettice Chaddon's type were the backbone of the British Empire. Behind all that harshness and seeming indifference to love, no doubt she was sincerely fond of her big, genial husband, and her efficiency was awe-inspiring to Veronica. Everything in the Chaddon household was fixed and ready; all cases packed. And she had a definite streak of kindliness which she showed Veronica in this hour which she knew to be a difficult one for the girl who was so crazily in love with her handsome young husband.

When Mrs Chaddon arrived at the Hallards' bungalow she found Veronica looking white and listless, struggling with a case of books and some of Charles's music manuscripts. Letty Chaddon immediately took note of the situation. This 'ridiculous girl' as she called Veronica, with her great grey eyes and tiny hands and feet and absurdly glamorous clothes, had at first annoyed Lettice. She had told Tom she thought her 'soft' and that all those baby ways of hers were 'put on' just to attract men. But after months of close association with Veronica out here on the West Coast, which was a difficult place even for a seasoned traveller, Mrs Chaddon had changed her mind. She had come up against courage and sweetness in the girl's nature and had been more than once astonished by her absolutely sincerity. It was not all a pose. It was the real thing, this incurably romantic side of Veronica ... and her passionate adoration of Charles Hallard. It embarrassed Letty Chaddon a little. Even twenty years ago when she had first loved and married Tom Chaddon it had not been love of *that* kind; doubtless she would never experience the 'roses and the raptures' which coloured Veronica's whole existence. She was and always had been too cold and reserved, and marital bliss had always seemed to her an overrated pastime ... fond though she was of Tom. He, himself, was scarcely a romantic man. He used to say even in their early days that a good pipe and a game of snooker held more charm for him than what he vulgarly liked to call a 'canoodle' in the back of a car. Letty Chaddon supposed that they were just an average British couple, lacking imagination. On the contrary, Charles and Veronica Hallard appeared to have stepped right out of the pages of a sentimental book. What had at first irritated her had soon begun to amuse Letty. She always had been feminine enough to appreciate the good looks and charm of Charles. And in the end she could no longer resist Veronica's appeal. That 'ridiculous girl' was really a pet.

The Chaddons were a childless couple. What latent maternal streak Mrs Chaddon possessed began to assert itself ... towards Veronica, and she was genuinely sorry for her this week, being torn away from husband and home. But it was necessary, and whatever was necessary in Mrs Chaddon's opinion should be done with as little fuss as possible. Tom said there was a war brewing and that it was the accepted opinion out there that the women should go back, so back Letty was going without demur. But she could see how hard it was on a girl like Veronica.

She had been edified this week by the way in which Veronica was trying to keep cheerful for her husband's sake.

'Poor little brute,' she thought this afternoon, as she looked at the girl. 'Really, it's all beginning to get *me* down. I shall go all soft and potty on Tom if I'm not careful. It's positively infectious.'

She greeted Veronica in her usual loud,

boisterous fashion, wiping her steaming red face.

'Goodness, it's warm today. What *are* you doing, Veronica, lifting all those heavy books? Where's the boy?'

'Nicholas doesn't know which books I want. I simply have to get down to it myself,' said Veronica.

Lettice glowered at her, but her eyes were kindly. Silly creature, she thought, in her childish cotton frock, with bare brown legs and red sandals; brown curls tumbled, threaded through with a ribbon. Looked about fourteen … and just about to have an attack of something. White-faced little ghost! Time she got back to the old country. All that rubbish about not sleeping. It took more than a pest of noisy crickets to keep Letty Chaddon awake.

'Come on,' she said tartly, put down her shopping basket and held out both hands. 'I'll help you. We don't have to go back, Tom won't be home for another half an hour. Let's finish this damn case.'

Gladly Veronica allowed Letty to take charge. In a few moments the books were packed. They were Charles's favourites and hers. On top, they put the precious music manuscripts. Charles's own works. Veronica looked at these sorrowfully.

'It's so awful,' she said. 'I shan't hear him play for so long. Oh, Letty, six months *is* a long time.'

'Nonsense,' said Letty briskly. 'Anybody'd think it was six years to hear you talk. Tom and I were apart for two years soon after we got married. He went out to Canada and I stayed with my old father who was dying at the time, and in the end didn't die but became a permanent invalid, and as my mother was dead he had no one but me, and I couldn't join my husband who was doing good business in Vancouver. Months ran into years before I saw him again. But it passed.'

Veronica shuddered.

'Two years without Charles... I couldn't *bear* it...'

'Nonsense,' smiled Letty Chaddon. 'You could.'

'Never,' said Veronica with conviction.

Mrs Chaddon shook her head. She had not really grown used to Veronica's exaggerations, even though she knew they were founded on sincerity.

Veronica, glad of the respite in the damp and grilling heat, sat back for a moment and watched Letty continue with the packing. The precious concerto ... as far as it had been written ... the earlier sonata for piano and violin which he thought one of his best works ... and that little song he had written for her recently... Her gaze rested upon it fondly as Letty lifted it up. Charles had found the words in the *Oxford Book of English Verse* ... Douglas Hyde's poem from the Irish... Charles had written such a charming, plaintive, Celtic melody for it. It was one of the songs Veronica liked most to sing for him. Today it had a special significance, she thought, and wondered if Charles had been moved by any psychic presentiment when he chose those words.

She began to sing the song softly, and Letty stopped to listen:

'My grief on the sea,
How the waves of it roll,
For they heave between me
And the love of my soul!

'Abandoned, forsaken
To grief and to care,
Will the sea ever waken
Relief from despair?

'On a green bed of rushes
All last night I lay,
And I flung it abroad
With the heat of the day.

'And my love came behind me–
He came from the South;
His breast to my bosom,
His mouth to my mouth.'

Letty Chaddon had often heard Veronica sing the songs young Hallard played for her. Neither she nor Tom understood good music. But they both liked to hear the Hallards perform.

Listening this afternoon to that mournful, sad, impassioned little Irish song, Letty Chaddon was reduced to an unusual state of embarrassment. Her eyelids were actually stinging. Veronica had an enchanting voice, she had to admit. Darn the girl!

'Sloppy, I call it,' she said fiercely at length, and continued the packing with fresh vigour. 'Why on earth didn't your husband find something jolly?'

Veronica's lips quivered with sudden laughter.

'Oh, Letty dear, you do me good! But isn't it queer that we *did* find those words ... two months ago? Now it's so appropriate.'

'Bit out on the latitude and longtitude,' said Mrs Chaddon, sniffing. 'When your love joins you it won't be from the *south*. And I don't know where your bed of green rushes is coming from ... you'll be crammed in a cabin with me among a lot of other females, my dear...'

Veronica laughed.

'Dear, practical Letty! Oh dear, I suppose you're right.'

'You send Nicholas for your suitcase and come along home and have a nice bath and rest before dinner,' said Mrs Chaddon, with a quick look at the girl's exhausted face. 'And stop brooding about your Charles. He'll be okay and so will you, and the six months will pass much quicker than you think.'

'Letty,' said Veronica suddenly, 'do you think it's wicked to love anybody as much as I love Charles? Some religious people would say that it was ... that one should only worship God, and I absolutely *worship* Charles.'

'Well, I don't know much about religion and I'm not given to worshipping. I just don't worship people. But I'm sure it's not wicked, my dear. Only silly.'

'Why – silly?'

'Because,' said Letty Chaddon, her plain gaunt face a trifle red, 'it reduces a person to ... well ... to what you're going through now, and it's not worth it.'

Then Veronica smiled and looked dreamily with her grey luminous eyes at the older woman.

'Oh, yes, it is, Letty – it really is. I'm willing to go through anything so long as I see Charles again.'

'Why the dickens shouldn't you see him?'

'Well, I mean ... so long as he really does get home to me in six months' time.'

'I'm sure he will,' said Letty, trying to be comforting.

Veronica walked on to the verandah. Through the date-palms the burning brightness of the sky was being gradually darkened by enormous clouds. The atmosphere was heavy, humid, breathless. A roll of thunder echoed in the distant mountains. She sighed and turned back to Mrs Chaddon.

'Another storm coming up.'

'Perhaps it'll clear the air a bit,' said the prosaic and practical Letty, mopping her face. She shook out a creased fold of a faded cotton frock which had long since ceased to be fashionable, and made a dive into a canvas bag for a packet of cigarettes. 'I think we'd best get cracking before the rain comes, my dear. Come along.'

Veronica walked into her bedroom. She looked a trifle wistfully at the twin beds so sedate and unruffled under the mosquito-netting, at Charles's dressing-chest (his brushes had gone). He had gone. He was at this moment half-way to Tafo, and she could only hope the 'plane in which he was flying would meet with none of these violent electrical disturbances. Oh dear, she thought, what use was it continually worrying about the person one loved? Charles would be all right. He would be back the day after tomorrow. And then ... her heart constricted. Then that dreaded good-bye for many months.

Veronica put on a big floppy hat, clapped her hands for Nicholas, gave the grinning black boy her bag and small suitcase and followed Lettice Chaddon out to the waiting car.

She managed to get to sleep that night in the Chaddon's house only because a thunderstorm cooled down the atmosphere a little, and Letty insisted on her taking a sleeping-draught.

Mrs Chaddon left the girl lying in her bed in the spare room, looking frail and small and forlorn in a shell-pink transparent nightgown with cobwebby lace over the breast, and a little pink net tying up the brown curls which had been neatly set and pinned. She looked ridiculously lovely, Letty thought, and went out on to the verandah to have a beer with her husband.

For a moment she stood frowning into the darkness which was lit up by occasional flashes of lightning. The whole place was vibrant now with the chorus of the crickets. It had never entered Letty Chaddon's head before to worry about them, but now they annoyed her because she remembered the girl in the guest-room with her white, tired face.

'I hope that kid gets some sleep – she needs it,' said Letty.

Tom Chaddon stretched his legs and took a sip of his beer.

'She's a pretty thing, I must say. Looked a picture at dinner. But not enough of her … absolute wisp.'

'Lagos has got her down. Ought never to have come out to this climate. She's a bundle of nerves. Much too highly strung and delicate generally for the West Coast.'

'Damn' silly of Hallard to have let her stay.'

'Don't be silly, Tom. She wouldn't leave him. I've never seen the like of those two. Crackers about each other.'

'H'm,' said Tom Chaddon, and yawned. 'Just like us.'

Mrs Chaddon's eyes, which were rather like a bird's … bright, small, investigating … softened the merest bit as they rested on her husband's bald head.

'None of your sarcasm.'

His yawn was repeated.

'We're too old for those sort of goings-on anyhow.'

She put her tongue in her cheek, amused.

'What d'you mean … "goings-on"?'

'Love-stuff, my dear. All that billing and cooing the Hallards go in for.'

Mrs Chaddon seated herself in the basket chair by her husband and drank thirstily of her own beer.

'Tell you the truth, Tom, I've never believed in that twaddle till I met those two, but they've got it good and proper, *and* mean

75

it. That kid in there is as upset because her husband's gone off for a couple of days as though he's gone for a year. I'm going to have one hell of a time with her on Sunday when we leave.'

'Well, after listening to tonight's news from home, I daresay there'll come a time in the not-far distant future when she may have to say an even longer good-bye to him,' said the D.C. reflectively.

Mrs Chaddon stared.

'You mean...'

'I mean there's going to be a war and a bloody one in Europe, Letty, and young Hallard'll go home and go for one purpose only. To join up, like other young men of his age. You mark my words.'

Letty did mark his words. A curiously cold shiver went through her. Phlegmatic, un-romantic she might be, but she had grown fond of the Hallards, and she felt a spirit of protectiveness towards Veronica which might almost be termed tenderness. Such feeling as that girl had for Charles Hallard literally frightened Letty Chaddon. The idea of a war ... of Veronica losing her husband in a war ... and Letty's throat felt dry. She took another hurried sip of beer.

'Oh, shut up, Tom, and don't be so pessimistic,' she growled.

He did not answer. He was busy lighting a pipe. Mrs Chaddon stared through the darkness in the direction of Veronica's bedroom. She thought:

'Lord save us... I wouldn't like anything to happen like *that* ... not for anything in the world.'

## 6

During that next two days Letty Chaddon began to feel that taking Veronica Hallard under her wing was a responsibility indeed. She really dreaded Sunday much more for the girl than for herself. She was devoted to old Tom, but she could live without him, and she took the coming parting in a philosophical spirit. Tom would be getting back to the old country about the same time as young Hallard. Six months' separation was nothing. But it seemed a form of torture to the Hallards.

It gave Letty a queer feeling that she was witnessing something almost sacred, as she afterwards told her husband, because she happened to witness the reunion between Veronica and Charles when he returned from Tafo.

Veronica was sitting on the verandah, mending a pair of silk stockings which had laddered the night before.

Letty was tidying out a cupboard in the dining-room when she heard a car drive up to the bungalow. She looked out, saw young Hallard. He must have come direct from the aerodrome. They had expected him about this time. It was mid-afternoon – sweltering. The storm and heavy rains of yesterday had done nothing to modify the heat. Might as well be working in the hottest of the hot-houses in Kew, Letty told herself, grimly wiping the sweat from her brow.

She stood a moment watching Charles Hallard get out of the car. Good-looking boy, to be sure, she thought. He wore khaki-coloured shorts and shirt. As he ran up the steps on to the verandah where Veronica stood waiting for him with outstretched hands, he took off his wide-brimmed *terai* and flung it on the floor. Letty Chaddon caught a glimpse of Veronica, radiant, flushed, her expression rapt as she flung herself into her husband's arms.

As they kissed, Mrs Chaddon turned away and went on with her tidying of the cup-board. Her weatherbeaten homely face was a trifle more red than it had been, and embarrassed. She thought;

'Good lord ... those two!'

She was beginning to wonder if she – and old Tom too – had not missed something in life...

Veronica, locked in Charles's arms, was murmuring:

'Oh, darling, darling, you're *back*.'

78

'Darling,' he said, kissed her again and again, then with an arm about her, led her into the Chaddons' sitting-room. 'Am I to stay to tea, then take you home?'

'Yes.'

'It's marvellous to see you. I missed you absurdly while I was in Tafo. That damned conference ... how I cursed it!'

'So did I,' she said, laughing, her shining eyes fixed on him. 'It was awful ... two whole nights without you.'

'Are you all right?'

'Fine. Letty is such an angel to me – made me stay in bed for breakfast and spoiled me atrociously.'

'You were meant to be spoiled, my poppet.'

She stood smiling up at him, then on tip-toe put her hands on his shoulders, pulled a handkerchief from his pocket and dabbed his wet forehead and neck. She often did that for him. It always enchanted him. She was such a gentle, tender little idiot about him. He adored her. It was fine being back with her. That long, dreary conference on the Gold Coast had wasted so much of the little time they had left together out here. He began to think about Sunday. Only forty-eight more hours, and Veronica would be gone. It made the muscles of Charles's face tauten. She saw his expression and knew at once what he was thinking. She

79

nearly always knew. And wasn't the same dread thought at the back of her mind?

She pressed close to him, shutting her eyes.

'Oh, Charles ... my darling...'

'Don't let's talk about it, darling,' he said shortly. 'Let me tell you about my trip.'

She swallowed hard, smiled and nodded.

'Yes. What it a good flight?'

'Grand. Met a lot of interesting people out there, as a matter of fact ... scientific representatives of the Cocoa and Chocolate Association ... leading experts on virus diseases ... ye gods, what I don't know about cocoa diseases isn't worth knowing!'

She giggled, and rubbed her cheek against his shoulder.

'It sounds so comic. I can't ever really connect you with cocoa-planting, darling.'

'Neither can I, darling...' He laughed with her. 'Come and sit down and tell me how you got on her with old Chaddy and his Lettice.'

'They were sweet. D'you remember when they first came to dinner with us how I dreaded her ... and thought them such a menace, snapping at each other? Now I understand them. They *do* care for each other in their own way. It just isn't our way.'

Charles pulled her down on to the sofa and looked at her with that quick deep passion in his eyes which never failed to excite and delight Veronica.

'Come here and tell me ... what is *our* way, my Nic?'

She shook her head, her breath quickening.

'Not here. Letty will be in any moment. I'll tell you ... when we get home, darling Charles.'

So the hours flew by. Another night ... another night of passionate happiness for these two ... then the last night before the Elder Dempster liner was due to call at Lagos and pick up passengers for England.

In the Hallards' bungalow there was an unusual disarray. A wardrobe trunk packed, locked, stood ready in the lounge. Suitcases were on the floor in the bedroom, still open, waiting for the last small articles to be packed. Nothing was left in the house that belonged personally to Veronica. It had become bare and unfamiliar. Charles Hallard hated it. Veronica talked and laughed a lot, but it was all rather strained and artificial. Charles knew it. *She* knew it. But she tried desperately not to give way, because she realised how much worse it would be for him.

They made marvellous plans for the future. He would be home early next year. February. She was sure there wouldn't be a war. It was all a big scare. But even if there was a war, she and Charles would be together. He must try and get a job in the

London offices of his firm and not have to come back to West Africa. They could never be separated *again*. She would stay with Mummy at Monks Rest for a bit, then start looking for a furnished place for themselves … a little flat, perhaps, in town near Iris and Mervyn. That would be marvellous. There was no need for depression. As Letty said, six months was *nothing*.

And so on … all on a note of forced gaiety, aided and abetted by the odd drinks. Then some music. Charles must play to her on their last night. She wanted to hear 'Veronica's Concerto'. She loved that theme. And she sang for him. Not his new song. It was too sad. Some Bach. Bach was pure and passionless and not too emotional.

They played and sang together until late. It was almost as though they dreaded breaking up the evening. Once they went to bed, they would sleep … and morning would come. Veronica was sailing in the morning.

But at midnight they *had* to put an end to the evening. They were both so tired. There were black shadows under Veronica's big grey eyes and under her delicate make-up no colour at all. Charles had a look of strain in his eyes and avoided meeting her gaze too often. He had been like that the whole evening.

Both of them tried to be casual as they started to undress. Charles pulled his shirt over his head, and ruffled his hair. Veronica took off the black chiffon *négligée* with the gold belt which he had asked her to wear, and cast a quick unhappy glance at him. She worshipped that ruffled boy's head ... and all the heavenly intimacy of their life together... Tomorrow she would be in a cabin with possibly two or three other women. She would be moving farther and farther every moment away from Lagos and *him*.

She felt choked. Sudden hot tears blinded her eyes, and she listened in a despairing silence while Charles talked ... rather more sharply and clearly than usual, as though he were forcing the words.

'I think we've done everything, darling ... you've got all your papers and passport, and your money in your pigskin bag, haven't you?'

'Yes,' she managed to get out the word.

'Old Letty Chaddon will keep an eye on you, my pet. And you'll cable me as soon as you get to Liverpool?'

'Yes, of course.'

'Hope you'll find your mother fit and all that. It ought to be pretty nice in Princes Risborough this time of year.'

'Yes, it will.'

'I'll keep you well posted, darling. Lots of cables and letters. You'll be seeing the Williamses almost at once, I expect. Give old Mervyn and Iris my love.'

'Yes.'

It was all she could say ... just that one word ... without bursting into tears. She hurried suddenly into the sitting-room on pretext of fetching a book, and stood there a moment, trembling from head to foot, face hidden in her hands. She was struggling for mastery of her emotions. She had taken a vow not to cry or upset Charles. But oh, how difficult it was! Too difficult. To leave him tomorrow would be like dying.

She tried to think of the benefits of this alteration in her life and temporary separation from Charles. Her health would improve in England. She would grow well and strong again for him. It would be lovely seeing the old home, too, and poor Mummy; and her many friends. A pleasant change after the appalling heat and monotony out here. Nice to see her old nurse – Mummy only had 'Nanny' to help her these days ... but she would miss the black boys... Nicholas's grinning face... Jack Jackson's marvellous curries... Oh, *how* would Charles get on without her? Would they look after him when he was alone? Would he be all right?

She heard him calling her:

'Darling ... what are you doing?'

She made another big effort, snatched up a book – she did not know what – and returned to the bedroom. Now the tears had dried on her lashes. She was stony-faced. She even smiled at Charles, who was already in bed.

'Darling,' he said, 'do you really think I ought to change that last movement and bring in the "Veronica" theme again ... just before the last bar ... you know...?' He hummed a stanza to her.

She nodded.

'Yes, I do think so, darling. Work it up to the *cadenza* ... where the piano part comes in.'

'You're right,' he agreed, and lay back on his pillow, hands behind his head, reflecting.

Veronica went to her dressing-table and began mechanically to take off her make-up and cream her face. The night was, as usual, sweltering, breathless. The same old roll of thunder far away. The same din of crickets. Suddenly she felt a new sense of despair because she would not be here to listen to the crickets tomorrow. She had hated them. They had got on her nerves and stopped her from sleeping. But would she ever be able to shut her eyes and sleep again ...without Charles? she asked herself. With Charles thousands of miles away from her?

She said suddenly in a high-pitched voice:

'Darling, do you really think there's a war coming?'

'Things look bad, sweetheart,' he said. 'A

lot of trouble is blowing up between Germany and Poland. We'd be forced to intervene if Hitler attacks Poland.'

'But Daddy always said another war was impossible.'

'Darling, all our fathers thought so. That's the trouble. We haven't been aware of what is really going on in Europe.'

'I'm so ignorant. I *must* try and learn something about politics,' said Veronica, in her vaguest voice.

Charles Hallard looked at his wife's slim, enchanting figure and watched her, fascinated as always, while she smoothed the cream into her face.

'Don't bother your adorable head,' he said. 'And certainly not tonight. And give over doing that face massage, my beloved, and come and make love to me,' he added gaily.

His gaiety did not find any response in her overcharged heart. But she smiled at him.

'Don't be so impatient. It isn't decent.'

'Who wants to be decent?'

*'Charles!'*

'Well – do you? With me, I mean?'

'Charles Hallard, behave yourself.'

She was smiling in earnest now. She loved it when they were 'silly' together. She wiped her face on a tissue, powdered it lightly, then turned to him. A great moth flew through the open window. She beat it off with both hands.

'Go away ... brute!'

'Thank the lord you'll soon be away from this infernal climate,' said Charles, with a sudden frown. 'I envy you, darling. It'll be getting cooler for you every day next week.'

She dared not meet his gaze. The strain of keeping up this show of courage was sapping every shred of her vitality.

'Yes, it'll be nice ... to be cold again, I mean.'

'Darling, will you come to bed or shall I get up and beat you? You're dilly-dallying about tonight like a reluctant Victorian bride.'

'Charles, don't be so silly,' she laughed.

He grinned at her and held out a hand.

'Come on, angel.'

She went to him, feeling no joy but only a crushing sense of misery. He knew it. He was in the last stages of misery himself! It would be hellish here ... tomorrow ...without her. But she had to go. At Tafo this morning they had been discussing the European situation and one of the big men, just out from England, had said that war was inevitable. If so ... shipping would become difficult and dangerous. And Veronica's health would never stand an indefinite period out here. She *must* go ... while the going was good.

In the darkness, lying with his arms about her, he thought how desperately happy they had been together, this year of their marriage. They had been one ... not two. One in body and mind.

His lips brushed her eyelids and found them wet. He was sick with longing to comfort her, but could not. He needed comfort himself. He was more worried about the future than he would let her know.

'Darling ... my little Nic...' he whispered. 'Don't be too unhappy ... *please*. Try to accept the inevitable.'

'I know,' she said in a choked voice. 'Letty has said it dozens of times ... remember it's only for six months. I will remember. But I ... I can't somehow ... say good-bye to you easily.'

'Then don't say it, darling. We won't either of us say so. We'll pretend it's just a trip you're taking for your health – which it is, really. Darling, your poor lovely eyes are popping out of your little head with fatigue and insomnia. You'll sleep like a top on the boat when it gets cool and feel so much better.'

She nodded speechlessly. He threaded his fingers through the curls which she had refused to pin up tonight. She didn't care what she would look like tomorrow morning. She couldn't bother to put on a net tonight. She had only creamed her face for something to do. She didn't care about *anything*...

She held on to him with feverish little hands. He covered her with caresses, whispering his love, his adoration.

'You know I'll only live to join you again, sweetheart. I'll be thinking of you … night and day.'

'And I … of you, Charles darling.'

'Don't let it hurt you like this, my darling, darling. I can't bear you to be hurt.'

She made the final effort, squeezing back the scalding tears, driving down the bitter longing to weep. She said:

'I'll be good… I'll be awfully bright and gay tomorrow when you see me off. Oh, my *darling*…'

'It's been such a happy year for us, Nic.'

'Incredibly happy.'

'Thank God we met … and got married…'

'Oh, yes, I couldn't do without you. Nothing must ever happen to you when I'm away, Charles … nothing.'

'Nothing will,' he said.

For a moment they lay in each other's arms without speaking, so close … and yet already separated by their secret griefs and fears for each other. Life was so cruel. It didn't seem that people were meant to be happy for long. Fate might have something frightful in store for them. They kept saying 'only six months', but what would they do if he couldn't get home in February … if their

parting should be prolonged? Or ... permanent. Death might come between them. *He*
might die... *She* might...

Without passion, yet more utterly in love
with each other than they had ever been,
these two spent their last night together.
And this time it was not only Veronica who
lay sleepless, but Charles too. Only when
dawn came ... banishing the hot, brilliant
moonlit night ... and a little wind sprang up
to cool the breathless humid air ... they
drifted into oblivion for an hour or two.

When Veronica woke it was broad daylight
and she knew that the dreaded day had
come.

How she kept going until she finally left
Charles she did not know. Somehow she
managed it. There was not much time,
fortunately, for last-minute agonies. The
ship came in unexpectedly early. That
meant a frantic rush. Veronica drove away
from the house leaving a disconsolate
couple of black boys standing on the
familiar verandah ... took a last backward
look through a cloud of dust at the garden
and the cocoa plantation. Then they joined
the Chaddons, and after that Veronica was
hardly conscious of what was going on
around her. She only knew that Charles
held one of her hands very tightly all the
time and kept up a flow of advice ...
warnings to her not to lose her bag ... to

give her valuables to the purser as soon as she could ... to take her *vassano*, if she felt seasick ... to let Mrs Chaddon look after her ... and so on. To all of which she answered, 'Yes, darling,' without really knowing what she promised. She was in a daze of misery.

Somehow they got through the customs ... and got Letty's and her luggage on board... Then they faced new trouble in the form of discomforts with a vengeance. The ship was crammed to capacity ... war rumours were driving home a great many women and children. Army officers were being recalled. Veronica and Letty were not even together. To her dismay, Veronica found herself separated from her kindly and helpful friend and placed in a four-berth cabin with three strange women, two from Freetown, one from the Cape, with an infant – a sickly, wailing little thing, the sight and sound of whom filled Veronica with fresh despair. It boded no better nights for *her.*

Charles fumed and protested to the purser and the captain himself, to no avail. Apologies were given, but they were assured that Mrs Hallard was lucky to have got a berth at all ... with the present state of tension in Europe.

What with all this fuss and palaver, Veronica found that she had to spend the last few moments with Charles in giving *him*

91

consolation rather than taking it herself. He looked so upset and dejected and was so worried about her.

'That damned baby … you'll never get any sleep … and three hags with you and not even Letty Chaddon … my poor angel!'

'I don't mind. I'll be all right. It's only for a couple of weeks,' Veronica kept reassuring him.

They sat with Letty and Tom in the bar, having farewell drinks. The bar was packed. There were several people from Lagos on board whom Charles knew. One or two women whom Veronica recognized. The sea looked like blue oil glittering in the sun. There was no air even with all the doors and portholes opened. Charles looked at Veronica's exhausted face and felt his spirits at lowest ebb. He kept a tight hold of her hand.

Letty Chaddon gave the pair a quick glance and felt more wretched herself than she had thought possible. It wasn't really funny leaving old Tom … and as for the Hallards … lord … they looked like death, the poor kids! As for this 'something' ship … *she* was in a four-berth cabin with a nurse and two children and anticipated a voyage of purgatory. Everybody seemed to be going home today. And everybody was talking 'war'. It was enough to depress anyone.

When the bell sounded and the voice

called, 'All visitors ashore, please,' Lettice Chaddon saw Veronica go a greyish colour, and even while she, Letty, was bidding Tom good-bye she kept an eye on the girl. She reckoned Veronica was going to faint in a moment.

But Veronica did not faint. She clung to Charles for a despairing moment, the bitterness of the parting tearing her heart in two. She felt his last hard, passionate kiss on her upturned mouth, heard him say, 'So long … not good-bye … darling, my darling … look after yourself…'

Then he was gone, with Chaddy. She did not remember saying good-bye to Chaddy. Her head was splitting with pain. The noisy, crowded ship was blurred from her.

She felt Letty take her arm in a firm grip.

'Come on, my lamb, I'm going to take you down to your cabin and get the doc to give you a dose of something to make you sleep. Come on … there's a duck.'

Veronica soundlessly shook her head, broke away from Mrs Chaddon and tore through the crowd, out on to the deck.

'Charles!' she gasped in an agonized voice. *'Charles…'*

She could see him going down the gangway with Tom Chaddon. Once on shore he turned and looked up at the ship. Veronica, her face streaming with tears, leaned over the rail and waved at him. He

93

waved back. Then she could bear no more. She let Letty lead her down to her cabin.

In her mind only one poignant question was uppermost now.

'When shall I see him again ... oh, when?'

## 7

For the first three days out at sea, Veronica did not leave her cabin. Reaction after leaving Charles and Lagos set in, and coming on top of the many weeks of insomnia was too much for her, just as Letty Chaddon had expected.

The heat in the small crowded cabin which they had to share with three strange women did not help, but with the aid of a sympathetic ship's doctor, who at once fell under the spell of Veronica's large grey eyes, and the indefatigable Letty, Veronica survived; more particularly so as he removed the mother with the infant.

Perhaps the sheer physical weakness that kept Veronica to her bed, and a certain amount of sleep induced by drugs, took the edge off the keen mental pain of leaving Charles.

She lay like one in a stupor, gasping in the heat that seemed to pour mercilessly off a glittering sea through the porthole into her cabin. Letty spent long hours beside her, wringing bandages out in iced water and eau-de-Cologne for the feverish forehead of her young protégée, and refusing to let Veronica sink any further into her state of misery.

'I can't have it, my dear ... it's a lot of rubbish ... you'll see your Charles again in six months' time,' she would say briskly. Then when Veronica looked at her with large, haunted eyes full of suffering and reproach, and said sweetly, 'All right, Letty – I'll try to be good,' it was Letty rather than Veronica who blinked the odd tear away. She wrote to Tom:

*That child gets me down. She's like a sick little animal taken away from its surroundings, or a kid on her first night at boarding-school. What the devil is the use of being in love to such an absurd extent?*

What, indeed? Veronica asked herself the same question dozens of times during those days and nights of sickness on board. But there was no answer to remedy the sickness. She pined unceasingly for her Charles. She hated every throb, every revolution of the engines which took the ship farther and farther from Lagos. She sat up daily, weak and ill though she felt, to write to Charles. She had vowed to write daily. And at Freetown she wired to him. There was a

95

telegram awaiting her:

*All my love goes with you, Charles.*

That was a lovely surprise and made her feel better. So much better, in fact, that that night she insisted on getting up to have her first meal in the dining-saloon with Letty.

She had seen little of her three cabin companions. They were all in good health and up and out early and back late, which was a blessing, because it had left Veronica alone.

Two of the women were friends – older than Veronica, South Africans with husbands on board. They were, it appeared, seasoned travellers and spent most of the voyage in the bar and playing bridge.

They were mildly sympathetic with Veronica, but thought her rather pampered and stupid. They spent what little time they had in the cabin wrangling about their bridge hands. Veronica hardly spoke to either of them, and did not even remember their names when the journey ended. But she often used to thank heaven she did not play bridge when she awakened to hear the two come in, undress and reproach each other in fierce whispers.

'You ought to have known I was asking for a diamond, my dear Madge...'

'But, you fool, Olive, I doubled that no trump.

*Why didn't you show your diamonds then...?'*
And so on...

The third and younger member of the party in Veronica's cabin, however, was a nice girl with whom she made friends in the desultory way of fellow travellers, although it was not a friendship likely to endure once they got to England. Pam Dalton was a South African and this was her first trip to England. She was going to join her fiancé, a young engineer from Liverpool who had met Pam when he visited the Cape six months ago. He had hoped to get back to South Africa and marry her there, but threats of this European war – and certain business complications – prevented him from leaving England. So Pam was going to him. She had an aunt in London and she had arranged to stay with her and be married almost at once to her Edward.

Veronica heard a lot about the said Edward, and was a willing and sympathetic listener. But Pam was not a very emotional type. Sometimes Veronica marvelled at her unsentimental attitude. Eddie, as she called him, was 'one of the best'. (She produced a photograph of a serious, rather heavy-featured young man for Veronica to see.) They had a lot in common. They had met at a tennis party in Durban. Edward played a beautiful game and Pam was crazy about tennis. She was a big, fair, hefty girl with a healthy colour and strong limbs. A thorough sports-girl. Her engineer was a sportsman, too. It was 'sport' they appeared to have in common. But what else? Veronica wondered what kind of a marriage it would be. One could not play much tennis in England … except in the season, which was short and uncertain, and if Pam settled down, as she announced she was going to do, in the dark and gloomy atmosphere of a city like Liverpool and produced a large family … sport would surely cease to be a link between her and 'Eddie'. What then would they have between them? Pam said they were both so stolid and unromantic. All this writing of daily letters and sending wires and cables made Pam laugh. Neither she nor Eddie would dream of behaving in such a way. Edward was saving for his future family and Pam thought that sort of thing a waste of money or 'sloppy'. (Letty Chaddon's word.)

Veronica, however, with her fragile beauty, the glamour which clung to her lovely clothes and entrancing perfumes, fascinated the big sports-loving Pam, who was most kind to her all through the voyage and frequently waited on her when she was ill in bed. She liked to hear Veronica talking about Charles. It half amazed and half amused her.

'You are *killing* about your husband. I've

never met anyone so much in love...' she observed on one occasion.

Veronica looked sad and said:

'So many people seem to feel like that. Charles and I must be unique. Except for some great friends of mine ... they are the same.'

And she thought about Iris and Mervyn. *They* were just as bad as she and Charles. Thank goodness there were others, or she would begin to feel that her passionate adoration for Charles and his for her an abnormal affair.

She liked to see and talk to the cheerful Pam, and half envied her that bursting health and energy and lack of imagination.

'Won't you feel absolutely sick with excitement when we dock and you see your Eddie?' she asked her, when they were talking on one occasion.

Pam laughed and said: 'I'll be terribly pleased, of course. After all, I've left my own country and people to marry him.'

'Then you must love him a lot, Pam.'

Pam – running a comb through a mop of corn-coloured hair – grinned and nodded.

'I do, but I know when we meet he'll just say "Hello, Pam," and I'll say, "Cheers, Eddie," and we'll snatch a kiss and start discussing the tournament I played in just before I left Durban.'

Veronica shook her head and groaned.

'Oh, how could you!'

Pam smiled down at pretty little Mrs Hallard, who looked as though a wisp of wind would blow her away ... so tiny and frail and lovely ... and laughed aloud.

'Well... What would *you* do?'

But Veronica was speechless now; always on the edge of tears these days, and not daring to say too much about Charles. But if Charles were waiting for her at Liverpool after this separation of only a few days (already it seemed like weeks), she would run to him and be held close, close, and she would hear him whisper in his husky voice: *'Nic ... my precious little Nic...' Oh, if only it could be!* Lucky Pam to be meeting her future husband, unsentimental though her reunion might be! No doubt they *felt* sentimental. Everybody was different. But somehow Veronica was thankful that she and Charles were not like Pam and her fiancé ... or like the Chaddons. Better to suffer as they suffered now and to know the high-pitched ecstasy of their eventual reunion.

During her first evening up on deck, Veronica made a new friend. It was cooler, but still very warm. The coastline of Africa was no longer visible and they were now well out at sea. Under an awning, in her deck-chair, Veronica sat dreaming, looking out at the smooth deep violet of the water.

She could see the pale churning cream of the furrow cut by the liner as it ploughed ahead. From the salon came the sound of a gramophone record which one of the passengers was playing. A tune to suit Veronica's present melancholy: Jean Sablon singing, *'J'attrandrai'*...

She thought:

'I wonder what my darling Charles is doing. He won't be at the house. He promised to dine every night at the Club with others. He'll be drinking his *stengah* now, perhaps ... and thinking of me...'

Tears welled into her eyes, but she blinked them away. She had promised Letty to be sensible and to try her best to be gay tonight. But she still felt so weak and listless physically. If only she had some of Pam Dalton's magnificent animal vitality, it might help.

Letty had been roped into a game of bridge and had not been seen on deck since she had left Veronica here. After a while Veronica decided to go, herself, into the bar and see if there was anybody on board she knew. One so often ran into associates. And it was really time she began to take an interest in life and this voyage. Charles would hate her to sit like this alone, grieving, brooding.

She got up and, carrying a cushion, some magazines, and her pigskin bag under her arms, began to walk slowly along the deck. She felt ridiculously tired after being up for only an hour. She saw for herself that it was as well she was going home. Her health was really in a very low state. Mummy would be horrified at the way she had lost weight lately. All her trousseau things were hanging on her.

She dropped a magazine and in her vague way walked on for a moment without noticing it. Then she heard a man's voice, very English and courteous, behind her.

'Pardon me, I think you dropped this just now…'

Veronica turned. In the dim evening light she saw a tallish man, wearing well-cut flannels, holding out her magazine. She took it and smiled.

'Thank you so much. How silly of me…'

He smiled down at her.

'You seem to be rather laden … are you going in? May I carry something for you?'

Veronica feeling suddenly shy, stammered:

'Oh … it doesn't matter … I can manage … really…'

'Let's have the cushion. I'd be delighted…' he said.

She found herself handing it to him. Regarding him more closely, she saw that he was the type that Iris always described as 'typically Army'. About thirty, with a brown lean face, broad shoulders, straight back;

102

crisp brown hair; lazy blue eyes that crinkled at the corners when he smiled. And she recognised at once the R.A. tie which he was wearing. That placed him for her at once. She had so often seen Mervyn Williams wear it. She said impulsively.

'Oh, you're a Gunner ... aren't you?'

His smile broadened.

'Right first go. You know the tie?'

'Yes. My best friend's husband ... you may know him ... Captain Williams ... Mervyn Williams ... is a Gunner.'

'Good lord, of course! Mervyn and I were at "The Shop" together. He was in Egypt some time back, wasn't he?'

'Yes. But that was a year ago. He's at Woolwich now, as a matter of fact.'

'Good old Mervyn. He has a charming little wife, too ... you know Iris... I was at their wedding, as a matter of fact. And you're a great friend of hers, are you?'

'Yes.'

'Well, that introduces us, doesn't it?' the man in grey flannels smiled down at Veronica. 'How very nice. My name's Mansell – Boyd Mansell.'

'A captain ... like Mervyn?'

'Yes...' He nodded, smiling. 'We were contemporaries. Matter of fact, we took our promotion exams much about the same time, I remember. I've been spending some sick leave in South Africa, visiting a brother of mine who has a delightful farm near Johannesburg. Now on my way back to my job. Looks as though they might need the soldier any moment.'

'Oh dear,' said Veronica. 'Are you another person who thinks there's going to be a war?'

'Not much chance of anything else if I know the Hun, and I do. Spent some time in Dresden in my extreme youth,' said Boyd Mansell.

'Oh!' breathed Veronica. 'My husband studied music in Dresden. We must talk ... do let's go in and talk.'

Mansell said:

'Of course. And your name is...?'

'Veronica Hallard. My husband is Charles Hallard. You didn't meet him in Dresden, I suppose?'

'Hallard,' repeated Mansell. 'No – no, I don't think that name rings a gong. But look here ... what about a drink? I'm sure we'll discover a lot of mutual friends before we're finished. For instance, you must know a great pal of mine, James McDowell, who is with Mervyn Williams's lot ... big hulking major chap...'

Captain Mansell went on talking as he walked with Veronica down the steps into the bar. Yes, she did know Jimmy McDowell, she said. She had met him at one of Iris's parties. And did he know the

Williamses' great friends, the Spallings?... Geoffrey Spalling was in the R.A.M.C... No, Captain Mansell had not met the Spallings.

They were both talking eagerly when they reached the bar and found an unoccupied table. Veronica sat down feeling suddenly much better and brighter. She looked round the crowded smoke-filled saloon at all the unfamiliar faces ... one or two men still in shorts and open-necked shirts; girls in a similar attire ... little groups drinking, smoking, laughing. Veronica knew none of them. She began to realise how lonely and depressed she had felt since she left Lagos and what a good thing it was to come out of her shell. It was definitely a treat, meeting and talking to an old friend of the Williamses.

How awfully nice Boyd Mansell was. A very good-looking young man, too. She watched him collect two pink gins and come back to her table with them. A clean, thoroughly British type. A touch of Irish in those blue eyes of his. And he had charming manners. He said, as he sat down:

'Where have you been hiding yourself? I can't think why I haven't seen you before.'

'Oh,' said Veronica, 'I ... I've been ill. I was rather ill, as a matter of fact, when we left Lagos. I've just got up for the first time this evening.'

'Good show,' said Boyd. 'Then we must celebrate. Here's to you!'

'Thanks awfully, and here's to you,' said Veronica, and raised her glass with his.

He smiled at her over the rim of his. He had not been able to see her very plainly on deck. Now, in the bright lights of the saloon, he got a clear picture of an exceedingly lovely small person with enormous dark-lashed grey eyes and dark brown curls tied up with a blue ribbon. She wore a light blue frock under a camel-hair coat. His gaze wandered a moment from the fascinatingly large and luminous eyes to the full red mouth ... then down to the smallest pair of feet in red sandals that he had ever seen. He could see that she did not look well and also that she looked unhappy. But his first impression of Veronica Hallard was that she must be a very gentle creature. Boyd Mansell liked a woman to be gentle. He loved pretty women, but he had never had much use for the hard-boiled modern girl who liked to think she knew everything and to assert her independence by drinking hard, rushing a man into an empty and briefly passionate affair and gaining what she liked to call 'valuable experience'. Boyd had suffered from one or two young women like that on the voyage out to South Africa. And in Durban he had almost (but not quite) lost his head about an exceedingly experienced attractive married woman who wanted him to involve himself in a divorce and take her away. But shoddy intrigues and public scandals were, in Boyd Mansell's mind, things to be avoided. He had got away unscathed. But it had decided him that he must be more judicious in his choice or acceptance of women friends on the way home. Consequently he had kept rather clear of the one or two who had tried to 'start something' from the moment the ship left the Cape.

Meeting Veronica Hallard was something akin to an electrical disturbance in his life. He sat talking to her, entranced by her physical beauty and even more so by the sincerity which shone out of those grave eyes of hers. She was telling him about her husband. That was another slight shock to Boyd Mansell, who liked to call himself a bit of a cynic about love. For it was obvious that here was a girl who was head over heels in love with this Charles to whom she had been married for a year.

Long after the moment of their first meeting, Boyd remembered the actual sense of frustration and disappointment he experienced because he was fated for the first time in his life to fall deeply and hopelessly in love with another man's wife.

# PART II

## 1

Boyd Mansell was the youngest son of four children. His eldest brother, James, ten years older than himself, had gone out to South Africa when Boyd was still at public school, married a South African girl and settled there.

There were two sisters, both married. Audrey, who came between James and Boyd and had, at a young age, tied herself up to a Lincolnshire doctor and settled in Market Rasen; Gillian (known to the family as Gilly), who was only eighteen months older than Boyd. Audrey was a little staid – 'pompous', the family called her, although a very good sort, and making an exemplary wife for her medical man and excellent mother to a lovely pair of twin boys whose photograph was carried around by Uncle Boyd and duly exhibited with pride. Gilly, however, golden-haired and blue-eyed – blunt little nose powdered with freckles, wide laughing mouth – had always been his playmate when they were children, had always shared Boyd's secrets and he hers.

109

But a major tragedy had befallen pretty, laughing Gilly.

At twenty-four she married a charming young man in the Royal Air Force. During the second week of their honeymoon, driving through Cornwall, their car, driven by Gilly's husband, crashed into a lorry at a hairpin bend made specially dangerous by the tall Cornish hedgerows. Dick, Gilly's good-looking and adored husband, died at once. Gilly was taken to hospital with multiple injuries and she had come out of that hospital a wreck; a girl who would never walk again. For her it was a spinal carriage for many long months and afterwards a wheeled chair. The light had gone out of those dancing eyes and the *joie de vivre* had died and been buried with the husband to whom she had belonged for a few short days.

Boyd, a gay young subaltern at the time, had been stationed in Palestine. The news from home had shocked and sobered him for many a long month. It had seemed impossible that he could say or do anything that could comfort poor little Gilly. Boyd, who had always done a lot of laughing, found it a little less easy after the tragic news of his favourite sister.

Trained by a mother who was a regular churchgoer and the best of women, he was like the average young man of the same upbringing – a Christian at heart – but loth to express his religious views, and attending the services with Mrs Mansell when he was at home mainly to please her; and because he liked the lovely old Priory church in the Sussex village wherein Boyd was born and where the Mansells had lived for the last thirty-five years. The awful thing that had happened to Gilly had somewhat shaken what faith the boy possessed. He remembered on the day he received his mother's first letter relating the tragedy he had felt embittered against the God who allowed such things to happen to good, kind, innocent people like Gilly. He had sat down and written in that vein, hotly, to his mother. Her answer had come ... typical of herself ... gentle, understanding, but endeavouring to heal his wound and at the same time to restore his confidence in the religion which meant so much to her. He never forgot her letter:

*Don't lose your faith, my darling boy. Gilly has not lost hers, anguished though she is. In fact, it seems to have drawn her nearer to Him than she was before. He will help her to bear this cross. Pray for her, darling, as I do. Prayers help when all else fails...*

He had tried to pray ... choking down the hot, difficult tears of a sensitive boy who had for the first time come up against the grim side of life. But he had never really quite recovered his full belief in the kind God of Mrs Mansell's teaching. The ways of that God were beyond his understanding. He was willing now to sit back and be glad that people like his mother – and poor Gilly – were the richer and happier for their simple and rather pathetic beliefs.

In the years that followed he saw Gilly as a kind of saint; always the most cheerful of the whole family, jesting, teasing, from her wheeled chair. She set a high standard for him ... as his mother had done. Boyd was going to find it difficult to meet any woman who could begin to come up to either mother or sister. But such is human nature, he had to admit, somewhat shamefacedly when he was on leave, that after a few weeks down at Chidding Manor with the family he grew restive. He could not quite 'live up' to them. The impeccable mother, steeped in good works; and the heart-rending patience and cheerfulness of Gilly. His father had died when Boyd was still at Sandhurst. James was in Kenya and Audrey rarely at home. Boyd found it dull nowadays. Much of his leave was spent abroad. He was crazy about winter sports. Christmas often found him with a party in Davos or Wengen. In the summer after duty visits to Chidding, he travelled to France, Austria or Spain.

Money was plentiful. Mr Mansell, a stock-broker, had died a rich man and James and Boyd had already inherited a handsome income from their maternal grandfather who was 'in oil' in his day. The life of an Army officer with a nice private income was congenial to Boyd. It satisfied his love of travel, supplied ample opportunity for sport and for meeting people. He was a sociable person.

Now, in his early thirties, he knew it was time that he chose a wife and 'settled down'. His mother was anxious that he should do so. He, personally, wanted a wife and children. He was popular with women and a great admirer of beauty. But so far *the* one woman had escaped him – perhaps because of that high standard set at home, and his deep-rooted belief that a woman should be like his mother and sisters, fundamentally good and of highest principle. Perhaps because he had had two unfortunate affairs which had made him a little cynical and wary.

Two years ago whilst stationed in Egypt he had formed his first really serious attachment for the daughter of a Government official living in Cairo. Until Boyd met Tessa Richardson, he had divided women into two categories in his mind: the good and the bad; the decent and those whom one did *not* introduce into the family circle. (He had

had a brief and somewhat disturbing affair with one of the latter type ... a lovely cabaret dancer ... but it had been entirely physical, taught him a great deal, and left him unscathed.) But Tessa was a revelation. Most decidedly she belonged to the 'good and decent' class. Her parents were well known and highly respected. But Tessa was a bad character. She was twenty-three when Boyd came across her, devastatingly pretty with her milk-white skin, glorious auburn hair and a pair of greenish eyes – blacklashed and wicked – which could look meltingly soft when she wanted to make them so.

She had already lived in Cairo a year when Boyd – then a subaltern – came out to do his foreign service. He was handsome and well off, had a car and a lot of charm in his quiet way. Tessa made a dive for him. She had already been through the hands of half a dozen Army men in Cairo and there were those, older and wiser than Boyd, who might have warned him. But they did not. It was not their business, and the boy must learn through his own experience.

He fell madly in love with Tessa. For a month they were inseparable. They dined together, danced, rode, went on Nile picnics; joined every party that was going. And during that month Boyd made up his mind to marry Tessa. But she toyed with the idea of marrying Boyd Mansell only for a brief spell. Then he began to bore her. She saw that he put her on a pedestal. She gathered from various conversations with him that he would expect a degree of loyalty and good behaviour from her which she knew she could not achieve. If 'amoral', she was at least honest, and true to herself. She knew that she could never satisfy Boyd; the Boyd who spoke with such reverence of his mother and invalid sister and that quiet home in Sussex which he would one day inherit, since brother James intended to remain in Kenya.

Tessa sheered off. The time came when Boyd woke up and discovered that the girl whom he had pictured as his wife was insatiable for pleasure – passionate without depth – faithful only for the moment. He arrived one day at her home to call for her, and was given a note which told him that their affair was at an end. Tessa had gone with a party to Luxor. In that party was a well-known American author ... Tessa's latest conquest. She told Boyd bluntly that she had 'fallen' for the American and that she and Boyd must 'call it a day'.

That was a stunning blow to Boyd ... to his vanity, his love, his faith in women. Fortunately for him, he was sent up to Khartoum and did not have to see any more of Miss Richardson. But her fascination remained with him for a long time, and he found it lowering to his morale in general to remember how responsive a girl could be in a man's arms and not mean it, and how entirely he had believed in her. She had promised so much. It was not good to know how shallow was the receptacle into which he had poured his first, ardent worship of a woman.

Time passed. Tessa became a memory. Boyd Mansell, once he got over the first bitterness, indulged in light-hearted affairs here and there, but was a little less inclined to 'worship' and a good deal more cautious.

Still he remained unmarried.

The next serious affair was this recent experience, which had disturbed him considerably, in Durban.

Ann Pumphrey was a very different proposition from Tessa. She was in her thirties, not particularly beautiful but extraordinarily charming. She had one of the most attractive personalities Boyd had ever come up against. A clever, vivid woman, full of lights and shades, with an exquisite figure unimpaired by maternity. She had two children of eight and ten, a boy and girl whom she adored. But she was desperately unhappy; married to a man whom Boyd, when he first met him in a bar in a Durban hotel, sozzled with drink and making advances to the barmaid, despised immediately. The Hon. Wilfred Pumphrey had at one time been a cavalry officer. Then there had been a scandal ... mainly over a drinking party and a woman ... he had been forced to resign his commission and come out to Africa with his wife and children. His father, grieved and disappointed in him, had given him the money and opportunity to start life afresh on a South African farm. Wilfred knew Boyd's brother, James, and thus Boyd and the Pumphreys had met.

From the start, Ann Pumphrey roused all that was chivalrous and compassionate in Boyd. At first, it was her pathetic loyalty to her husband, who was rarely sober or faithful, and her pitiful attempts to keep up appearances in public for his sake and her children's, which impressed Boyd. Then when she fell hopelessly in love with him, he responded more from pity and admiration than real love, although Ann was fundamentally good as well as a fascinating woman and offered more depth and quality of loving than Tessa had ever done.

He was drawn into an affair ... temporarily blinded to reason by Ann's charm and her desperate need of him. After years of misery in the hands of the weakling she had married, Ann Pumphrey flung herself whole-heartedly into this, her first real love-affair. Boyd was fine and strong and all that Wilfred was not. She begged him to take her away. Wilfred would give her the children, she said. He would not want to be bothered with them. If Boyd would go through the divorce for her she would see that he never regretted it. They could start life afresh in England.

But here, Boyd came to a full stop. The mere mention of the word 'divorce' pulled him up with a jerk. His mother would be heartbroken if he became involved in a scandal. Gilly would never believe in him again. Audrey and her husband would be horrified.

He felt a prig and a cad for ever having encouraged Ann. But he had drifted into the affair. Certainly he had not meant it to get this far. They had a painful scene when he told her how he felt; she broke down and cried until he almost decided to take her, no matter what the result. But it was the woman herself who made the final decision. He knew that he would never forget the deep pity and concern which he had felt when she had said good-bye.

'You don't love me enough. I see that. If you had cared as I do, you'd have taken me away and the divorce wouldn't have mattered,' she had said in a heartbroken voice.

He knew that was true. For a woman whom he really loved he would gladly have figured as co-respondent ... risked losing his commission ... made any sacrifice she asked. Even if it meant hurting his family. But Ann – sweet and pathetic though she was – was not *the* one. *She* knew it, now.

For a little while she had sobbed in his arms. He had said:

'Forgive me, Ann. I can't forgive myself ... but it wouldn't work with us ... I know it. But thank you ... for everything...'

She had tried to laugh and said:

'You needn't thank me. You brought a lot of happiness into my miserable life for a bit. I'll just have to put up with Wilfred. I dug my own grave when I married him. But he was different then. Everything was different. Oh, Boyd, Boyd, why does time change people and things so dreadfully?'

Long after he left her, he asked himself the same question. It made a fellow uneasy ... damned uneasy. The awful way men and women altered ... the way in which passions flared up ... then burned out. The times vows were broken; and ideals smashed.

He left Durban and poor Ann Pumphrey, doubting himself ... his own capacity for permanent affection ... and wondering if he would ever marry. It seemed too unsafe. True love was a snare and delusion. Better to remain a bachelor.

Now, on his return voyage to England, he must needs meet another married woman and fall in love with her. But this time, it was not to be for an hour or a day ... but for always. Somehow Boyd Mansell sensed that fact within an hour of knowing Veronica Hallard, and was dismayed by the thought that she was not only already married but in love with her husband.

Yet – incongruously – he respected her because of that very fact. Entranced, almost awe-stricken, Boyd Mansell sat listening to this distractingly lovely girl talk about her Charles. They had been married a year, but were still so much in love that they apparently found even this temporary separation intolerable.

Veronica admitted, without embarrassment, that she was unutterably miserable apart from her husband and that this voyage so far had been an agony to her. Boyd could see it; her sincerity was undoubted. Those great grey eyes of hers glowed at the mere mention of her husband's name. She seemed glad to be able to talk about him; to pour out stories of his music, his books, his charm, and the wonderful way he had put aside his ambitions to become a composer behind him and start a fresh life – uncongenial to him – as a business man; how well he was running the cocoa plantation in Lagos.

'Can't you imagine how he hated it to begin with?' Veronica said. 'His heart and soul were in music.'

'But he had you with him – that was his

compensation, and no small one, if I may say so,' observed Boyd.

Veronica blushed a little, looked over the rim of her glass at Captain Mansell and thought that he was very nice indeed and that it was pleasant, after days of lying half-dead with seasickness and misery alone in her cabin, to feel better and sit here talking to a man who was such a charming and sympathetic listener.

'I've been rambling on about me and my Charles. Now it's your turn. Tell me about *you*,' she said.

Boyd's blue eyes crinkled at the corners.

'Oh, my story would fill a book, and not a madly exciting one, I assure you.'

'But tell me something,' she said, with the upward tilt of the red lips and grey eyes which he found so delicious. 'Are you married? Have you a girl friend?'

'No to both questions.'

'Oh!' she exclaimed. 'You are not one of these confirmed bachelors, surely?'

'Almost.'

'Oh, you mustn't be. It's so lovely to be married to the right person.'

'But not so lovely to be married to the wrong. How can one guarantee the right?'

'You just have to trust to luck. Charles and I were lucky. We met ... at Mervyn and Iris's cocktail party. Just like that ... a lightning flash ... and it was all over.'

'H'm,' said Boyd, and looked at her speculatively and fingered his empty glass. That was how it *should* be, of course. How it might have been if Veronica Hallard had been *Miss* Hallard, he told himself wryly. He would have known this very evening all about the 'lightning flash' of which she spoke ... known that it was all over. She was the girl for him. Oh, confound it!...

'You'll meet someone *one* day,' Veronica was assuring him with her sweet seriousness. 'Don't despair.'

'Have another drink,' he said abruptly.

'No, thank you, really. I've had enough.'

'Do you mind if I do?'

'Of course not. But oughtn't I to be going down to my cabin to get ready for dinner?'

'Don't,' he said impulsively. 'Stay and talk a bit longer.'

She stayed, gladly, enjoying his company.

He drank his pink gin and told her about Chidding Manor ... his mother ... and poor Gilly. He had never seen anything, he thought, so entrancingly soft and luminous as Veronica Hallard's eyes when she sympathized about Gilly.

'It must have been so awful ... for her and for all of you who loved her.'

'It was.'

Veronica breathed a little sigh:

'Oh, such horror... I can't picture it... I can't *imagine* what I'd have done if my

122

Charles had been killed like that on our honeymoon. Your sister sounds so brave ... facing life. I'd have *died*...'

He honestly believed that she would have died. This Charles was a lucky devil. How many men could rely upon their wives loving them as Veronica loved her husband? Not many he guaranteed. He said:

'Gilly certainly stood up to things very pluckily; I daresay you'd have done the same.'

'No – never. I'd have died,' she repeated.

She was quite pale and moved, and he began to see how vulnerable she was and to wonder in a half-cynical fashion what life had in store for *her*. What grim jest of Fate lay in waiting. Gilly had once been vital and young and madly in love. Like Veronica. Then he told himself not to be morbid. There was no reason why Veronica should not retain her happiness. She and her Charles would probably live to be Darby and Joan together.

He changed the conversation from poor Gilly and spoke of his other sister who was married to the doctor in Market Rasen. Out came the much-admired photograph of Audrey's twins – David, so-called after his father, and Jonathan. Veronica was as enthusiastic as most women to whom Boyd showed the likeness of his young nephews.

'They are *darlings* – what angelic curls and

123

eyes! – oh, I do think little boys of that age are so sweet.'

'So do I when I don't have to cope with them. Audrey finds them a handful,' laughed Boyd, 'but she's a damn good mother.'

'Charles and I want a son one day,' said Veronica simply. 'But not until he has got on a bit more with this new job and we can live in a place where the climate is better. He's going to try and get transferred to London.'

'My dear, there's a war fast approaching and he may have to get himself a uniform,' said Boyd drily.

Veronica caught her breath.

'Oh, I couldn't *imagine* Charles in the Army. I don't believe it will happen, anyhow. It mustn't. Not another war like the last.'

'Worse than the last. I don't wish to depress you, but...' Boyd paused significantly and drained his glass, then added: 'Don't let's talk of it. "Sufficient unto the day." This is your first evening up. Let's celebrate tonight. How about dining with me? We'll open a special bottle of something. Yes?'

She bit her lip like an excited child.

The fear of war and of Charles having to be a soldier vanished into thin air. At the moment, after all, it was all such a nebulous affair. She expanded like a flower in the sun to Boyd Mansell's quiet charm and the friendliness which was such an intrinsic part of his make-up. Nobody could feel strange or embarrassed with Boyd. He had a genius for making friends and Veronica had never been more in need of a little masculine support and friendship. Letty Chaddon was a dear and had been exceedingly kind. Pam was kind and attentive, too. But Veronica felt that both the women, behind their sympathy, failed to understand wholly her intense love and longing for Charles. They probably in their hearts thought her a little idiotic, but Boyd Mansell *understood* ... she was sure of it. She could talk to him of Charles without feeling that he would sneer privately, or be bored. He *knew* ... and was extraordinarily sympathetic.

She decided to accept his invitation.

'Charles would want me to,' she said. 'I do feel so much better. And I'd love to celebrate with you, Captain Mansell.'

'Boyd, please.'

'Boyd,' she repeated the name, and standing up, looked at him with her enchanting smile. He looked down, clutching his empty glass and a half-smoked cigarette and felt his heartbeats quicken absurdly. 'And please call me Veronica,' she added. 'Everyone does except Charles. I'm "Nic" to him.'

Boyd thought suddenly of that far-off passionate interlude with Tessa Richardson. Very far off ... with the ghost of poor, unhappy Ann between them. And Ann, too, seemed a long way away now. He had cabled 'good-bye' to her but no more. It was better he should not write again. But during the first few days at sea he had remembered uncomfortably her broken weeping in his arms, and her desperate wish for him to take her away from Wilfred Pumphrey. It had worried him. But tonight the ghost of Ann was laid. Veronica Hallard, little, lovely, and quite crazy about the man she was married to, was fast blotting out the memory of all other women for Boyd Mansell.

He watched her walk away ... and murmured her name aloud.

'Veronica...'

Then he ordered his last before-dinner drink and with knitted brows watched the rest of the crowd in the bar.

'Oh, damn,' he thought. 'And *damn* that lucky fellow Charles!'

## 2

From that time onward life on board ship changed for the better for Veronica. The enforced rest, the sea air and comparative quiet of the cabin at night – even with the irksome presence of the other three women – did her good physically, and the sudden friendship which sprang up between her and Boyd Mansell was no small comfort spiritually. For the rest of the voyage he would not allow her to be lonely or miserable. In fact, as Letty Chaddon put it, he became her shadow.

'My word, I think that young Captain Mansell has fallen in love with you, my dear,' Letty remarked in her blunt fashion when she and Veronica were discussing the possibilities of going ashore at Madeira where they were due tomorrow morning. 'What *would* your Charles say?'

Veronica flushed. A rare look of annoyance flashed into her grey eyes. She turned from Letty and continued with her dressing. Pam and the other two bridge-playing inmates of the cabin were already up and on deck. It was a bright, crisp morning and a good deal cooler now that they had left the West Coast so far behind them. The sun poured radiantly through the porthole. Letty, smoking a cigarette, looked good-humouredly at Veronica's flushed face and added:

'There! I was only teasing. We all know you have no eyes or ears for anyone but your Charles. But Captain Mansell *is* attractive, and he *does* haunt you, my dear. One must notice it. The young cats are all jealous – he's the best looker on board, and you, with a husband already, get him. Spoiled child!'

This was where Veronica put in a word.

'I haven't "got him", Letty, and don't want him except as a friend. He's been very kind to me and we have mutual friends and–'

'Oh, come, don't lose your sense of humour, duck,' Letty Chaddon broke in with her strident laugh. Her gaunt brown face was creased with laughter. Veronica, mollified, swallowed her annoyance and tried to smile back. She supposed old Letty meant no harm. But somehow it irritated her even to be told in fun that she was being talked about and 'envied' because of her so-called conquest of Boyd Mansell. Charming, attractive though he was – Boyd was not Charles. There never could be another Charles. She was still most unhappy because of her separation from her husband. But admittedly the young Gunner officer had helped to make the hours seem less long and weary. He was always friendly and helpful. Meal-time was something to look forward to now. They sat together in the dining-saloon, with Letty and Pam and two other men. It had developed into quite a gay little party. They had danced once or twice and got up a concert ... and Veronica had played and sung and been a tremendous success. Especially with Boyd. She knew, of course, that Boyd liked her very much. He did not attempt to hide the fact. But Letty was hinting at a flirtation. That upset Veronica. For her there had never been nor could be anything approaching an 'affair' with any other man. She was completely in love with her own husband. She wrote to him every day. He knew all about her new friend. She was sure he would not disapprove. He would be glad that someone was taking care of her and making life as pleasant for her as possible under the circumstances.

But of course she realised that in a ship like this, among a lot of catty women, there was bound to be gossip. But Veronica decided that she would be stupid to take Letty's 'ragging' too seriously. She changed the conversation from Boyd to Madeira.

'We must all go and do some shopping when we're there. One can buy such lovely things in Madeira. I remember when Charles and I went ashore on our way out to Lagos, we had a marvellous morning,' she said.

'One thing I'm sure about,' observed Mrs Chaddon, with a look of real kindliness at the girl, 'Charles would be glad to see how much fitter you're looking already. West Africa was killing you by inches, my girl.'

Veronica agreed. But she sighed as she put the finishing touches to hair and face. She would give a lot to be back in that awful climate ... even to be lying awake listening to the crickets ... in the suffocating, drenching heat ... if only she could see Charles, feel his arms around her. It seemed years instead of days since she left him. It was *awful*, how far he was away now, she reflected.

Letty Chaddon looked at her with almost maternal pride. Bless the girl! Why, she was pretty as a picture this morning, with a touch of natural colour in her cheeks; slim figure seen to advantage in a neat grey flannel suit, crisp white blouse. She had tied her dark waving hair up in a white scarf. She looked altogether more animated than she had done in Lagos, although still much too thin.

'Well, let's go up...' said Letty.

They walked round the deck together, and Veronica sniffed appreciatively at the keen, salty air. The sea was a deep greeny-blue and the sky radiant. One or two young couples were playing quoits; several were sun-bathing; the swimming-pool was already in use, and shouts and splashes issued from that direction. Everyone was up and doing this morning. It was calm and at the same time invigorating. Madeira tomorrow, thought Veronica. The voyage was nearly over. Well, thanks to Boyd Mansell, she had not found it the awful experience she had anticipated.

Ah! There he was ... coming towards her, always so well turned out in his smart grey flannels (the complement of her own), blue silk scarf round his neck, pipe in his mouth.

He took the pipe in his hand and waved to her.

'Hello! Good morning...'

Letty Chaddon grinned and said:

'Run along and play, honey-girl. I'm going to fetch my knitting and sit in the sun.'

Veronica felt annoyed again. Was Letty openly inviting her to have a *tête-à-tête* by being 'tactful'?

'Silly old thing,' thought Veronica crossly.

Boyd Mansell reached Veronica's side and noted at once that the penciled brows were knit and the sweet red mouth unsmiling.

'Hello! What's wrong?' he asked quickly.

'Nothing. What should be?'

Her answer was almost sharp and so unlike her gentle self that Boyd was pulled up with a jerk. He raised his own brows.

'Something has annoyed you...' he said promptly.

At once the cloud vanished from Veronica's face; she could never be angry for long. She laughed.

'Only my own foolish thoughts. Isn't it a heavenly morning!'

'It surely is, and you look pretty smooth, if I may say so. Wretched girl, I believe your grey flannels are better than mine. I must speak to my tailor.'

He always managed to make Veronica chuckle. She liked that expression of Boyd's, 'pretty smooth'. They strolled together to the ship's rails and hung over them, looking down at the glittering opalescent water. Veronica said:

'Madeira tomorrow ... isn't it amazing? The voyage has gone quite quickly.'

'It's fairly flown since my meeting with you,' he said. 'I can't tell you what a difference it made meeting you.'

'For me, too. Charles will be terribly grateful ... you've looked after me so well,' she said.

Boyd gave a swift look at the charming profile under the white turban, then stared at the water again. Of course, he knew he was all kinds of a fool ... and more ... to fancy himself in love with this girl. But he could not help himself. It was going to make a difference to his whole life. He knew that. Veronica typified all that he had ever wanted in a woman. He had got to know her well ... her adorable gentleness; that enchanting childlike simplicity of hers ... *and* her deep-rooted passion for her husband. She was such a fascinating mixture. He could plainly see how crazy a man could become about Veronica Hallard. There was such a depth of passion, of intense feeling, in her, despite all that 'little girl' atmosphere which he had learned was no affectation in Veronica but a sincere part of her make-up.

He was crazy about her now. But he knew he must master that passion or be hurt by it. Veronica belonged body and heart and brain to her husband. Whenever she spoke of her Charles (which Boyd encouraged her

132

to do) it caused him a bitter pang, and yet he loved her all the more dearly for it; adored her for the very reason, perhaps, that he would not dare to take her hand or attempt one of those 'ship flirtations' in which he would have indulged with any other woman who attracted him … but Veronica.

'Will you let me take you on shore at Madeira and give you lunch?' he asked, after a pause.

'Of course. It would be lovely,' she said. Then added: 'Oh dear, I suppose it will soon be getting colder and we'll all have to unpack thicker things. After all – the first week in September can be very cool in dear old England.'

'I rather look forward to the grey days and the rain,' said Boyd. 'Had enough of sunshine and parched earth after four years of foreign service.'

She nodded.

'I agree. My home – Princes Risborough – should be at its best.'

'And mine. I want you to see Chidding Manor and meet my people,' said Boyd.

'I'd love to – especially your poor sister,' said Veronica softly.

'We must fix it somehow. Gilly would love you.'

'How much more of your leave have you got?'

'Practically nothing. I took the couple of months due to me, but I'm afraid I neglected the family by flying out to Kenya to see James and his farm. I feel rather guilty about it. But I hadn't seen my brother for so long.'

'Of course. Tell me … is James like you?'

'Not at all,' smiled Boyd. 'He's a plump fellow with fair hair, rapidly growing bald on top, and a passion for animals. Got a regular menagerie on his ranch. His wife is a big, bouncing South African girl rather after the style of your friend on board here, Pam. They've got a nice little kid, Bunty. Rather sad for my mother – she's never seen her grand-daughter, and I doubt she ever will. James is a bit of a stick, and having got to Kenya won't ever come away. But I'm more restless. I like getting around the world.'

'And you won't ever keep a menagerie, eh?' smiled Veronica.

'I don't fancy so. I like a dog in the house, but not all these weird animals James goes in for.'

'What do you like doing best, Boyd?' she asked suddenly.

He cast a wry smile at her.

'I've no particular hobbies, Veronica. Nor can I lay claim to any talents. I ride a bit, shoot, fish, climb mountains, and now and again buy books. Yes … I'm keen on reading. Got rather a decent library at Chidding Manor.'

'You don't like music, do you?'

'I like it, but don't understand it. I mean … your husband is a musician … composes … and you play and sing … and very exquisitely, if I may say so … but although I appreciate it, I'm no critic and couldn't for the life of me do what you did the other day, for instance, tune-in on the wireless and put a name to everything you heard played.'

'That's all a question of training.'

'I think I'd be a bit stupid about music, always,' he said.

'But you have a sense of rhythm. You dance awfully nicely, Boyd.'

'Do I?' He looked pleased. But when he looked down into the luminous grey eyes raised to his, he felt a queer stabbing pain. To hold Veronica's small slender body in his arms and dance with her had been a delightful experience the other night. To do so again might become torment as well as delight. He had never wanted, more intolerably, to kiss any woman than he wanted to kiss this one. But it would be sacrilege … those lips of hers belonged first and foremost to Charles Hallard.

One day he might have to meet Charles. He would feel nothing for him but the most primitive form of jealousy. In fact he did not really want to meet Veronica's husband.

He forced himself to say:

'I suppose you and your Charles dance a lot together?'

'M'm yes ... we do ... but he isn't terribly keen on dancing. He and I spend more time at our piano than anything.'

Boyd felt absurdly pleased. Veronica had praised *his* dancing... Hallard didn't dance much ... that was something.

'You're a doggone fool, Mansell,' Boyd admonished himself and abruptly suggested that they should go and find a couple of deck-chairs and have a cigarette.

They were sitting there, stretched out in the warm sun, smoking, when a short stout man with greying hair and moustache, a very sunburned round face and wearing khaki shorts and shirt, came up to Boyd, excitedly waving a pair of smoked glasses.

'Mansell, Mansell ... looking for you, my boy. Heard the news? Just been radioed to us.'

Boyd rose.

'Oh, hello, sir...' He turned to Veronica. 'This is Colonel Dakers, I don't think you've met... Colonel Dakers, may I introduce Mrs Hallard...?'

The Colonel and Veronica exchanged greetings, then the little man addressed Boyd again, obviously in a state of emotion.

'It's war, my dear fellow ... war...'

Simultaneously Boyd and Veronica echoed

the word.

'*War?*'

Colonel Dakers nodded agitatedly, removed his glasses and blinked a pair of jaundiced eyes.

'Just come through ... been talking to the Captain. It's September 1st, y'know. Things have been at high tension all this week. At half past five this morning Germany started bombing Poland. We're for it now. Hitler's made up his mind and we'll have to intervene. *Have to*...'

Boyd remained standing silent a moment, his blue eyes grave and speculative. Those eyes wandered instinctively to the girl in the deck-chair. She looked pale, frightened.

'Oh, no,' she said breathlessly. 'It can't be. It mustn't be. We didn't intervene when Hitler attacked Czechoslovakia.'

'Weren't ready to. Couldn't be done then, my dear lady,' said the Colonel. 'But this is different.'

'But ... but my husband told me about Chamberlain and the Munich peace–' began Veronica in dismay.

Colonel Dakers interrupted.

'Scrap of paper. Not worth the ink written on it. Like the scrap the old Kaiser tore up in 1914. Same thing. Hun aggression. Can't get away from it. We didn't finish them off properly in 1918 when we had the chance.'

'You think it's inevitable, sir?' asked Boyd.

'Absolutely. At 8 p.m. the German Army crossed the Polish frontier. Today we'll protest. Germans won't give in. Day after tomorrow we'll declare war. You'll see.'

Veronica sat up stiffly.

'Oh, heavens, then we'll be in a state of war when ... when we land!'

'Undoubtedly,' said Colonel Dakers. 'Second world war in my lifetime. Damn me, I'm on the retired list, but I'm going to get back into *this* show! As for you...' He clapped a hand on Boyd's shoulder. 'Envy you your youth ... like to be your age and right in it again, Mansell my boy.'

Boyd nodded. He was a soldier. He both expected to and wished to be 'right in it'. But he had an uncomfortably vivid imagination. He loved beauty and the pleasant things of the world, and now he saw violence, bloodshed, untold misery ahead. This war would be as his father had prophesied, 'in the air' this time. A far more terrible war than the one which had scorched the face of the earth when old Dakers was a subaltern.

The Colonel moved off, ready and anxious to pass his news round the ship. Boyd sat down again. For a moment he was silent, filling his pipe. Veronica, wide-eyed, still curiously frightened, watched him. She had thought from the first time they met what nice hands Boyd had. Not as slender

138

and sensitive as Charles's ... but hard, brown, masculine, with long fingers and well-shaped nails. Charles had the hands of a dreamer, an artist; Boyd's were of a more practical, perhaps more efficient, type. But at the memory of those well-loved hands of her husband's and the thrilling touch of them, a pang shot through Veronica's heart. She said:

'Oh Boyd ... how *awful!* To be at war when we reach England. Oh, Boyd, I wish I hadn't left Charles.'

He turned to her, his bright-blue eyes gentle, as they always were when looking at Veronica.

'My dear, it's just as well. Things will be tightening up all round now. Shipping ... travelling ... the whole show. Your Charles, when he hears this news, will be more than thankful that you're safely back in the old country.'

'But *he* isn't safe, Boyd. He'll have to travel in February some time, and by then – if we really are at war – there may be a submarine menace like there was in the last war. I remember Mummy telling me about the *Lusitania* ... those horrible Germans go for passenger boats ... oh, Boyd...!'

'My *dear* little Veronica,' he said, 'you mustn't jump your fences till you come to them.'

'I always do,' she said, with a half-shamed

laugh. 'I get so nervous about Charles.'

'He'll be all right,' said Boyd. 'There's no earthly reason to suppose he'll get torpedoed or anything else. Don't even let such a thing prey on that funny little mind of yours.'

'Is it funny?' She smiled.

Boyd's quite authoritative manner and sense of humour always calmed her down. The creases were soon smoothed out on the lovely forehead again and the grey eyes laughed at him. He stuck his pipe in his mouth and wondered how much more he would be able to stand of this sort of thing. He would soon begin to dislike the very name of Charles Hallard. Yet for Veronica's sake, he wished most sincerely that the fellow were here now, with them; that there need be no cause for her alarm and despondency concerning him.

They talked animatedly about the German attack on Poland and the dire consequences as prophesied by the old retired Colonel. Veronica, listening to Boyd, realised what a first-rate officer he must be. He knew his job thoroughly and was keen on it. He was so interested in this new crisis that he took the trouble to go down to his cabin, fetch a map and, spreading it over his knee and hers – showed her the scene of action; told her more about the Danzig Corridor ... made rough guesses at Hitler's next move. Finally Veronica sat back with a deep sigh and said:

'Oh dear, Charles and I have been living in a world of our own all this year out in Lagos. A world of music, mainly. We never thought of all this brewing ... although Charles did mention something about it just before I left. I must admit I realised then how ignorant I was about current events. Being with you, who are a soldier, shakes one up a bit, Boyd. You seem to have expected this ... like Colonel Dakers.'

'We all thought that war was likely after the *Anschluss*,' said Boyd.

'What will happen to you as soon as you get back?'

'If war has been declared, I shall have to get into uniform and report at once for duty. Our lot are at Borden at the moment, I believe. I shall go down there.'

'Does that mean you won't get home at all?'

'I shall see the family because I have to run down to Chidding Manor to get my kit. I left it all there before I flew out to South Africa.'

Veronica's thoughts travelled back to Lagos, to Charles ... picturing his reactions to this news which would have reached him over the radio. She thought, too, of her mother. Lady Lowring would be thankful to get her home. And poor Iris ... it would

141

affect her seriously if war was declared. Mervyn would report for duty ... another regular.

Veronica said:

'Let's be optimists. Let's hope there *won't* be war. There's still hope.'

He smiled at her.

'Right. We'll hope. Nothing like hoping, my dear.'

Their hands touched under the map as Boyd drew it away to fold it up. She did not seem to notice the fact. But the man's face reddened. He drew a quick breath and thought:

'Lord, what a fool I am ... to love her so much! It's just as well we shall be separated once we get to England. I couldn't go on seeing her ... being near to her every day ... like this...'

In ironical contradiction to those thoughts and feelings, Veronica turned to him with that warm, friendly glow in her great grey eyes which half thrilled, half saddened him, and said:

'I do hope when you're on leave you'll come and see me at my mother's house.'

He squared up to it.

'Of course I will,' he said.

But he did not return her smile.

That next morning – a cloudless September day – they put in at Madeira. Despite the immediate threat of war between England

and Germany – everybody who went ashore was determined to have a good time – and did.

Veronica, Boyd Mansell, Pam and another young man who had been playing a great deal of deck-tennis with the South African girl, made up a party and lunched together.

They had an excellent meal washed down by good wine. They sat in the sun. They drove through the beautiful town, so full of glorious flowers and trees. Everything radiant under the blue sky. They bought presents for those at home from the gay colourful shops. And Veronica, for one, thoroughly enjoyed herself. That day in Madeira was a tonic and in her mind cemented the friendship between Boyd Mansell and herself. They would assuredly meet again after this voyage was over, she thought, and Charles would one day also meet and thank Boyd for his delightful care of her. That he had fallen desperately and hopelessly in love with her never somehow entered Veronica's mind. He kept a tight rein on his emotions, and was far too serious to attempt even a mild flirtation. For that she was grateful. She was in need of friendship ... but nothing more. When men tried to make love to her – as one or two had done, covertly, in West Africa – it merely worried her. She had nothing emotionally to give any man. Charles possessed her entire heart. But she had grown to like and respect Boyd Mansell during this voyage home, and was most anxious that their friendship should endure.

He bought a great armful of carnations for her at Madeira and she accepted them with delight. But for him the joy of buying flowers for Veronica was spoiled when she reminded him that Charles had done exactly the same thing on their trip out.

Certainly, he was beginning to dislike Charles, Boyd told himself gloomily. But he did not let Veronica see that. He was so well aware that he had not the slightest right to be jealous. Neither had he any hope for the future. Veronica Hallard was not for him. But he loved her … everything about her … and he asked himself several times whether he was glad or sorry that he had met her. She was spoiling all other women for him.

A chance conversation with Mrs Chaddon on board that same evening after leaving Madeira further strengthened Boyd's own conviction that it would be better for him not to see much of Veronica in the future.

Letty had found the young officer standing by himself, looking down at the dark violet water, while the ship ploughed its way steadily towards England. Veronica, over-tired, had gone down to her cabin for an early bed. Letty had just finished a rubber of bridge and come out of the card-room for a 'breath of fresh air' and a cigarette. She

144

greeted Boyd, and with his customary politeness he offered her his cigarette-case.

She was a quaint, unattractive woman in his opinion. Typical of the type of her age one met out East ... dull, dried up ... a little dangerous. But he also appreciated the fact that Letty Chaddon was a good sort and a genuine friend to Veronica.

She grinned at him and said:

'Sulking because your girl friend has gone to bed?'

Boyd flushed.

'Hardly my "girl friend", Mrs Chaddon.'

'Tch!' she laughed. 'I was only teasing. I know Veronica. Ye gods, I ought to know her! Seen enough of her at Lagos. She's a lunatic about that husband of hers. But you're good for her. She's bucked up no end this trip ... thanks to you.'

'I'm glad,' said Boyd a trifle stiffly.

She gave him a sidelong look. She could see plainly what was written on that brown, handsome face. Poor Captain Mansell was hard hit. Fallen properly for Veronica's charm and beauty. She said, quite kindly:

'Veronica *is* a fascinating person, but I don't think any chap will ever get anywhere with her. Far too interested in her husband.'

Boyd suddenly turned and faced her squarely.

'What *is* Hallard like, Mrs Chaddon?' he asked.

145

She gave a harsh little laugh and good-humouredly patted his arm.

'Can't cheer you up by telling you he's no good and cross-eyed or bad-tempered, and that she'll soon get sick of him. He's the best-looking man I've ever seen and she adores him. He has a remarkable face and tremendous charm. Plenty of brains, too. One of these musical geniuses, you know. Yes, I must say Charles Hallard is a heart-breaker. My husband dotes on him.'

Boyd essayed a slightly wry smile.

'That's *that*...'

'Yes,' said Letty thoughtfully, 'it is. They're a remarkable couple. I scoffed at 'em to start with, but I don't any more. It's too genuine. Don't know what they'd either of 'em do if one lost the other.'

'I certainly don't know what *she'd* do,' said Boyd. 'But we mustn't anticipate anything like that.'

Letty Chaddon patted his arm again.

'You're rather a nice boy. Aren't the girls all crazy about you?'

He put his tongue to his cheek and flung a half-smoked cigarette into the water.

'Queueing up for me, Mrs Chaddon. But I just love 'em and leave 'em.'

'That's the way,' she said heartily. 'This burning love-stuff gets me down. Doesn't seem to make for happiness.'

He shrugged his shoulders. He felt suddenly depressed ... an unusual state for him. He said:

'Let's go and have a drink.'

He wanted to put the thought of Veronica and Charles out of his mind for a bit.

Down in her cabin, Veronica was sitting up in bed feverishly writing her daily bulletin to her husband ... she wanted to get it finished before the other three women came down.

*Darlingest, we did have a good day on shore, but – oh, despite everyone being so kind, and Boyd in particular, I missed you desperately and remembered our day in Madeira. Oh, Charles, I can't do anything without missing and wanting you. And now this awful war is going to happen. I wish I had never left you. Darling, darling ... it's so hard being without you.*

She stopped writing for a second, and picked up the leather-framed photograph of Charles which stood on the table beside her. She looked long and passionately at the clear-cut features, so dear and familiar; the fine dark eyes, the beautifully shaped lips. She pressed her mouth to his pictured one, the hot tears starting to her eyes. The red carnations filling the cabin ... the carnations Boyd Mansell had bought for her ... were blotted out by those tears.

Perhaps she was still overtired, overwrought; but she could not finish her letter.

147

She put it away, laid the photograph down, and for the first time for several days, hid her face in her pillow and wept like a broken-hearted child for the man she had left in West Africa.

When she met Boyd again that next morning it was already half past eleven. She was later than she had been because she awakened with a headache and stayed in bed. She met Boyd coming out of the purser's cabin. The moment she saw his grave face she knew that there was bad news. He took her arm and told her as they went out on deck that the Prime Minister had just announced to the world that Great Britain and Germany were at war again.

## 3

Veronica had telephoned Lady Lowring from Liverpool and said, 'Don't meet me – I must just catch a train whenever I can get one,' so it was alone in the taxi that she finally drove with her luggage from Princes Risborough to her mother's new home.

For Veronica it was in a way a real home-coming because of the familiar countryside, steeped this afternoon in the mellow light of a fast-fading September day. She felt like one almost in a dream as she looked at the little town which she had known since her babyhood; the market place, the winding streets with their charming Queen Anne cottages, and finally the green rustic lane flanked by trees which led down to her mother's cottage, Monks Rest.

Nothing had changed. But *she* had changed; she felt a totally different being from that Veronica who had lived quietly, sedately, such a well-ordered existence here for so long with her father and mother. After her year in Lagos as Charles's wife, she was so much more mature and experienced, so much richer, she thought, for the tremendous love which was now an integral part of her life.

It seemed extraordinary to look at Whitelands Hall as she drove by the gateway; her old home in which every stick and stone, every shrub, tree and flower, was so familiar. Those days when poor old Daddy was alive had gone. Mummy was living in a cottage now with only one servant, she said – old Nanny, who had been Veronica's nurse and who had come back to help her ladyship with the cooking. The other maids had gone. Already they had gone, right at the beginning of the war! – anxious to go into munitions and have their nights free. 'Horrid girls,' Lady Lowring had said to Veronica on the telephone during that Liverpool call. 'Running away as soon as they get the chance.'

Veronica had laughed. It was so typical of her mother to be 'down' on the servant class. She had said:

'You can't blame them for wanting to do war work, Mummy…'

But of course she knew her mother would be certain that the motives of her staff in leaving were not of the highest. Veronica had her private theories about the attitude of the cook and house-parlour-maid who had just 'walked out'. She knew her mother. She was a martinet and maids respected but did not like her. Well, times would change with a war on. Maybe there would *be* no maids in a few years' time.

Veronica looked ahead of her. She knew Monks Rest, of course. It belonged to the Lowrings, and before Veronica went out to Lagos it had been occupied by a young couple with a baby. They had since moved to Scotland. It was altogether charming, and Veronica really preferred it to the big Hall. It was such a fairy-tale place, like an illustration to a Hans Andersen fairy-tale, she always thought, with its tumbledown irregular lines, its famous old chimney-stack which leant backwards as though about to fall, its lichened tiles and rosy Elizabethan bricks.

A hedge separated the small garden from the village churchyard. It was not a sad view in Veronica's opinion, but a peaceful, even comforting, one. She liked to look upon the old grey tombstones with their quaint inscriptions, the dark graceful yews, the rose bushes in full bloom, here and there little bunches of flowers on remembered graves.

The small grey stone church had stood up bravely against many storms in life; the tall elms at the far end where the rooks nested and cawed had witnessed the passing of one century after another.

'One war after another, too,' reflected Veronica, and sighed at the memory of the London she had just come through. A very changed city from the one which she and Charles had left twelve months ago. Already trenches had been dug in the parks and there were air-raid precautions, gas-decontamination centres; mobile ambulances, national fire services, organizations Veronica had never imagined or heard of. Air-raid sirens and enemy bombers. Black-out regulations. More than ever, Veronica had been struck by her own ignorance that such a state in her own country had been brewing all these months, and preparations being made for emergencies even while the English people slumbered on, shielding themselves from the storm under the symbolic umbrella raised by Mr Chamberlain.

Princes Risborough, however, seemed unchanged. For that, Veronica was thankful.

Then she saw her mother standing at the

little wooden gate, waving a pair of gardening-gloves, a basket of cut flowers on one arm. Behind her lay the glorious purple of a herbaceous border vivid with Michaelmas daisies, gay with golden rod and blue with the last lovely delphiniums. Veronica's mother was and always had been a keen gardener, and it had not taken her long to make much of the little plot of ground belonging to Monks Rest.

A rush of warmest affection for her mother came over Veronica as she jumped out of the taxi and looked with sparkling eyes at Lady Lowring. She, too, thank goodness, was unaltered. The same tall regal figure, exquisitely groomed. Even when gardening Beatrice Lowring never looked untidy. Grey hair immaculately waved and dressed under a black straw hat. She wore a hat both in and out of the house on most occasions. Well-cut grey suit. Well-polished tan shoes. (Goloshes protected her when the ground was damp.) A handsome woman, with the beautiful pale skin and finely pencilled dark brows which Veronica had inherited. Hers was, however, a much harder face, and she usually wore horn-rimmed spectacles these days. She had a determined mouth and chin and a haughty tilt to the head. Beatrice Lowring had never been a woman to whom anybody could come close. Neither did she give way an inch in any matter on which she formed a decided opinion. She had had to stand aside when her only daughter made what she thought a 'poor marriage', but it had disappointed her and she had never really got over it. Now, however, when Veronica had come home alone because of her health and this new, terrible war, Lady Lowring was genuinely pleased to see her, and it was with a greater warmth of feeling than she had ever shown in the past that she dropped the basket and clasped the girl in her arms.

'Veronica, my *dear* child...'

Veronica hugged the tall figure, always so unbending in her youth ... and there were tears in her eyes. She felt suddenly tired and lonely and in need of a comforting embrace.

'Dear Mummy! How lovely to be back!'

They kissed several times. Then Lady Lowring looked over Veronica's shoulder at the taxi-man and said in her imperious fashion:

'Good evening, Barnett. Bring in the luggage, please.'

Barnett, an elderly man, scratched his head and looked at Veronica's wardrobe trunk.

'Anyone to give a hand, mum?'

'Certainly not,' said Lady Lowring. 'You must manage.'

'I'll help–' began Veronica.

'Certainly not,' interrupted Lady Lowring

153

again, and taking Veronica's arm, led her down the flagged path towards the portico which was covered with trailing creeper. 'Barnett will do it. You will only hurt your inside, lifting heavy luggage.'

Veronica smiled. Dear old Mummy! *Certainly* unchanged. The same old autocrat. And she herself, a pawn on the chessboard... Mummy making all the moves. She was Mrs Charles Hallard now, yet almost at once she felt herself slipping back, instinctively, to the old, shy, diffident girl who was completely dominated by a determined mamma.

An old woman with white wispy hair and wearing a dark-blue dress and spotless apron appeared in the small dark hall. Veronica ran to her and this time the embrace was long and spontaneous.

'Nanny … my darling old Nan!'

'Mercy on us!' exclaimed the woman, peering at Veronica through gold-rimmed spectacles. 'If it isn't my little dear come home! Let's look at you, Miss Veronica darling.'

Lady Lowring held the basket out to the old woman who, alone out of her whole staff, had stuck to her and lived under her patronage for over twenty years.

'Take this, Nanny, and put the flowers in the sink. I'll do them as soon as Miss Veronica – I mean Mrs Hallard – and I have had a chat.'

Nanny clicked her tongue and shook her head, eyeing Veronica's slight figure.

'Mercy ... she's as thin as a lath ... and yellow in the face!'

'I hope not,' laughed Veronica.

Her mother took her into the drawing-room and surveyed her critically.

Veronica. The last rays of the setting sun slanted through the low casements and showed up the fatigue on the small sallow face. Yes, thought Lady Lowring, Nanny was right. 'Thin and yellow' described it. Cheekbones standing out. Salt-cellars in her neck. Skirt hanging on her; no hips. Just a wreck of her old self. The most beautiful girl in Risborough at one time. And that was what came of marrying a more or less penniless young man and going out to an outlandish country like the West Coast of Africa. Lady Lowring was always insistent that it was the 'white man's grave', no matter what improvements had been made out there.

She kept her counsel, however, determined not to criticize but to be very sweet and kind to her daughter. After all, since her husband's death it had been very lonely here for Beatrice Lowring. She had disliked intensely 'coming down', as she called it, to Monks Rest, and living the quiet frugal life she had had to lately. It was a real pleasure to get her one and only child home. And

155

much as she liked her son-in-law, she was more than a little pleased that Charles was still in West Africa and that she would have Veronica to herself for at least six months.

'You *are* thin,' she said. 'You need fattening up. But a few weeks' rest and my care and you'll soon be a different girl. That climate did *not* suit you. I knew it wouldn't.'

Veronica took off her hat, smoothed back her hair, and sitting on the arm of the nearest chair, gazed around her. How cool it was, almost cold to her blood which had grown so thin in West Africa. And how quiet. Such peace after the feverish activity on the ship, getting through the Customs and that awful journey. She couldn't have done without Boyd Mansell. He had been a tower of strength and seen her through it all. Letty Chaddon had been met by a sister who had soon carted her off, and Pam, by her Liverpool boy friend, the famous Eddie. A dull, prosaic-looking young man, Pam had insisted upon introducing him to Veronica. But she had taken little interest in that humdrum, unromantic couple. She had let Boyd take entire charge of her, feeling not at all well. She had caught a cold in the last two days before they got into port; it was the unaccustomed dampness and chill after the intense heat of Lagos. Her head had ached violently all the time they were disembarking, and her spirits had been at lowest ebb. She had felt so far from Charles; and it was all so queer and frightening in England without him. But Boyd had helped in every conceivable way. He had travelled as far as London with her; had taken her in a taxi to Paddington and finally seen her into her train for Princes Risborough. Dear, kind Boyd.

Thinking of him now, Veronica had a fleeting sense of uneasiness. There had been something rather queer about his behaviour just before her train went out. He had seized her hand, squeezed it until she winced, and said in a kind of rough voice:

'Good-bye ... my *dear* ... anything I can ever do in this life ... let me know ... I shall miss you, Veronica...'

Then, stammering, his brown face red, he had turned abruptly and marched away. She had thought at the time (as she thought now) that it would spoil a marvellous friendship if Boyd Mansell were to fall in love with her. She was not conceited ... but really ... his farewell had been a little peculiar for a man whose feelings were purely platonic. It had worried her all during the journey down here. It worried her now. Then she cast aside the memory of Boyd and tried to concentrate on what her mother was saying.

Seated in a tall winged Queen Anne chair (it used to be Sir Giles's favourite chair, with its fine old tapestry cover), Lady Lowring was holding forth on the present situation.

Food was going to be difficult. It would shortly be rationed. They must grow more vegetables here. Nanny was full of rheumatics and always grumbling. It was all work now and no play. Lady Lowring did most of the housework and Nanny the cooking. Impossible to get daily help. The women just would not come out. Transport was dreadful now they had no car. She had, of course, sold the Daimler when Daddy died. Sold a good bit of furniture from Whitelands Hall, too. Only brought her favourite things to Monks Rest, the small pieces which fitted into the place. It was so tiny ... so restricted. Lady Lowring did so miss her big rooms, the space, and the old days when she was a social light. She could not entertain now. Only a few of her oldest women friends came to Monks Rest. People were different nowadays. Already a great many of the young men had joined up and the girls were taking Red Cross lectures. Lady Lowring was head of this committee and that ... there was plenty to do with this new, dreadful war in progress.

Veronica listened, but with only half of her here, it seemed. The other half was away ... thousands of miles over land and water ... in the turgid heat of her bungalow ... with

Nicholas, grinning ... asking for 'dash' ... with Charles coming home, which he always did at this very time ... ready and eager for her kiss. Oh, Charles, *Charles!*...

Her head drooped. The hot tears stung her eyelids. Lady Lowring, short-sighted, did not see, but went on holding forth in her clear, authoritative voice. It was obvious to Veronica that few of her own particular friends in the locality were available and that life would be much more restricted than it had been. But what did she care? It was a mere hiatus this existence ... until she saw Charles again. Until he came as he had come once before, to take her away and lift her up to the stars.

She felt a sense of grievance suddenly because her mother had not once asked after Charles. She was talking about everyone, everything, else. But that was so like Mummy. She had never wanted this marriage...

Veronica looked round the charming room with its huge open fireplace over which hung an exquisite piece of Jacobean tapestry. On the high mantelpiece stood some rare old Dresden china figurines and a Nankin bowl full of rich yellow roses. The curtains were soft gold and green, the rugs faded Persian, the furniture Queen Anne walnut polished until the veneer looked like dark-gold glass. It was all very restful and beautiful. Lady Lowring had always had perfect taste. In one corner there was a recess full of leather-bound books. Flowers on the low window-sills, flowers on the painted spinet. Through the open door, a vista of the dining-room with its lovely dark-oak refectory table and tall carved Jacobean cane-backed chairs. Still farther, through open french windows Veronica could see the loggia ... the one anachronism in an otherwise perfect Tudor cottage. But a very pleasant one, since the loggia got all the sun and one could fold back the doors, until it was like sitting on a verandah.

It was all lovely, tranquil and satisfying to an artist's eye. But Veronica, her heart aching badly, was thinking of that *other* verandah in the blinding heat, Charles's arms about her and his kisses on her lips and throat. She swallowed hard, desperately trying to control herself. She knew her mother so well. Lady Lowring would be hurt if Veronica wept on her first evening home. She was not a sentimental woman. She would say: 'Isn't your mother enough ... just for *once?*'

Suddenly Veronica became alive to the fact that there was no piano in the room, only the spinet. The tears dried on her lashes and she sprang up.

'Mummy ... my *piano*...'

Lady Lowring frowned.

160

'Yes. I'm afraid your big Steinway wouldn't go in Monks Rest, my dear. But it's in store ... quite safe. I haven't sold it, of course.'

Veronica breathed again.

'Thank goodness! I was terrified ... but how awful to have no piano ... oh, Mummy!'

Beatrice Lowring smiled a little.

'Still the same music-mad child?'

'More so than ever. Charles and I have such wonderful musical evenings together.'

'Oh, well, you will again, when he comes home. You will have to find a home of your own and put your Steinway in it,' Lady Lowring sought to console her. Then added: 'There's Mrs Jacobs living at Whitelands now. Her husband is a little fat Jew who makes kitchen-sinks or something deplorable ... they're rolling in money. Our lovely home! ... but they offered a big rent... I had to accept it. So hard hit, my dear. Your father left me none too well off. Mrs Jacobs wants to be friends, but I don't get on with the *nouveau riche*. I rather cold-shoulder her, I'm afraid. But if you like to call on her, I know she has a grand piano – I saw it being carried in when they took possession. I daresay Mrs Jacobs would be only too pleased if you asked to play it now and then.'

'Then I shall,' murmured Veronica. 'I don't mind whether they are Jews or not ...

if they love music.'

Lady Lowring looked at her daughter and coughed.

'Darling ... if you don't mind ... it does so ruin chairs to sit on the arms...'

Veronica slid off. Now her full red lips curved into a genuinely amused smile. This took her back to childhood's day with a vengeance! Mummy was always so particular about the furniture. One scratch on a polished surface, one mark on a cover ... and it was a major disaster.

'I'll go to my room if I may and get washed and changed, Mummy,' she said.

Lady Lowring took Veronica upstairs. The upper landing was beautiful; wide, with a tall window, recently put in, leading on to a balcony from which one could look down on an enchanted garden, and an old stone bird-bath surrounded by rockery plants. Beyond the curved green hedge was a little orchard full of apple and plum trees, laden with fruit.

On either side of this window tall French taffeta curtains swept gracefully to the polished oak floor. There were old gilt candelabra against the whitewashed walls; on one side stood a William and Mary chair with soft-hued green and gold brocade; on the other an old French walnut cupboard. There were green-painted shelves in one corner bearing some exquisite china. The

162

same old perfect taste Mummy had always shown, thought Veronica, recalling and admiring all these choice relics from Whitelands. How well the things had gone into this tiny cottage, despite Mummy's dislike of its confined space.

Veronica's bedroom was a real sign of Lady Lowring's wish to make Veronica happy and comfortable She had taken the trouble to furnish it with all Veronica's old things; the pale green painted furniture (bought originally at Fortnum's), delicately touched with gilt; her own bed with its rose-and-green chintz headboard and quilted glazed chintz covers; curtains to match. The gilt-framed painting over the mantelpiece was a reproduction of da Vinci's 'Head of Christ' which Veronica had chosen herself, soon after her 'coming out', and used to adore. The well-remembered and beloved mezzotint of three noble heads: Beethoven, Brahms, Wagner, hung over the bed. (She had found that in Rouen, on a summer holiday with her parents, when she first began to study singing so ardently.)

Veronica, dewy-eyed, looked around the little low-ceilinged room so full of treasured possessions of the past, and flung her arms round her mother's tall, stately figure.

'It's *lovely*. You're a darling to have done all this for me!'

Lady Lowring looked pleased and patted

the girl's shoulder.

'There ... I'm glad, my dear ... now get changed and come down and I shall do the same, then I shall help Nanny with the supper. Only some hot soup and a cold chicken and salad. Will that do?'

'Of course,' said Veronica. 'It sounds marvellous.'

Lady Lowring shut the door. Veronica stood a moment in silence looking out of the casements down at the bird-bath in which an intrepid young thrush was dipping and shaking its wings vigorously, sending a diamond-like spray into the air. The evening was full of bird-song. The sun was fast sinking and a bluish mist already veiled the green fields. Soon it would be dark.

It was all peaceful and familiar – like the things in this room. Yet it was all strange. For she was no longer Veronica Lowring. She was Charles's wife. She ought not to be here really. She should be out there, in Lagos, welcoming Charles home from work at this very hour. What was he doing this evening without her?

Veronica bit her lip, turned and unstrapped her suitcase. The first thing to come out was her photograph of Charles. Long and passionately she regarded it.

'Darling, darling...' she whispered. 'You are never out of my mind for a single moment. You know that. I shall live only for

164

you to come home to me…'

Again she stifled the inclination to cry. She hastily found her way to the bathroom and ran some hot water into the bath. She could hear her mother calling down orders to old Nanny. She thought of the things she must unpack first … the length of silk she had brought home for Mummy; a leather purse made in West Africa, for Nanny. And tomorrow she must call on Mrs Jacobs. Fat Jew or not … she had a piano … and Veronica wanted to use it. To play and sing Charles's songs. She must not allow herself to get out of practice before he came back.

While she lay in the bath she tried to keep her emotions under stern control and not think too much and too sentimentally about her husband. She forced herself to concentrate for a moment on the man who had been so kind to her during the voyage home. She wondered if Boyd had reached Chidding Manor; how he had found his mother and poor sister, and what his fate would be … coming back, to be plunged straight into this war. As a regular soldier, he would be well and truly 'in it'.

Perhaps that funny farewell of his had meant nothing. She hoped not. She wanted his friendship and to be able to ask him to Monks Rest if ever he should be stationed near by.

A tap on the door and Nanny's voice said:

'Miss Veronica...' (she could never remember that it was Mrs Hallard), 'something for you, dearie.'

'What?' asked Veronica, getting out of the bath and wrapping her slight, dripping figure in a bath-towel.

'Open the door ... something her ladyship says you'll be wanting...'

Veronica unlocked the door and held out a small wet hand. Nanny thrust a piece of paper into it and withdrew. Veronica, her heart beating fast, saw that the 'something' was a cablegram. She tore it open. Her big grey eyes glowed as she read the message which had been so excellently timed.

*Welcome home stop my love goes with you wherever you go my darling stop Charles.*

Veronica read the cable several times, then suddenly her spirits rose. She began to feel elated, almost at peace again. He loved her, he thought of her as much as she loved and thought of him. They were very much one in spirit. The months would soon pass and their reunion would be ecstatic, a glorious thing to look forward to. She must not grieve or mope any more. It was wrong of her.

She kissed the cable and tossed it in the air, then vigorously drying her slender limbs, began to sing in her high sweet voice a song that Charles had composed...

## 4

On that same fine September afternoon – the momentous first week of the new world war with Germany – the Mansell car was to be seen parked outside Horsham Station. A quiet, old-fashioned Rolls-Royce, it had been in the family for the last fifteen years and chauffeured by the same man, Scott, who used to come every evening to this same station to fetch Mr Mansell, back from his daily journey to London.

Scott, stern-faced, grey-haired, bespectacled, looking, as the young Mansells used to say, like a humourless headmaster who had got into uniform by mistake, stood this evening by the bookstall with an air of expectancy on his face. He was waiting for the London train to come in; meeting the 'Captain', as Scott called Boyd these days. He had known Boyd from the age of eight.

In the back of the Rolls, Mrs Mansell waited, knitting a pair of khaki-coloured socks. From the hour that war had been declared she had decided that Boyd would want plenty of these socks now. No more mufti for her poor darling boy for many a long month. It would be all uniform henceforth.

Violet Mansell's delicate white fingers

moved fast, flicking the slender bone needles. She was fond of knitting. She had made every pair of socks her two boys had worn in the past and every jumper Audrey or Gilly possessed. Knitting soothed her, and she could read a book at the same time (which used to seem like a miracle to her husband).

Now and then she looked through the glass window at the other cars rolling into the station yard to meet this same London train. There were a lot of people here tonight. The September sunset was lovely, she thought, and she was glad that the grounds of Chidding Manor were looking so perfect. Old Dempster, the head gardener, said that the chrysanthemums were the finest they had had for many a year. Dear Boyd loved the chrysanthemums.

Violet Mansell lived for and through her children now that her husband was dead. And when not busying herself about one or the other of her family – or her grand-children – she was busy doing kind deeds for other people! She was devoted to her Church and all its causes.

She had been left a large income by her husband, a fine house, everything – and more – that she needed. But she had never been spoiled by luxury. The more she got the more she thought of those less fortunate and interested herself in their their trials and tribulations. She had had her own

168

misfortunes, of course, and bore them with fortitude. The tragedy that had befallen her youngest daughter had been a severe blow from which she had never, in her heart, recovered. She adored Gilly and spent her life nowadays endeavouring to make her burden a little lighter. She was bitterly disappointed, too, because James, her eldest and favourite son, had taken so little interest in his own country and old home, and had decided to remain in Kenya. She had never seen, would never now see, James's daughter. But Mrs Mansell counted her blessings. She still had Boyd, her handsome soldier son, and dear Audrey, who made such a good mother, and those adorable twin grandsons, David and Jonathan.

Audrey and Roger, her nice husband of whom Mrs Mansell thoroughly approved, and the twins had been down to Chidding Manor recently for their summer holiday. The big place seemed quiet and deserted again since they had gone.

Now this war had come... Mrs Mansell could judge from the news and from what the rector of Chidding Priory Church had told her, last night at dinner, that things were serious. This was a war which would not be over as quickly as the optimistic liked to think, he had said. She, of course, would have the worry of Boyd as a Regular being in it from the start. He was sure to be drafted abroad. Wars were never fought on this island! He would inevitably go overseas. And he had only recently finished four years' foreign service. They had seen so little of him. Gilly was devoted to Boyd, and it would be hard on her if she must lose sight of him again.

Still, Mrs Mansell tried to cheer herself up, it *might* all be over sooner than the rector thought. She was anxious to hear what her son had to say on the subject.

Ah! The train was in. People were coming out of the station, carrying luggage. Mrs Mansell's heart fluttered with excitement. She took off her horn-rimmed glasses, put away her knitting and stepped out of the Rolls. Dear Boyd! So lovely to have him home again, even for one night. He had telephoned them from Victoria whilst waiting for his train to warn them that it would only be for tonight and that he must report for duty to Borden Camp tomorrow.

There he was ... followed by a smiling Scott (most rare for Scott to smile!). How tall and sun-bronzed and well Boyd looked. The mother's heart swelled with love and pride. Boyd came up and in his charming, spontaneous way, seized Mrs Mansell in a hug, not ashamed to embrace her in public.

'Hello, Mother darling ... how are you...?'

He kissed both her pale soft cheeks, then stood smiling down at her. She always

170

looked like a faded tea-rose and smelt as faintly sweet as one, he thought. A little dainty creature, with ash-blonde hair which even in her sixtieth year retained a glint of gold; eyes which had once been as blue as his, now faded; and delicate complexion. She was very small and dressed as a rule in subdued colours, grey or black, often with an Edwardian black velvet ribbon about her throat. Violet Mansell was not smart according to the fashions of 1939, but always beautifully turned out. Boyd, from his earliest childhood, could not remember his mother without a piece of lovely lace at her throat; or a charming ribbon or that cameo brooch which she wore this evening and the locket on the long gold chain round her neck. In the locket was a miniature of James as a baby, with golden curls and seraphic face. It made Boyd smile to look at the familiar locket, know what was inside, and remember the fat, bald-headed James whom he had just visited in Kenya.

Scott put the luggage on the car. Boyd took his mother's arm and led her to her seat.

'Still running the old chariot, I see.'

'Yes, my dear, I suppose we shall be allowed petrol, even though there *is* a war on.'

'At the moment. But one never knows. It may be severely rationed before we're through.'

'Oh, Boyd dear,' said Violet Mansell,

raising anxious eyes to her son as he took the seat beside her and slammed the door, 'are we not going to beat those horrid Germans quickly?'

'I honestly don't know, Mother,' he said.

They moved away from the station and into the town, driving through the narrow main street and out on the open road. The village of Chidding was some five and a half miles west of Horsham.

Mrs Mansell looked at her son tenderly.

'I am so thankful you're home, dear. I hated your being away just at this time. With this terrible war in Europe, it is nice to have one man in our family close to us. Gilly and I have so looked forward to seeing you again.'

'How is my Gilly?'

'She has a surprise for you, Boyd.'

'What? A new cat or dog or bird?'

'Something much better than that, but wait till we get home. She wishes to tell you herself.'

'Okay,' smiled Boyd.

'Now I want to ask so many questions, mainly about James and his wife and Bunty. How wonderful to think you have seen them, Boyd dear. Tell me all that you can.'

He nodded and began to give her what news he thought might interest her about the little family out in South Africa. But he spoke mechanically. His eyes looked ahead with a slightly vacant expression. He frowned now and again, and restlessly took out a pipe and began to toy with that.

Mrs Mansell soon noticed this restlessness and the fact that her son was unusually *distrait;* inclined at moments not to hear the questions she asked, or to answer haphazardly. It did not take her long to decide that all was not as well with Boyd as it had appeared when she first saw him. He looked well enough physically, but he was not *quite* the old Boyd, she thought, full of chatter and high spirits. She wondered if perhaps the outbreak of war accounted for his gravity. She made no comment. Violet Mansell had always been a woman of discretion and was never one to invite confidences but liked to wait in her gentle soft fashion and hope to receive the confidences, then offer her help and advice.

Boyd stopped talking about James and listened to the little pieces of news Mrs Mansell had for him. Alan Willsom, the young son of one of Mrs Mansell's oldest friends in the district, had upset his mother only this morning by rushing to a recruiting depot and joining up as a 'Tommy'. Mrs Willsom was very distressed because her uncle, who was a major-general, could easily have got Alan a commission. To which Boyd said:

'I think it was rather a good show on

Alan's part.'

Mrs Mansell agreed.

Then there was Heather D'Arcy, one of Boyd's girl friends of years ago – she was being married next week to a man in the Navy because he expected to sail for the Mediterranean at any moment.

Such a nice girl, Heather, and none of us really care for *him* ... much older than Heather, and a widower with a grown-up son ... it was rather a pity, Mrs Mansell sighed ... but of course Heather was Gilly's age and getting on – just as well she should marry now if she wanted children.

'Of course, Gilly and I believe she has never married all these years because she was so fond of *you,* my dear,' Mrs Mansell murmured at the *finale* of the recital.

'Oh, nonsense, Mother,' said Boyd, with a laugh.

'Oh, but she was *very* attached to you, Boyd dear. Mrs D'Arcy hinted the other day when she announced Heather's engagement and forthcoming marriage to this naval man that she had been terrified at one time that Heather would stay an old maid because of *you.*'

Boyd laughed again, but his eyes were unsmiling. Briefly he recollected Heather D'Arcy and the mild flirtation they had had when he was home on leave, many summers ago. He had known, of course, that the girl

174

had become too fond of him, and he had regretted it. Boyd would never willingly hurt anybody. But he could not summon up any enthusiasm at her memory ... he was disinterested in her and all other women ... except one. And he was haunted by the memory of her; of a pair of lovely luminous eyes, grey and shadowed under sweeping lashes; of a sweet, piercingly sweet, voice; of an unbelievable gentleness and passionate devotion ... to another man. After he parted from Veronica Hallard at Paddington he had realised to the full how badly he had allowed himself to fall in love with her. He felt lost without her this evening ... vaguely irritated because Fate had decreed that she should go in one direction and he in another. Had he not sworn to himself that he would try not to see her again ... that it would be the best thing for himself in the long run? Yet, fool that he was ... scarcely had he dropped the small hand to which he had clung so tightly at Victoria, and stammered his good-bye, than he had found himself planning to get to Princes Risborough, by hook or by crook, and see her again in the near future.

He tried to concentrate on what his mother was saying. Now Scott had turned the big smooth car through the wide-open wrought-iron gates of Chidding Manor. They passed the little ivy-covered lodge. Mrs Nicholls, the lodge-keeper's wife, and her

175

small boy stood outside and waved as the Captain and his mother passed by. There was no lady in the district more liked and respected than Violet Mansell, who did good to everybody, was head of the Women's Institute; and was already organising knitting parties on behalf of the soldiers and encouraging the village to take part in the war. Her staff adored her.

Boyd looked with mingled feelings at the park through which they were now driving; he had always loved this broad, handsome drive flanked by chestnut trees, and the green pastureland on either side skirted by low iron railings.

The last red rays of the sun were catching the plate glass of the windows of the Manor, now visible round a bend in the drive. The place looked its best on an evening like this, when the beeches were turning to russet shade and the flower-beds fringing the front lawn were brilliant with red and golden dwarf dahlias.

Everything seemed touched with red to-night, thought Boyd, including the flaming brightness of the virginia creeper which covered half the house. Chidding Manor was a noble-looking Georgian mansion with a portico which was covered with wistaria in the spring. The house was one of the finest specimens of Georgian architecture in Sussex. It had belonged to Boyd's grandfather, old James Mansell, after whom Violet's elder son had been christened, and had been in the family for a century before that. Boyd was proud of his home and interested in the garden, as his father had been before him. Mrs Mansell knew that the first thing Boyd would do in the morning would be to examine the hot-houses (famous for Dempster's Muscat grapes), the equally famous peaches and greengages on the south wall in the orchard; the chrysanthemums which every year won a prize at the local flower shows and would have taken a prize in much bigger shows had anybody in the family taken the bother to exhibit them. Yes, Boyd loved the gardens; the hard tennis court; the fishpond in which he and James boasted they had kept goldfish for twenty years. Big, reddish-golden fish with black fins; so tame that they swam up to one to be fed.

Boyd was always fond of his home out of doors. But not so fond of it indoors. He read a bit, had a good library, mainly of travel books; but for the arts – music, painting and such hobbies as Violet Mansell and Gilly liked – Boyd had no use. It was, she supposed, because he had spent most of his life soldiering and was such a sportsman – so thoroughly masculine.

As they drove up to the front door, Boyd remarked:

'The old place is looking a dream, Mother.'

'Yes,' said Mrs Mansell sadly, 'it is hard to believe there is a war on here. Of course, it has only just begun and we haven't had time to feel it.'

Boyd took a suitcase, left Scott to tackle the rest of his luggage and followed his mother into the hall. Here, lights had been switched on to dispel the shadows of evening, which was now darkening rapidly. Boyd, depressed though he was, felt a glow of appreciation as he saw the familiar gracious house; the wide handsome staircase with its carved rosewood banisters, at the foot of which stood a fine bronze of Mercury holding a lamp, now brightly shining. The walls down here and up the staircase were panelled and hung with oil-paintings of the Mansell family throughout the ages. Everywhere there were soft, thick-piled carpets, rich satin draperies across tall windows; an atmosphere of luxury, of tranquillity, of dignity; echo from a past graceful age.

The panelling in Chidding Manor was historic and valuable. Boyd knew and appreciated both the beauty and value of his home. But it had always been here and as a rule he took it for granted. After a short time on leave he felt a little suffocated by the ritual of living in dignity, being waited on hand and foot by well-trained servants, eating the best of food; entertaining and being entertained by all their neighbours in the county. At times he felt a little in sympathy with old James who had turned his back on it all and chosen a life of freedom and simplicity on a Kenya ranch. Life at home *could* be irksome; vaguely annoying, like his mother's drawing-room, which in Boyd's opinion held far too much furniture; too many pictures on the walls; too many cabinets of china, vases of flowers, satin cushions, silver-framed photographs and ornaments in general.

It was quite a relief sometimes to go back to life in the mess.

But tonight he was pleased with it all.

Now for his poor little sister.

'Gilly! Gillo!' he called, tossing hat and gloves and coat on to a chair, and smoothing back his crisp brown hair.

An eager voice answered from the direction of the room in which the family always sat when they were alone; one of the smaller rooms overlooking the back garden; Boyd's favourite, since it contained little else but desk and books and a few big comfortable chairs. The room was known rather grandly as the 'library'.

Boyd opened the 'library' door.

'How's my Gillo...' he began in the cheerful and affectionate voice he always preserved for his tragic little sister. Then he stopped, stood still, staring, round-eyed, astonished to silence by what he saw. Not Gilly in the accustomed wheeled chair in which he had seen her for so many long painful years. But Gilly standing upright on two crutches. On crutches ... but *also on her feet*. Those small feet which to his certain knowledge had not touched the ground since her accident.

He stared amazedly at her slight figure. She wore a short black dress which made her look tall and very thin. Her face was still the pretty, fair face of the old Gilly. The golden hair which Boyd remembered as a mass of tangled curls in her childhood was beautifully done; set in soft waves, tied with a blue ribbon. She looked, as Boyd afterwards described it, positively *radiant*. In a shaking little voice, she said:

'Do you see, Chumps? Do you *see?*'

Chumps ... the old family name for the youngest Mansell son. It evoked so many happy memories of childhood for the man standing there, staring at his sister who for nearly nine long years had been a hopeless cripple. Then he ran to her side. She dropped the crutches and fell forward in his arms. He lifted her up ... so much too light, that poor wasted figure. He said:

'Gilly-flower ... Gillo, old girl ... but how *miraculous!*'

She sobbed, tears raining down her cheeks, even while she laughed.

'I know. I told Mummy what a surprise it would be for you, Chumps. While you were abroad I've been having treatment … a new kind of wonderful electrical treatment which has never been used before. Someone recommended Mummy to try this man – he's an alien, Chumps, an Austrian … they interned him … but he has an English partner who is carrying on his work.'

Boyd, slightly bewildered, laid his sister down on the broad, comfortable chester-field which stood at right angles to the Adams fireplace in which a log fire burned merrily this September evening. Gilly wiped away her tears, blew her small snub nose and reached out for the precious crutches which had given her a real *élan* for existence now, inspiration in no small measure. Boyd sat down beside her, filled his pipe and listened to her excited chatter. Mrs Mansell joined them and put in a word now and then in her quiet, soft voice while she continued her knitting.

Yes, it was wonderful … a friend … some-one Boyd didn't know … had told them to go to this Dollfuss (historic name indeed … a relative, perhaps, of the ill-fated Chan-cellor). The doctor was in practice here, but not naturalised, so of course he had been interned as soon as war broke out. But his partner, Dr Frobisher, hoped they would soon get him released. He was pro-British, absolutely anti-Nazi and doing marvellous work in this country. He had invented the wonderful electric apparatus which had been used with such miraculous effect on Gilly's paralysed body. It was only at the beginning of last week that she had been able to walk, with aid, for the first time. But Dr Dollfuss had prophesied that by the end of this year she would be walking without crutches or even a stick. Her gait might be a bit awkward and shuffling, but she would *walk*.

'I shall be like other women again, Chumps,' Gilly said, smiling at her brother, her eyes like rain-washed violets. 'I shan't be a helpless wreck watching people wait on me any more. I shall be able to go for walks with the dogs again. Oh, *Chumps!*...'

Boyd leaned forward and patted her shoulder.

'I'm damned glad, darling. Damned glad,' he said huskily.

'Our prayers have been answered,' put in Violet Mansell gently. 'I always told you children to believe in prayer.'

Boyd puffed at his pipe, his brows drawn together. It was a grand surprise ... finding Gilly on her feet again and likely to be cured before Christmas. His spirits rose considerably at the sight of her, practically cured and so happy. He was and always had been devoted to Gilly. But now his thoughts turned again to Veronica. A little bitterly, he asked himself if it would be sacrilege to pray that one day he might get Veronica for his own … yes, his mother would not approve of a wild prayer of that kind. She would call it sacrilege. Veronica belonged to another man, and only through death or divorce could he, Boyd, gain the right to ask Veronica to marry *him*. Either way was unthinkable.

Gilly smoked a cigarette and chattered to her brother, but she noticed, as her mother had done at the station, that Boyd was un-usually grave and silent; unlike himself. They had always had such fun together, joking, laughing … it was always so gay at Chidding Manor when Boyd was home on leave.

What was wrong with him? She, too, wondered if this sudden outbreak of war was responsible for the change.

An elderly maid wearing dark-green uni-form and coffee-coloured frilly apron came into the library with a tray bearing glasses and a decanter of sherry. The late Mr Mansell had been a connoisseur of wine and had an excellent cellar; encouraged his sons to drink and appreciate good wine. But cocktails he would not have in the house, and Violet Mansell kept to these traditions.

Boyd greeted the old parlourmaid, and she retired beaming. The 'Captain' was a great favourite with the staff. Then he and Gilly drank sherry, and Boyd had to tell her all about James and his family. Later, a muffled gong sounded. Mrs Mansell rose and said:

'Half an hour to dinner, children ... are you going to change tonight, Boyd? Perhaps not, your first night home.'

He looked down at the dark-grey suit he was wearing, with the 'Gunner' tie, and said:

'I'll stay as I am, if you don't mind, Mother.'

'Of course not, dear...'

She went out, smiling. She was happy to have him home. He could do as he chose. But she had changed into a long dinner-dress for the evening meal every night for as long as she had lived in this house, and she never swerved from that custom, no matter how tired she was.

Brother and sister sat alone. Gilly lit another cigarette and looked thoughtfully at her tall handsome brother. She said:

'Chumps, old boy ... something's bitten you. Tell Gillo. What is it?'

He moved uncomfortably and turned his gaze from her. Looked, without seeing it, at the familiar picture hanging over the fireplace. An oil-painting of his grandfather's horse which had won the Derby sixty years ago. He and James used to laugh at the painting. It was so funny, they said ... the horse's head looked so small and his body so big. Not at all like the thoroughbreds of today.

He could not answer his sister for several moments. She could see that he was having a struggle with himself. Suddenly she, who was closer to him than to anyone in the family, *knew*. She said impulsively:

'It's a girl, isn't it, Chumps?'

Almost relieved that she had mentioned it before he did, Boyd turned back to her, knocked his pipe against the fender and nodded his head.

'Okay, Gilly ... you've said it.'

'Oh, Chumps,' she said sadly, 'is it some girl who doesn't care for you? I can't believe it. If I weren't your sister I'd snatch at you.'

'Thanks, darling,' he laughed, his troubled brow clearing a little. 'But in this case it is rather a hopeless situation. She is madly in love with her own husband.'

An instant's silence whilst Gilly digested this. Their mother would have been shocked, of course, at the mere thought of her son falling in love with a married woman, but Gilly was of Boyd's generation and more broad-minded. At length she said:

'Oh, lord, Chumps darling, that does seem rather hopeless. Why fall in love with a girl who's married and in love with her husband? You can't even contemplate a divorce

– getting her that way. She wouldn't co-operate...' Gilly tried to speak lightly.

'Perhaps it's just as well,' Boyd said, with a short laugh. 'You know what Mother would think of divorce.'

'But would you have taken this girl away if she had wanted to go?'

Boyd had an instant's uncomfortable recollection of Ann Pumphrey sobbing in his arms ... of his own relief when *that* affair had ended ... how he had recoiled from the mere thought of being involved in a scandal with her. But with Veronica ... oh Veronica ... so small, so exquisite, dancing with him on board ship ... Veronica with the maddening perfume of her dark, cloudy hair ... the incredible smoky greyness of her eyes ... that was different... He said harshly:

'Yes. If *she* had wanted to go with me, I'd have taken her away, Gilly.'

Gilly gave a little whistle.

'Phew! You *have* got it badly, old boy.'

'You couldn't be more right.'

'Yet there hasn't been an affair between you? She loves her husband?'

'With all her heart and soul. I think it was her amazing devotion to him as well as her beauty and gentleness which first attracted me.'

'Oh, poor Chumps!' said his sister sorrowfully. 'I'm awfully sorry, old boy.'

He poured out another glass of sherry.

'Chump is my name all right. I've had many affairs, as you know, but I've never really loved any woman but this one, and she is as inaccessible as the stars. Bright of me, isn't it, sister mine?'

'Tell me about her, Chumps, if you'd like to.'

There was nothing he liked to do better. Gilly lay back on her cushions, smoking, watching, listening to the torrent of words ... mainly words of praise ... that issued from her dearly beloved brother's lips on the subject of Veronica Hallard. Veronica ... a sweet name. And she sounded a sweet person. Gilly had a vivid imagination and she could picture the girl just as Boyd described her.

'I've never known a more charming person, Gilly,' he finished. 'You'd think so, too. Mother would adore her ... if only she were free and cared for me. It's devilish, isn't it?'

'Devilish,' agreed Gilly. 'How cruel life can be. Unnecessarily so. One just has to square up to it. You must try to forget her, Chumps darling, and find someone else.'

'I shall never find another Veronica.'

Gilly sighed. She wished Boyd was not quite so serious. It was hurting him, this new love. She hated him to be hurt. After all, who better than she should know how bitter and agonizing love can be when it is unfulfilled?

As for forgetting ... the Mansells were not good at forgetting. They had long memories. They were faithful to heart to those they really loved. How many years was it now since Dick had died ... crashed in that terrible accident ... three days after their marriage ... driving from Redruth to their hotel in Portreath? Nearly nine now. Nine long empty years of physical misery and mental suffering almost beyond endurance. She had been so happy with Dick. For three days and nights she had belonged to him, utterly. Yes, she had known what it was to love and be loved to the uttermost. They had adored each other. Life had stretched in front of them offering golden, glorious opportunities; perpetual delight. Just before that hideous smash, Dick had stopped the car to kiss her and say:

'Light me a cigarette, sweetheart ... and, by the way, I don't think I've told you for the last half-hour how adorable you are and how much I love you...'

She had put the cigarette between his lips, then taken his hand and held it against her glowing cheek. She had thought that life could hold no greater happiness than being married to the right man. Then ... disaster ... darkness ... grief unspeakable... Dick gone from her... Dick, so straight and fair, like herself, so full of the *joie de vivre*. Dick, the tender lover, the perfect comrade. She had suffered weeks and months of despair ... she had wished to die, too, and go to him. She could not live without him, she had said. But her mother had made her live ... *made* her by sheer force of indomitable will-power and unshakable faith which burned in that small, delicate frame. Religion was the rock on which Mrs Mansell had founded her whole existence ... and through that religion she had helped to save her daughter's life; to make it possible for her to face the loneliness, the anguish of living without Dick ... doomed to widowhood, chained to an invalid's spinal-carriage ... without hope of recovery.

Yes, she had survived it; she had learned to laugh again. And now, she was learning to walk again, after all these years. One need never despair, thought Gilly. Time made such an incredible difference. Sometimes – even though her young husband's photograph stood beside her bed – and was here in this very room (it had been taken on their wedding-day, Dick standing beside her in her bridal gown) – she felt that that marriage had never been; that she had never known him. Nowadays she could not even remember the sound of his voice. He had gone from her ... completely, even though Mummy assured her that they would meet again ... in another and better world. But it was queer and little heart-breaking to realize how memories could fade. Poor Boyd, he would forget his Veronica in time. Of course he would. But futile to tell him so today.

She said gently:

'Try not to think too much of Veronica as it is so hopeless, Chumps darling.'

He gave her one of his swift, charming smiles.

'My dear old Gilly, fool that I am, I'm already hoping against hope that I might be stationed somewhere near enough for me to call on her.'

'That would be unwise.'

'Nevertheless I shall see her again. I know it. And I want her to come here ... and meet you.'

'You know I'd like that, Chumps ... anyone you love ... I should love.'

'Anyone in the world would love Veronica.'

Gilly sighed and smiled.

'Poor old Chumps!'

He said:

'She's devoted to music, Gilly. Husband composes and she sings. She sang at a concert on board – voice like a lark. Wish I knew something about music. I must try to learn.'

'Whatever for, darling?'

'Don't know ... just would like to learn. We must tune-in to some good concerts, eh? Veronica is wonderful. Recognises every damned tune she hears ... it's incredible!'

Gilly shook her head. Poor Chumps! He

had got it badly. What a shame! Then, trying to take his mind off Veronica Hallard for a moment, she said:

'I haven't told you *all* my news yet...'

'What else? Seeing you walk was enough.'

'People in love are so self-centred,' she grinned at him, wrinkling her small nose powdered with golden freckles ... in a way very familiar to her brother. 'Don't forget that I'm no longer a bed-ridden misery and I *might* indulge in a bit of romance myself. I feel my darling Dick would want it – that it is no disloyalty to him after so long.'

'Good lord, Gilly, I'm sure of that! I've always said it was damnable you shouldn't have another chance ... why, you aren't thirty till next year...'

'Quite elderly ... but I've found an elderly admirer,' she laughed. 'Mummy doesn't know yet. I shan't tell her till things are a bit further ahead; but she will approve, I know. She loves doctors. Audrey is married to one and I may be – one day – to another.'

He put aside the memory of Veronica. Sincerely interested in her sister's welfare, he questioned her further.

It appeared that the man of whom she spoke was the English partner of the Austrian who had helped to cure her. John Frobisher, M.D. Aged forty. Unmarried, she said, with no relations except an old mother in Devonshire. He lived in a flat over his consulting-room in Welbeck Street. He was a successful doctor and an idealist. That was what Gilly had first liked in him. He was not a 'quack' or the smart ladies' doctor who liked to take big fees from hypochondriacal old ladies and Society neurotics. He was mainly devoted to research work and on the staff of one of the big London hospitals. His ambition was to go eventually to China and work out there among the missionaries. But (as Boyd grimaced), Gilly hastily added, John was no prig. He had a terrific sense of humour. He was not good-looking as darling Dick had been ... broad-shouldered, rather heavily built, with dark, untidy hair and deep-set intelligent eyes. But he had great personality and the most wonderful hands ... gentle, sensitive, healing. From the first time he had seen her (he had come down here to Chidding Manor with Dr Dollfuss in consultation) Gilly had put all her faith in Dr Frobisher ... in him even more than in the Austrian, although John said Dollfuss was a genius and had the greatest admiration for him. But John had charge of her now. Once a week Scott drove her and Mother in the Rolls up to Welbeck Street and John gave Gilly this wonderful new electrical treatment.

'John is a very rare person ... as you'll see one day when you meet him, Chumps,' she added.

192

'Is he in love with you?'

Gilly's charming face ... still so youthful despite the lines that age and pain had etched round the blue eyes and at the corners of the sweet-tempered mouth ... was fiery red now. She said:

'Yes, I think he is, Chumps. He ... more or less said so when we were alone the last time. He said I was the only girl he had ever met who came up to his ideals. He has never wanted to marry before.'

'Do you mean to marry him soon, then?' asked Boyd incredulously. After all these years of thinking of his sister as an incurable invalid, it was wonderful and unbelievable to connect her with marriage.

'Yes, if he asks me, Chumps ... which I fancy he will do ... and if I feel I can help him in his career. But I shall never be able to run or walk too quickly. He knows that, of course.'

'My dear, if he gets you, he'll get a prize.'

'Thanks, Chumps ... and I think the same about the woman who gets you.'

Gilly regretted the words as soon as she had said them. For the cloud returned to Boyd's handsome face. He got up, moved to the fireplace and rather sullenly kicked a log into place.

'No woman will get me, Gilly ... unless Veronica Hallard is ever free to marry me,' he said.

*Extract from a diary by Veronica Hallard at Monks Rest at the end of September, 1939.*

'I haven't kept a diary since I was a little girl when Mummy bought me one of those lovely leather "Five Year" ones and I used to keep an account of all my doings at school, or write my secret thoughts and describe my deepest feelings which I always kept so much under control those days. Daddy was a dear kind nebulous sort of person who used to pat my head and give me a ten-shilling note when he thought about it ... but I would never have confided in him. Mummy was always much too dignified and grand and "managing", and I certainly never attempted to confide in her. I would have been much too shy. She never understood the sentimental side of me.

'Now, even though I belong to Charles and have experienced the ultimate happiness with him, I cannot always write to him as I feel. I don't want to worry him and let him know how wretched life is without him, so once again I take refuge in my diary. One day I shall read it to my darling Charles. I love him so much that it frightens me. Since leaving him, a month ago, I have been terribly lost without him and so lonely in myself, it has been like a nightmare. Never, never must I be parted from my husband again. And yet when he comes home next year will he not be called up? He is so young. He will have to go into the Army and take part in this terrible war. The mere idea makes my blood curdle.

'Mummy – seeing sometimes how upset I get when such a thing is suggested by herself, or someone else – scolds me and says I am unpatriotic and that I mustn't wish my husband not to take part in the war. But Charles is not a soldier. He has none of the fighting qualities of one. He is not like Boyd Mansell, for instance; he is first and foremost a musician. It would be terrible to Charles to have to take part in violence and bloodshed. Still, he is no pacifist. I can see from the last letter of his in which he wrote that he envied some young man who is coming back almost at once to join up. He both expects and wishes, himself, to take an active part in the war.

'Oh, why must it be so? The world is full of such lovely things – music is one of the loveliest – and those wretched Germans are musical to the bone. Why must they turn to aggression and beastliness? Noble men like Bach and Beethoven and gentle creatures like Schumann and Schubert would have loathed wars. Only Wagner has more than a touch of the Nazi martial spirit. I hate Wagner nowadays. But musicians on the whole are men of peace. They want time in which to study and compose. Like my Charles.

'Already dreadful things have happened. Death and disaster are sweeping over the world and I am petrified when I read about the sinkings ... the *Athenia* ... sunk off the Hebrides.... The *Courageous*, that lovely aircraft carrier, has gone. One of Mummy's old school friends lost her only son on it. And there will be more sinkings. I know it. Charles comes home by sea in five months' time. Oh, my knees tremble and my head spins at the prospect. Charles, my beloved darling, I shall not know an instant's peace of mind until you are safely back.

'Sometimes I wish I had inherited Mummy's marvellous *sangfroid*. Her philosophical streak which I do not possess in any degree. I'm a horrid little coward ... about Charles. I would be far braver if I, personally, were facing danger. I know that. But I am terrified for him. I want him to live. Oh, dear God, *let him live*.

'Life at Monks Rest seems queer and unreal after the year in West Africa with my darling. I have become Veronica Lowring again ... a meek girl, doing what her mother wishes; and flying, as of old, to Nanny for consolation. Nanny is very understanding. Withered old maid as she is, somehow she realises what my husband means to me. She tries to comfort me, she thinks a good cup of tea or a compress of eau-de-Cologne for my forehead are certain cures when I looked fagged or miserable. Dear old Nan! Mummy *does* bully her. No wonder none of the servants stays. Mummy was very jealous, I'm afraid, when I read her that letter from Boyd telling me all his news and how well run Chidding Manor is. The staff there have all stayed on. Mrs Mansell must have a 'way' with her.

'Dear kind Boyd, I was so thrilled for his sake to hear the wonderful news about his sister's cure and her possible engagement to her doctor. He must be so happy about it. I like Boyd's handwriting and the way he writes. A firm, masculine hand and he has a natural, boyish way of putting things. Not a bit like Charles. I adore his letters. He writes untidily, sheets and sheets, to me ... illustrated here and there with funny little pen-sketches. He is so brilliant. If he hadn't been a composer he could have been a painter. He's a beautiful draughtsman. He says the loveliest possible things. And he writes like a poet. I wish I could publish some of his letters, only of course I couldn't – they're only for me. I lock them away. But the world is missing something very beautiful.

'In his last letter he said that there was perpetual night in our bungalow now; that a Stygian gloom has spread over the place since I left. The sun no longer shines. No flowers bloom. The world has died because his Veronica has gone. He goes about his job in a mechanical way, a kind of dark, sad dream (that is how I feel here, at Monks Rest), and the shadows will lift only, he says, when he sees my face again. I remember one paragraph by heart:

*'I need you unbearably at times, my darling love. I lie awake and toss and turn and hold out my hand, thinking I might touch you, as I used to do, but your little bed is empty and I cannot hear your gentle breathing, nor switch on a lamp and see the perfection of your alabaster body – your small, haunting face. I want to hold you and kiss you, my Veronica, my own, my darling wife. We must never be parted again ... it is torture...*

'Those words are merely the echo of all that lies in my heart, only I cannot put it as perfectly as Charles. Oh, my own Charles, I am just as hungry for you as you are for me. We shall die of mad happiness when we reach each other again.

'Five more months. I strike every day off my calendar, I want 1939 to end quickly. Then on New Year's Day I can say, "My beloved will be back *this* year ... in February ... please God."

'I've started doing some war-work. Mummy made me lie up and rest for a fortnight, but I couldn't stay doing nothing any longer. I get too depressed. So I went to see Mummy's crony, Lady Forringale of Brampton Hall. She is organising a local mobile canteen which takes books and sweets and cigarettes to the troops stationed around and about. At the moment there is not a lot to do. I go to Brampton Hall three afternoons a week and help buy the food, get the vans packed up. But later, when I'm stronger, I want to go out with the canteen and take a more active part. There are a lot of soldiers training round this area and new aerodromes being built and tremendous aerial activity. Oh, what a hateful thing war is! It destroys peace and leaves so little time for the pursuit of real truth and beauty ... which is the artist's aim. One is almost ashamed to be artistic these days.

'But I go over to Whitelands in the evenings. Ruth Jacobs is as Mummy described her – a fat little Jewess. But infinitely kind with the dark, sympathetic eyes of her race and a pathetic wish to please; to "get in" with Mummy and me. She loves and understands music, and her Steinway grand is a beauty. I have played and sung many of Charles's compositions to her and she thinks, as I do, that he is a genius in his way – that his talents are horribly wasted. My poor cocoa-planter in Lagos!

'Mummy still sniffs at the Jacobses, but I am friendly with them. Mr Jacobs is a funny little fat man who goes up to London every day; has a smart car and a lot of smart friends down for the weekend. He is, of course, a vulgarian. But he is as kind as Ruth. And they have a son, Benjy, who has joined up and is doing his bit, and they are so pathetically proud of him in his uniform. Mr Jacobs made me laugh when he showed me Benjy's photograph, mournfully shook his head and said: "Vot a cut, that suit, *hein?* Vot a cut...!"

'One feels one ought to be specially kind to the Jewish people because they are having such a dreadful time. The Jacobses have a brother whose family in Berlin have recently been turned out of their home. The father and sons have been taken to a concentration camp and tortured. One boy has died. It is horrible, and Mr Jacobs said he will use every penny of his fortune he has accumulated to aid our country and avenge that poor boy.

'Last night I sang *My Grief on the Sea,* and poor Ruth wept. The Jewish people are heavy with grief these days.

'Another letter from Boyd yesterday. His second. I am glad he wants to maintain our

200

friendship. Charles had said that he isn't in the least jealous of Boyd, because he *knows* me and how I feel about him, and he likes me to have a man friend. "Enjoy yourself with this chap now and then – he sounds a good fellow and I don't want my poor Veronica to become hag-ridden..." He wrote that when he acknowledged my first letter describing Boyd's kindness on board.

'Boyd is at Borden ... terribly busy, doing an adjutant's job. He thinks he may be moved any moment and "go up a pip", as he describes it. Major Mansell will sound awfully grand. Of course, promotion is rapid in the Army these days.

'It's my birthday on October 2nd. I must do as Charles wants, make an effort to cheer up and have a little party. I'll ask Boyd to try and get over. He has a car and he could stay the night. We'll put a camp bed in Mummy's room for me and he can have mine. He might be able to. And I'll have a good dinner... Nanny and Mummy and I can manage it between us. Lovely fresh vegetables and fruit from the garden, and Ruth Jacobs will, I know, save me a pheasant. She seems to be able to get anything she wants. Such is the power of money. Her husband has a friend with a big shoot near here. I don't mind asking. It gives Ruth such pleasure to do things for her friends. She has the nicest nature.

201

'I'll ask Mervyn and Iris to come down and stay at the "Buckingham Arms" the night. And I'll ask Molly Forringale. She's on the spot doing V.A.D. work, but can get a night off, no doubt. She's a pretty girl and will do for Boyd. Mummy can have in her old Brigadier Bletchley for her *vis-à-vis*. I don't want anybody but Charles ... I shall just be odd man out ... it's my birthday, and I'll sit at the head of the table and smile benignly on everyone else.'

## 6

*Another extract from Veronica Hallard's diary, written at the end of October.*

'I haven't been writing in my diary regularly. I've been too tired. I'm one of the ones who go out in the mobile canteen every day now, and by the time we get back I'm so stiff and cold all I want to do is have a hot bath and lie down. It is stupid, being so delicate. I never thought I was, but Mummy and Nanny say I was always prone to colds. I get such dreadful ones and my throat closes up and I just have to go to bed. I feel ashamed of myself with everyone else working so hard. All kinds of women's services are being formed, but Charles says he doesn't want me to join any of them. I enjoy the canteen, even when it's bad weather. The boys are so grateful for their chocolate and cigarette rations, and such dears. They look terribly young, the ones who are training now. Makes me feel how old Charles and I are getting.

'On a fine autumn day it is lovely here. Monks Rest garden has the most glorious variegated kinds of Michaelmas daisies and dahlias. And Mummy's special brand of zinnias. I like the violent hues of the zinnias because they remind me of West Africa and the exotic flowers that used to climb up our verandah. But when it is cold and wet (as it was a week ago) it's hatefully depressing. I suppose I feel the climate more than other women here because I'm so used to the heat. They laugh at me, shivering like a sick little monkey, they say, in the canteen.

'It's queer to think of my Charles panting in that awful scorching heat. They're getting heavy rain in Lagos now, and it is often unbearable out there at this time. I remember it last year. I suppose I was wise to come home. That climate did try me sorely. But the longer I'm away from my darling, the more I miss him.

'It makes me sick to meet people like that woman who came to help while our Miss Butler at the canteen was away. I told Charles about her. She has a silly sort of nickname – Cootie or something. Very good-looking and smart, with long red nails and overdone golden hair in a pageboy's bob and far too much paint. Her husband is in France and they've only been married six months, but she openly says she is sick of him and is thankful he's gone, and that she's got a new boy friend, a Polish flying officer. When she had a wire to say the husband was on his way home with superficial wounds, she actually announced that she was fed-up because it would mean a row over her 'Polski' as she calls him and she won't give him up. That poor husband coming home to *her*. Such women oughtn't to exist. If only you would wire me to say *you* are coming home, my Charles! But it's always the wrong people who have the luck. Another four months to go before I see you again.

'And then ... what? Already Charles is preparing me for the worst. One of his letters warned me that he has spoken to his chief and told him that whether men of his age are being called up or not, he will offer his services when he gets home. Typical of Charles and his idealism. Even though he loathed every inch of the way, he would travel the hard road rather than stay behind with the slackers. I'm so proud of him and yet ... so afraid. I wish I thought I would make a good wife for a soldier. Perhaps one day I shall have to learn.

'We are all learning to do things we have

never done before. Mummy is magnificent the way she stands at that kitchen sink and attacks greasy dishes and sweeps and dusts and never complains. I must admit she is not only hard on others but on herself.

'My birthday party was a success. Mrs Jacobs came to the fore (as I knew she would) with a brace of hen pheasants, presented as a present plus a wonderful album of records – the Sibelius Symphony No.1 – which I have wanted for a long time. I'm longing to play it to Charles and so thankful Mummy kept Daddy's radiogram as it has a good tone and is still going well.

'Mummy allowed me to move things round so that we would have plenty of room to dance on the polished floors in both drawing-room and dining-room. I slept with Mummy, and Boyd had my little room. He managed to get away and come to the party. He was fully expecting to go overseas, and at first thought it hopeless, but at the last moment he was posted to Woolwich on a course. He was very pleased because the course didn't start till October 3rd, so he managed to dash down here on the 2nd.

'He was a great success with Mummy. I knew he would be because he has such charming manners, and of course Mummy hinted that she wished I'd chosen a man like Captain Mansell for a husband. Just because he has money and a large estate. It's so hateful of her. She knows I'd rather have my Charles and no money. But she can't help being what she is any more than I can help being *me,* so I don't quarrel with her.

'Boyd seemed awfully pleased to see me, and raved about Monks Rest. He said how his sister would love it. Gilly is now officially engaged to Dr John Frobisher. We saw it in *The Times* the other day and Boyd says she is blissful and learning to walk a little more every day.

'Dear Boyd. He is so tall – he had to stoop in lots of places in this funny old cottage – the beams in the drawing-room are far too low for him. He looks nice in his uniform. Smart and always wears such well-polished shoes and Sam Browne. He's so funny about that belt. It is cracked and darkened by much polishing. It was with him in the Palestine campaign in 1935. He has worn it since he was a subaltern. He says he wouldn't for the world change it for one of those awful, smooth, light-coloured ones the "new boys" wear as soon as they get commissions.

'We had a talk, and he was just as sweet and sympathetic about my Charles as ever. He seemed to think it quite right for Charles to want to join up. Of course, Boyd is every inch a soldier and doesn't really understand the artistic temperament. But I was surprised and touched when he brought me down some records for a birthday present. A bit hackneyed and on the dramatic side, dear old Boyd ... a lot of Puccini ... *La Tosca* ... *Madame Butterfly* ... things he said he had been listening to on the wireless in the Mess. I honestly believe he is flattering me by trying to take an interest in music.

'Dinner was grand – beautifully cooked by Nanny. The dining-room looked heavenly with three tall green candles burning in Mummy's candelabra. All our lovely Georgian family silver shone, and the cut glass Mummy saved when she sold so many of our things at Whitelands glittered exquisitely. I could see Boyd liked it all.

'Mummy looked regal in black lace and pearls. I wore a long black skirt and pale yellow chiffon blouse, and found a late yellow rose from the garden to pin in my hair. Boyd had that queer look in his eyes when he looked at me as I came into the room. The look I fancied I had seen at Victoria. It rather disconcerted me. Oh, I don't want Boyd to be attracted by me *that* way. I don't! I tried hard to make him see how attractive Molly Forringale is. She looked sweet in her blue velvet dress. She's taller than I am – and very fair, with naturally curly hair and hazel eyes. She shares many of Boyd's interests. She's a great sports girl and used to win all the local tennis championships in the old days. But

Boyd and she didn't seem to get on particularly well. He talked a fair amount to Mummy at the table, but mostly to me. Molly must have been so bored. The old Brigadier paid her a lot of attention, and so it was Mummy who became odd man out in the long run and not myself, as I intended. I do wish Iris and Mervyn had been able to come, but Iris wrote a sad little letter from her mother's house in Farnham to say that Mervyn is overseas already. Poor Iris! I pity her. I pity all women who love their husbands and have to see them off on active service.

'After dinner, another young couple came in. The Angertons, who live in Risborough. He's a chartered accountant and was once an old admirer of mine. Now happily married to a Risborough girl – Anne Eccles. They've just had a baby and are frightfully happy. It positively hurt me to see how they looked at each other during the evening. Now and again I caught him surreptitiously taking her hand. It brought a lump to my throat. My Charles is still so far, far away and I need him so desperately.

'After coffee we put records on the radiogram and danced, as Mummy planned. Then after my first dance with Boyd Mansell things went wrong.

'He dances beautifully. I told him that on the boat. Our steps match so well together.

The dining-room, with furniture pushed back, was dim and romantic with the soft candlelight burning in the lovely old silver sconces against the walls. Mummy has a passion for wax candles and hates electric light. I love the subdued effect, too. Molly had just put on an old tune, "Night and Day". It used to be one of my favourites. It's a haunting melody. I closed my eyes and gave myself up to that dance, and for a moment, with Boyd's arm holding me close I was stirred – nothing but physically stirred, of course, Charles my darling – you know that! It was just the sensuousness of the room full of flowers and candlelight, and that unforgettable tune:

Night and Day ... you are the one...

'Charles! We have been separated for so long. I am sick of life without you. Perhaps it was that I tried to imagine for a mad moment that it was *you* holding me ... dancing with me ... anyhow, I felt suddenly breathless and excited. I allowed my hand to tighten round Boyd Mansell's neck. His response was unexpected and devastating. He clasped me quite roughly with both arms and kissed my hair, and I heard him say: "Oh, lord ... Veronica ... I can't bear this ... you're too sweet ... far too sweet..."
'Charles, you said those very same words

to me on the first night we met after Iris's party. Oh, *Charles* ... and oh, *Boyd!* I didn't want *him* to feel that way. I opened my eyes and saw his brown face was pale and his eyes the eyes of a man struggling with some gigantic problem which he could not begin to solve. Thank goodness the music stopped then. I drew away from Boyd sharply. A frill of my yellow chiffon blouse caught in one of his tunic buttons and tore ... and that saved the situation. He pulled himself together and gave an apologetic laugh.

'"Oh, lord ... I'm sorry ... how dreadful ... your lovely dress, Veronica..."

'"It's nothing," I laughed back. "Nanny will soon mend that. Isn't it hot all of a sudden?"

'"Very," he agreed, and took out a khaki silk handkerchief and mopped his forehead. His Sam Browne he had already unclasped and put over the back of a chair.

'Mummy called from the drawing-room: "Wouldn't you young men like some beer?"

'Boyd seemed to think that a first-rate idea. So we joined the others. Boyd attached himself to Molly. Later, when I was talking to Brigadier Bletchley, I saw them dancing. Boyd looked quite normal again. So good-looking and charming; laughing with Molly. I was relieved, but I could not forget that revealing moment when he had lost control and kissed my hair and uttered those passionate words.

'I knew that night Boyd had fallen in love with me.

'I have tried my best to ignore that knowledge, because I still want his friendship. He is one of the nicest men I've ever met. I must say he appeared to be quite ordinary and friendly for the rest of the evening. When he said good-bye to me early in the morning just before he drove back to London he thanked me heartily for a "whale of a party", as he put it, and said quite casually, "See you again soon, Veronica. So long. Take care of yourself, my dear."

'And he drove off, leaving me slightly upset and bewildered. Poor Boyd! I don't want him to be hurt by me. I have absolutely nothing to give any man – except my husband. I must have been crazy – allowing myself to be stirred even for a second while I danced with Boyd. I must never do anything to encourage him again. But I would hate him to go out of my life.

'I haven't seen him for three weeks now but he has not deserted me. He writes brief notes now and then to tell me how hard he is working on this course. It is all "hush-hush", and he can't explain what it is, but when it is ended he says he may be sent to any part of the British Isles, but not abroad. It is something to do with anti-aircraft. He also says when the course ends he hopes to run down and see Mummy and me. I wrote and told him that we would love to see him.

'Mummy still talks of "that nice Captain Mansell".

'Meanwhile, October has rolled on. Another month gone; four weeks nearer my Charles. But it has been another month of sinkings at sea, and each time I hear of one my blood congeals.

'The leaves are fluttering down. The tall poplars at the end of the garden are stark again and have a wintry aspect. The little churchyard, like our lawn, is brown with decaying leaves. The flowers are dead. Last night a storm of rain and wind stripped the last petals from the last roses, flattened the herbaceous border and turned our lane into a sea of mud.

'I'm awfully depressed at the moment. Mummy and I are getting slightly on each other's nerves. Nanny isn't well. She has a "chest". One day that poor old soul will crack up. She's a good seventy and she oughtn't to be working. It's so sad that the old people of the poor have to carry on with manual labour long after they're unfit for it, in order to earn their living.

'I am awfully lonely. I meet heaps of people at my war work, and know every-body in Risborough. But I'm desperately alone. Only half of me is here. The half that counts is in Lagos with Charles. He is getting desperately impatient, too. I know it. I can tell from his letters.

'I've crossed off two more weeks. Charles my darling. Soon now it will be Christmas. You know how I long for 1940 since it means your homecoming.

'Today the first German bombs to fall on British soil fell in the Shetlands and killed a rabbit, so the report says. I wonder how many human rabbits will be killed by bombs before this war is over! People are not so sure now that it will all end quickly.

'Boyd has been posted miles away, up near Edinburgh. He's in some anti-aircraft job on the Forth. He says it's bitterly cold and unattractive, but that he's very interested in the work. He came down to say good-bye before he left. He seemed depressed, for Boyd. He used to be so cheerful and confident when I first met him on board ship. He *has* changed, I think. I do hope not because of me. Molly Forringale worried me terribly the other day by telling me she is quite sure Boyd is crazy about me; that he did nothing but talk about me to her at my party, and some rubbish too about the way he looked at me. But *is* it rubbish? I must say he was a bit subdued and constrained when we last saw each other. Perhaps it's just as well he has gone up to Scotland. But I am sorry he's so far away. I feel lonelier than ever. Boyd is the only man friend I have now that my darling is away.

'Brigadier Bletchley came in for a cup of coffee last night. He is very gloomy. He says Holland will be the next country to be invaded by Hitler. It seems unbelievable. The whole world is being dragged into chaos and misery.

'It is no longer the sane, lovely world in which my darling and I first met. I am only content now when I am out with the canteen, doing my "bit", or playing Ruth's piano. Poor Ruth! Her Benjy is in France and she is so worried. Mr Jacobs doesn't like or trust the French. Nor does he believe in the invincibility of the Maginot Line. Everyone depresses me. Charles, I want you horribly badly, my darling.

'It will be no Christmas for me without Charles. I shall have to try and get up the party spirit. Iris wants me to go up to town, but I would rather stay here. I seem to have lost any desire for "fun". There *is* none without my darling.

'*December 13th.*

'One cheerful day to record. The Navy has sunk the *Graf Spee*, Bravo the Navy!

'Charles's letters are still very desperate and impatient. He says he really will not be able to live without seeing me again soon. I love him to write those words, because I feel the same. He said old Chaddy wanted to know if I had seen anything of his wife, but I haven't. Letty wrote once after we landed and said she was going into some new organisation – I really don't know what – and is living with her sister in Newcastle-on-Tyne, so our ways never meet. I told Charles I had had a letter from that girl I shared a cabin with ... Pam... She is married to her Eddie and cheerful and happy in her matter-of-fact way as ever. I really believe the matter-of-fact people get along more easily in this world than the ultra-sensitive, silly ones like myself. Either way up or way down. But it's so lovely ... being way up ... and life *is* marvellous and intoxicating as lived with my Charles.

*'Christmas Day.*
   'Isn't it typical of me? I'm in bed with a streaming cold and temperature. Mummy says it's flu and won't let anyone but Nanny or herself come near me. She had fixed a Christmas dinner with the Brigadier and the Forringales and had to put them off. I'm sorry to disappoint everyone. I'm disappointed too, because the Jacobses, although not Christians, were celebrating tonight with a huge party and had asked a young violinist – a prodigy – down especially to play to me.
   'My head aches. My eyes stream. I submit meekly to Nanny rubbing my chest and

Mummy stalking in with innumerable inhalants. My little room reeks of camphorated oil and friar's balsam and through a mist I see my beloved Charles's photographed face smiling tenderly at me. I used to have awful colds even in Lagos, and he always gathered me in his arms and said: "Hell to the infection! Let me kiss that dear little flushed face..." I can hear you saying it, Charles ... feel your lips on mine. Oh, darling, even with flu, I'm hopelessly in love with you. That settles *all* doubts, doesn't it?

'You had Christmas dinner today in the breathless heat, and I drank milk and can't get warm even with two hot-water bottles and piles of blankets and an electric fire full on. My casements are blurred and rimmed with frost. It is bitterly cold. Not even a white Christmas ... just a black frost. Icy winds. Misery! I suppose I'm better off in bed, but I've let the canteen down again. I'm furious with myself.

'I had a letter from Boyd wishing me a happy Christmas, with a huge tin of short-bread from Edinburgh. He is so thoughtful and generous always. His letters seem normal and friendly. I don't think I need worry about my birthday night. We were both just a bit het-up then.

'Boyd says it is a sad Christmas for his mother. Mrs Mansell apparently is spending it quite alone in her huge house. Boyd could not get leave. Her eldest daughter is in Lincolnshire and Gilly was married two weeks before Christmas to her doctor, who has taken her to his old mother's house in Devonshire for their honeymoon. Apparently Gilly, still far from strong, wished that instead of an hotel. I am sorry for Mrs Mansell. It must be awful to have a huge place and all one's children away. I must try to go down and see her one day. She sounds a perfectly sweet person. Boyd's devotion to her is the nicest thing.

'New Year's Day.

'1940 at last. Now only two months off seeing you, Charles, my darling. Your last letter was full of plans for our reunion. It thrilled me to the depths of my being. I really begin to feel you *are* coming. The middle of February, you think. Charles, Charles, what heaven!

'I must start collecting clothes … some very special undies, a new nightie … to devastate you with, my Charles. You like black chiffon. You shall have it. You want to take me right away from here … from everyone we know. Oh, yes, darling. Let's go to Land's End … anywhere … miles into the blue. I want only you and you will want only me. *And* a piano. We must sing and play together. I am crazy to hear you play "Veronica's Concerto" again.

'Charles ... I can hardly breathe for excitement today. *January 1st.* The tide has turned. Two months – eight weeks, then you. Oh, I don't care what happens now; I feel gloriously egotistical. I am waiting for, living for, you.

'What will you say to me, Charles? What will your first words be? Where will we meet? London, I suppose. You'll land at Liverpool, but for security reasons you won't be allowed to tell me when to expect you. But one day I shall hear the telephone bell ring here at home and I'll hear your voice. You'll say: "Darling, I'm back..." Then I shall faint. I know I shall ... just pass out from sheer bliss.

'Charles, Charles, *Charles!*...'


7


*Letter from Boyd Mansell to Mrs John Frobisher, written on February 14th, from 'Somewhere in Scotland'.*


'My dearest Gilly,

'I owe you several letters, and when you hear my news I know you will forgive me for the long delay. I am writing this on my old typewriter in my room. There's a beer-party in the Mess and the other chaps are getting down to it, but I couldn't for the life of me

218

go to any party tonight. I have just got back from forty-eight hours' compassionate leave, which I spent half in Princes Risborough and half in London. Gilly, if I live to be ninety I shall never quite recover from these two days. I feel like hell even now. I haven't been able to write to poor old Mother. But I must write to you. It will help a bit. And also, as you'll see when I've finished this letter, I need *your* help.

'I'll start from the very beginning of this sorry tale. I was sitting in the Mess two – no, three – nights ago (I've almost lost count), and was told there was a personal call for me. It was snowing and bitterly cold and I was trying to get warm, having been out on a gun-site all day. I answered the call. It was from Lady Lowring, Veronica's mother. You know ... I've told you all about her and that charming little cottage. Well, Gilly, she is a cold, self-contained sort of woman – I admire her, but never thought till that night that she had much heart. She could hardly speak to me for emotion. She said, "Boyd, am I asking too much, or could you come down to Monks Rest at once? I think if somebody like yourself doesn't come and take charge, Veronica will go out of her mind. Indeed, she is out of her mind already." I asked what had happened. She told me that it was Veronica's husband, Charles, who was on his way home from

Nigeria. I hear regularly from Veronica, and she had just written an ecstatic letter last week to say she had had a cable telling her that Charles had left Lagos. I made a long-distance call to her the next evening and she had sounded on top of the world. Poor, tragic little Veronica! Gilly, you can guess what has happened. Charles Hallard will not be coming back to Veronica. The ship was torpedoed, sunk somewhere between Lagos and Madeira. Nobody knows where and hardly any details through yet. Lady Lowring said they had just had the bare information by way of an official telegram, deeply regretting, etc. Apparently very few passengers beyond a boatload of women and children were saved. One eye-witness landed said that those who were clinging to rafts or lifeboats were machine-gunned by the Germans who came to the surface to watch their fiendish work.

'Lady Lowring sounded absolutely panic-stricken. She said Veronica was demented and trying to rush out of the cottage and that she and the old nurse could do nothing with her and that she had now locked herself in her room and wouldn't even let the doctor in. They wanted to give her a hypodermic. She appeared to be suffering from acute shock, but instead of it prostrating her, she was in a half-crazed state and Lady L. was petrified of what she might do. She said, "Boyd, you are her friend and she likes you and relies on you. You might be able to help where I've failed. Do come if you can."

'Needless to say, I went straight to the C.O. and explained the position, and he let me off at once. I took the night train down to London, and without waiting for breakfast caught an early-morning train to Princes Risborough.

'Gilly, you alone in this world know how much I love Veronica, and those next few hours were so excruciatingly painful to me, I don't like to remember them, and yet must tell you about it. Must "get it off my chest", so to speak. It's like a terrible burden weighing me down. Gilly, I must say that not for one moment did I feel the slightest thankfulness that the woman I loved was free... God forbid! In my maddest moments I never wished her husband, who was a young, fine chap, to die like that, actually on his way home. It is too grim to contemplate. And I will also say in defence of myself that when I first saw Veronica that morning I would have given my right arm for Charles Hallard to walk into the house safe and sound.

'I shall never forget her face. It haunts me now. Poor little Veronica!

'It was a raw winter's morning when I got to the cottage. The country lay under a pall of snow and the trees round the cottage were rimmed with it. They were stark and dreary under the leaden sky still full of heavy snow-clouds. I used to like the little churchyard next door, but that morning it looked grim and full of foreboding. The sight of those snow-covered graves made me think of that poor fellow, struggling for his life in icy water … perhaps being shot as he attempted to get to a lifeboat. It was a horrible thought for me, and I did not know him. What it must have been for *her*, God alone knows. *You* will understand. You know a bit. And here I thank heaven you are so happy with your John. From your letters, your marriage appears to be so very successful, my dear.

'To continue, I reached Monks Rest, feeling pretty jaded after a cold, grim journey – I couldn't get a first-class sleeper to King's Cross at a moment's notice – so sat up in a carriage with a lot of naval chaps who played poker all night. I felt unshaven and in no state to enter a lady's house, but I thought Lady Lowring's call had been so urgent I had better not wait for a meal or a shave in town.

'I was right. Lady Lowring opened the door to me, looking like a corpse, herself; eyes red-rimmed with crying. None of her usual rather "bossy" manner, poor old Lady L. She fairly fell into my arms and wept and thanked God I'd come.

'She and the old Nanny had been up all night drinking cups of tea and trying to cajole Veronica behind the door. The local doctor had called twice, but been refused admittance. They were a couple of scared old women, expecting Veronica to throw herself out of the window or cut her throat at any moment, I think. Lady L. said to me: "It's horrible, *horrible*, Boyd. She had a presentiment, weeks ago. She kept saying she was afraid of Charles being torpedoed, and I always pooh-poohed it. Then she seemed happier about him and she prepared a trousseau as though she were a bride – she adored that man, her love for him was almost abnormal, in my eyes – and now this. This disaster. It will kill her, Boyd. I know it will. Or she will kill herself."

'Well, Gilly, you know me. I'm not a very highly emotional and excitable person. I generally face the odds pretty coolly, but I will admit I stood outside Veronica's locked door that dreary winter's morning with the icy fingers of death gripping my own heart. I fancied I heard a sort of soft singing and it made my blood run cold. I was afraid Veronica had, in truth, gone out of her mind. I listened a moment. Lady L., huddled in a fur coat and looking blue with cold, nodded at me meaningfully. The old Nanny was there, too, weeping. I told them both to go

downstairs and prepare hot coffee and food.
I asked them to let me tackle Veronica alone.
She obviously wouldn't listen to either of
them, and I asked Lady L.'s permission to
break down the door if necessary. She said I
could do anything I liked.

'Well, Gilly, I stood for a moment, rubbing
a pair of very cold hands, listening to that
awful singing. I knew the song, as a matter
of fact. Heard her sing it once or twice when
I've been on leave in Risborough. She used
to take it to her old home, Whitelands Hall,
and use the Jacobses' piano. It was a sort of
old Irish lament. I can hear the words now;
absolutely pathetic, Gilly, and so eerie, too,
her singing away like that alone in her room:

'My grief on the sea,
How the waves of it roll,
For they heave between me
And the love of my soul!

'Abandoned, forsaken,
To grief and to care,
Will the sea ever waken
Relief from despair?'...

'She got as far as that, and then I knocked
on the door loudly. The singing stopped.
She said in a dead sort of voice, "It's no use.
I won't let you in, Mummy. Go away. I only
want Charles. You can send Charles when

224

he comes. You don't understand how much Charles and I love each other. Go away, Mummy ... you, too, Nanny ... please. And I don't want a doctor. I'm not ill."

'Then I said:

'"It's Boyd ... Boyd Mansell, Veronica. Will you let *me* in?"

'She answered in a changed sort of voice:

'"You, Boyd? I wasn't expecting you. Why have you come?"

'"I want to speak to you, Veronica," I said. "About Charles."

'I suppose it was a bit of a trick, and gave her false hope, because without hesitation she opened the door and let me in. But immediately she locked it again, gave me an almost sly look, and whispered:

'"We won't let Mummy or Nanny in. They don't understand about Charles. You do. You always did. What news is there? Is he in England yet? Have you heard, Boyd?"

'Gilly, I couldn't bring myself to answer for a moment. I could only stare at her. What I saw was pretty frightful. The lovely bedroom – they used to give it to me whenever I stayed there on leave – was in a most awful state of disorder. Clothes chucked all over the bed and hanging out of the drawers; a suitcase half packed and photographs of Hallard – dozens of 'em – snaps, studio portraits of all kinds, dotted all round the place. And Veronica. Oh, Gil, how awful she looked! Like a little mad thing. (Like I imagine Ophelia in that awful scene from Hamlet.) Hair all tangled, hanging over her face. A tailored skirt on; no blouse; she stood there in a little pink thing that showed her lovely neck and small bosom and bare arms. She didn't seem conscious of being in such a state of undress. She looked at me with crazy eyes; huge great eyes burning in a deathly white little face. She seemed to me to have shrunken even in a few hours. She had changed terribly, anyhow, since I last saw her. When I didn't speak she came and clutched my arm.

'"Tell me, Boyd," she said. "What news of Charles? Mummy is so stupid. She keeps telling me to try to be brave because he is dead … drowned … never coming back to me. It isn't true, Boyd, is it?"

'I wanted to say "No" to her, Gilly. My throat ached. I can't describe to you my feelings in that moment. But I thought it best to be firm and try to make her snap out of that unnatural state. I took her poor little thin arms – they were frozen – and held them tightly. I looked down into her beseeching eyes and said:

'"Veronica, my poor little darling, you've got to face up to it. You've got to. The liner Charles was travelling home in has been torpedoed and there are only a few survivors – some women and children and a few sailors. They told your mother that the ship sank rapidly in heavy seas and there is little chance that other survivors landed. Charles may, of course, have been taken on board the submarine. He may eventually be a prisoner of war. You may hear yet. There *is* that chance. Hang on to that, but try to face up to the fact that it is a slender hope, my dear."

'Gilly, she looked at me as though she did not take in a word I said. She backed away from me, sat down on the edge of her bed and started to shiver. Her bare arms and neck were bluish with cold, like her lips. It was the first time I had ever seen Veronica without rouge on her lips or any powder on her face. All her beauty had gone. She was livid and haggard and yet I had never loved her more. I felt the most boundless compassion for her. It was almost my undoing. I wanted, in an unmanly fashion, to burst into tears. I admit it to you.

'She looked up at me with those terrible eyes of hers and said:

'"I don't understand you. *Where is Charles?*"

'I saw a coat on her bed, a camel-hair coat. I recognized it. She used to wear it on board. I wrapped it gently round her shivering little body. She huddled in it like a sick child, her teeth chattering. I said:

'"Veronica, darling, do try and under-

227

stand. There's been a terrible disaster and the official telegram your mother opened says that Charles has lost his life through enemy action at sea. That is all at the moment, my dear. But I tell you – there may be hope ... he may still be alive and–"

'Then she interrupted me, Gilly, with a stifled sort of cry. She said through those chattering teeth:

'"I don't believe it and I don't want to hear any more. Mummy keeps telling me stupid things. They are not true. I've been packing ... all night ... getting ready for our reunion. He should arrive at the end of the week. I thought I'd go up to London and meet him. We used to like that funny little hotel in a *cul-de-sac* off St James's Street. Duke's it is called. We always had that ground-floor bedroom there with the lovely powder-blue satin bedcovers and our own bathroom. We stayed there just before we went out to Lagos. I'm going up to Duke's and I'll take our old room and wait in it for Charles. You'll help me, won't you, Boyd? Mummy won't let me go. I've tried once or twice to go out and she forces me back. I know she wants the doctor to give me something to make me sleep. She's never cared for my Charles and I think it's hateful of her ... trying to keep me away from him now. I'm glad you've come, Boyd. You'll help me, won't you?"

'I looked at her with despair in my heart, Gilly, but I saw nothing for it but to humour her at the moment. I said: "Yes, I'll help you, Veronica."

'Then she sprang up her face colouring with excitement. Her teeth stopped chattering and she spoke quite gaily:

'"Run along down then and order breakfast. I'm hungry and you must be, too. We'll eat something, then go straight up to London. You can always manage Mummy. She loves you. And Boyd, it's wonderful that you've come at this moment just when I need your help. How did you know?"

'I shook my head. I couldn't answer. That colour in her wan face and the unnatural brilliance of her great eyes unnerved me again. I felt sick at heart and wondered what the end of this would be. It could only be a complete nervous breakdown for *her*.

'We carried on with the farce. I said I'd order breakfast and she said she'd get dressed. Before I left the room she seized my arm and dragged me round, showing me all kinds of pathetic things. Lovely lingerie she herself had made for "her Charles"; a new, smart little fur hat; a new pair of shoes. (What tiny shoes she wears, Gilly – like a small kid's foot!) She showed me everything so proudly with that crazy light in her eyes. It was all for Charles ... *for Charles* ... how he'd like it ... what they'd do together in town... Honestly, it almost sent me off my own rocker. Don't know how I stood it.

'I went downstairs and told Lady L. what had been said. The old nurse rushed to boil eggs and make strong coffee and they both seemed to look on me as a sort of saviour of their treasure. At the same time Lady L. was very naturally apprehensive about this trip to London. Why did Veronica insist on going up to town? Much better keep her here in bed. She would only collapse, etc.

'I argued then that I thought it best to give V. her head and let her do as she wanted. The madness would die down. I was confident of it. I promised to look after her and never leave her side.

'Lady L.'s eyes filled with tears and she put a hand on my shoulder and said: "I trust you absolutely, Boyd. I am so grateful."

'I rejected the gratitude. I had done nothing – yet. But I thought poor Lady L., usually so stately, so domineering, had shrunk considerably in stature and demeanour.

'Shall I ever forget that breakfast? Veronica came down in her new tailored suit. A pale blue tweed which she had had made for the "spring", for Charles's home-coming; a little absurd blue hat at an angle over her eyes; dark hair curled more neatly than I had seen upstairs. She was very much made up, but one thing I had never before seen on that well-loved face. A smear of lipstick; of eyelash black; too much rouge. As though the hand holding the cosmetics had trembled.

'She was in high spirits; eyes abnormally bright. She chattered without ceasing, about Charles and his home-coming. Her mother watched, half in misery, half in fear, and said nothing. I answered her as ordinarily as possible. She then concentrated on me. Gilly, I had no clear idea what was going to happen when we left Monks Rest. I didn't know, you see, how far Veronica's mind was deranged and when or where the collapse would come. But of one thing I was confident – she must be humoured. Resistance seemed to make her worse.

'Poor Lady L. looked heart-broken, when the taxi came for us, but I pressed her hand and whispered: "Don't worry. I'll ring you from London..." and tried to smile as I added: "At least she ate a big breakfast and that is something. It will help her body if not her mind."

'So, Gilly, we took that strange journey together to Paddington. Unforgettable. Almost uncanny ... like a couple going on a holiday. Our suitcases with us. God knows what lay in *her* mind. She talked feverishly of her husband and their meeting. He would come to Duke's. She knew that he would. That was the arranged hotel.

'I listened, smiled, nodded, let her have

her way. But I watched her closely. How long would this unnatural state continue? When would she wake up and realise the grim truth?

'She seemed endowed with more than usual stamina, physically Veronica is really a delicate thing. That February morning she was like one possessed. Nothing deterred her from that trip. Neither the snow, which had begun to fall again in large feathery flakes, the chill north-east wind, nor the crowded train which happened to be a popular one. People read their papers ... men discussed the main topic of the day (the trade pact which had been signed yesterday between Germany and Russia). Another triumph for Ribbentrop. It was disgraceful, they said. But little I cared, Gilly. My whole soul was concentrated on Veronica; that pathetic little figure in the blue suit, the gay little hat; the short fur coat. She said once or twice: "You must buy me a flower when we get to town, Boyd. Charles adores me with flowers on my coat. Violets – they would look heavenly on the pale blue – don't you agree?"

'I found myself promising to buy her violets. And I looked at her reckless, lovely little face with its smeared make-up and groaned inside me. My poor, unhappy Veronica. So much misery in store for her when she came out of this trance and realised what had happened. I wished to God I could bear the pain for her. There was no jealousy in me of Charles Hallard then, I tell you; there was no passion in me, Gilly, save that of pity and the genuine wish that I could bring that poor drowned fellow back to her. Another b–y murder done by the Germans. Another score for me to pay when I really get down to it.

'We reached London. I took Veronica's arm as we walked down the platform on the taxi rank. I could feel her trembling slightly. Her gait was, I thought, a little peculiar; like that of a somnambulist. I wondered once or twice if I had been wise in letting her come so far from her mother and home. She was really a pathological case.

'We got a taxi and she insisted first on stopping at a florist's. Then I went through the farce of buying her a festive-looking bunch of flowers! There were no violets on sale: I got pink carnations, and put them on her lap. She seemed to have forgotten then that she had asked for flowers and did not even thank me, but sat listlessly staring out of the window. The snow drifted drearily against the windowpanes. It was bitterly cold and I feared she would catch a cold, and took off my khaki great-coat and put it over her knees. Her eyes went on staring as though she did not see. I began to wonder how near she was to caving in.

'When we reached Duke's they said they were full up, no room having been booked for Mr and Mrs Charles Hallard. Veronica frowned but seemed less perturbed than I imagined and said:

'"Then we'll go somewhere else, *Charles darling*…"

'That was when I got my biggest shock, Gilly. Veronica had reached a stage in which *she imagined I was her husband!* I tell you, she had me pretty worried then, but I carried on – thinking it best to go through with it to the bitter end.

'I found a small hotel near by – Lord knows I never want to enter the place again. The memories are too painful. But it was a nice quiet little place near the park. The quieter the better, I thought, until I saw what Veronica was going to be like. She was beginning to look very ill. The rouge stood out on her face, on the high cheekbones. Her large eyes were sunken.

'In the hotel she went straight to the lift. She said:

'"You register, darling … follow me up. I've got such a queer headache."

'I told the woman at the reception desk that I'd register later; gave my name hurriedly as Hallard (I thought it best) and rushed after Veronica, carrying up our suitcases myself.

'They had given us a small comfortable

room furnished in the usual dull conventional manner. I couldn't tell you what the furniture was like. I only remember rather dreary blue chenille curtains and a lot of net over the window which looked out on a quiet street at the end of which one could see Piccadilly and the trees. Twin bedsteads with wooden head-boards each of which had a little striplight. An arm-chair; a luggage rack on which I placed our two cases.

'Veronica sat down on the edge of one of the beds. She stared at me rather blankly and smiled. I could not bear that smile. It was too heart-breaking. I went and sat beside her. I said:

'"Veronica, darling, don't you know me?"

'She took off her hat and twiddled it in her small gloved hands. (The carnations, I noticed, were in a heap on the carpet.) She nodded.

'"Of course…"

'"Veronica…" I said, then could say no more. Words simply would not come.

'Suddenly she flung off her fur coat and the tweed coat of her suit and peeled off her gloves as though coming terribly alive. Her eyes glittered in her flushed face. She flung herself into my arms. Like a frenzied creature. She…'

*Boyd Mansell stopped typing.*

235

For a moment the muscles of his face – a haggard young face in the grey February light – worked. His fingers twitched and dropped into his lap. He stared without seeing it – at the Forth Bridge – spanning so miraculously and in sheer mechanical wonder the grey icy water of the Forth. In a moment it would be dark. He must draw the curtains, switch on a lamp. He could hear hearty laughter and voices issuing from the Mess. The beer-party was warming up.

Suddenly he leaned his head on both his hands. He was tormented by the memories this pouring out of his heart to his sister evoked. But even to her, the beloved understanding Gilly, he could not write *everything*. Could not bare secrets that were poor little Veronica's as well as his own. Somehow he must complete this letter – gloss over that bedroom scene – rewrite the last page; Gilly must not know all ... it wouldn't be decent ... he could not tell her exactly what had happened just before Veronica's collapse. But the man would remember it – carry the memory to the day of his death. He loved her. Those had been damnable hours for a man with a woman he loved.

He could feel Veronica's arms about him now, straining him passionately to her breast. Her lips had clung to his with a passion he had never before experienced; she had kissed him with the eager thirst of one who was dying for love. And in between the kisses she called him 'Charles' ... *Charles*... (How that name grated on him now!) She thought still that he was that poor, dead, drowned fellow, Charles. It was horrible! And he, loving her, had held and returned her kisses, trying to help her; trying desperately not to lose his head and take advantage of her madness. But he had never known, would never know again, such sweet terrible caresses. She lay there, fully dressed, in his arms on that hotel bed, recklessly crushing the silk spread, her flushed face wet with passionate tears, her dark hair tumbled about her eyes. 'Charles, Charles,' she kept on calling that name. 'Kiss me again, my darling, darling...' she had moaned. And he had kissed her repeatedly, held her closer trying to bring warmth and comfort to the broken mind, the starved young body.

Then suddenly her moaning cries ceased. She lay back on the pillow, all colour fading from her face. He had raised himself anxiously on his elbow, staring down at her, his face red from her fierce kisses, his heart pounding, passion and pity running a neck-to-neck race within him. Pity won, deepest concern. He called her name, 'Veronica.'

*Boyd Mansell lifted his head wearily and returned to his letter, altering the last page; telling Gillian briefly of Veronica's piteous love-*

237

*making, with no detail; and the fainting fit that followed it.*

'I revived her, dabbing her forehead with ice-cold water from the bathroom which adjoined our room. She opened her eyes but seemed not to see me. Then she said in a heart-broken voice:

'"Oh, don't leave me again, Charles, *Charles ... don't,* darling..."

'I realised that madness was still gripping her. I took her in my arms again, kissing her very gently. I begged her to sleep. Gilly, it was pathetic; she shut her eyes and fell asleep at once, like a child, against my shoulder. I watched her in agony; the sweeping silk of her long lashes on her hollowed cheek; she was so pale, so fragile, lying there on that strange bed in a strange hotel. Fate had allowed me to bring her there, I thought ... to become, momentarily, her guardian, her protector. I must not fail her now. And for all I knew this deep sleep, following her tempest of passion, might be the saving of her reason.

'I lay listening to her soft breathing, not daring to stir until cramp sent shooting pains down my arm and shoulder. Then I gently disengaged myself and laid her on the pillow. I got up and switched on the electric fire. The room had a radiator in it, but it was only luke-warm. The morning was wretchedly raw and cold.

238

'I covered my darling with an eiderdown from the other bed. Then I looked at myself in the glass. I wasn't good to see, Gilly. I think I aged ten years that morning. I rang for a chambermaid, went out in the corridor and waylaid her and told her my "wife" had been taken ill, and that I wanted hot milk and whisky sent up to our room at once. I told her that "Madame" would be going to bed and asked her to try and find a hot-water bottle, fill it and bring it back.

'The maid was an amiable woman and returned with the hot bottle. Later, a waiter came with the milk and whisky. After they had gone, I put the covered bottle at Veronica's cold little feet and poured half the whisky into the milk and put the glass down in front of the fire. I thought she might need it when she woke up. I drank the rest of the whisky, thankful for the raw stimulant. I was "in a way", Gillo, my dear, I can tell you. Half off my own rocker by then.

'Veronica did not stir. So I lay down on the other bed. I was damned tired after the journey from Scotland, no sleep, down to Risborough and up again, and then that scene with my poor darling ... enough to tempt St Anthony himself, Gil. I still don't know how I managed it. But I kept the trust she and Lady L. both put in me. I *had* to...'

*Boyd Mansell abruptly stopped typing* and rose to his feet. He was shivering as though with cold. The cold grey mists of the February dusk blotted out the Forth Bridge and the little smutty coaster which was slowly passing up-river towards Rosyth. Boyd suddenly needed a strong drink. He felt a kind of nausea. What was prompting him to write all this to Gilly? Some queer urge... He had to write it. And she alone on earth would know the hell through which he had passed. Heavens! His limbs felt as though he had the ague. A touch of fever, perhaps. His head ached badly. And he was obsessed with the thought of Veronica as he had seen her lying there in that bed in that tragic, exhausted slumber.

An orderly knocked on the door, came in and closed the shutters. The raw Scottish night was shut out. A light dispelled the gloom in the room but not in Boyd Mansell's heart. He ordered a double whisky. When the man came back with it and retired, saluting smartly, Boyd returned to his desk. He sat down and took a long drink of the stimulant.

*He went on typing his letter to his sister:*
'I must have fallen asleep, Gilly, myself, and some hours later I opened my eyes and got a bit of a shock. Veronica was up and standing beside me. She was fully dressed even to her little fur coat and blue hat. She

240

looked ghastly pale but there was no madness in her eyes. They were deeply sunken. She was looking down at me in a wondering sort of way. I sat up and slid off the bed on to my feet. My heart was pounding. I said:

'"Good heavens … are you awake? You oughtn't to be up. You ought to go on resting…"

'She stopped me with a gesture of the hand. She spoke in a perfectly natural, calm little voice … very much more herself.

'"Boyd," she said, "do you mind telling me where we are and what this" – she indicated the room – "all means. Why are we here together like this? I woke up just now and found … myself here … like this…"

'I told her as gently as possible. At the end:

'"You were a bit unhinged, I think, my dear," I said. "You insisted on coming up here. You thought I was … Charles. I'm so damned sorry, Veronica darling. But I thought it best. And you are, indeed, much better for that sleep."

'She went on staring at me with great haunted eyes. She said:

'"I … see. Thank you, Boyd, very much. It was … very good of you. I … don't seem to remember much … about anything…" She passed a hand across her forehead and gave a deep unhappy sigh. "Except … Mummy telling me about Charles."

'"Veronica, my dear," I said. "Would you

241

like to go home now? Will you have some lunch ... it's only one o'clock ... you have only been asleep a couple of hours. Have some food, then let me take you back to Monks Rest."

'She did not answer for a moment but rubbed her forehead again in that anxious, bewildered way. Then she shivered and muttered:

"How awful! I don't remember coming up to London at all. I must have been quite mad. What hotel is this?"

'I told her. I added that Duke's had been full up. The mention of that hotel sent a painful flush to her face. She said:

'"Duke's ... yes, Charles and I meant to go there together. He always liked it ... it was *our* hotel..."

'I was afraid for her. Her calm was almost as frightening to me as her wild hysteria had been. I could see that she recalled nothing of those mad moments in my arms, abandoning her poor little self to such wild passion. My own blood coursed feverishly at the memory of those caresses...'

*Boyd stopped, tore that page savagely out of the typewriter and began again:*

'I could see that she recalled nothing that had happened since she had been told the tragic news by her mother, so I said:

242

'"Will you be all right? Do you feel fit enough for the journey home?"

'She put the back of her hand against her lips. Lips that she had touched with bright vermilion. Her teeth started to chatter ... as they had done when I saw her first thing that morning. I took a step towards her, anxiously watching ... expecting another collapse at any moment. Then she gave a low moan which I shall never forget ... it broke my heart in two, Gilly. She said:

'"He's dead. He isn't coming back. Oh, Charles ... Charles ... let me die, too ... let me die and come to you ... oh, *Charles!*"

'Then down she went, Gilly, like a ninepin ... at my feet. And this time I knew Veronica was very ill. I lifted her on to the bed and moistened her lips with whisky and milk that was still warm. It had no effect. Then I telephoned down to the reception bureau.

'"Send for an ambulance at once," I said. "My ... wife ... has been taken seriously ill."

'After that it was a nightmare, Gilly. My poor darling lay like one completely dead. Indeed, her colour was so bad and breathing so poor, I was petrified that her wild prayer to die and go to Charles might, indeed, be granted. She was no longer crazed. She knew the truth and it was too terrible for her to endure. Do many women love in that way, Gilly? God help them if they do. I swear I felt mad with misery myself ...

wishing I could bring the poor fellow back to her. It was so inhumanly cruel …. his being taken from her on his very way home.

'I telephoned to Monks Rest and told Lady L. what had happened. She said she would take the next train up to London, and I suggested I should phone your John and put the matter in his hands. She agreed, so I did so. Gilly, I wish you'd been in London that day, but you were down at Chidding with Mother. Still, your husband was of inestimable help. I never knew a better chap in an emergency.

'I remember sitting by the bed in that hotel bedroom which had been allotted to "Captain and Mrs Hallard" for such a brief, tempestuous period, waiting for John. I held my darling's icy little hand and loosened her collar, took off her shoes and stockings and rubbed her cold feet – I covered her with blankets and tried to restore her circulation. She did not move. She lay like a statue … a little statue of grief … too near to death for my liking. I kissed her hand once or twice and I spoke to her, knowing she could not hear. I told her how I worshipped her; how desperately I wished I could recall that man from his watery grave, for her sake. My poor, poor little love…

'Then John arrived and took immediate charge. He understood the situation at once. Bless the fellow – he left an important patient to come to my aid. He seemed to grasp the seriousness of it. He gave Veronica a brief examination and said: "Bad collapse, of course. But don't worry, old chap. We'll get her right. You've done the best thing keeping her as warm as possible. When the ambulance comes I'll have her taken to my own nursing home."

'So Veronica was taken away from me on a stretcher and driven to the home in Manchester Street. I felt pretty done up by that time. I remember taking a last look round that room as I left and shivering. What an experience, Gilly! I felt whacked. As though I'd been beaten all over. I knew the hotel thought it all very peculiar and possibly wondered if I'd taken my wife upstairs that morning for the express purpose of trying to murder her! Anyhow, I paid the bill they gave me (very sour looks I got, too). Then I drove to Paddington to meet Veronica's mother. When she saw me, she gave an exclamation and said: "Good gracious, Boyd, you look awful! Are you all right, my dear boy?" I smiled at her and said: "Fine, thanks, and don't worry about the child. She's in a good nursing home run by my brother-in-law, Dr Frobisher. He says she'll be okay. I'll take you straight there..."

'In the taxi, driving to Manchester Street, of course Lady L. asked all kinds of questions: where we'd been; what Veronica had said and done before her collapse. I told her a little. No more. I could never tell her ... no one but you ... what had actually happened...'

*Boyd stopped typing.* His headache was worse. He had felt ill when he got back to Edinburgh after another all-night journey; this time spent in a third-class sleeper ... sleepless ... conscious of nothing but the desire for oblivion but not getting it. Haunted by the memory of that grey cold morning in London ... of a small trembling body in his arms ... of lips passionately demanding his kisses ... of caresses unremembered by her ... never to be forgotten by him. He had a calm, practical nature, but that had been too much even for him. He had come back to his job in a state of high tension hitherto never experienced. This morning he had been out on the gun-site, doing his job. But tonight ... he was done. He knew he would have to report sick, get a sleeping draught from the M.O. and go to his bed.

Briefly he finished that letter to Gilly. He told her how he had left Veronica's mother at the nursing home in John's kindly hands, then betaken himself off. He wanted more than anything to stay ... to see *her* again. But he dared not. He could no longer trust himself. He was too strung up. So he consoled

246

himself by the news John gave him that Veronica had recovered consciousness and would be all right ... but that she must stay in the home a week or two seeing nobody but her own mother. But at least he knew she was not going to get her heart's desire, poor darling, and die.

He left the home and went to a florist's and ordered a huge bunch of flowers. He knew how she loved flowers. With them he sent a short note to Veronica.

*You must try to face life again. You must, my dear. Charles would wish it. You are so young and have so much in front of you still. Get well. God give you courage. Anything I can ever do ... call on me... Bless you.*

*Boyd.*

Not the ordinary sort of letter he wrote to women. Not at all. It had been written with his whole heart in it. He had felt, after sending it, that he would like to go out and get drunk.

Instead, he went to his Club, and later to King's Cross to catch the night train to Edinburgh. The sooner he got back to his job, the better.

Now ... what? This damnable insomnia and a chill that seemed to have settled in his very bones.

Boyd put the sheets of typing paper which

he had covered into a long envelope and addressed it to Gilly. He added a P.S:

*I want you to go to the home and see Veronica. John will let you. I know you of all people can help her most ... you, alone, know how. Say nothing about me but that I am her friend ... when she needs me...*

He posted that letter himself. He was shaking with fever when he returned to his room. The M.O. came and took his temperature, found that it was 103, diagnosed 'flu' and sent Captain Mansell straight to his bed.

## 8

Veronica was trying hard to go to sleep. That was one of the most difficult things which she had to do these days. Sleep ... that wonderful act of Nature described so aptly by a great poet as *'a blessed thing, beloved from pole to pole'*. Sleep ... which is *'a forgetting'*. Only when she slept could Veronica begin to forget her grief and pain and even then she dreamed ... night after night, she woke up sweating, shuddering, after some dreadful vision of Charles struggling in an icy ocean... Charles with blanched despairing face, and hands clutching at the side

248

of a raft... Charles being machine-gunned by the devilish enemy... Charles calling her name just before he sank. Oh, ghastly nightmares! Hopeless awakenings to the old searing agony of knowing that he had gone from her and that she would never see him again!

The nurse who had just tucked her up with a fresh hot-water bottle and drawn her curtains had begged her to 'try and get a little rest' because she had a visitor coming to see her later today. Boyd Mansell's sister ... Mrs Frobisher ... wife of that wonderful doctor with the healing hands who had done so much for her, Veronica, since she became his patient.

Veronica wanted to see Gilly.

She had refused every other visitor. Nobody except Mummy was allowed to come. She did not really want Mummy very much. The poor woman looked so worried and tried so hard to comfort Veronica but didn't know how. That once self-confident lady admitted defeat in this crisis. She could think of no possible way of rousing her daughter from the terrible lethargy into which she had sunk since her husband's death.

What use to tell Veronica how young she was, how lovely, how much she yet had in store for her; how wrong it was to let sorrow bring her so low; how cowardly not to face up to it like thousands of other women who had lost their husbands through 'enemy action' or in battle?

Veronica knew all these things ... admitted them. But they did not help. She had tried to conquer her sorrow. She tried to be brave. She even hoped at times that Charles would yet appear; that he might have been rescued and would communicate with her shortly. But in her heart of hearts she was sure that he was dead and that it was no use hoping. All the frantic letters Lady Lowring had written to the authorities concerned had brought nothing but negative replies. Charles Hallard was on the list of those 'lost at sea'. He was not likely to come back.

Veronica did not know that it was possible for any human being to go through such agony of mind and heart and survive. She had prayed at first to die. But as she lived, and, according to doctor and nurses, grew physically stronger, she knew that she had to endure the torment. Life stretched in front of her seemingly an arid waste; a world of shadow and pain without Charles or hope of Charles. She was quite sure that she would never recover from this mortal blow, never be herself again. The Veronica who had lived life to its fullest as Charles Hallard's wife had died with him. This girl who lay here in the Manchester Street home was merely a shell; a body that answered to the name of

Veronica Hallard and tried automatically to obey the behests and commands of those in charge of her.

She had been here for three weeks. The February of snow and ice and bitter frost had gone. March had come in 'like a lamb'. It was a mild day in London today. A grey still day of damp fog; depressing, dreary. London at its worst.

Veronica did not care. She did not notice the weather. Her room was warm, roseate with electric fire and gay with flowers. Such wonderful flowers. Mummy wrote all the letters of thanks. Veronica lay in her bed like a dead thing, incapable of sitting up, of putting pen to paper. Totally exhausted in body and mind. But today she was better. She had eaten a little more; John Frobisher had told her this morning that she was looking more normal. But when she gazed in her mirror she seemed to see a stranger's face; thin, transparent, with huge eyes that held little or no expression.

On her bedside table there were always red roses sent fresh from a florist every other day. They came from Boyd Mansell. Kind, devoted Boyd. She had been told by Mummy how well Boyd had looked after her on that dreadful day of her breakdown but she remembered little or nothing. Everything was a haze, from the time she had been told about Charles's death until she had recovered consciousness to find herself in a strange hotel bedroom alone with Boyd. Even that moment was hazy: she was not quite clear about anything until she actually woke up in bed in this room.

She had taken much longer to recover from the shock than John Frobisher had predicted. But Mummy said she was better off here in this luxurious warm nursing home than down at dear little Monks Rest just now because it was so cold there and Nanny not well, and Lady Lowring could not have given Veronica the attention she needed. It was at night that Veronica appreciated the nurses; someone to creep in and lay a kind hand on hers, rearrange her pillows; refill her hot bottle, say a reassuring word. The days passed ... she read a little ... not novels ... she could not face romantic or sentimental tales ... but magazines; newspapers; history. Veronica had always had a certain love for history; it was impersonal, unemotional, what she needed just now.

But the nights were long and bitter. Dr Frobisher gave her drugs that first dreadful week. But now she had to do without them. He said that she would never get well unless she stopped taking 'dope' and made an effort to sleep naturally. That was the hard thing ... to sleep without drugs. Always, as soon as she was alone and shut her eyes, she began to summon up all the thousand and one dear memories of her past life with Charles. The grim knowledge that those days had for ever gone and that he was dead would return in full force. She, who thought that by now she had no more tears to shed, could yet feel the moisture trickling from her agonised eyes; oh, what hours of terrible, hopeless weeping she had known here in this room ... weeping for Charles!

She had been offered a wireless set but refused it. She did not want music; could not bear it. She would never play or sing again. *He,* with all his passionate love for music, would never play another piano nor compose another theme. That lovely flame of genius had been put out by the bestiality of war. Music to Veronica had virtually grown to mean *Charles.* So, without him, music for her could be no more.

She lay this afternoon restlessly turning from side to side, every now and then opening her eyes and looking round her darkened room. From the street below came the incessant sound of cars and footsteps. Life went on ... that was the appalling part of it. For her, it was the end of the world; but life went on around her just the same. Nothing had changed, but the core of her own existence had vanished. She felt like a phantom having little or no contact with those who moved and breathed around her.

People had been very kind. Boyd Mansell ... unforgettably so. Between Boyd and herself must always be a link of friendship that could never be broken; they were knit by this sorrow. He loved her ... she knew that ... but had sunk himself and his own need ... and stretched out to her the firm hand she had needed in her hour of extremity.

She was touched and pleased, always, by his roses.

There were carnations here from Letty Chaddon. Letty had heard the news, of course, and sent a letter full of distress, deep sympathy and praise of Charles. Veronica had had dozens of such letters. A cable expressing great concern from Phillips – Charles's old chief in Lagos. Lady Lowring read all the correspondence to her. Sometimes she listened stonily. Sometimes she could not bear them and made her mother stop and turned her face to the pillow to stifle the sobs. Praise of Charles was welcome yet always painful. To be told how wonderful he *used* to be brought home so poignantly the realization that he was dead. To hear people speak in the past tense; he *was* always so charming ... he *was* so clever...! oh, terrible, unbearable thought ... that he *was* ... but *is* not. Would never more be spoken of as here in the present.

A week ago Iris Williams came to see her

but Dr Frobisher would not let her in. She was told that she could come later. He was anxious that Veronica should not be faced with an emotional scene which might distress her all over again. But Veronica had decided to go and stay with Iris down in Farnham when she was better.

She hoped to be allowed up for a little while this evening. The last time she had attempted to get out of bed she had fallen over; so ridiculously weak.

She never asked for war news and nobody discussed the war with her. She was disinterested. Now that Charles was dead she did not mind about anything. But this afternoon as she lay waiting for Gilly Frobisher she began to ask herself whether she was not being horribly egotistical, feeling and behaving this way.

What was she in this world ... what, indeed, had her darling beloved Charles ever been?... Nothing but a tiny cog in the great wheel ... a midget among giants... Neither he nor she really counted. No individual counted. It was only the country as a whole that mattered. The country was fighting for its very life. That Charles Hallard had lost *his* could be of no ultimate significance. It was a cruel thought, it hurt, rankled. She shrank from it; yet had to admit it as her mind and body grew stronger and calmer.

When she was strong again, she reflected,

she must really get down to some work for the war. She must throw herself into a really useful job. Frail, useless though she felt herself to be, she knew that even the smallest effort was of significance. The Germans had done Charles to death. She, Veronica, must help now to do the Germans to death. In her feeble way she would avenge him.

This idea grew; and the more she thought about it, the more vitality there seemed to seep through her being.

Certainly, she decided, she would get a more absorbing job than that one she had had in the canteen down in Risborough.

Perhaps Boyd's sister would suggest something. She would ask her.

Veronica rang her bell. She could no longer lie here brooding in the dark. She wanted to sit up and write a letter. Yes, she suddenly felt that she could write ... for the first time. To Boyd, first of all, to thank him for the wonderful, regular supply of roses.

Yet at the thought of Boyd her cheeks flushed and her forehead creased. It was rather dreadful ... about Boyd... She wished she had a clearer recollection of that day he had taken her up to town. In heaven's name, what had made her lose her reason and drag him ... poor man ... to an hotel like that? She could recall, vaguely, Boyd, lying on his bed ... exhausted, dishevelled; and herself sitting beside him.

He must have had an awful time with her and had been so good. Mummy thought Boyd one of the most wonderful young men she had ever met. She said so.

The nurse who had been looking after Veronica came into the room.

'Can't you sleep, Mrs Hallard?'

'No,' said Veronica. 'I want to sit up and write a letter.'

The nurse looked pleased. Dr Frobisher had told them that as soon as Mrs Hallard wanted *to do anything* within reason she must be allowed to do so. It was that dreadful inactivity of hers which worried him most. Let her write a letter and a good thing, too, nurse reflected. Poor little soul. They were all so sorry for her in the home. Such a slip of a thing and so beautiful, and that handsome young man whose photograph stood beside her bed ... to think that he was dead ... had been torpedoed on his way home ... what a ghastly affair!

In a few moments Veronica's flower-filled room was full of light aided by the electric lamp. The March morning was on the dull side. Nurse propped Veronica up with pillows, put her little pale blue swansdown bolero around her and found her a writing-pad and a fountain-pen.

'All right now?' she smiled.

'Lovely, thanks,' said Veronica, and gave the woman that heart-breaking smile which always upset her, as she told the other nurses.

Veronica sat for a while with pen suspended, staring ahead of her. It took some time for her thoughts to flow with any ease these days. Always they returned to the same focal point. Charles. It seemed strange and awful that for three whole weeks she had not written *to him* ... nor in her diary *about him.* She could not do the former; the latter she had no further interest in. For he would never read it now and in any case she could have written nothing but words of despair. So let it go.

Now, even to write a friendly note to Boyd Mansell was going to cost her a pang.

She began with difficulty:

*My dear Boyd,*
*I can never begin to thank you enough for all you did for me on that dreadful day. Mummy has told me how grand you were. I remember very little. But I do thank you, Boyd, and I...*

A rush of wild grief surged over her, blotting out her desire to thank Boyd; her new-formed resolution to be brave; her sudden wish to take on a big job of work. She laid down pen and pad. She hid her face in her hands and for a moment her small body shook with hopeless weeping.

'Charles,' she moaned aloud, 'Charles, you

258

must come back. You *can't* leave me like this. Darling, darling, I can't bear it...'

Someone knocked softly on the door. Veronica did not hear. The door opened. A slender woman in tweeds and wearing a short ermine coat and cap to match stole in.

For a moment Gillian Frobisher looked with some dismay at the small huddled figure in the little blue bolero sitting up in bed and crying like a desolate child. For a moment Gilly thought of tip-toeing out again and leaving the younger girl to her grief. Then she remembered something John had said last night. John who was so wise and understanding.

'Make Veronica Hallard see that there is something more for her to live for. You can do it, Gilly. You were broken on the wheel yourself once, my darling, and learned to live with courage. Help her. She's such a pathetic small creature.'

So Gilly did not go. She shut the door behind her, came to the bedside and said in a low voice:

'Veronica...'

Veronica's hands dropped. Gilly saw a thin, drawn young face, woebegone and wet with tears; dark cloudy hair, which had grown long, tumbled about a slender neck; and large eyes dulled by much weeping, veiled by those long silken lashes which Boyd had described ... (poor Chumps, who

259

loved this woman so madly and hopelessly ... she would never forget his long letter telling her about that dreadful day with Veronica ... it had almost broken her heart).

Veronica said in a small voice:

'Oh ... who are you, please?'

Then Gilly opened her arms and drew the small quivering figure close. She said:

'My dear, my dear, I'm Gilly. Boyd's sister. I know what you're going through... I've been through the same hell. It's a long damnable road, a dreadful road to travel, Veronica. But there *is* an end to it. It doesn't go on for ever. I can promise you that if you'll only believe it will end, my dear ... poor little thing!'

Veronica was speechless for a moment. She had had a blurred glimpse of Gilly's charming face and blue, tender eyes (Boyd's eyes), of the way she walked ... that slow, rather shuffling gait ... and she remembered all that Boyd had ever told her about his sister. *Her* particular Gethsemane ... the awfulness of losing her young, attractive first husband in that car smash; and the years of illness afterwards when she had had to face life as a cripple. At least *she*, Veronica, was not doomed to a spinal chair. Her lot was not as hard as Gilly's had been. But Gilly's courage had shone through it all like a star ... Boyd had said so. Veronica could believe it ... she could feel the strength and warmth of this woman's personality even in this brief embrace.

Suddenly she responded to Gilly and hugged her back like a lost child, starving for affection, longing for help. She sobbed:

'Oh, Gilly, help me, help me...'

'I will, darling,' said Gilly, and disengaging herself for an instant, flung off fur coat and hat, and then took Veronica's small figure back in her arms and held her there ... she talked to her ... talked ... talked ... telling her about Dick, deliberately reopening her own wound (which time ... and John ... had healed so astonishingly well). Told Veronica how suddenly the answer to all these problems came; how infinitely kind the passing of Time can be; how certain sure Time's fingers blot out the first unbearable vision of agony and grief; how slowly but surely there returns the will to live, the strength to endure, even the ability to forget.

Gradually Veronica ceased to weep, to tremble, she sat back against her pillow, small crumpled handkerchief pressed to her lips and looked at Gilly, listening ... believing...

'It isn't that one ever really forgets,' went on that firm, gentle voice of Boyd's beloved sister. 'I haven't forgotten Dick nor ever will. My dear John knows that. But one forgets the *pain* ... the awful ache attached to one's memories. Just as one forgets physical pain once it has passed. The scar is there but it does not hurt. And in the weeks and months ahead you'll gain courage, Veronica, my dear ... and you'll be able to remember your Charles without this bitterness. You'll laugh again. Yes, *I* laughed, Veronica ... even when I was in a spinal chair and thought I never would walk again. See how I am now...' Gilly spread out her arms and drew a deep breath... 'I go everywhere alone, without even a stick. It's a miracle. God performs miracles. Believe in God, Veronica. He will perform one for you.'

Veronica shook her head.

'Oh, I haven't your faith... Mummy keeps telling me to have faith ... to believe in another world ... and that I'll meet Charles again. But I find it so difficult. I only know that I want him now *here* in this world that I *know*...'

'Yes, my dear. We all need proof, tangible evidence of the thing we crave to see. But we can't always have them... That is when the importance of blind faith comes in. But I am not wanting to preach religion, my dear. Each one of us must discover that for himself. What I do preach is the certainty that you will get over the initial blow. Also that one of the things which helped me most was the knowledge that Dick of all people would have loathed me to cave in and abandon myself to grieving for him.'

'Oh, I know,' said Veronica with a shame-faced little smile. 'Charles would feel the same about me.'

Gilly pulled a packet of cigarettes from her bag.

Bless the girl ... what a sweet child she was ... and what fantastically lovely grey eyes ... no wonder poor old Chumps had got it so badly...!

'Have one,' she said. 'Smoking helps a lot.'

Veronica accepted and smoked the first cigarette since she came into the home. Gilly's presence was wonderfully stimulating. She began suddenly to ask Gilly all sorts of questions. What she had done to make herself sleep at night ... what sort of books she read ... all manner of small, unimportant details which Gilly gave her and rejoiced in giving. It seemed to her that Veronica was waking up at last. *Veronica was going to be all right.*

They smoked and talked ... and later a nurse brought in tea for two ... and they went on talking as they drank the tea; until Veronica's pale face was flushed and her eyes more animated than they had looked for days. And Gilly Frobisher thought:

'When she's well she must be ravishing ... my *poor* old Chumps.'

She turned the conversation, tactfully, to her brother. And here she met with a warm response. For Veronica was obviously fond of Boyd in a platonic way and deeply grateful for his friendship. She asked Gilly to tell him so; showed her the letter she had just begun.

'I shall always be glad we met on board coming over,' she said her great eyes dewy, grateful. 'You must be proud to have such a grand brother, Gilly.'

Gilly dabbed her freckled nose with a powder-puff and rearranged a burnt-fair curl and sniffed and smiled.

'Chumps is all right.'

'Chumps?' repeated Veronica and smiled a little.

'That's what I call him. He and I were of an age. James and Audrey were older. Chumps and I were always the best of pals.'

'He's very good-looking and charming,' said Veronica reflectively. 'I feel surprised he hasn't married.'

'He will find the right girl one day, perhaps,' said Gilly and looked at Veronica, at the lovely little head drooping like a fragile flower too heavy for its slender stalk, and thought: 'One day it may be *you* ... who knows...?' She added: 'When you're well again, Veronica, will you let me take you down to Chidding Manor to meet my mother? She's rather a gem. John has to go up to Edinburgh on a medical conference in a fortnight's time. Maybe you'd come to my

264

old home with me. We have such a lovely garden. In a week or two the parkland should be a mass of daffodils. The crocuses are all out now. My mother says it's heavenly even though still cold.'

Veronica stretched out a hand to Gilly, who took it in her warm capable one and pressed it. She said huskily:

'I'd love to come to Chidding Manor with you, Gilly.'

And long after Gilly Frobisher had gone, Veronica, feeling stronger, more certain of herself, finished her letter to Gilly's brother and said:

*I think your sister is absolutely wonderful. Who, to look at her now, would dream she has been through so much? She puts me to shame. I must ... I will make the effort from now on, dear Boyd. But I do know one thing ... Gilly was lucky being able to love again in this world. She is happy with her husband. But I shall never, never replace Charles. Of that I am certain...*

Of so many things are human beings certain ... for the time being. Later they change ... faith is restored, the will not only to live but to love again is revived ... but no woman in Veronica Hallard's shoes, in the initial stages of such sorrow, could begin to believe that.

Boyd Mansell received that letter, but not

in Edinburgh on the following morning, as she had expected. Nor did she see him again for a long, long time. For Gilly dropped in at the nursing home to give Veronica some very unexpected news. Boyd was no longer in this country. Apparently he had not been in Scotland for several days but for security reasons had been unable to communicate with his family or say good-bye. A brother officer, at his request, had just let them know that at a moment's notice, and under special orders, Boyd had flown over to France.

Gilly was a little anxious. Veronica sat up in a chair, dressed for the first time. She looked colourless and as though a breath of wind would blow her away. But ironically enough it was she, this time, who comforted Gilly.

'Don't worry,' she said. 'Boyd will be all right, I'm sure. I expect it's a staff job he's doing – he won't be in the front line. Besides, there's no fighting in France, really, at the moment, except in the air, is there?'

'Oh, of course there's nothing to worry about and Boyd always wanted to be right *in* it. I'm glad he's gone across,' said Gilly stoutly. Then added: 'Do write to him, Veronica. He'd like it.'

'I certainly will,' said Veronica.

And wrote her second letter within twenty-four hours to Gilly's brother.

She missed the red roses which no longer came as a regular tribute. But soon after that she left the Manchester Street home. Quite suddenly she had begun to get well. Lady Lowring came with a special hired car to drive her down to Monks Rest. There Nanny received her, shaken by the sight of her 'ewe lamb' looking so frail and white, but thankful to get her back. At one time she knew her ladyship had feared for Miss Veronica's life.

The Jacobses had sent flowers, fruit, and a note of greeting which touched the girl. The cottage was gay with the first daffodils from the garden. It was all fresh and shining and big log fires had been lit to welcome Veronica. Lady Lowring took special note of the fact that on this day of return Veronica did not mention Charles's name, neither did she ask where the photograph of herself and Charles, as bride and bridegroom, had gone. It used to stand on the spinet, but Lady Lowring had put it away.

Veronica had changed. She was quiet, subdued, *older*. All that was very young in her seemed to have died … with the man she loved so desperately. But Lady Lowring could see for herself that the girl had pulled herself out of that awful slough of despond and was now able to face up to things, for which her ladyship was supremely thankful. She did not wish a repetition of the last few weeks; nor did she wish Veronica ever in her life again to be so utterly wretched.

To the old nurse when they were alone, Lady Lowring said:

'Nanny, I think our girl is going to be all right now, don't you? She's talking a lot about war work and joining the services when she is fit enough. Of course she'll never be strong enough, in my estimation, to get into uniform, but I'm glad she wants to do *something*.'

But Nanny said wisely:

'Maybe it'll be the saving of her if she *does* go as a WAAF or WREN, my lady. She wants something to throw herself right into. Poor little dear ... if ever a child's heart is broken, hers is.'

But Lady Lowring had hopes for the future, having seen and talked to her daughter today.

'There's something in store for her still, Nanny, mark my words,' she observed.

And her thoughts leapt to that nice Captain Mansell. A pity he had gone over to France! But he would come back and see Veronica. And who was to know ... oh, well ... she stifled this last thought speedily, somewhat ashamed of herself. With that poor boy, Charles, hardly cold in his grave, it really was not decent.

Upstairs in her little room, Veronica unpacked her suitcase. She took out her photograph of Charles and placed it in its accustomed place by her bedside. For a moment she stood looking at it with intense melancholy. The old pain rent her through and through, threatening to overcome all her resolves to be brave and beat her down to her knees again. But she stiffened and drew a hand quickly across her eyes.

'No,' she said aloud. 'I'm not going to cry any more. Charles, my darling, I've got to learn to be brave ... and to live without you. Gilly is right. You'd want me to. You'd be ashamed if I went on being such a little coward ... but I'm not forgetting you, if I don't cry. You know that, don't you, my darling, darlingest Charles! I shall want you and love you always – all my life!'

All her muscles were taut and her lips quivering as she finished unpacking, but when she went downstairs to join her mother, she managed, somehow, to enter the sitting-room with a smile.

# PART III

## 1

One warm summer morning in the August of 1942, Veronica Hallard returned to Monks Rest from the W.V.S. centre at which she had been working for the last eighteen months. Finding her mother out she went up to her bedroom.

Mummy, she supposed, was still in Aylesbury at Mrs Toynbell's house. She went there three times a week to help pack parcels for prisoners. She could not go more often because she had all the cooking and work of the cottage to do these days with only a woman coming in twice a week to scrub. Old Nanny had died last Christmas of bronchial pneumonia. She was an irreparable loss to both Lady Lowring and Veronica. They missed her sorely. She had been a faithful friend and nurse to them both.

Veronica wore the green-and-wine-coloured uniform of the W.V.S. She was a full time paid worker and had charge of all the Comforts for the Bombed-Out and Evacuees for her district, which was a twenty minutes' bus ride from Risborough. It was the only job which her health had permitted her to take up after she had recovered from the first dire effects of her husband's death. It satisfied her wish to enter one of the women's services, and although long hours and hard work at times, it was not too much for her health.

Certainly for the last six months or so she had been gaining weight and looked better than she had done since she went out to West Africa. Lady Lowring had remarked only last night at supper how Veronica had 'filled out'; her face had a rounder curve; her step was more buoyant; and she had gained one of the most important of all things – peace of mind. She was calm and resourceful – much less neurotic and dependent, these days. The passing of the long months and years had achieved the habitual miracle of Time and healed the wound. The sharpness of grief had been dulled. The deep pain of losing Charles in that sudden and frightful fashion was still there, in the background. A sense of loss, of frustration, came back to her at intervals, depressing her horribly. But Gilly had been right; one could learn to endure, to face up to the most appalling disasters … and laugh again.

It seemed a long, long time since Charles had died. Veronica was thinking so this afternoon as she took off her uniform, put on a pair of linen slacks and a cotton shirt, and sat down at her desk. Two and a half years since she had been waiting here in this little cottage for Charles to come home. Like a lifetime ... and that other life, which she had known with *him* ... was no more than a radiant dream. She had awakened from it ... and could never dream it again.

There by her bed, Charles's photographed face still smiled at her with the old handsome eyes. His books, his music, were there on her shelves. There were so many evidences of his love and of their marriage still with her. But he had gone...

It was astonishing, even frightening to her at times, to consider how very far Charles *had* faded from her immediate existence. And as incredible to think that he would never now grow old as she would; but stay always that young, ardent-eyed, brilliant Charles she had loved and married. For her had been the struggle and heartache ... but for him a kindly oblivion. She could see now how kind it was. Life these days would not have been easy for Charles. So much had happened in the war since he had died. The fall of France; Dunkirk; terrible gargantuan battles in Russia; the agony and loss of Singapore. The bombing of London. So much that would have horrified and perhaps broken him. Better the end as he had known it, rather than being wounded badly ... or done to death in some hideous way on the battlefield.

Yet many men had survived all the horror and come back. Boyd Mansell amongst them. Boyd had been 'missing' for a month, in June 1940. Veronica, having only just begun to recover from her own shock and grief, had been roused to fresh anxiety over him, her dearest friend. She had shared with his mother and sister the awful suspense of waiting to hear if he were dead or alive. But he had come back ... unscathed. He had been miraculously spared. And now he was in this country again on a special job in the War Office. He was a frequent visitor at Monks Rest and an ever welcome one.

Veronica opened a drawer and suddenly pulled out her old diary. For a moment she sat very quiet, reading one or two of the pages she had written when she first came home from Lagos. She had not opened this book since Charles died.

It made her feel old; it seemed so very young and eager and full of pathetic hope. She glanced at the last entry ... made just the month before Charles had started on that tragic and fatal journey home. Written in the New Year of 1940. When she had decided that she must start collecting a trousseau for Charles.

She had written:

'One day I shall hear the telephone bell … hear your voice … you'll say "Darling, I'm back" … and I shall faint…

'Charles … Charles … *Charles*…'

Veronica lifted her head. There was a lump in her throat. She looked out of the casements at the little churchyard which was dappled with sunlight. Down in the bird-bath a thrush dipped its wings noisily. The air was full of the sound of bird-song and of humming bees.

Veronica thought:

'How happy I was then … how full of hope…'

Hope! A thing she had lost for a time … along with faith, self-confidence, everything that had made life worth while. All that was ardent and joyous in her had been tem-porarily buried in that watery grave with *him*. Yet she had recovered. Here she was today, able even to read this tragic record of her love and longing and not burst into tears. She felt almost ashamed of her com-posure. Yet she knew that *he* of all people would be thankful that she had begun to live again. *Even to love again.*

Was *that* possible? Sometimes when Veronica thought about it she was horrified with herself. But unbidden, uncontrolled, came the memory of Boyd Mansell's last visit down here. A walk with him through

275

the summer evening after Lady Lowring had gone to bed.

Suddenly Veronica bit her lip, lit a cigarette and smoked hard for a moment. Mechanically her gaze wandered to her W.V.S. uniform on the bed. She must put it away, then go down and lay the supper-table. There was always so much to do with no servant in the house, and Mummy would be tired when she got back. But it was only cold fare tonight ... a treat actually ... Ruth Jacobs, bless her, had sent in a brace of grouse and Mummy had cooked them mid-day. There was only the salad to prepare. She could be idle a little longer.

The old longing to pour out her heart was gripping Veronica. For so long she had been repressed; tied up in herself, as it were. With her grief for her adored husband she had said good-bye to so much of the old impulsive Veronica. Not even to Boyd (to him, least of all!) had she been able to bare her innermost feelings. So long and faithfully he had loved her. She knew that, even though he had never actually said so. She knew it from his wonderful devotion, a service that was and always had been self-less. She knew it, too, from Gilly ... today one of her dearest women friends. Gilly had told her how much Boyd loved her.

She wanted to say more than she could say even to Gilly.

*Suddenly with a little smile, she reopened her diary and began to write in it quickly, eagerly:*

'I thought I could never do this; that it would hurt too badly to write another line in the book that had been meant for you to see, Charles; that I would let it lie in a drawer closed for eternity. But I was wrong; just as I was wrong when I thought in the nursing home that day I first met Gilly Frobisher, that although she had married again, I, personally, would never replace you.

'Charles, my dear one, this is rather like a confession. I am talking to you, wherever you are in the vast Universe ... whether in some queer dim spirit-world ... or some definite Heaven. In hell you cannot be. You were too kind, too good, too much an idealist. Whatever the ultimate fate of us poor mortals may be, you, I know, are happy and at peace. Charles darling, many long, bitter days passed before I even began to learn the meaning of peace or happiness. Your death was nearly mine. For a while I descended with you into the shadows. Charles, I loved you beyond all people and all things. You know that. And what I gave to you I can never give to another man. The virgin me! The girl who has since become a woman. That Veronica whose dearest wish was to say by your side, bear your children and grow old with you. That Veronica who must have had a premonition of disaster because she was so reluctant to leave you in Lagos and come home alone. My beloved Charles, there were many moments when in my bitter misery I wished to God I had insisted on staying with you...

'For a time I entertained a vague wild hope that you might be alive and come back to me. People said you might ... that I could hope ... that it was possible you were rescued and would eventually write to me from a prison camp. But you didn't. Gradually all hope died ... with you. I knew that you had gone from me beyond recall.

'Once I was well enough to leave the home and my physical strength returned, I was able to get back some of the spiritual force and courage that I needed. Today I feel that just as I wanted the living you to read this diary as far as it was written, I now wish the dear dead Charles to read ... and to understand and forgive my weakness. I have never been a very strong person, have I, Charles? I have always wanted comfort and help and love and laughter and all that you once gave me. Forgive me, darling, for this seeming infidelity to your memory if I say that I need those things again. But I do. Some human beings may misunderstand – because people in this world are uncharitable and unkind. But not in your world, Charles.

There, all is understood and nothing hidden. You will sympathise with me and forgive me. I am still your Veronica in so many ways, darling. To no other man can I ever be what I was to you. To you I gave my first and my best love. What is left, Charles, I want to give to Boyd Mansell, because I am very lonely and in need of him. Is that all right? Will you be glad? I think so. You were never a jealous, selfish person. You were fine and sweet and you loved me. So for my sake you will be happy if another love has come into my life. I know that, otherwise I would never marry Boyd Mansell. Wherever you are, my darling, I could not make *you* unhappy. Boyd loves me very much and has waited for me a long time. He is coming at the end of this week, Charles, to ask me to marry him. He has told Gilly so. I am glad she passed on that knowledge to me so that I can have a little time in which to think and to make up my mind … and time in which to talk to *you*.

'You know all about Boyd. In that world of yours you know everything. You like him, don't you, Charles? I always wanted you two to "get together". Now you will never meet on this earth, but one day in that place where "there is neither marriage nor giving in marriage" you may yet be friends.

'Is it queer of me to think like this, to write like this … in a diary which you are not here to see with earthly eyes, my darling? I know Mummy still thinks me a "funny person". She often says I'm too introspective, too quiet. But that's "me". A little bit like the "me" you used to know. Only I'm much older, Charles ... years and years older. Not just two and a half years. Your going from me knocked the ground from under my feet, and, Charles, I found some grey hairs in my head the other day. A lot of little crows' feet around my eyes ... no, I am not at all the young, ardent Veronica whom you loved. Suffering changes a person, doesn't it, Charles?

'When I look back on these years which lie between us I remember very special moments but a great deal of it seems a haze. Life is like that. We are supposed to remember every incident, but only certain ones stand out for me. My first visit to the Mansells' home, for instance.

'I went down to Chidding Manor with Gilly soon after leaving the nursing home. I shall always remember that because of the mixture of grief and happiness I experienced there. Intolerable grief, still sharp and new, my darling, intensified perhaps because of the poignancy of that spring which you were not there to see. The exquisite flowers; the lovely old Manor, and Boyd's mother, who must surely be one of the most sweet and gentle women I have ever met. I don't wonder she produced fine children like Gilly – and Boyd.

'I stayed with the Mansells for a fortnight. John Frobisher, who is such a clever doctor and a brilliant psychologist, full of understanding of women, came down at weekends to join Gilly. I loved to see her happiness with him unfolding like a flower in front of one's eyes. Even though it hurt me to see it; to know that mine with you had irretrievably vanished, I was glad that Gilly had come into her own.

'Mrs Mansell could not do enough for me. She is a very religious woman. As you know, Charles, I never was very religious, but her deep-rooted faith and perseverance did much to strengthen me, to help me on to a more even keel in those days. Just as the knowledge that Gilly, who had lost everything ... and more than I lost ... had regained happiness. Those things were, at such a critical time, of inestimable value to me.

'I missed Boyd's friendship and was sorry he had gone abroad but I wrote to him and he to me. What happened on the ghastly day on which I learned of your death I shall perhaps never know. He may not tell me. But I remember enough to realise that he was unforgettably good to me with no thought for himself.

'I was down at Chidding Manor again that

summer, and this time Audrey and her two children were at home. She, typical of the Mansells, gave me a warm welcome and made me feel that the Manor was my second home. But she has not that "spiritual" quality of Gilly or her mother. She is just a nice, amiable, ordinary girl, typical of hundreds of such women in this country. They make the best wives and mothers, really. They are the backbone of our Empire. Like Letty Chaddon. Not useless, dependent, neurotic creatures such as your poor Veronica. But I did try to pull myself together, Charles, and after Dunkirk I changed a good deal, for the better I fancy.

'I was with the Mansells while Boyd was in France following the collapse. I prayed with Mrs Mansell that he would be safe and spared to his family; and to *me*. It was I who was able to comfort and give hope to Gilly. She so adores her "Chumps". She was shattered by the ghastly fear that he would never come back.

'When he came, I was still at Chidding. That is a morning I shall remember always. One of those glorious summer days when the gardens of the Manor lay sweet and fragrant with flowers; the first lovely roses opening under a benediction of sunlight. The sky was a radiant blue and the newly-clipped and rolled lawns, emerald smooth. I remember walking through those grounds

282

(we were all still waiting for news of Boyd and desperately worried) thinking: "This is one of the stately homes of England for which men are dying amidst unbelievable horror and violence. To keep this peace, this beauty, for the next generation, they are dying…"

'Then I thought of Boyd; so fine and good to look at with his gay blue eyes and brown cheerful face and strong tall body. And I thought: "God, he mustn't die. Bring him back… I've lost Charles. Don't let me lose him, too, my dearest friend … bring him back to his family and to me, God, *please.*"

'And he came, Charles. In an old station taxi he drove straight from Horsham Station. He had not even time to warn us of his coming. In stained uniform, with a growth of beard, dirty, disheveled, half-dead from lack of sleep, but still smiling, Boyd came home in one of the last of the "little ships" that brought our men back from that hell. He landed at Newhaven and had taken the first train to Horsham … and to his mother.

'But I was the first person he saw. He told me afterwards that it seemed like a miracle to him to find me in the garden waiting at Chidding Manor as though I knew he was coming home.

'I was the first person he took in his arms and kissed; and I kissed him back. It was without passion. I had no passionate love then, so soon after you had gone from me, to give to any man. But like a friend, a devoted sister, I hugged and kissed him. And it touched me poignantly because it was he who wept. Not I. Poor Boyd ... he wept the slow difficult tears of a man tired to exhaustion pitch, worn out after fighting one of the most awful rearguard actions in military history.

'I remembered the feel of his damp, rough, bearded face against my neck; the sound of his voice murmuring my name over and over again.

'I left him later alone with his delighted mother and sisters. Although they begged me to stay, I left Chidding that same afternoon. I felt I must. I could not bear too much emotion in those days. It upset me so much. I wanted to get back to Monks Rest and be alone. I used to crave to be alone just then ... with my thoughts, my memories of you, my lost darling.

'In the years that followed I spent many happy holidays at Chidding. I came to be a frequent guest; to love the Mansells as much as they seemed to love me. Poor Mummy ... she was always jealous of my deep affection for Mrs Mansell, but she never lost her first admiration for Boyd, and she did not discourage my visits there.

'Oh, the dreadfulness of this war; Dunkirk

was only the beginning. There was the Battle of Britain; the martyrdom of London ... of other great towns and ports in the "blitz"; the grim and hideous fighting in Russia.

'I worked as hard as I could in those days in my little green-and-wine-coloured uniform ... proud to be a member of the W.V.S., yet sorry I was not strong enough to emulate the example of one or two of my contemporaries and join the A.T.S., the W.A.A.F. or the W.R.N.S. I just could do so much and no more. Poor feeble thing that I am, with those awful chest colds that I get, and a "tired heart" after you left me, Charles, combined with the ill-effects of living in West Africa for a year. I could not stand up to much.'

## 2

Veronica's diary continues:
'Time went on ... bringing many changes in the lives of all those around us. I watched the staff at Chidding Manor gradually disintegrate. First one gardener was called up – then another. Gradually the beautifully kept gardens which used – so I was told – to be Mr Mansell's pride, began to go to rack and ruin. Lawns were dug up for vegetables. Chickens were put on the beautiful tennis

courts. Herbaceous borders disappeared in a choke of weeds. Mrs Mansell worked like a slave but could not begin to cope with the work. Then her well-trained staff was taken from her ... all but an old and faithful cook and a "daily".

'Mrs Mansell was marvellous. Like Mummy, used to living the life of a "lady", much waited on, she now spent most of her time in the scullery washing up greasy dishes; or on her knees, polishing floors which, she insisted, must be kept as shining as they used to be.

'Then came the evacuees; half the Manor was given over to mothers and children from the East End of London. Chaos and disorder reigned where all was so orderly. Yet I never saw Boyd's mother look annoyed or lose her temper. She accepted every fresh tribulation put upon her with sweet resignation, as her "war work". She counted herself fortunate. James was in Africa, excempt from military service because of his age and his farm; Boyd had come back from France and since been lucky enough to hold jobs in England.

'At Monks Rest, Mummy and Nanny and I carried on ... until poor Nanny's passing. Poor old darling, she went down with a dreadful attack of bronchitis in the winter of 1941 and was taken to the local hospital where she died of pneumonia. Her old heart gave out. It was the saddest loss. I was her "baby" and she had always been so good to me. I often wonder if she found you, wheresoever you were, darling Charles … if so she would have told you all about me .. and you would have given her a great welcome. I like to think so, anyhow.

'We could not replace Nanny. The selfless sort of devotion she gave us is rare in these times when women in domestic service appear to dislike doing more than the minimum for us and demand a maximum wage in return.

'We have a Mrs Rubble (isn't it a lovely name?) who comes and scrubs the stone kitchen floors and polishes the place up generally twice a week. A good-tempered, untidy creature – one of the kind that always has a torn overall, wears no stockings (showing hideous goose-fleshed legs), down-at-heel shoes, and a jumper pinned to the bosom with a garish brooch. The kind that arrives with an empty shopping-bag and departs with a full one Mummy watches her waddle down the path and says in a sinister whisper: "Now I'd like to know what she's taking away. She *says* it's rubbish and pieces for her chickens. But I'd like to take a look…!"

'The New Year was disheartening. I was laid up for a fortnight with one of my worst attacks of flu. Mummy had to cope without

Nanny this time, and Mrs Rubble didn't turn up for a week because one of her children had had an accident. I must say women like Mummy and Mrs Mansell are marvellous. They are at an age when they ought to be resting and waited on hand and foot. I meet so many in the W.V.S., elderly women with white hair – staunchly doing their 'bit'. There ought to be a special medal for the over-fifties. They haven't the strength and resilience of the very young and they went through a terrible war before this one. Hats off to them!

'On the whole it was a poor spring for me. Life seemed to grow sadder and more difficult as the months went by. Tragedy has befallen Whitelands Hall. My poor friends, the Jacobses, have lost their one and only son ... their Benjy ... light of their lives ... heir to all that they have. He lies buried in the Libyan desert. One of the first to reach Benghazi ... never now to return to England and his adoring parents. Ruth has shrivelled up; mourns her son unceasingly with all the passionate sentiment of her race. Poor Mr Jacobs is a broken man. They have gone away, which I regret, as I had grown fond of them both – liked them despite all their shortcomings and ostentation. They have let Whitelands to a big art gallery for the time being and it is full of rare, valuable paintings which are being hung and stored there whilst London is in danger of being 'blitzed'.

'Ruth asked me if I would like to have the Steinway – squeeze it somehow into Monks Rest. But I refused. I never play now. I haven't sung since you died, Charles. Somehow, I don't think I will ever sing again. YOU were the very core of music to me. With you, my urge for music seemed to die. I don't even like hearing classical music on the radio nowadays. That, more than anything, brings you back too poignantly. I don't want you to come back too close ... just to torture me, darling. So I try to forget that I ever loved to sing or play. Your own compositions, including *Veronica's Concerto*, lie at the bottom of a trunk ... locked away ... with my memories of the glorious evenings you and I used to spend at our piano.

'I had a letter from dear old Lettice soon after Christmas. Chaddy is home now, of course. He wanted to come and see me, but ... is it awful of me?... I got out of it by saying I would be away at the time he suggested. He has retired from West Africa and bought a little place in Devonshire and he and Letty have gone down there. I couldn't see him, Charles. I didn't trust myself. I don't want to lose the tranquility of mind and heart that I have lately achieved. Old Chaddy is far too closely connected with *you* … and Lagos. In a funny way I have built up a new world for myself; like a sort of high wall which shuts out my former world. It is better so. Even Iris is outside that wall and I don't grieve particularly because I can't see much of her. Dearly though I love her … once again, she brings *you* back whenever I see her. It is better for me to lay the ghost of my Charles … lest I should be hurt again. But I am so terribly glad Mervyn has been wounded in Libya and is now back in England. Iris, bless her, had a baby in the New Year. A daughter whom she has called Susan-Jane. I am godmother. Iris and Mervyn are blissfully happy once more and living on a farm in Somerset. For them the horrors and separation of the war are over. I am so thankful for little Iris and I hear my god-daughter is enchanting.

'Poor Molly Forringale has had wretched luck. I often see her, as she is still doing her V.A.D. job in the district. She was engaged at the beginning of last year to a charming boy whom she met at an R.A.F. dance in High Wycombe. He was killed flying over Berlin a month after they announced their engagement. My heart bleeds for her. Oh, my Charles, I know that dark valley into which a woman descends when she loses her beloved … it's very nearly unbearable. Molly took it wonderfully well – so much braver than I was ... but it had a bad affect on her. She flung herself into a round of dancing and gaiety which shocked the neighbourhood. I understand ... she had to develop some sort of armour ... and she stood up to grieve by defying it in that way. It takes us all differently. But she still hasn't replaced her flying man. Poor Molly!

'Soon after Christmas this year, Boyd Mansell was sent to Russia on a secret mission. Rather a tribute to him, being picked out for the job. He was full of cheer about it. He wrote me marvellously interesting letters from Moscow. He has a great admiration for Stalin, he says. He came back bringing us all great pots of caviare and we made pigs of ourselves down at Chidding and here at home.

'Each time Boyd goes away and comes home again I realize how important he is beginning to be in my life. How necessary. How dreary England seems without him. Sometimes I marvel at his patience. I know he loves me, but not once since my darling died has he forced himself or his feelings upon me. Just sometimes he weakens ... lets me see what he feels when he looks at me or touches my hand. But Gilly is quite frank on the subject. The other day she said: "When are you going to put Chumps out of his misery, Veronica darling?" When I asked for an explanation, she said: "You know. You know he's been in love with you ever since he first met you on that ship. He's the best chap in the world, Veronica. I wish you'd marry him."

'That gave me a bit of a shock. Until then the thought of marrying Boyd ... of exchanging *your* name ... your wedding ring ... Charles, had never entered my head. Or if it had, I did not let it stay there. It seemed such flagrant disloyalty to our love ... our memories...

'But I was beginning to need Boyd.

'I am young and emotional and lonely. Poor Mummy could never begin to supply what I need. No mother can – no matter how dear to her daughter. I know that. I've had to own to it, too, during these summer months. The craving for love and the richness of life as it should be lived between a man and a woman is growing more and more urgent within me. Bit by bit it is seeping into my deepest consciousness ... until I have ceased to feel it a disloyalty to you, Charles. It is a natural thing ... and you of all men would say, *"I understand... I don't want you to live alone for the rest of your life."*

'To know that a man like Boyd Mansell has been in love with me for two and a half years without hope or encouragement ... is an ever increasing temptation. A few weeks ago I began to toy with the idea of marrying him, Charles. Yes, I began to think of him *differently* ... and when we last met, which was a fortnight ago ... to *feel* differently ... when he looked at me ... took my hand...

'We were here together. He had snatched twenty-four hours from the War Office. He is a busy, important man these days, and his promotion has been very rapid. He was a major when he went out to Russia. He is a lieutenant-colonel now. Such a young-looking colonel. But there are plenty of them in war-time and Boyd is a "regular" and always was a keen soldier. I never know what he does. Neither does his family. It is always rather "hush-hush". Largely Intelligence, I think.

'Mummy was out at her Prisoners' Parcel Depot. It was my half-day home. A lovely summer's afternoon at Monks Rest. Boyd and I sat drinking our tea in the loggia. The windows were wide open, letting the sun pour in on us. Glad to be out of uniform, I wore these blue linen slacks which I am wearing as I write this, and a gay cotton shirt. I suppose I looked young and attractive because Boyd suddenly leaned over the tea-table and said so.

'"It's hard for me to realize you're rising twenty-seven," he said. "Seventeen is what I'd guess if I didn't know."

'I laughed and said:

'"Don't be so silly. I am an old woman now."

'"Then you're a very attractive old woman," he laughed back, then thumped his chest and said: "And what of the old man? Crusty old colonel ... what?"

'I looked at him. At the crown and "pip" on the shoulder of his tunic which was hanging over a chair. Boyd was having tea in his shirt-sleeves. I gazed at his finely-shaped head; the brown hair touched to gold by the sunlight; he was lean and fit but a little pale. Definitely, the long months of war had aged him. The long trying hours at the War Office, working underground in artificial light ... had etched a few deep lines about eyes and mouth. But it suited Boyd to look mature.

'And he had never seemed more physically attractive. The look in those very blue eyes of his as they rested on me ... the flicker of passion ... quickly controlled ... the longing ... swiftly banished. I couldn't help seeing it. For the first time, this radiant afternoon, something in me leapt in response. I found myself thinking it would be very sweet to feel those firm lips of his upon my mouth ... those strong, supple fingers in my hair...

'I was almost aghast ... never having let my thoughts run riot like that before with Boyd ... or with any man except you, Charles. (That was as long ago ... oh, so long...!)

'Boyd put down his tea-cup, suddenly stood up and came round the back of my chair. He rested his hand on my shoulder and said in a queer sort of voice:

'"Veronica, my dear ... there are moments when you look adorable enough to tempt St Anthony, and this is one of them. In that absurd checked cotton shirt, with your ruffled hair ... your brown feet in red sandals ... good lord, married woman of twenty-seven? Not you – just a schoolgirl!..."

'I felt myself trembling a little and laughed to cover my confusion. I could feel the warmth of his fingers on my shoulders. I was glad he couldn't see that my face was one hot blush. I said:

'"The schoolgirl has several grey hairs. Your eyesight must want testing, Chumps..."

'(I had fallen lately into the habit of calling him by Gilly's nickname. He seemed to like it.)

'An instant's silence, then he kissed the top of my head. I could feel that light caress tingle through me. I knew then that I loved Boyd Mansell ... as he wanted to be loved... But the moment had not yet come when I could say so. He, as usual, kept his feelings under iron control. He had once told Gilly that no matter what it cost him he would never frighten me away from him because he held me so dear. I respect and admire him so much for that. So many other men, feeling as he did, would have tried to get me long ago… He certainly is a past-master in the art of "waiting". And it had worked. The very fact that he didn't pull me into his arms and kiss me at that moment fired my imagination … challenged my own restless heart.

"Let's take a walk," he said abruptly.

'I stood up and could feel myself still trembling slightly. I felt suddenly on top of the world. I wanted to raise my arms above my head and shout for joy. My blood raced as it had not done for long, weary months. Impulsively, I turned to him and said:

'"You're the dearest, most lovable person on earth, Chumps. I can't *tell* you how much I like you."

'He looked astounded … poor Boyd … so used to my being casual and unaware of him.

'"Why, Veronica!" he stammered.

'Then I got scared … of myself … of him … of my new disloyalty *to us, Charles*… I ran out of the loggia and up to my bedroom. I flung myself on the bed and cried… I don't know why. But I just cried and cried. And Boyd took his walk alone. When he came back Mummy had turned up. I was subdued – I suppose – looked a bit red-eyed. Boyd avoided looking at me and later he had to go back to London. He was so patient, so tactful, darling Boyd. He didn't even comment on those tell-tale eyes of mine nor ask me what had upset me. But I had never cared for him more than when he left me that evening. I suppose it was the general emotional upheaval; my discovery of my true feelings for him that had distressed me so. When he said good-bye, I tried to be my old self.

'"So long, Chumps dear," I said casually. "Come again soon."

'His blue eyes looked at me with mingled bewilderment and sadness. I almost forgot myself and flung my arms around his neck in that moment. He answered:

'"Okay, Veronica. Look after yourself, my dear. I'll probably run down on the first if I may. I'm getting my leave then and I'd like to put in a night at Monks Rest before going down to Chidding."

'"Lovely," I said.

'After he had gone, the cottage seemed extraordinarily quiet and deserted. I missed the sight of the tall figure in khaki; the sound of the deep, cheerful voice; the smell of his pipe and cigarettes; the essential *masculinity* of him. He was such a thorough man, Boyd. So integral, so nice. So good to me.

'All that night I thought of him … and wanted him. The first time I have wanted anyone but you, Charles. Dear, you *will* understand and forgive me, won't you? But I knew that night that from now on there would, inevitably, be a subtle change in my relationship with Boyd.

'Gilly, whom I met for lunch in town that following week – settled any lingering doubts in my mind. Over our coffee and cigarette she mentioned her brother, and with a queer look in her eyes she said:

'"Look, Veronica, my dear ... don't mind my being frank ... but I saw Chumps last night, and I don't think this business is fair on him. I mean I *know* you've never encouraged anything but friendship from him. He knows it, too. But he's dreadfully in love with you, Veronica. He'll never look at another woman. And he ought to marry and have children. He *ought* to, Veronica. What can you do about it?"

'I felt my heart-beats quicken. I looked with affection at Gilly's sweet, serious face. I said:

'"Gilly, would you *like* me to marry Chumps?"

'A light flashed into the blue eyes so like *his*. She exclaimed:

'"Good heavens, you know I would...! Mother would, too ... we *all* adore you, Veronica. But you're such a deep, strange little thing. You suffer so: feel things so much more intensely than many of us. I know your husband's tragic death knocked the bottom out of your world. I could see that you would be a long time getting over

298

it. So was I – over Dick. But I am terribly happy now with John. Veronica, couldn't *you* be happy with Chumps? Couldn't you ... put aside that life you led with Charles and start another one ... with Chumps? It would be so wonderful if you could. I know how faithful you are ... but it seems to me sometimes that you owe Chumps something, too."

'I leaned over the table and took Gilly's hand.

'"Darling Gilly," I said, "you're right. Don't worry. I agree with every word you say."

'"Oh, Veronica," she said, "Chumps was so miserable last night. He said he found it increasingly hard to go on seeing you and being a 'brother' to you. You're much too attractive. It really isn't good for either of you two to live alone. You're *both* too attractive. He said he was going to tell you what he really felt when he saw you on the first, even if you send him away for good. He's going down to you for the night, isn't he?"

'I whispered, "Yes."

'Gilly added: "Will you send him away, Veronica?"

'I shook my head. I could not speak. My eyes were full of tears. But I hung on to Gilly's hand ... that firm helping hand that had done so much for me already. And I felt that if Boyd Mansell wanted me ... and all the Mansells wanted to accept me ... I could not say no, and that I must surely be the luckiest girl in the world.'

## 3

*Veronica's diary – final entry*

'I shall never write in this book again. It was commenced for you, Charles. It ends ... with the breaking of all my earthly ties with you.

'This afternoon – a few hours ago – I promised to marry Boyd Mansell. I am writing this late at night when the little household is asleep.

'He came down to Monks Rest – as anticipated – on this the first day of his leave. He was very tired. He had not taken any leave for six months; he would work like a lunatic as I always told him, but he is like that; he will never "let up" while there is an important job to be done. The Army comes first with Boyd. Even I, whom he loves, come second. I know that. But I like it. I do not admire a man who weakly puts his personal feelings before his country's need. I am content to be second to Boyd's beloved career. But it is a very good second, and I am so very, very happy. You are glad, too, aren't you, Charles, wherever you are?

Because I was so dreadfully miserable for so long.

'Boyd came in time for tea. I had only just got back from the W.V.S. and was still in my uniform when he arrived. It always makes Boyd smile to see me in that green coat and skirt and wine-coloured shirt. But it suits my slenderness; I must say one is thankful not to be too plump when one has to wear any kind of uniform. And the colouring is good for my dark hair and pale skin. But Boyd says I look like a child dressed up. He will never admit that I'm "rising thirty". He just flings back his head and roars with laughter at me when I try to be very elderly. I love to hear it. Boyd is such fun when he forgets the "serious soldier" side and laughs like that.

'Mummy, I think, had an inkling that something was "in the air" because she was her most charming to Boyd – and to me – and had taken special pains with the flowers. They were everywhere; a great china jar full of delphiniums and beech leaves on the upper landing. Bowls of sweet-smelling dark red roses in the drawing-room, on the spinet and the high mantel-piece; a low crystal vase of mixed flowers on a mirror in the centre of the refectory table. Flowers even in Boyd's bedroom. (We have turned old Nanny's room into our guest-room these days.)

'It was by no means a perfect summer's afternoon. Mummy had picked the flowers only just in time. There was thunder in the air and it was very sultry. The sun had vanished by the time Boyd's taxi came chuffing down the lane and a few big drops of rain were already spattering against the casements. There was certainly going to be a storm. It was quite breathless. But I didn't mind. Mummy hates storms. She disconnects the radio, draws curtains to shut out the lightning and swears the cottage will be struck any moment. That is one of her "phobias", but I am used to storms after the awful ones in West Africa. This sort of thing is child's play.

'I was feeling extremely well and excited. My heart seemed to beat at twice its normal rate as soon as I heard the taxi drive up to the cottage. For two and a half years Boyd had been coming to this place as a guest. But *this* time was different. It was full of significance. I knew what was going to happen and I was, myself, astonished by the force of the emotion, the breathless tension in me.

'I went out to meet Boyd. He stepped out of the taxi with a suitcase in one hand … and something I couldn't see very well at first in the other. Then I gave a gasp.

'"Chumps! A *puppy!*"

He grinned at me – looking very young

302

and sheepish, despite the fact that he was so exhausted, and held out a small brown body which was wriggling with excitement. It was a baby dachshund. He pressed the little thing into my arms and said:

'"You ought to have a fierce dog here to guard you and Lady L. when you're alone. How about this creature? I saw it in Bond Street as I passed by this morning and just walked in and bought it for you. Quite mad."

'I looked at the baby dachs. It looked up at me with anxious golden eyes ... its absurd long body still wriggling ... its pointed tail wagging furiously; long ears flopping. Then it squeaked and struggled to get down. I put it on the pathway and it scampered over the grass and proceeded to show what a clean puppy should do. That made me laugh. I said:

'"Oh, what a little *poppet!* Chumps ... how *could* you!"

'Mummy, coming out of the cottage, seeing the dachs, flung up both hands in horror.

'"Boyd, you *evil* young man! Veronica will be crazy about it, of course, but it means the end of my carpets and covers. *And* my flowers ... shoo ... shoo...!' She clapped her hands, violently, chasing the dachs off a precious shrub.

'Boyd and I exchanged glances and both

roared with laughter. I felt oh, so gloriously happy all of a sudden, with a lightness of heart I had not experienced for years. I was glad Boyd had brought the puppy because it eased the tension and somehow it *needed* easing that afternoon.

'It was beginning to rain quite definitely now and we heard a distant growl of thunder.

'"Oh, dear!" exclaimed Mummy. "I must go and disconnect the wireless."

'I picked up the adorable puppy and asked what its name was. Boyd said promptly, "Winston. Let's call it after our P.M."

'So "Winston" it was … and a moment later the newly christened member of the household was running, or rather slithering, all over the polished oak floors of Monks Rest, causing Boyd and myself a lot of amusement and Mummy a good deal of anxiety. She did not know whether to follow Winston with a mop or put both hands to her ears to deaden the sound of the thunder. Finally a flash of lightning made her shut both eyes tightly and stand in the hall, and so Winston careered madly around, showing this time what an untrained puppy could do … unseen by my mamma.

'I picked up Winston and followed Boyd to his room. He set his case on the floor, flung his cap and gloves on the bed and un-buckled his belt.

'"Ugh ... it's hot and sticky in Town and I'm glad to be here," he said.

'Then he smiled down at me. My heart shook suddenly. How dear he was ... how more than ordinarily attractive, my tall, fine colonel ... smiling at me from those blue eyes which were so steadfast, so deeply intelligent and sometimes so tired. I could not bear him to be tired – or sad. I was not going to let him be sad about *me* any longer

'Confused by my own thoughts, I kissed the top of Winston's silky head. I heard Boyd say:

'"Lucky tyke!"

'I looked up. I felt an extraordinary rush of passionate love for Boyd Mansell surge through me. And suddenly, without further restraint, I put the little dog down. He scampered out on to the landing and did not come back. He was probably up to some mischief, but I did not care. I said:

'"Shall I kiss you, too, darling?"

'He looked almost stunned for a moment. (Afterwards he told me he had come down to Monks Rest with a grim burden on his mind: the fear that I was going to send him away for good and all. It had never really entered his head, he said, that I had grown to care for him as he did for me.) Then the stunned look was replaced by a light of intense joy and hope. He said:

'"Good lord, Veronica ... why ask me that

when you know I'm crazy about you ... that I love you with every drop of blood in my body ... and always have done since the first time I set eyes on you?"

'Then I walked straight into his arms. I whispered:

'"Chumps ... darling, darling Chumps ... *I love you, too.*"

'He held me frantically close as though he would never let me go again. I could scarcely breathe. My breast hurt, bruised by his tunic buttons, but I didn't care. I liked the pain. I *wanted* to be hurt. I realised in that moment how starved I was for physical love ... sweet, clean, overwhelming passionate love such as flamed into a white-hot fire between us then. He said:

'"Say that again... Veronica, *Veronica* ... say it again."

'"I love you," I said.

'He looked deep into my eyes for a split second, then I shut them. I felt his kiss on my mouth ... just as I had imagined and *wanted* it. A fierce, possessive kiss, draining my vitality until I could no longer stand. He lifted me right up in his arms and laid me on his bed. I opened my eyes and saw him for a moment. His face was no longer weary and anxious. It was flushed and his eyes were shining. He looked quite wonderfully handsome. The little room was dark; the rain had begun to pour torrentially from the surcharged skies. It was coming in through the open casements, spattering the sill. The chintz curtains waved wildly, getting drenched. The storm had broken right over Princes Risborough. We neither of us cared. We did not even notice the lightning. We only saw each other. It was a miraculous moment for me after the long pain and grief and loneliness of the past two and a half years. And later Boyd told me that for him it was like seeing a gate open, and that he walked through it into paradise; a paradise he had longed for interminably, in vain – so he had thought!

'He knelt beside me in the little storm-filled shadowed room. Picking up one of my hands and crushing it against his lips, he said:

'"Veronica, darling ... *darling* ... I can't believe it yet. It seemed so long. Do you *really* love me, darling?"

'I whispered "Yes." He added:

'"Veronica, you won't remember it very well ... but once before I saw you lying like this, and held and kissed you. But you didn't love me then. You didn't even realise whom it was you kissed. Darling, that was hell for me, but I never forgot it. I've remembered the sweetness of your lips for days and nights ... been tormented by it. I used to fear that you were not for me and would never want me as I wanted you. I told

Gilly I was coming down today to ask you to marry me because I couldn't go on like this. The strain is too much. But, my darling, I never dared hope to find you like *this*."

'I put up my arms and drew his head down to mine.

'"I love you," I said for the third time. "I can never thank you enough for your devotion and patience. Darling, forgive me if I've hurt you – worried you – I don't honestly remember anything about ... those other kisses. I don't really want to now. The past belongs to my poor Charles. I'm quite frank when I say that a part of me is buried with him and always will be. But I've got a lot left ... for you. It's the present and future that I offer you, Chumps, darling."

'"It's more than enough," he said. "Will you marry me soon, Veronica? Don't make me wait any longer."

'"I'll marry you whenever you like, my dear," I said.

'A loud clap of thunder shook the little cottage. I was in Boyd's arms again. Our lips clung ... exchanging the sweet deep kisses of our mutual love and passion. I knew, then, that I need never be unhappy or lonely again. And even while I was in his arms like that, I thought of my lost Charles ... yes, ... Charles... I remembered *you* and I believe I could see your eyes watching me without jealousy – with only kindness and under-

308

standing. I could hear your voice saying: "You have my blessing, Nic…" (no one else will ever call me by *that* name). "I want you to be happy … always…"

'"For a moment or two I stayed in Boyd's ecstatic embrace. He said so many wonderful things. He told me how long he had worshipped me; how no other girl had meant a "row of pins", as he called it, since our first meeting; and how his family loved me, and what a wonderful thing it would be when we could go down to Chidding Manor together as man and wife. It had been grim, he admitted, struggling to maintain a platonic friendship all these months when he was so much in love. But he had watched me growing stronger and better and less melancholy and neurotic. He had seen the gradual improvement and the return of my old gaiety and he had told himself that *perhaps* one day I would forget my grief and love again … love *him*. This hour between us was, he said, incredibly wonderful to him. It was the same for me. I told him how much his friendship and consideration had meant ever since Charles died. How I had grown, gradually, to love and need *him*.

'He said:

'"I'll never ask for more than you can give me, my darling. I don't even know if I shall satisfy you… I'm no musician and you're so artistic and…"

'But I interrupted that. I said:

'"Music doesn't mean to me what it did, Chumps. You needn't worry about that. It's one of the things that I said good-bye to ... two and a half years ago. You'll satisfy me absolutely. I love everything about you. Have no doubts, darling."

'He kept smoothing back the hair from my face which I felt to be flushed and hot, and looking into my eyes as though at some wonder he could not fathom ... my darling old Chumps! He said:

'"Those glorious grey eyes of yours! Veronica, you are the most intoxicating person. Do you know that? You've often driven me crazy without realising it."

'I laughed and bit my lip and pulled his warm cheek down to mine. I whispered:

'"I want to drive you crazy, darling..."

'"Not just now ... for heaven's sake," he said, laughing. He stood up, set me on my feet and pulled me into his arms, kissing my hair, my throat, my lips. Then a little roughly he put me away from him. I could feel him shaking.

'"Let's go down and tell Lady L.," he said in what I call Boyd's "military" voice; rather curt and authoritative when he wanted it to be. I was glowing with pride in him; with happiness; with glorious prospect of the future as his wife. I took his hand and went downstairs with him. I knew how happy

310

Mummy would be. This was the sort of marriage she had always wanted for her daughter. I knew her so well. Poor snobbish Mamma. I can hear her saying to everyone, "Yes, my girl is going to marry Colonel Mansell ... such a fine man ... a brilliant soldier ... a wonderful place, Chidding Manor, too, which will belong to him one day. Very well off ... oh, yes, *very* ... and so well connected..."

'Mummy would say all that. But I didn't care. I would have married Boyd Mansell tomorrow had he been a common soldier. But Mummy never did understand *that* "me". She never understood why I married a "penniless" musician like Charles.

'But Charles ... listen ... wherever you are... You know how much I love you. What I gave to you, my first husband, my dear lost love, I can never give to this man I am going to marry now. I will keep faith with you, Charles ... even while I lie in another man's arms. You know that. And now, good-bye, Charles. I shall never write in this diary ... or open it again. It is my good-bye to you on this earth.

'Till we meet again...'

## 4

*Letter from Iris Williams to Mervyn Williams written from Winniford Farm, Nr. Dulverton, on September 2nd, 1942*

'My dearly beloved,

It seems such a shame that just when Veronica chose to be married you should have had to rush up to your mother's place, but I was glad to get your wire, darling, saying she is better and no longer in danger. Also terribly relieved that you will be home for the weekend. The farm is absolutely heavenly in this fine weather. The beech trees are turning golden brown and your daughter is almost as brown. She has just learned to say "dada", which is a terrific thrill. Only she said it first as she saw a perfectly strange American officer when I was wheeling her pram past the post office, so I don't know *what* she means!!! But, darling, she is incredibly attractive and clever and *undoubtedly* your child.

'I got back from London last night and found everything perfect here. Nanny had looked after everything, including our offspring, so well. Now I must describe the wedding to you as you won't be home till the end of the week. Mervyn, you *did* miss a lovely day, darling, although I admit I had several awful pangs about poor Charles Hallard.

'Mervyn darling, it isn't that I criticize our poor darling Veronica for marrying again. I'm only too thankful she has done so. I know how she *adored* Charles. It is just that when I remember how happy *they* were, and how nearly Veronica died when Charles was torpedoed, it gives one a funny sort of feeling that things should be transient ... even great love. If Veronica can get over losing Charles ... anyone can get over *anything*. But two and a half years is a long time and Veronica was terribly lonely. She hadn't a baby like mine to live for.

'But to continue... I must say I came away feeling thankful Veronica has a husband like Boyd Mansell to look after her now. He's such a grand person. You always liked him, didn't you? And it's nice to think V. has again married a friend of ours. But how it is going to suit V. to be a soldier's wife, I don't know. She used to pooh me when I had to cope with all those awful moves and having no settled home and all the drawbacks of Army life. I remember *every* part of it with *no* pleasure, I assure you, darling. It's heaven to think you are a civilian now ... and that Winniford is our settled home.

'Darling, Veronica looked an absolute knock-out yesterday. You know they were married in the dear little church in Princes Risborough next to her home (the same church, of course, in which she married Charles). They gambled on the weather and won. A gorgeous September morning and so they were able to do as Lady Lowring had planned and have a sort of informal reception in the garden ... where there were lots of borrowed tables and chairs... The herbaceous border was a perfect picture with all the mauves and dark purples and pale pinks of the Michaelmas daisies, and the scarlet and yellow of the dwarf dahlias. Lady L. is so clever at gardening. She does most of it herself and that cottage is a gem.

'There were not many people. Veronica told me when I got down there (I arrived long before any of the others – we'd planned that so we could have a long talk) that they only wanted a very quiet wedding. The Mansell family came *en masse*, of course. I thought them quite charming. Mrs Mansell is such an angel, with snow-white hair and the sweetest expression – and she seemed more than delighted with her son's choice. Gillian, Boyd's sister, whom you know had that awful disaster years ago and has recovered her health, although she walks in rather a funny way, is charming ... and has such a clever husband. He's the doctor who helped to cure Gillian, which is so romantic. And there was Boyd's elder sister, Audrey.

Her husband couldn't come because he's in the R.A.M.C. and couldn't get leave. But she brought the most adorable pair of twins with her. David and Jonathan. Audrey and I had a serious discussion as to whether we might make a match between one of the twins and our daughter, darling. I'm already developing, like Lady L., into a match-making mamma.

'Lady L. looked superb as usual – regal in pale blue and silver fox stole and huge black hat. Absolutely in her element as the grand hostess. And (so she told me) better pleased with this marriage than the last. She never did want V. to marry poor Charles.

'Mervyn, darling, I must tell you, as soon as I arrived at Monks Rest where there were "borrowed" maids and everyone rushing around in circles (the cottage looked heavenly, full of flowers) I went up to V's. bedroom. Lady L. said V. needed a sort of "bridesmaid" and that as I was V.'s oldest friend I must cope. Darling, I didn't feel very bridesmaidy – such an elderly mother of one these days … but I'd put on that best pre-war three-piece … the blue and white *crêpe* you like so much, and my blue foxes and a new hat, and V. said I looked pretty good. But when I first saw her I thought *she* looked rather odd. She *is* so highly strung, Mervyn. When I entered her bedroom she was still in a pair of divine white satin

315

caminicks, with her hair swathed in a scarf, and she was "doing" her face. The room was quite tidy, really, for a girl who was about to be a bride at any moment ... suitcases neatly packed ... all her things laid out on the bed, ready for the wedding ... then I saw a huge photograph of old Boyd in his Colonel's uniform, by the bedside. (That saddened me in the silliest way, but I haven't been in V's room for ages and I am so used to seeing a photo of Charles on that bedside table. It *did* seem sad.) Then V. held out her hands to me and said: "Oh, Iris, darling, I'm so glad you've come. I must have someone to talk to. Iris, I feel so *awful.*"

'I asked, "Why?" and sat down beside her, and we talked and she went on doing her face, and you know, Mervyn, she is the *loveliest* person ... even in that early stage of making-up she looked beautiful with those huge grey eyes of hers. She isn't so thin and drawn as she used to be. Her figure is absolutely perfect now. Well – you know when she wrote to us about Boyd she said how blissful she was and what a pet he was, etc., etc. But on her wedding morning she seemed almost uncertain of herself. She said:

'"I love Boyd. I know I love him. I want to marry him. I want it with all my heart. But I feel a presentiment, Iris ... just as though

316

I am doing something I shall regret bitterly. Something *wrong*...”

'Mervyn, darling, that gave me the "willies" and I ask her to explain but she couldn't. She was just nervous and ill at ease and she said she didn't understand herself ... that she had been terribly happy ever since her engagement to Boyd was announced, that the Mansells were terribly good to her, her mother awfully pleased and Boyd absolutely ecstatic. But suddenly on this, her wedding morning, she had got this uncomfortable feeling. I tried to laugh and make her get it out of her head but it stuck there. That odd feeling that she would one day be sorry if she married Boyd. I took the bull by the horns and asked her if it was because of Charles ... if she felt that *he* would dislike it. She said no; not in a way. She was sure Charles would say she *ought* to marry again and not live like a nun for the rest of her life. She was only just twenty-eight, after all. A year younger than I. So I said: "Then why feel it wrong, Veronica. It can't be ... if you love Boyd."

"'I do," she said. "It isn't that..."

'I took a few moments, Mervyn, getting at the truth. And then with her hands nervously locked and her face – now perfectly made-up and exquisite with its golden summer tan and slight flush – screwed up as though she were going to cry, she said in

317

that heart-breaking husky little voice of hers:

'"Iris, *you don't think Charles will ever come back now,* do you?"

'I was really shocked and said so. I said:

'"My darling Veronica, get a grip on yourself. Why let such a notion enter that ridiculous head of yours? Of course he won't come back. After two and a half years ... why, what utter nonsense! How could he? If he were alive you'd have heard from or of him months and months ago."

'She looked unhappy and almost ashamed of herself but obviously still worried. The haunted look I used to see in her eyes when Charles first died had returned to them. She said:

'"Oh, well, I expect I'm a fool. But people *do* lose memories and things and oh, it would be so awful if he came back to find me married again. Awful for him ... for me ... for Boyd."

'"But it won't happen," I told her. "You've been reading about Enoch Arden or something ... or seeing a thriller on the films. Darling, there's no chance of Charles coming back. If you love Boyd, marry him today without a care in the world and be happy. For *heaven's* sake, be happy."

'A glimmer of humour returned to her face and made it wonderfully young and fresh again. Veronica always had a sort of radiance about her, delicate though she was as a young girl. She lost it when Charles died. But yesterday she seemed to get it back again. She began to breathe more easily and admitted that she was stupid. Especially as she had been so happy during her brief engagement. Boyd, having waited all these years, had refused to wait a day longer than was necessary and had swept her right off her feet into this marriage today. But she loved him, she assured me of that. She would never regret giving herself to him.

'I said:

'"Veronica, you wrote and told me you had finished and shut the diary you had written for Charles, and that you meant to devote the rest of your life to Boyd. Do keep to that, darling, and don't let any ghosts spoil this moment for you ... or any of your future moments with Boyd."

'She promised me. She seemed relieved now that she had "got it off her chest". She cheered up and spoke no more of Charles. Only once, when she was dressed, she did something which I must say upset me more than I let her see. She came close to me and asked me to take off her wedding-ring. Charles's. She said that she had tried to take it off last night and hadn't been able to. She had worn it up till now, with the lovely emerald engagement ring Boyd gave her.

She said, with a queer, twisted smile:

"'Once it's off … I shall feel quite dissociated from my poor Charles. Take it, Iris. I can't keep it, somehow. Not now that I'm going to wear another man's ring. Do what you want with it. But take it, please."

'I drew the ring gently from her finger. It left a little whitish circle on the sunbrowned flesh. I fancied she flinched a little as that ring came off. But she looked calmly at the narrow gold circlet which I was holding on the palm of my hand.

"'Good-bye, little ring. The new one is not like it at all, Iris. It is platinum. Mummy always disliked gold and said platinum was smarter and more modern. So Boyd's is platinum."

'I slid Charles Hallard's wedding-ring into my bag and tried to speak lightly, although I admit there was a lump in my throat. I have an awfully vivid imagination and a long memory, as you know, darling, and I seemed to see Charles Hallard's slender, charming figure standing beside Veronica in the very same church in which she was to be married to Boyd that morning. How he had adored her! How wrapped up in each other, in their music, they used to be, those two. Poor little golden wedding-ring. I've got it in my jewel-case. I can't bring myself to part with it, Mervyn. Just as sentimental as Veronica!

'Veronica kissed me and gave a little laugh.

320

'"No more ghosts now, Iris darling. I'm all Boyd's. And I'll make him a good wife. He's the dearest thing and I love him ... indeed I do..."

'I am sure she does, Mervyn. And I'm sure the marriage will be a great success. She was just a bit overwrought that morning and I don't wonder, really. It must be peculiar ... marrying again for the second time when you have loved your first husband very dearly. A sort of rebirth ... and birth-pangs are, after all, always painful.

'From that moment onward Veronica did not look back. She made a joyous bride. "Radiant" is the word to describe her. I stood in the pew of the little church and the tears dimmed my own eyes as I watched her come up the aisle with her mother. Boyd was waiting for her ... so tall and good-looking in his Colonel's uniform ... beside a frightfully nice Major – Edward Rochester by name – who was best man. (He works with Boyd at the W.O. I don't think you know him, darling. Not a "Gunner" ... R.E.'s). Boyd had the expression of a man about to enter heaven. Veronica looked as though she were miles and miles away – seeing nothing and nobody. Slightly "fey" (you know that look she used to get when she was very emotional). I can't tell you how beautiful she was. She wore a new three-piece suit – autumnal colouring. Leaf brown with a pale yellow exquisitely cut blouse and an enchanting Juliet cap of the same yellow on that dark head of hers, with leaf-brown veiling, and a diamond clip. Her spray was just right – big mauve orchids. She wore little high-heeled brown suède shoes, and she looked so small and sweet beside the tall soldierly Boyd. I suppose Lady Lowring and the Vicar and I were the only three in the church who were present at that *other* wedding ... nearly four years ago. A much more pretentious affair with Veronica in bridal white and that huge garden party at Whitelands Hall afterwards. I don't know quite *what* I felt, Mervyn ... except that I'm sure it doesn't do for one to compare the two ... one wedding so gay and festive and carefree and the other under the shadow of a terrible war... Veronica was a war-widow ... and yesterday everything was on a subdued note. I certainly felt subdued, sort of sad, darling. I could not forget what V. had said to me upstairs before the party started. What would happen ... *if Charles came back?* Although, of course, such a notion is fantastic.

'I was quite glad when that marriage service ended and Veronica came down the church on Boyd's arm, her small, lovely face smiling, her grey eyes shining with happiness. Boyd Mansell looked immensely proud and happy, too, and I walked back to

Monks Rest with Major Rochester and tried to smile like everyone else.

'The "reception" was certainly delightful. Everything went without a hitch. We drank some marvellous champagne which I understand had been sent to Veronica by a funny little Jew who used to rent Whitelands from Lady L. We sat in the garden in the warm sunshine and Veronica talked to everyone and seemed in high spirits and to have forgotten her "presentiments" entirely – thank goodness. The most adorable dachshund, "Winston" V. calls him, was there with a comical white bow, helping to entertain the guests.

'Boyd Mansell came and chatted for a moment but never took his gaze off Veronica ... my goodness, how faithfully and devotedly that man has loved her! He asked me if I didn't think him the luckiest fellow alive and I said quite sincerely that I thought he was. Veronica is a lovable fascinating person and when she gives herself ... she gives whole-heartedly. I'm sure she'll make him as happy as she made Charles and I said so bluntly. (I don't know whether I really ought to have mentioned him, was it tactless of me, darling?) but Boyd took it awfully well and said: "My dear, you're right. She was a marvellous wife to that poor fellow and my one wish is to make her as happy as he did." Wasn't that sporting of him, Mervyn?

'That nice doctor – John Frobisher, who is now sort of related to Veronica – made a speech, and Boyd made one – and then Veronica beckoned me and we went up to her room and closed her dressing-case. She put her little short fur coat over her arm and stood ready for her "going away". They were to spend the ten days' leave which Boyd had for his honeymoon in some lovely hotel Boyd knew about in the depths of Worcestershire. The late September days were warm but the evenings were cold. She would want her furs, she said.

'She looked at me with dewy grey eyes and said:

'"Thanks, darling Iris, for all your help today. And Iris … I *am* lucky. Two such wonderful men in my life. I don't deserve it…"

'I kissed her and told her that she did. We clung to each other for a moment. Her lips were trembling and I fancied that at the back of her mind there was something else she wanted to say. *Something connected with Charles,* But she did not say it. It was as though she had firmly made up her mind that … with Boyd's platinum wedding-ring replacing the little gold one … she would dedicate herself entirely to Boyd now.

'She drove away from Monks Rest with her husband, smiling gaily and waving at us all. Lady L. blinked and blew her nose and said how happy she was and how she adored her new son-in-law. Everyone said how enchanting Veronica was. Mrs Mansell joined in and said she couldn't be more pleased than she was to have Veronica for her daughter-in-law. And I said how splendid it all was, too. But Mervyn darling, I had become stupid and fanciful then. I could not forget Charles ... and that little ring that lay so desolately in my bag.

'All the way home I kept remembering what Veronica had said, and even while I tried to concentrate on the memory of Veronica's radiance as she drove away with her second husband, I was unable to shut out that awful thought:

*'Supposing Charles Hallard did come back...*

'Mervyn, he couldn't, could he? Oh, he mustn't, now!

'Hurry home, darling, and tell me I'm a little fool. Just as I told Veronica.

'Your most devoted Iris.'

5

*Letter from Veronica Mansell to Iris Williams written from the 'Lygon Arms', Broadway, Worcestershire, during her honeymoon.*

'Darling Iris,

'I don't think I really thanked you properly on my wedding day for leaving your baby and coming all the way from Somerset to "bridesmaid" me and help me the way you did. But I do appreciate it, my dear. And now I feel I must apologise to you, too, for behaving the way I did. I mean – all those foolish fears of mine casting a shadow on such a lovely day. I know it was only between you and me, but it was wrong of me, as well as silly, to allow my poor lost Charles to become a "spectre at the feast" when he should be only a lovely friendly memory. And that is what he will always be now, Iris, for the rest of my life.

'I want to tell you how terribly happy I am with Chumps (you know that is the nickname Boyd's sister gave him when they were children and I use it, too). My dear, very dear Chumps, is the world's most perfect husband. I have no words with which to describe to you what I feel towards him or how wonderful he is to me. But he always has been – from the first moment we met on that fateful voyage coming home almost three years ago.

'If I had any lingering doubts as to whether or not I should have married again, they no longer exist. Chumps has blown away my shadows like a marvellous fresh breeze. There is something so sane and wholesome and *shining* about him. He radiates good temper and good sense and I do so admire and respect his attitude towards the Army. I will, I trust, never develop into one of those Army wives who grumble all day and try to seduce their unfortunate husbands into resigning their commissions. Long after this war is over I want Chumps to carry on with his career. He loves it and he will most certainly end up as a Major-General, bless him. He makes me laugh when he starts being all dictatorial and assertive about military matters. When we walk down the street together and he replies to all the salutes, there's something about him which is so *soldierly*. I feel so proud of him.

'Iris, he is a thrilling person altogether. As marvellous a lover as he was a friend. No girl could be anything but content as his wife. This week we've had has endeared him to me all the more. I want nothing better now than to be the world's best wife to him and to have an infant as soon as possible. Yes, Iris, I want his child and he wants one, too. He's sweet with small children and I can imagine how grand he'll be as a father. He has the right make-up. He adores electric trains, meccano sets and puzzles. I can see him sitting on the floor of some nursery playing soldiers with his small boy. Yes, I hope I have a child soon, Iris. I've envied you your motherhood ever since you had Susan-Jane. And I'm so much stronger now – I feel I could cope with having a child.

'When our ten days are up the hardest thing is going to be our separating even for a short time, but I've got to leave Chumps and go back to Monks Rest alone for a variety of reasons. First of all he expects to go to Minley Manor this month – he is to take the senior officers' course. You know he's had all these special jobs all this time but not taken a staff course since the junior one a year ago. He must do it, because although he is still so young he is a Lieutenant-Colonel and may be wanted for more important jobs still. Once in Camberley I shall find a house and live with him. But for the few weeks he remains in London he wants me to stay with Mummy. He works till all hours and he dislikes the possible bombing for me and, as he says, the amount we would be able to meet doesn't make it worth while. Then there is my W.V.S. job which I must carry on with until they find a relief. After that I'll settle down to running a house for Chumps. They tell me it is almost impossible to get maids in Camberley so I may find myself doing the cooking and housework, which appals Chumps, but I tell him I shall enjoy it. I'm sick of being fussed over and waited on, and its time *I* stood at a sink and faced greasy dishes like poor Mummy ... or my dear mother-in-law and a million other women. I've been spoiled up to now.

'Iris, dear, this is such a charming place, full of lovely old furniture and the countryside is heavenly. We've been so happy, Iris. Gorgeous walks ... you can see five counties from the hills ... Winston with us ... bless him ... growing longer and fatter in the tum every day. But a good walker is our Winston ... fairly walks *us* off our feet. We have had lovely misty autumn evenings in front of big fires getting drowsy... Chumps drinking his last beer and me my feminine cup of tea. Then up to our room which is full of flowers. Boyd always sees there are flowers for me. He thinks of every little thing for my happiness. He has just come up behind me and kissed the top of my head and told me to hurry up and finish my letter so we can post it. He has just written one to Gilly. So I must end this, Iris darling.

'Chumps sends you his love. He looks brown and so much less tired after his week's respite from the W.O. Extraordinarily youthful without those lines on his face. He's wearing grey flannels and a check shirt and blue pullover. His eyes look as blue as forget-me-nots.

'Iris, I'm very much in love with my husband and so grateful to God for my new happiness.

'My best love to you and dear Mervyn – and my godchild.

'Your loving
'Veronica.'

*Letter from Lieutenant–Colonel Mansell to Mrs John Frobisher, written from the 'Lygon Arms'.*

'Gilly dear,
'This won't be much of a letter because writing is too much like hard work and I'm being entirely selfish during this honeymoon of mine, devoting every second of it to my adored and adorable wife.
'But I want to tell you how happy I am, old girl. It seems almost too good to be true … that Veronica is actually my wife at last. Miracles certainly do happen, Gillo. There was a time you will remember when I never dreamed I'd be lucky enough to get her. Ye gods, the longer I live with her, the more I realise my luck and understand why that poor chap who died was so crazy about her! She is an amazing person … all the things a man wants in a woman. But I knew that. I've loved and watched her for two and a half years. I wasn't likely to be mistaken.
'Gillo, our honeymoon is perfect. That about sums up the situation in a nutshell. *She* is sitting near me, also writing a letter. She looks wonderfully well, like a kid in her

330

pair of dark blue slacks and a little blue and white woolly jumper. Her hair is tied up in a gay sort of scarlet handkerchief thing. (Not quite sure it isn't one of mine!) She's just turned her head and smiled at me. I admit my heart misses a beat when Veronica smiles at me like that. Gilly, you of all people must know what I feel about her and how particularly satisfying it is to me to know she loves me as much as I do her. Thanks, sister mine, for your past goodness to her – and tell Mother how much I love her for taking my Veronica so completely to her heart.

'I'm right on top of the world.

'Your proud and happy
'Chumps.'


## 6


It was the last night of Veronica's and Boyd's honeymoon. They sat in the fire-warmed shining dining-room at the 'Lygon Arms' finishing dinner. They had reached the coffee stage and had just lighted cigarettes.

Neither of them had the least desire to leave Broadway and return to London. They dreaded their brief separation. And both had agreed when discussing things this afternoon that they could so willingly have spent another ten days in the charming hotel in this glorious piece of country, away from everybody who knew them; away from work and a world at war.

But the war was on. Lt.-Col. Mansell had an important conference at the War Office at two o'clock tomorrow afternoon. Mrs Boyd Mansell had an important one of her own at her W.V.S. centre in High Wycombe the morning after.

It was, indeed, the end of their honeymoon. And as though Nature were in sympathy with them, the spell of fine dry weather which had graced the whole of their holiday had broken this evening. It was a wild wet night – a typically depressing night of autumn. Ever since 'black-out' the rain had been falling in torrents and there was south-west gale blowing. It would mean the end of the last flowers of summer; a wanton stripping of leaves from the trees; a sad churning of little rugged lanes into tracks of squelching mud. Certainly, there was some consolation to the Mansells to know that even could they have stayed here, there would be no sunbathing tomorrow; no lazy strolling across fields or picnics on the hills.

Veronica poured out a cup of coffee and handed it to her husband. He changed every night from a civilian into a soldier again. She liked Chumps in his well-cut uniform with the little dark purple and green 'Palestine' ribbon over the tunic pocket. All the women always turned their heads twice to look at the tall, handsome young Colonel. Veronica was immensely proud of him and much to his embarrassment (and pleasure) told him so, several times a day.

But this evening she was subdued, and so was he. Their dinner had lacked the usual jokes. Boyd's effervescing spirits and humour were dimmed. Now and then Veronica's large grey eyes looked sad ... which was a thing he could not bear. He had taken a vow that Veronica must never be allowed another moment's sadness now that she was his wife.

He leaned across the table and touched her hand.

'Up with the corners of that fascinating mouth of yours, Mrs Mansell,' he said. 'Smile at me.'

At once she smiled ... her finger caught and held his a moment.

'Darling, was I looking miserable?'

'Definitely.'

'If I am, it's only because I know that this time tomorrow we won't be together.'

'The mere thought is enough to drive me to drink, darling,' he said with a short laugh. 'But it's just got to be. I can't let you stay in London by yourself, and you've got your job and I've got mine ... so we must be parted for a week. But no longer, sweetheart. We should be together again by then. By the way, I've asked a chap I know who is an instructor at the Staff College to send you some addresses – you might as well start looking for rooms or a house at once. They're pretty tricky to find, I'm told.'

'I'll find something even if it has to be a caravan,' said Veronica, smiling. 'I shall just long to be back with you, darling.'

Boyd Mansell felt his heart swell as he looked into the luminous eyes of his wife, and heard what she said. It was wonderful to him as he had written to Gilly – to know that Veronica cared for him like this and belonged to him at last. These ten days had been a revelation. He had not dreamed that the possession of an adored wife could be so thrillingly sweet. Once or twice during this honeymoon with Veronica warm and yielding in his arms, he remembered that grim day when he had taken her to a certain hotel in London ... a Veronica half-crazed with misery, mistaking him for her first husband ... himself, half crazy, trying to comfort her. A grim memory. But now she had got over *that* ... and she was *his* wife. It had all been worth while, the waiting and the pain and the long-drawn-out test of his endurance. She was an enchanting creature to live with and life with her in the future ... life of peace after the war, promised to be even more perfect.

He said:

'Do you mind if I tell you you look pretty smooth in that rig-out tonight, Mrs Mansell...?'

She dimpled at him. Darling Chumps! He just loved calling her by that name ... as though he could not hear it often enough. She said:

'The rig-out, as you call it, Colonel Mansell, is not a new one. You've seen it before.'

'I like it, anyhow.'

'You're very appreciative of my clothes. I know wives who'd envy me. Some men never notice what their better halves are wearing. You are a model husband.'

'I've got a particularly attractive wife.'

She sipped her coffee happily. She could not be depressed for long. Boyd would never let her. He added:

'It's still raining like hell, darling. I can hear it. No walk for us. I'll have to collect Winston and let him out for a moment, then let's put on the fire in our room and stay up there. I can't bear to share you with anyone else tonight.'

Her pulses thrilled ... as always nowadays to that deep, adoring look in Boyd's blue eyes. She nodded, her cheeks flushed.

'All right, darling. I agree.'

'When you look like that,' he said in a low voice, 'I am tempted to keep you in London with me, raids, W.V.S., War Office or not.'

She laughed and shook her head – a small graceful head with dark hair springing back crisply from the pretty broad forehead and brushed into a smooth roll round the back.

She wore a plainly cut black wool dress tonight. There were pearls in her ears, and about her throat a lovely creamy double row of pearls with a small emerald clasp which Mrs Mansell had given her from her own collection of jewels. She looked older in this than in her sports clothes. Prematurely, there were grey threads in the darkness of the hair above both those small ears. Although so young, hers was the face of a woman who had suffered deeply. But in Boyd's eyes this touch of maturity made Veronica all the more attractive. He wished to make it his particular aim to protect Veronica from any further suffering.

He knew that he had succeeded so far ... that she was not disappointed in him as lover and husband. For that he was supremely thankful, and he had no longer any need to be jealous of the man who had been first in her life, her heart. He could afford now to pity poor Charles Hallard who had lived with Veronica for such a short while. He, Boyd Mansell, please God, would spend all the lovely years of their youth with her; watch her grow old ... grow old with her ... and their children. A glorious thought.

The waitress came to clear the table.

'More coffee, darling?' asked Boyd.

'No, darling, thanks.'

'Then let's collect Winston.'

Arms linked they walked up the staircase to their room. The 'Lygon Arms' was full of lovely old Jacobean furniture. Their room was no exception. The curtains were drawn and the bed-table lamp shed a soft rosy glow over everything. The wild wet night was shut out. Winston sat on his rug on the bed. He greeted them ecstatically, waggling his long brown satiny body. Boyd picked him up and ruffled the foolish ears.

'Come on, young feller … out we go.'

Veronica sat down on the edge of the bed and pulled a cigarette and her lighter from her bag.

'You're getting as silly as I am about that dog, Chumps.'

'Quite,' agreed Boyd without hesitation.

She lit her cigarette and put the lighter back in her bag. She smiled up at him with the lustrous grey eyes which had such power to stir him.

'I'll wait for you, shall I … if you want us to stay up here tonight and talk. I might begin to pack. We've got to make such an early start.'

'Okay, sweetheart,' he said.

The door closed behind him. A moment later Veronica heard Winston's shrill bark. Boyd had let him out into the garden. She smiled and walking to the dressing-table, opened the top drawer and began to sort a few oddments, cigarette between her lips.

She must find her suitcase. But oh, how miserable to be saying good-bye to the 'Lygon Arms'; to this honeymoon which had been so sweet, so friendly, so entirely satisfying to them both.

She pulled open the next drawer. Boyd's drawer; khaki collars and ties; civilian silk handkerchief; white collars; things Boyd had worn during his leave. A tobacco pouch and a couple of pipes. She lifted up one of the pipes and fingered the briar bowl tenderly. *Dear* Chumps. Darling husband! His pipes were so much part of him. She loved all his set masculine habits. She wouldn't want to change one of them.

She found her case and putting it on the bed, began to pack. Thank goodness this separation from him would be brief; a week at the most. Then Camberley ... Minley Manor for him ... housekeeping for her. A complete change from any life she had led before. Veronica ... an officer's wife. One of the 'Regular Army', too. Not too easy an existence. She knew that from Iris. But she wanted, with the absorption which Veronica put into everything she tackled, to lead that life with Boyd and enjoy it.

Suddenly the sound of music drifted into the room. It came from the room below. Somebody had switched on a wireless. Instinctively Veronica stood still and listened. A few bars more and she knew ... this was a

B.B.C. Symphony Concerto. Exquisitely played. Who was the pianist? she wondered. Moiseiwitch... Myra Hess...? Some great master of the art, anyhow.

For a moment Veronica did not move. Holding a pair of stockings in one hand and her cigarette in the other, she listened, lost in reverie. She knew every note of the Concerto. She and Charles used to have the records. They had played it often. It was one of Charles's favourites.

It was a long time since Veronica had listened to and taken note of any good music. She had not heard the Brahms since she left Lagos. Standing here now, concentrating on the familiar, haunting strains, she was inevitably drawn by her memories out of the present ... back into the past. There is nothing so poignant, so full of remembered joy or pain, than familiar music.

She could even recall in detail the last time she and Charles had listened to this particular Concerto. It had been broadcast from some foreign station. She and Charles were in their bungalow ... it was a hot, breathless night ... with the white brilliance of the tropical moonlight flooding them ... and the customary background of thunder growling in the distance, portending a storm.

She lay on the sofa, limp, exhausted by the heat, one hand hanging down, the other behind her head. (A head that ached violently, as usual.) But she was transported with pleasure in the music and Charles was sharing her transports. He sat on the floor, his head leaning against the sofa. She could see him as plainly in this moment as though she were back with him in that room, reliving that incident.

*Downstairs someone turned the radio up a little higher.* Piercingly sweet came the remembered melody. Veronica flinched and gasped a little with the sudden and un-expected pain that gripped her heart and wiped the happiness from her face.

*Charles ... Charles...* (he had turned sud-denly and kissed her hand ... his brilliant eyes rapt with feeling. He had said under his breath: 'Oh, Nic ... what sheer heaven ... *listen...*')

Her poor Charles! ... such a born musi-cian ... he used to know so much about the theory of music, too ... loved it so well. And he was dead. He would never hear the Brahms No. 2 Piano Concerto again.

Veronica dropped the stockings and drew the back of a hand across her eyes as though trying to shut out her vision of him; of that night in Lagos. *Of what had happened afterwards.* When the Concerto was over ... keyed up to a high pitch of excitement and intense emotion, he had taken her in his arms ... (oh, God, why remember it? She

340

was no longer his. She was Boyd Mansell's wife and this was her honeymoon with Boyd. It was madness to let music reawaken old passions ... bring back dead dreams...)

She wanted to drop down here on the floor beside this bed and cry ... as she used to cry for Charles ... with a broken heart.

An awful thought seized Veronica in that moment. A blinding moment of self-revelation. She had married again. Charles was dead. She loved Boyd. *But not as she had loved Charles* ... no, never as she had loved Charles ... with whom she had been one in mind, body and spirit.

Terrified at this thought she stood transfixed, and prayed that the music would cease before Boyd came back into this room.

Then suddenly as though in answer to her prayer the Symphony Concert was abruptly switched off. It was replaced by a gay feminine voice singing 'They're Either Too Young or Too Old'. The contrast – and the relief – was too much for Veronica. The colour surged back into her cheeks. She burst into laughter. She was still laughing when Boyd came in followed by a pleased and wagging Winston. Boyd shut the door and gave his wife a surprised look.

'What's the joke, darling?'

She looked at the tall, soldierly figure, the handsome kindly face of the man she had married ten days ago, and felt guilty because of the storm of emotion which had swept across and so nearly submerged her. She ran to him and hugged him close.

'Oh, Chumps … darling, do I make you happy … *do* I, darling? Are you glad you married me?'

He regarded the top of the dark little head with amazement. His arms went round her.

'My adorable darling … of *course* … why on earth do you ask? You must know it by now, surely. You know how crazy I am and always have been about you.'

'You've always been terribly sweet to me, Chumps, I certainly know that! And I want to make *you* happy – too.'

'You always will, my poppet. Good lord … can't Winston and I leave you to yourself for ten minutes without you going all doubtful and introspective, you ridiculous child?'

She leaned her cheek against his shoulder, composed, comforted again. He was so solid, so real … her new and charming husband. She was indeed ridiculous she told herself ruefully … allowing that music to upset her… She must not let the memory of Charles disturb her again. It was unfair to Boyd, unwholesome, too. She disapproved of it strongly.

But the dangerous and difficult moment had passed. Veronica and Boyd spent a happy evening packing their few things, then sat in front of their fire, and smoked a last cigarette. Boyd went downstairs and returned with a mug of lager beer. Veronica, warm now from her exertions, sipped some of the frothy golden liquid, then sat on a pillow at her husband's feet and with her head resting against his knee, listened to his stories. She loved Boyd's stories about his boyhood at Chidding Manor ... days when James was at home; when the two boys were on holiday; and when Gilly was a little girl. Boyd always had a store of cheerful memories to draw upon. He told Veronica tonight about the time when he had been dared by James to do some climbing on the roof and how he had crashed through one of the greenhouses and escaped miraculously with a few cuts, and how his poor panic-stricken mother had rushed out of the Manor having heard the noise of breaking glass and feared someone had been killed. Then later, how Boyd's father had lectured him and docked his pocket-money for a month to help pay for new glass.

'Dad was a just man and a damn good father,' Boyd finished that little tale. 'I owe him a lot. We all do in the family.'

Veronica shook her head.

'Goodness, you were a mischievous boy, Chumps! Who would have thought you would grow into a good, well-behaved Colonel!'

He laughed and pointed to the uniform coat he had just taken off.

'They wouldn't have made me one had they known the full extent of my wickedness.'

'Wickedness ... pooh!' she laughed at him, grey eyes sparkling. She felt warm and happy and content again. 'I don't believe you've ever done a really wicked thing in your life, Chumps.'

He took his pipe from his mouth and grimaced at it.

'H'm. I daren't begin to tell you of my peccadilloes as a subaltern ... my love-affairs in Cairo and South Africa, for instance, and...'

'Now, darling, don't boast,' broke in Veronica, tugging at his tie. 'And don't try to make me jealous, because you can't.'

He put down mug and pipe and enfolded her small figure closely, letting his lips rest on her hair, drawing in its fragrance.

'Darling ... *you* need never be jealous of any woman on God's earth. I love only you. All of you ... with all of me.'

She shut her eyes and sighed.

'What a lovely thing to say.'

'You're a lovely person to say things to. Sweetheart, I don't know how to part with you tomorrow.'

'Nor I with you darling.'

'I love you more every day, every night we

spend together, Veronica. Do I make *you* happy, darling? Do I?'

She raised a flushed, grateful face.

'Terribly happy, darling.'

'Then I don't want anything else in the world.'

'I do,' she said.

'What, Veronica?'

She pulled his head down and spoke against his ear.

'A son ... of yours ... like you...'

Boyd Mansell's face flushed a little and a look of indescribable happiness came into his eyes. He drew Veronica up on to his lap and kissed her sweet, yielding mouth.

'Darling,' he said. 'Darling ... my love...'

The room was wrapped in silence then. The radio downstairs had been switched off. There was no sound except the relentless rain beating against the windows. Winston, the dachs, sat on his rug, head on his paws, golden eyes drowsily blinking. He could see that there would be no more 'walkies' tonight. These two human beings who were his god and goddess were engrossed in each other. They had no use for him at the moment. None at all. He might as well settle down to sleep for the night.

# PART IV

## 1

Violet Mansell stood in the portico of Chidding Manor on the morning of June 6th, 1944, and watched her eldest daughter, Audrey, push a perambulator slowly and carefully down the drive. It struck her that Audrey was ageing – growing very plump. It was a cold, damp, windy morning, not in the least what a June day should be. But for Mrs Mansell – as for the rest of the world – it was a day of such tremendous moment that it was hard to settle down to the ordinary routine of work.

This morning the British had successfully invaded Normandy.

The whole household had listened, breathlessly, to the early news. The Mansells heard that news with mixed feelings, remembering their personal share in it.

Audrey's doctor husband was with the 'invaders'. He had not been able to tell them; had not communicated with Audrey for weeks. But she knew ... and she alone of them had felt that sickness of unnamed fears as she listened while the radio com-

347

mentator gave his first brief picture of that epic landing.

Poor Audrey, thought her mother as she watched her daughter vanish down the drive. They could do nothing but pray for her ... for Roger's safe return. Thank God, Boyd was out of it. He had fully intended to be 'in it', and was bitterly disappointed because he was still in England. But unfortunately for him (or as the Mansell family, and Veronica in particular, felt, *fortunately*) he had gone down with an acute attack of sciatica a couple of months ago whilst on Salisbury plain. Veronica was convinced it was due to sleeping out in such wild weather. At the time, Boyd had suffered great pain and had been forced to enter a military hospital for special injections and treatment. He had hated his enforced idleness and separation from Veronica, but the wretched complaint seemed to her, at least, a blessing. For now in this 'invasion month' Boyd still walked with a limp and had to use a stick. He was by no means quite cured, but he had returned to duties at Woolwich. To him it was an exceeding bore except that it made it possible for him to live with his wife and child.

A son had been born to Veronica and Boyd Mansell eleven months ago. It had been a tremendous event in Violet Mansell's life. The first son for one of *her* sons. James had no other children except Bunty, his girl. The future heir to Chidding Manor was this important young man who had opened his eyes (bright blue like his father's) in the London clinic and who had Veronica's soft dark hair and, so Mrs Mansell declared, the broad forehead and strongly moulded mouth and chin of the Mansells. A typical Mansell, in fact.

He had been christened Giles (Veronica wished that, after her father) and Boyd, of course; but already he had a nickname which Mrs Mansell deplored. But his parents liked it. It had been given him on the first day that his father saw him. Bending over the white bundle which lay in the crook of his lovely young mother's arm, Boyd had touched one tiny curled fist and said: 'Good lord, darling, he really is a chip off the old block. I can see a resemblance to my old man. I swear it.'

Veronica had answered:

'Well, he's a very *nice* chip, darling... I'm terribly proud of myself...'

And from that moment onward young Giles Boyd Mansell was the 'Chip'. The Chip he would remain. As Mrs Mansell sighed: 'I gave my boy a lovely name like Boyd and Gilly calls him "Chumps". Now my grandson must be *Chip*. What *is* the use of choosing nice names?'

But she adored young Chip and thought

349

with deepest love and admiration of her daughter-in-law. Veronica had been all and more as a wife to Boyd than Violet Mansell had ever hoped for. Although she had loved Veronica at first sight she had at one time feared that the girl might turn out to be a little delicate and too highly strung; an anxiety for Boyd. But in these last two years it seemed that the girl had outgrown her delicateness. She had produced young Chip with little trouble and given her doctor and nurses a surprise in consequence. She had even fed him for four months, herself, with great joy and pride. Now, nearing his first birthday, Chip was a credit both to Veronica and his doting father. Only yesterday Mrs Mansell had received a letter containing some snapshots which Boyd had taken of his son in Hyde Park, sitting up in his pram. A handsome, manly little fellow with a mass of brown curls, sturdy limbs and mis-chievous laughing eyes. (Oh, so like her little Boyd had been, the grandmother had thought, when she studied those snapshots through her magnifying-glass.)

Veronica and Boyd had a furnished flat in Lowndes Square. Boyd was permitted a car for his work and drove down to Woolwich every morning and back at night. Veronica looked after her son entirely herself. Much to her own as well as her mother's surprise, she had turned out to be a capable and perfect mother. And – luckier than most of her relatives and friends – she had found a good maid to do the rest of the work, an old woman who had in her day been a cook in large houses and who completely satisfied the *cordon bleu* in Colonel Mansell. But she was no longer fit to take big jobs and could just manage the small comfortable flat. After being a few months with Veronica she was her devoted slave; ready to do anything and everything for her. Veronica had that 'way' with her.

Audrey was not so lucky. Mrs Mansell was sorry for Audrey. It had been a great hardship to her to be parted from her husband and she had had to give up her own home in Market Rasen. Roger had handed the practice over to a *locum*, and the house was wanted. So Audrey had brought the twins and Patricia, a small girl, born six months ago, down to her own home. She had little fun out of life these days, thought her mother. Nothing but washing and ironing for those three children; taking the twins to nursery school or fetching them back; putting them all to bed. Tired out at nights always, was poor old Audrey. But good-tempered always. She had a placid disposition, fortunately.

James had written several time suggesting that she should send the twins out to Kenya to his ranch to be brought up in sunshine and safety with his own child. But Audrey would not hear of it. She and Roger were British folk, she said, their sons were British. They must stay and risk whatever was coming to them ... on their own soil.

Now the invasion had started and Mrs Mansell wondered how long this dreadful war would continue. How long she would have the painful necessity of neglecting this dear home: of seeing chickens on the tennis court, weeds choking the big flowerbeds; the broad gravel drive was growing green with them, too. They just could not keep it all up with a half-time visiting gardener and evacuees running all over the place. Three lots of mothers and children Mrs Mansell had taken from bombed areas. The mothers looked after themselves, but the children were wild little Cockneys, shouting in the garden, or through the house, disturbing the peace, morning, noon and night. It was a trial which Violet Mansell accepted with the sweetness of her nature, but she had never really got used to it. She longed for the old, well-ordered times and wondered if they would, indeed, ever return.

She did the cooking for her family. She and Audrey, with a daily woman to 'scrub', managed the rest of the work. It was a lot for her. Sometimes Violet Mansell felt her age; very old and weary. She had lately seen her doctor and he had told her to rest more, that the muscles of her heart were 'tired'. But she could not rest. There was too much to do. Twice as much now that Audrey and the children were here. But she liked to have them. They were company for her and she adored her grandchildren. Little Pat was a sweet baby.

Mrs Mansell was never really so happy as when Chidding Manor was full of the members of her family. She encouraged Boyd to bring his wife and son down whenever it was possible. But Boyd rarely got a Sunday off these days. Like everybody else, he was working at full pressure.

Mrs Mansell felt almost guilty for standing here doing nothing. Audrey was now out of sight. She turned back into the house. She could hear the distant voices of the evacuees, and a child crying. She sighed and walked into the library. Better get down to some work. There were dead flowers to be thrown away and new ones must be picked. As long as there were flowers in the garden, she liked to see them decorate her rooms.

She had so many letters to write. She owed one to Veronica's nice mother. Lady Lowring was not at all well. Overworked, like many others of her age, she had now yielded to the entreaties of her daughter and shut up Monks Rest for a month. She was at present staying with a sister of her late husband in the Lake District. She adored her grandson. To Veronica, in private, she intimated that young Chip was *much* more a Lowring than a Mansell. His nose resembled Sir Giles's, she said. But what did it matter? Let dear Mrs Mansell think him like *her* side.

Mrs Mansell and Audrey had made the beds. Now there was the library to dust (the big drawing-room was shut up, white and desolate with dust-sheets), then Mrs Pryson would arrive by bus from Horsham. She must wash the kitchen and scullery floors today. But oh, to get down to the quiet luxury of her letter-writing, thought Mrs Mansell with a little sigh. The weekly letter to dear James. And it was Bunty's birthday in six weeks' time. One must get a parcel off to the child. James and his wife were so good about sending regular parcels to them all at Chidding Manor. She must tell him how much they appreciated that big tin of peach jam and the currants and raisins in the last parcel.

The telephone bell rang.

Violet Mansell went out into the hall and answered the call in her soft, gentle voice. She tried to save the time of caller and operator by avoiding the usual 'hello' and always began in the same way: 'This is Chidding 151.'

Veronica's voice replied.

'Is that the *Madre*...?' (She had given Mrs

354

Mansell the Spanish form of 'mother' one day during her brief engagement to Boyd, when she had seen Mrs Mansell at dinner with a black lace mantilla over her pretty white head, and it had remained.)

'Oh yes, Veronica, my dear. How are you?'

'Terribly well thank you, *Madre*. I'm phoning you from Lowndes Square. Chumps is at work. I want to know if I can bring the Chip down tomorrow for a few days. Chumps has to go away on some hush-hush job, and doesn't want me to stay here in the flat alone. I would have gone to Mummy but you know Monks Rest is shut up and–'

'But of course, darling,' broke in Mrs Mansell. 'You know I'd love to have you with us. One thing I've been thankful for during this war is the size of the Manor. It will take you all. Audrey will be pleased, too. It's boring for her with no young people around these days. When will you come?'

'In time for lunch. Can you do with all of us – Chip and Winston too?'

Mrs Mansell laughed.

'The inevitable Winston. We love him. And how is my grandson?'

'Blooming. Got another tooth, he wishes me to tell his Granny. He's so proud of it.'

'I'll be very happy to se you both, dear. Don't bother to bring too much. You can use Audrey's baby bath and he can sleep the other end of Pat's pram, can't he?'

'If Pat doesn't mind being kicked. Chumps thinks his son is going to be the football champion of the future,' laughed Veronica.

'Isn't Boyd thrilled about this morning?'

'We both are. It's terrific, *Madre*. Chumps has maps of France all over the floor and little flags stuck on them to show where we landed. He's as excited as a schoolboy. It's the sort of thing he used to do in a hypothetical fashion at Camberley when he was at the Staff College. Now it's all in deadly earnest. I think he wishes he were in it, *Madre,* but thank God he is not. I never knew sciatica could be so welcome. Poor Chumps!'

'How is the leg?'

'Better this week than it's been for ages. He will soon be able to walk without that stick.'

'You don't know where he's going now, I suppose?'

'No idea. He can't tell me. But he hopes to be back in town in about five or six days.'

'It will be lovely to have you and the boy down here for so long, my dear,' said Mrs Mansell.

She put down the receiver and stood a moment thinking what next to do. If Veronica and little Giles were coming down to Chidding tomorrow morning, perhaps the kitchen floor must be left again, and

Mrs Pryson must turn out the room that Veronica and Boyd generally occupied when they came. It used to be one of the 'best' double guest-rooms; with two sunny windows facing the gardens. There was that old cot that used to belong to the twins, up in the attic. Mrs Pryson must help her get it down for young Giles.

It would be nice having a houseful ... despite the lack of staff and difficulties in feeding. Veronica was a sweet person – easy to cater for and tidy (which poor Audrey certainly was *not!*). Gilly had always been the tidy one of her family. Dear Gilly! Mrs Mansell – going about the daily round – thought fondly of her youngest daughter, and never ceased to thank God for the health and happiness which had been restored to her through John Frobisher. Gilly was a very happy creature these days. John was busier than ever, and Gilly both wife and secretary, his right hand.

## 2

Boyd Mansell – he had been a Brigadier for the last twelve months – stood with his wife in the nursery looking down at their son, who had just had his bath and last cup of milk and refused to settle down in his cot for the night.

'You don't know how lucky you are, my dear fellow,' Boyd addressed the small boy who was kicking his legs together, throwing off fleecy blankets as quickly as his mother put them over him. He gurgled with laughter up at his parents. 'I'd give anything to be able to lie on a soft pillow like yours and have a bit of shut-eye. I'm worn out. Aren't you?'

Giles Boyd Mansell laughed some more and, seizing a bar of the cot, hoisted himself up and grinned at his father.

Veronica looked with immense pride at her son. He was so beautiful. She was enraptured with those fine dimpled limbs in the white sleeping-suit; at the rosy face crowned with silky brown curls; the laughing blue eyes with lashes as long and thick as her own. He was going to be devastating when he grew up, she thought. As fine, as charming, as his father. But he was an imp of mischief and she was tired, and it was about time the Chip settled down for the night. Boyd had to go off early in the morning. She wanted to settle down to a nice quiet evening with him. She hoped none of those horrid officers would ring him up and worry him. He never seemed to be away from his job even when he got back to the flat. But she was so proud of him. It was rather marvellous Boyd being a Brigadier. Five years ago, when she had first met him coming from West Africa, he had been only a Captain. He had done very well in this war.

Veronica put her son down and covered him up again.

'Now, my Chip ... you've *got* to go to sleep or you'll be in disgrace. Mummy will be angry. Good night, darling... Not another sound. Here, take Woggle; he wants to go to sleep too.'

(Woggle was a dilapidated woolly lamb, so christened by the Chip himself.) He clasped Woggle, looked angelic and shut his eyes. Veronica took her husband's arm and drew him out of the darkened room which was sweet with the scent of talcum powder and all the familiar nursery odours.

In the drawing-room Veronica took off her overall, screwed it up in a roll and flung it on the sofa. She smoothed out her flowered cotton frock she was wearing and patted her hair.

'Ooh! I feel a wreck. It's warm in the flat this evening. Chumps, my sweet, what about a drink?'

'Couldn't want anything more,' said the Brigadier, and following his wife's example took off his tunic and rolled up his khaki sleeves. 'We mustn't miss the six o'clock news,' he added. 'It's been a great day in all our lives ... the beginning of liberation for Europe – and for better things in the life of that rascal of ours, my darling.'

Veronica seated herself on the arm of a chair, lit a much-needed cigarette and nodded. Boyd, lighting his pipe, looked at her. She really had improved remarkably since the birth of the boy, he thought. He had dreaded her having that child. Much as he wanted one, he had been full of fear in case something should go wrong with his Veronica. He had thought of her then as an ethereal, fragile creature who might break at a touch. But her doctor – and her mother – had both told him that childbirth in Veronica's case had been a blessing in more ways than one. From the hour that Giles made his appearance she had seemed to improve and thrive. Motherhood suited her. She had lost quite a bit of the 'ethereal' look. Her cheek-bones these days were not so pronounced. Her face was a little fuller, like her small figure. But she was still slim and exquisite, and looked younger than her age; and to the man who worshipped her, still very much a person to be adored. He had always adored ... but since she had become the mother of his son, his passionate love had deepened; nowadays he experienced the ultimate happiness with Veronica. And deep down within him he was immensely proud that this child – her only child – was *his* and not Charles Hallard's. Whatever Hallard had meant to

360

her, *he* had not given her a son. The coming of Giles had wiped away the last ounce of Boyd's jealousy of Veronica's first husband.

He walked into the next room and came back with two cocktails, which he set down on a table. Veronica was standing at the window looking down at the square. She turned to him and said:

'Darling, I've got such a funny feeling.'

Her eyes crinkled humorously at the corners in the way he always liked ... Chip had inherited it.

'What sort of funny feeling? Hope it's directed at me, anyhow, darling.'

She came up to him and put her arms around his waist. Immediately he laid down his pipe and clasped her close, leaning a cheek against her dark, cloudy hair.

'Veronica, my angel ... what is it?'

'I don't really know. I think it's been too momentous a day – with the invasion and then you phoning up to say you've got to go away all of a sudden ... and fixing to go down to Chidding... I feel just a bit hectic tonight.'

'Darling...' he murmured, in a soothing voice, and stroked her white graceful neck, then dropped a kiss on it.

She raised her head and looked at him with the big grey eyes which were seldom sad these days.

'I never like you leaving me, Chumps.'

'I loathe leaving you, darling. But it's this ruddy war. It upsets all our lives.'

She smiled and pulled at his tie.

'I'm a poor soldier's wife, really. I never get used to sudden upheavals and separations.'

'You will before I've been in the Army much longer, sweetheart,' he said with a short laugh. 'Can you manage to get down to Chidding quite well by yourself with the Chip and Winston? By the way – where is our noble hound?'

'Eating his supper in the kitchen. Mrs Taylor loves feeding him. He's getting a horrible fat tum.'

'Won't Mrs Taylor take you down to Chidding?'

'She's not really any good, Chumps. She's always full of aches and pains and has a married daughter in Clapham who wants to see her whenever she gets off and she hates leaving London. I'm not even going to ask her. No ... I can manage. She can come to Victoria with me and hold Chips while I get the tickets, and put me on the train. *Madre* is sending a taxi to meet us at Horsham.'

Boyd sighed and released Veronica.

'Oh lord, I remember the days when Scott and the Rolls met one in comfort. The good old days. Sorry you couldn't have been my wife then, darling. You seem to have come in for all the hardships with me.'

'Darling Chumps, it's the war's fault, not yours. And I consider I'm having a very lucky war, really.'

He suddenly gathered her into his arms again.

'You *are* happy these days, aren't you, darling?'

'Absolutely,' she said with truth, and stood on tiptoe and kissed his chin. 'We've had two lovely years together, Chumps darling.'

His heart swelled with content. He kissed her lingeringly, then let her go.

'Come and have your drink, darling,' he said. 'And tell me what you've been doing today.'

They sat together on the chesterfield, sipping their cocktails, arms around each other. Mrs Taylor let the dachshund into the room. Full of supper and *bonhomie*, licking his chops, Winston bounded up to his master and mistress, received little or no attention and retired to sulk on an armchair over which Veronica had spread a rug. She was careful of other people's furniture and this was a charming flat furnished in modern style. With the luxury of constant hot water and central heating, it was a real treat after the awfulness of the uncomfortable rooms in Camberley; of the dreadful little house they had rented after the Chip was born (in Newquay, where Boyd had been stationed) and later on the dreary hotel in Newcastle (that had been the worst of all) until that attack of sciatica had sent Boyd to hospital and Veronica back to her mother at Monks Rest. Since then had come the Woolwich posting and this flat. A glorious relief. But Veronica wondered how long she would enjoy it and how soon Brigadier Mansell would be moved again. She knew that she need not have any of these dreaded moves and discomforts in strange dwellings. She could always go to Monks Rest and stay there. But she did not want to be parted from Boyd. This husband of hers had grown very dear. And she did not think it fair that he should be deprived of seeing his son in all the fascinating stages of 'growing up'.

She told him what she remembered of the day. Walking in the park with Chip in the morning; having a tussle with him at lunch over his rice pudding; then a visit early this afternoon from Iris and Mervyn who were up on a week's holiday from their farm. Nothing much else.

There *had* been one more thing; but Veronica had no wish to relate it to her husband. This was unusual, because she always told Boyd every little thing. They had no secrets from each other, other than those concerning his job.

At tea-time, soon after the Williamses had left, there had been a somewhat unpleasant affair. Not actively, *openly* unpleasant, Veronica decided now, as she recalled it, but it had contained an under-current of something not too agreeable which had upset her afterwards.

She had returned from wheeling Chip down Sloane Street where she had done some shopping, to find Lettice Chaddon here.

It had given Veronica a shock. She had not seen Lettice since they parted at Liverpool five years ago. She had not communicated with her either, since Lettice had written to say that Chaddy was home and wanted to see her, and Veronica – shying at that time from reopening a deep wound – had manœuvred herself out of the meeting.

Lettice Chaddon looked older and decidedly 'haggish', as badly turned out as ever and more inquisitive, if possible. She greeted Veronica with effusion. She had said:

'I've always longed to get in touch with you, my dear, but somehow our ways never met. Then I saw the announcement of your second marriage in the papers, and Chaddy and I both meant to write but you know what poor correspondents we are. Then I happened to be in town today and I thought... "Now I wonder how little Veronica Hallard is... I must see her..."'

Veronica had not heard the name 'Hallard'

for so long that it had been like a douche of cold water flung in her face. She had said, coldly:

'How did you find me?'

'Chaddy and I are staying at the R.A.C. Club and we met a friend of Chaddy's – such a coincidence – he's a General and we asked him if he knew a Gunner man named Mansell and he did, quite well, and said he was a member of the same club ... the "Rag", isn't it? So we got on to the "Rag" and they gave us Brigadier Mansell's home address. I should have phoned but hadn't time, so here I am...'

Lettice had gone on chattering in her twittering fashion for half an hour. Veronica – remembering how kind she had been in Lagos and during that painful voyage home – got Mrs Taylor to make her some tea and let her talk. But it had seemed strange and rather depressing to meet this woman again after all these years. Time rolled back in the queerest way; she might have been in the Chaddons' bungalow ... listening to that familiar voice ... seeing that angular, badly dressed figure, the nutcracker profile, the bright prying eyes. Lettice hadn't really changed. She still spoke disparagingly of 'old Chaddy' and said she was bored with home life these days and only happy when she was at her job ... driving her mobile canteen. And so on...

Then she had been introduced to the Chip and gone into raptures. 'Such a be-eautiful boy,' she had said, then added: Goodness, how queer to see *you* as a mother! And you look so well and happy, my dear. Your second marriage is turning out a big success, isn't it?'

Veronica, thinking things over now as she sat with Boyd, wondered whether she had not been fanciful and read a slight note of reproach into Mrs Chaddon's voice which had not really been there. The woman, eyeing Veronica curiously had added:

'I can't sort of imagine you as anything but Mrs Hallard, you know. I suppose it's only natural ... knowing you as we did in Lagos, with poor Charles, and not having seen you since.'

Nothing unkind, really. Just tactless. But it had sent a queer flame of anger and indignation through Veronica. She did not want Lettice Chaddon to come here and remind her of the past and to utter that name 'Charles' in this flat. Boyd's home... The ghost of Charles had been laid. Her last agony of longing for him had been healed by her small son's tiny fingers. She never really thought about Charles these days. Boyd and little Chip filled her life.

Yet when she looked at and listened to Lettice she was dragged back ... back to Lagos ... to the drenching heat ... the thick, green vegetation ... the grinning black face of the boy, Nicholas ... the slender, graceful figure of Charles ... the sound of haunting music ... *Veronica's Concerto* ... filling the bungalow with its unforgettable melody. *Unforgettable, like Charles.* But she had wanted to forget ... hoped to die and be born again in her new marriage ... in her little son. She had been filled with resentment against Mrs Chaddon for coming here ... bringing with her all the old nostalgia ... reviving dead griefs.

She had said, almost rudely:

'You must forgive me ... it's Chip's bedtime and ... my husband will be home any moment...'

Lettice had looked disappointed. Possibly she had wanted to satisfy her curiosity further and stay and meet Veronica's second husband. But Veronica did not ask her to stay. For a few moments after she left Veronica had sat motionless, watching Chip crawl over the floor ... playing with the dachshund. She had felt quite upset ... yes, as though Lettice Chaddon's words had reproached her for infidelity.

Yet hundreds of war-widows of her age (and much older) married again. Nobody thought anything of it. It was natural and right.

Suddenly she had picked up the laughing chubby form of her son and pressed him fiercely to her breast.

'Darling,' she had whispered. 'Darling Chip.'

Her eyelids had pricked with hot tears. She had found herself, for the first time for two years, uttering a voiceless cry to Charles.

'*You* would approve ... you would like my little boy, wouldn't you? You don't mind ... don't blame me ... do you, Charles?'

Boyd Mansell glanced at his wife.

'Penny for your thoughts, sweet one.'

She flushed and her lashes dropped. She picked up one of his hands and put it against her cheek.

'Nothing, darling. Nothing,' she said.

And she told herself as she sat there in this charming room, drinking and smoking with Boyd, that she had been a bit of an idiot this afternoon. Lettice had meant nothing ... nothing at all. The sooner she forgot the whole incident – the better.


# 3


Lady Lowring had returned to Monks Rest.

She sat at the table in the dining-room sorting her letters somewhat lugubriously, her hat still on her head, her suitcases in the hall, still unpacked. She had just come back from her holiday in Windermere. She had enjoyed every moment of it. The late Sir Giles's sister, Alice, had a charming house there – and a maid. (Lady Lowring had appreciated the latter even more than the former.) Monks Rest was charming enough in June. The garden was at its best – full of heavenly roses. But no maid. Not even a 'char' at the moment. And living alone was rather sad after one had had a big house and family and so many friends.

Sighing, Lady Lowring read the latest letter from her daughter. Dear Veronica! She was happily settled these days. Bless that baby ... what a little darling *he* was ... she longed to see him again. Her one and only grandchild. Veronica and Boyd must come down and stay now she was back. There was nobody to do the cooking – but she could manage, somehow. It was such a joy to see Veronica so content, so well, and of course, thought Lady Lowring, that son-in-law of hers was quite perfect. She often felt a little guilty because she was *glad* poor Charles Hallard had never come back. But it would never have done; Veronica spending the rest of her life with that poor young musician. Now, as the wife of a Brigadier...

Lady Lowring abruptly interrupted her own thoughts. She would be Christian and think kindly of poor lost Charles ... if she must think of him at all!

She reread her daughter's letter. Veronica

was down at Chidding Manor. Boyd was away on a job. She counselled her mother to remain with Aunt Alice as long as she could. But Beatrice Lowring was not one to outstay her welcome and she had felt that she had stayed with dear Alice quite long enough. It was such a business having a guest these days; what with rationing and so on.

Lady Lowring looked through a few bills, then rose, sighing again. How stuffy the cottage was! She must open all the windows. There was plenty to be done; dusting, then some shopping. She would go down to the shops before they shut. It was now four o'clock. A good thing Alice had insisted on her bringing back some eggs. A boiled egg would do for her supper.

She looked out at the bird-bath. Bless that thrush shaking its wings in a cascade of silvery water. She doted on those birds. They were company. It was lonely here … without Veronica …without anyone … she almost wished they would insist on her taking evacuees, but she had only one spare bedroom and must keep that for her daughter, for Boyd and her adorable grandchild, when they wished to come down.

She heard a taxi scraping down the lane and walked out to the gate. Who was this? It could not be for her.

But the taxi stopped at the gates of Monks

Rest. Lady Lowring fixed her horn-rims firmly on the bridge of her nose and stared. She hoped it was not an uninvited guest, who would be unwelcome, lonely though she was. She was dead tired after the long tiring journey from the Lakes. She had started out at the crack of dawn. She meant to have a good rest.

A man got out of the taxi. Lady Lowring, short-sighted, could not see his face plainly. She did not know him. He looked elderly. He had white hair, carried a stick and stooped badly. He took a small suitcase out of the taxi. She felt indignant. A strange man arriving at Monks Rest! What was he thinking of? Then a voice which she *knew,* said:

'Lady L. Don't you know me? No ... I daresay you don't. I've changed out of all recognition, haven't I?'

Lady Lowring felt her spine creep. She stiffened in every limb and then began to tremble. She peered through her glasses. *Who was this man?* She knew the voice. *Dear God! She knew the face.* It was white, cadaverous, changed, with dark hollow eyes.

*But it was the face of Charles Hallard.*

Lady Lowring swayed. She felt an arm grip hers.

'Hold up ... sorry if I've scared you,' said the Voice.

She could not speak She could only

mouth at the apparition and stare. He guided her gently into the cottage and into the dining-room. She fell weakly into the chair from which she had only just risen. He said:

'Terribly sorry. I suppose ... you thought I was dead. Everybody must have thought so. Is Veronica here?'

Then Lady Lowring found her voice. The blood came back into her cheeks but she did not stop shaking. She whispered:

'My God... Oh, my dear God!'

Charles Hallard looked down at her. Or was it the ghost of Charles Hallard? she asked herself affrightedly. She had been thinking of him. Yes, the sun had touched her. She was a little mad. But no ... she was sane. *It was he.*

She could see Charles more clearly now. The Charles who had married Veronica and been torpedoed ... four years ago. This was a much-changed man. He looked old with his white hair. (It used to be black.) And that tragic face ... heavens! What he must have suffered ... gone through...

'May I sit down?' he said. 'I am ... not very fit.'

She pointed with a trembling hand to the chair opposite her.

'Yes, yes, of course. You ... look ill. Can I ... get you some whisky? I keep a little ... for medicinal purposes ... it's hard to get now, you know…' she broke off, licking her lips. He smiled and shook his head.

'Nothing for me just now. Where is Veronica? I want to see her. You don't know how much I want to see her.'

That floored Lady Lowring and reduced her to a state of speechlessness again. She could only shake her head. Charles Hallard fixed her with a gaze which seemed to her terrible. A look so full of pain, of intense anxiety.

'Veronica … isn't dead, is she?' he spoke again.

Lady Lowring gasped.

'No … no … of course not.'

'Isn't she here with you?'

'No. She … she…' Lady Lowring gulped and covered her face with her hands. 'Oh heavens…' she added in a moaning voice. 'What are we all going to do?'

Charles Hallard said:

'Tell me. I must know.'

Lady Lowring wished a dozen things in that moment; all ridiculous things, of course. She wished this were a nightmare from which she could awaken herself; she wished that an earthquake would come and swallow up Monks Rest and herself and Charles Hallard, too. She wished Veronica had never married again. Never had a child (oh, heavens, that poor child … he was … *illegitimate*. Lady Lowring's blood froze at the thought. And Veronica, poor little Veronica, all unknowingly, had committed *bigamy).* She wished that Charles had gone to Chidding Manor and that Mrs Mansell, who was so tranquil and wise (Veronica said she always managed difficult situations with the utmost composure), were dealing with this ghastly *dénouement.* She wished anything but the thing that was happening to her, shattering her peace.

At length she raised her face and, taking off her glasses, drew a hand across her dazed eyes and looked at the man who sat opposite her, staring at her with such painful intensity. She said in a hoarse voice:

'My dear boy ... my dear boy ... we all thought you were dead. You were officially declared to be dead ... torpedoed on your way home. It's ... it's unbelievable. *After four years.* Charles, where have you been?'

'Please tell me about Veronica first,' he said.

Beatrice Lowring swallowed hard.

'I ... I'm afraid ... it will grieve you, Charles... But my dear boy, you can't blame Victoria ... she waited for two years ... and...'

Her voice trailed away. Charles Hallard's white emaciated face had flushed crimson, then whitened again. He winced as though he had received a blow. Then he recovered. He said:

'I think I understand. She has ... married again?'

'Yes,' whispered Lady Lowring.

Silence. Lady Lowring could remember no more awful silence. As she wrote to Alice, her sister-in-law, later on, it was a *hellish* moment ... for both of them. She had received a terrible shock, seeing Charles Hallard appear like this, in the flesh ... back from the dead. And no doubt he was equally brutally shocked by the news she gave him. Although he said at once that he did not blame Veronica.

'How could I blame her?' he said in a hollow voice. 'I was supposed to have drowned. Better that I had. I realise that now. Far, far better.'

Lady Lowring began to weep quietly, a handkerchief pressed to her lips. She was besieged by all the most dreadful thoughts about Veronica and Boyd and their child ... and this man. None of her thoughts would straighten itself out. She could only sit there, cry ... and although she had never borne Charles any particular love, she had once accepted him as a son-in-law and been mildly fond of him. Giles had liked him. Veronica had *worshipped* him. It was dreadful ... for he had always adored his wife... To come back and find her married to another man. He looked so ill, so old .... the *poor* fellow...

Charles said:

'Please tell me everything. Whom did she marry? When? Where is she?'

Lady Lowring told him what he wished to know. He listened quietly then nodded.

'I see. I know who you mean. She met this fellow Mansell on the boat coming home, I remember. He was kind to her. She wrote and told me.'

'Charles ... oh, Charles, my dear boy ... they have ... they have a child ... a son.'

He sat still. His face might have been carved from marble. He was an effigy of bitter sorrow, of despair. He said:

'Veronica has a *son*? Not mine? The other chap's?'

'Yes,' said Lady Lowring, wiping her eyes.

Charles Hallard stood up and turned his back to her. A bent back. The back of a man in physical as well as mental pain. His voice came thickly.

'What a damned thing!... What a damned thing!'

Lady Lowring looked anxiously through her tears at that back.

'Charles, she waited for two years. She suffered terribly thinking you had died. You know how she loved you. She nearly went out of her mind when the news first came through. You can ask the doctors ... she went into a nursing home ... almost a mental case. We were all afraid for her reason. Charles ... she did not get over it for two whole years. Boyd waited for her ... and finally she married him.'

Charles turned round.

'I believe you,' he said. 'I know that Veronica loved me.'

'Oh, she did, she did.'

'Two years is a long time. Four years is twice as long,' said Charles bitterly. 'In her mind I have been dead all that time. Oh, don't make any mistake. I understand. And does she ... is she ... very fond of this fellow?'

'Yes, very. They are ... devoted,' said Lady Lowring, wishing once more that the ground would open and swallow them up.

'He is a decent fellow, I believe.'

'One of the best. A ... a Brigadier...' said Lady Lowring, with a pathetic reversion to her natural snobbishness.

Charles Hallard's worn, suffering face broke into the faintest smile.

'A Brigadier. So he's done a good job in this war. As for me...'

'Oh, Charles, poor fellow, where have you been? For heaven's sake tell me ... tell me what it all means,' said Beatrice Lowring, unable to stem her tears. She was sobbing now.

'Don't cry, Lady L.,' said Charles. (How strange that sounded to her. He always used to call her 'Lady L.' in that half-teasing,

378

half-affectionate way.)

She hiccoughed into her handkerchief.

'It is so dreadful ... for you ... for us all. What will my poor girl say? It will be a *terrible* shock to her...'

'Yes,' said Charles. 'As it has been to me. Worse for her, perhaps. To know that she is not really married to the father of her child.'

Lady Lowring positively shuddered. Charles saw the movement and added, quickly:

'Don't worry. She soon will be. Poor little darling. She won't be troubled long with me. I'm a dying man. I've only come back to die. It was a mistake ... coming back at all. If I'd known ... abut her second marriage ... I'd have stayed away. But I knew nothing. I had to see her again. *I had to...*' He broke off, his voice rasping with pain.

Lady Lowring sniffed and wiped her tears.

'Oh, Charles, why did you say you are dying?' (She inwardly besought God to forgive her for the wild hope that sprang to life within her at the poor man's words.) 'Where have you been?'

'If you don't mind,' he said, after a pause, 'I'll accept that offer you made of a strong drink ... first of all. And a cigarette. I ... feel pretty groggy. I must apologize, too, for not warning you that I was coming, Lady L. But I telephoned several times this morning and there was no reply.'

'No. I've been away. I have only just come back.'

'The operator thought you might be away, but I had to come down to try and trace you. I had no other means of finding Veronica. I tried the Williamses' old flat, but they left years back and nobody could give me their address.'

Lady Lowring got up slowly and with difficulty. She was not young and her heart was not too good. This shock had taken it out of her, she thought. She felt suddenly an old feeble lady.

'I must find the key of my cupboard,' she mumbled. 'I must get you that whisky, Charles.'

She moved into the hall, and saw as through a mist an oil-painting of her late husband. She looked at the kindly intelligent face and thought:

'What would Giles have done about this? Oh, if only I had him here now … to help … to advise me…'

In the dining-room, with the June sun streaming through the casements, Charles Hallard sat waiting for his drink, his eyes looking out towards the spire of the little church. In that church, over five years ago, he had been married to Veronica Lowring. In that big Georgian house, Whitelands Hall, close by, their reception had been held. He could see it all as plainly as though it were yesterday! His small, exquisite bride in her creamy satin dress, her lace veil, her large grey eyes shining starrily at him. He could feel the touch of her hand, hear the sound of her soft voice; remember the golden rapture of their shared passionate love for each other. She had been all his. And she had said it was 'for ever'.

*For ever.* And today she was another man's wife.

He groaned and put his face in his hands.

Why had he come back? Why had Fate allowed him to live; live through the strangest of experiences; pass through one small hell after another ... only to come out the other side and find this bitter loss and pain?

'"*Until death us do part.*"' Charles Hallard repeated aloud the words of the marriage service. 'Of course ... she was faithful to me until she thought me dead, and long after. It isn't her fault that I have come back.'

He felt slow, hot tears trickling through his fingers; fingers painfully thin and transparent, like those of an old man.

Lady Lowring came back with the whisky and gave it to him.

'Drink this, Charles. Drink it all up, my poor boy, and tell me everything,' she said.

He wiped his face, drank the stimulant, then sat brooding in a heavy bitter silence for a while. Lady Lowring sat beside him looking at him with amazed and stricken eyes.

She could not stop thinking of Veronica and Boyd; of what this thing would mean to them.

Then Charles Hallard began to unfold to her the story of the last four years ... of the incredible adventures that had befallen him since the hour that the liner bringing him back from Lagos had been sunk.

# 4

Listening to Charles Hallard's story was to Beatrice Lowring like hearing the account of a fantastic dream; or reading the pages of a thriller. It sounded anything but the truth. Yet she knew the saying that 'truth is stranger than fiction'. Here it was ... actual fact. A history of illness, of lost memory, of mistaken identity; many strange things rolled in one, shadowed by grief and suffering and resolving finally ... into *this*. The end which to Charles was grief and loss more poignant than the loss of his own life.

It were better that he had died.

On that morning when the ship coming from the West Coast had been struck by a torpedo, Charles Hallard was, like the rest of the passengers, asleep. Following the explosion which rocked the ship from bow to stern, he had time only to put an overcoat over his pyjamas and rush up on deck.

He recounted briefly the awful tale of the last moments on board the sinking ship; the agonized rush for boats; the struggle for life in calm waters during that cruel and radiant dawn; and the brutal machine-gunning of the survivors by a ruthless enemy.

He, Charles Hallard, and a man whom he knew only by sight (a British officer returning from Accra; he had thrown on his khaki tunic and trousers), clung to a lifebelt. They were near the submarine, which had surfaced, and both expected death at any moment. The officer had already received a bullet in the shoulder and was being supported by Charles, himself not a strong swimmer. As they came within speaking distance of the submarine, Charles saw a face he knew ... the face of an officer on the U-boat. It was a young man who had studied music with him in Dresden. He called out the man's name and spoke to him in German. The young man was captain of the U-boat; less bloodthirsty than his companions. He gave the order to cease fire and took Charles and the officer on board. The U-boat moved on.

That night the British officer died. Charles who had seen him only once or twice in the bar on board ship did not even know his name. There was nothing in his tunic pockets to identify him. The uniform was dried and given to Charles to wear. The U-boat commander who had spared his life was not disposed to grant him further favours, but told him he must be taken to internment in Germany. But first the U-boat under orders was making for a certain base in Norway.

It was off Trondheim that the U-boat, which had surfaced, was in turn attacked by an R.A.F. bomber, and sunk. The ship in which Charles had sailed was avenged. But this time Charles did not come off so well. He was wounded in the head and flung into the water. He remembered, he told Lady Lowring, little beyond the fact that his German friend struggled in the water with him. What happened after that he did not know. *He did not know for four long years.* But the story as he told it now was this: he was picked up by a fishing-boat which was under German control and which found him lying on a raft with the U-boat commander. The latter had died, after receiving a fatal shot from the R.A.F. bomber. Charles was unconscious, but the German had apparently lived long enough to assist Charles on to the raft. The man had twice repaid the debt of friendship which they had shared in the days when music was sweeter far to his ears than the blast of battle.

Charles survived and was taken to a prison camp in Norway. Still wearing the khaki uniform, he was presumed to be a British officer. But he had no name and remembered nothing whatsoever of his past. He lay in hospital seriously ill for six months. During that time the Nazi authorities made enquiries which proved abortive. Nobody knew where he had come from or how he came to be on that raft with the German submarine officer. It remained an impenetrable mystery.

Charles Hallard ceased to exist. They gave him a new name in the prison hospital. The name of George Smith, after the King of England; Smith because it was the most common English name. There were two 'pips' on the shoulder of his tunic. Lieut. George Smith, he became. Later, the doctor said, he might recover his memory. Until then … everything that had happened to him in the past was a blank.

Of the years that followed this strange tragedy Charles Hallard remembered hazily. After he recovered he was removed to a German prison camp, from which he eventually escaped, only to be recaptured and put in a worse place where he was half starved and reduced to a poor state of health. It was there that his hair turned snow-white and he contracted the stomach trouble which had now become inoperable; a fatal malady.

But Lieut. George Smith had not yet finished with life. He escaped for the second time, successfully. Speaking fluent German, he managed to get over the border and eventually found himself in Poland. From Poland after a series of incredible adventures, he reached Russia and, still remembering nothing of his past, joined the Russian Army.

That was a year ago. He fought with Soviet troops until his failing health put an end to his activities. The convalescent home in which the Russian doctors were attempting to restore the unknown 'British officer' to health and strength was the victim of an air attack by the Luftwaffe during a German retreat. That bomb destroyed the home and 'George Smith' was injured for the third time. But this time, although the injury was slight, the consequences were momentous. Something in Lieut. George Smith's brain snapped. The mists cleared away; the strange fancies and phantoms which for years had pursued him but never became clarified were clear at last. *He knew who he was.* Bit by bit he began to remember... Veronica, his wife, his old life in Lagos ... everything up to the hour that he was wounded in the head when the U-boat sank.

The effect on Charles Hallard was to fill him with mingled joy and horror. For four years he had been living as another man. *What, meanwhile, had happened to his beloved Veronica?* What indeed? For a time he was too weak and ill to attempt to communicate with her. As soon as he was well enough, by courtesy of the Soviet Government he was flown back to England in an American bomber which had refuelled in Moscow and was on its way to England.

'I came back in that plane more dead than alive,' Charles Hallard told the woman who was his mother-in-law. 'I know from what the doctors all said in Russia that I have not long to live. But I had to come ... to see my Veronica ... if only once again. They brought me to London. I had to make a report to the authorities and explain my reappearance as Charles Hallard. Then I telephoned to you ... and came straight down here.'

Lady Lowring did not speak for some time after Charles had finished his long, painful story. When she looked at him her eyes were full of tears. She laid a hand on his thin bowed shoulder.

'My poor Charles,' she said. 'My poor old boy. It's a terrible tragedy ... terrible... I don't know what to say ... or do!'

He gave a ghost of a smile.

'Nothing much to be done, is there, Lady L.? It would really have been better if I had stayed as George Smith ... and died as George Smith. But once my memory returned, I could not keep away from England – and Veronica. Between the time – and it wasn't very long – that the convalescent home in Russia was smashed up, and my

387

flight back here – I thought of nothing but the hour in which I should see her again. Somehow it never struck me that I would find her married again, yet I might have known ... it has been so long ... and she was so ... very lovely and young...'

His voice trailed away. He sat bowed, mute, looking so ill, thought Lady Lowring, that she wondered, indeed, if poor Charles would live even now to see Veronica. Her mind whirled.

'I must telephone Chidding Manor... I must tell Mrs Mansell to break it to Veronica ... she must come ... whatever happens in the future ... she must come home at once...'

She knew that death had set its mark on Charles Hallard. He had been through too much. He could not live.

She stood up and said:

'Charles, you must stay with me here for the moment, anyhow. You must see my doctor. You...'

'I am incurable,' he broke in. 'Nothing can be done for me, Lady L.'

'Oh you never know,' she said with forced brightness. 'Come along ... up to ... to the spare room. You must go to bed now. You look very tired. I shall get you some supper. I will telephone Veronica. She must know about this at once.'

'I feel almost as though I ought to disappear again... I shall only cause her unnecessary suffering,' he said in a weary, bitter voice.

'Oh, no ... you can't disappear ... she must know. It ... it alters her position with Boyd ... it is all ... most awkward...' stammered Lady Lowring.

He smiled at that word. *'Awkward.'* What a funny conventional little light to throw upon this major tragedy. So typical of dear old Lady L.

He was too tired to argue further. He said:

'I'll ... do whatever you think best...'

But he thought:

'Oh, Veronica ... my *darling*...'

Lady Lowring left him alone for a moment. She must go upstairs – get out sheets – make up a bed for Charles. Heavens, how ghastly he looked! Whatever he said, he must see the doctor and at once.

Charles Hallard sat still for a long time, gathering strength. Then he rose, and walked, leaning on his stick, into the drawing-room.

'I wonder if Veronica still plays her piano and sings,' he thought apathetically.

He saw no piano, only the spinet in the charming little room which was hot and stuffy, after being closed up so long.

Then he noticed a photograph on the spinet. He picked it up and studied it with eager pain-filled eyes. It was Veronica with a baby in her arms. It had been taken when her son was three months old.

Incredulously the man stared at it ... examining every detail hungrily. She had changed, of course; this was not the thin ethereal Veronica who had left him in Lagos. It was a Veronica with a round face; a glowing, healthy-looking girl. She held her baby in her arms, her cheeks pressed to the baby's. A charming maternal picture.

To Charles Hallard it was unbelievable ... as fantastic as his own story. *His* Veronica ... with another man's child in her arms. She looked so well, so happy. *She had forgotten him.*

He laid the photograph down. He was shaking from head to foot; cold despite the June sunlight that streamed through the dusty casements. He felt a gnawing pain in his side. A pain that was always there.

But the pain in his heart at this moment, his feelings of bitter jealousy and resentment, were so fierce – so hot – that they swamped all other feelings and overcame him. He sank down on to the nearest chair. His stick fell on the floor. He groaned aloud:

'Veronica ... oh, God ... why didn't I die? Why was I allowed to live ... for *this*...?'

Lady Lowring heard the stick clatter. Fearing that Charles had fainted, she came running down to him. With difficulty she tried to comfort him. But it was all so impossible, so complicated. She was stricken with a sense of her own impotence to say one word that could possibly console this unhappy man.

She managed to get him upstairs to bed. That was the first thing. Then she telephoned for her doctor. And now ... to get on to Chidding Manor ... she must deliver this crushing blow to Veronica, through her mother-in-law. Mrs Mansell must be told first and must break it gently to the girl.

'My poor Veronica,' thought Lady Lowring, and shuddered at the thought of what would happen next. 'My poor girl who is still the wife of that unfortunate man upstairs ... what in God's name will she do? What will Boyd Mansell do?'

And at the memory of the little laughing-eyed boy who no longer had legal right to the name of Mansell, Lady Lowring's blood seemed to turn to water. She hardly had strength to lift the telephone receiver to her ear and ask for Chidding 151.

## 5

It was Mrs Mansell's birthday. She was sixty-five and – as she told the family – felt it, these days, but they could not let her get away with that. She looked so young still with her beautiful blue eyes, delicate pink and white complexion, and a figure still as slender as a girl's.

She was celebrating this particular birthday in the way that pleased her most. Amongst her children. Boyd had come back from his course and joined Veronica and the boy for forty-eight hours leave; Audrey was already here, and darling Gilly and John had managed to come down for the night. The Manor was packed. There was nobody to help with cooking or housework, but nobody minded. Everybody was happy and there were terrific secret preparations going on in the nursery for Granny's birthday party. The twins were making her 'something special'. Audrey had made a cake and iced it this morning. Every one had saved sugar for it. John had his car here and had gone off early with Gilly into Horsham to 'shop'. Veronica, after putting the Chip to sleep in little Patricia's pram, was 'doing the flowers'.

It was a lovely day. The last week in June. Veronica had been here nearly a fortnight. She had meant to go back to Lowndes Square before now, but a new danger had befallen Londoners. The pilotless 'plane was disturbing the peace and Boyd would not let her and his small son take any risks. They must stay at Chidding for the moment. True, there were these horrible flying bombs over the South Coast and Chidding was by no means a 'safe area', but much safer than London.

They had all discussed the affair at breakfast this morning and Mrs Mansell had begged Veronica to do as Boyd asked and keep little Chip down here. She had protested that she could not stay away from Boyd. Gilly was going back with John. But, Mrs Mansell reminded her, Gilly was not a mother. There was that precious little boy to be considered. Veronica knew that they were all right ... she ought not to expose the Chip to danger. But she felt deeply depressed at the idea of being separated from her husband.

It was spoiling the birthday party for her.

Boyd saw that she was depressed. He did all he could to cheer her up. The flying bombs would soon be stopped, he said; the anti-aircraft were already getting their measure; she would soon be able to return to London. But Veronica remained depressed.

'I can't bear living apart from you, darling,' she said.

Brigadier Mansell looked pleased, and *was* pleased. The very last thing he personally wished was to be in London without Veronica, but he remained adamant.

'I don't want you or our boy to take any risks, my darling,' he said firmly.

Most of the family were in their bed-rooms, putting the younger generation to bed, or changing for Mrs Mansell's dinner-party when the telephone call came through from Princes Risborough.

Mrs Mansell imagined (when Audrey, who had answered the call, told her where it was from) that Lady Lowring had been kind enough to ring her up and wish her many happy returns of the day. She knew that Veronica expected her mother to be back at the cottage tonight. She answered brightly:

'Hello, how are you, Lady Lowring?'

Then, when she heard Veronica's mother's strained, unfamiliar voice she was at once apprehensive. She closed the library door and sat down to take the call.

'Yes,' she said anxiously. 'Yes, Lady Low-ring. I am quite alone. No ... Veronica isn't near ... oh, what is it, my dear?'

It was a long call. They were cut off after six minutes, but Mrs Mansell did not move from the telephone. Lady Lowring was putting another call through at once. Violet Mansell sat rigid, white to the lips, her eyes full of horror. And while she waited for the second call, she prayed ... as always, in trouble she flew to the refuge of prayer.

'Oh God,' she said under her breath. 'Oh God, be merciful to my poor son ... to my grandson ... be merciful!'

The telephone bell rang again.

It was Gilly, in a dressing-gown, just out of the bathroom, who eventually had a feeling that all was not well and came down to the library. She had heard the two rings and knew that her mother had answered them. When Mrs Mansell did not return to her bedroom Gilly went in search of her.

She found her mother sitting by the telephone with a hand over her eyes. Gilly walked to her as fast as her slow legs would allow her.

'Mummy!' she said anxiously. 'Oh, Mummy, what is it? Have you had bad news? It isn't for Audrey ... it's not *Roger* ... is it?'

Mrs Mansell looked up at her daughter. She seemed dazed.

'No, darling,' she said. 'It's not ... Roger.'

Gilly sat down beside her mother and took one of the delicate, ringed hands.

'Tell me, dearest...'

Mrs Mansell's lips quivered. Her eyes filled with tears. The first tears Gilly remembered seeing in those brave blue eyes.

'Oh, Gilly,' Mrs Mansell said brokenly. 'It is terrible. *Terrible* ... I don't know what to do. God will help us ... but I don't know what to do just now. My poor Boyd ... my poor Veronica...'

Gilly stared.

'Chumps? Veronica? What's the matter with them? Chumps is upstairs singing in the bath, and Veronica–'

Mrs Mansell broke in.

'Call Boyd, Gilly. Tell him to come down at once. We must tell him before we breathe a word to Veronica.'

Gilly looked perplexedly at her mother. Never had she seen her tranquil mother so upset.

'Oh darling,' she said... *What is it?*'

Mrs Mansell in a trembling voice told her. Gilly stood still, a hand against her lips. Then she said:

'Oh, Mummy ... how ghastly!'

'Ghastly ... worse than that. For that poor fellow to have been alive all these years ... with loss of memory ... serving in the Russian Army ... believing himself to be another man altogether ... oh, the *poor* boy, Gilly. And then to come home and find his wife married again ... and with a child. It's the *child* that makes it so much worse. Do you realise what this means to poor little Giles?'

Gilly's face went scarlet.

'Oh, lord, Mummy ... you mean ... he isn't... Veronica and Chumps aren't really married; so the Chip...'

'Don't!' broke in Mrs Mansell, covering her face with her hands.

'It is nobody's fault ... nobody's ... it's just an appalling disaster, Gilly. And poor Veronica is so well and happy. What this will

396

do to her, let alone our poor Boyd, I dare not think.'

Gilly's sweet freckled face crumpled as though she were going to cry. She said:

'I must get my John ... John will help ... he always knows what's best to do.'

'My darling girl, there isn't much he can do. Veronica must be told and go at once to ... to Charles Hallard. Lady Lowring says he is a dying man.'

'Oh,' breathed Gilly. 'Then it ... it won't be for long?'

Mrs Mansell shook her head, her thoughts sad and confused.

'Call Boyd, darling,' she said.

Boyd Mansell came down into the library cheerfully, his tall body wrapped in a plaid silk dressing-gown, face glowing after his bath, bright brown hair ruffled like a boy's, pipe between his teeth. He grinned at his mother and sister, looking from one to the other.

'What's up, you two? You look pretty gloomy. Why, Mother, on your birthday, too? What's happened? One of your evacuees stolen the family jools?'

Mrs Mansell and Gilly exchanged glances helplessly. Both heavily burdened with their knowledge, hating to drive the good humour and happiness out of the man they loved so dearly. Mrs Mansell seemed unable to speak. Gilly came forward. She put a hand on her brother's shoulder.

'Chumps,' she said. 'You've got to prepare yourself for a shock, old boy.'

His smile faded. He took the pipe from his mouth. His mind leapt to all kinds of possibilities; bad news about Roger, his brother-in-law who was in Normandy; or James in Kenya; anything but the right thing. He said:

'What is it? What's happened?'

Then Gilly told him – exactly what her mother had heard from Lady Lowring. For a moment Boyd Mansell looked stunned. The healthy colour faded from his tanned face. In a flash, thought Gilly sadly, the boyishness vanished; he looked fully his age and more. He said:

'Good God!' Then again, incredulously: *'Good God!'*

Violet Mansell put a handkerchief to her lips.

'My poor Boyd,' she whispered. 'You didn't deserve this.'

Gilly hastily added:

'But it's only a temporary blow, Chumps. Lady Lowring told Mummy that … that Charles Hallard is desperately ill. So ill that he can't live. She … she has sent for Veronica. She must go to Princes Risborough at once.'

Boyd sat down heavily in a chair. His strong body was shaking. His mind was in turmoil. He stared at his sister and his mother, blue eyes dazed. At length he said hoarsely:

'Charles Hallard ... still *alive*. A case of lost memory ... of his living all this time under the name of George Smith? But, lord, how? ... why?... I don't understand the half of it. Tell me some more.'

'Oh, Chumps, we don't know any more,' said Gilly. 'Mummy says Lady Lowring sounded very confused and distressed over the phone and was cut off after six minutes and had to come through to Mummy again, and then Mummy says she told an incredible story about Charles Hallard's being saved by the commander of the U-boat that sank his ship ... and he was sunk again off Norway then taken to Germany, but eventually escaped to Russia... He had this head injury and did not remember for four years. Then he was bombed in Russia recently and his memory came back...'

'It all sounds fantastic,' broke in Boyd. 'It doesn't make sense...'

'But things like that do happen. Don't you remember that book *Random Harvest?*' said Gilly slowly. 'We saw the film in Horsham. That was all about a man who lost his memory and became someone else, but eventually regained his own personality.'

There was silence. Boyd stared at his pipe. His mind was whirling. He was conscious of two salient and desperate facts. The first that he had married Veronica bigamously. The second that his unfortunate little son was, by letter of law, illegitimate. Of course the law would do something about that ... in a case like this they wouldn't let the Chip suffer ... he had every right to the name of Mansell. Why, good heavens, Veronica had been fully entitled to marry again. According to the law, she had been a widow for two years before she did so Hallard had been *officially* declared dead. It was a damnable thing to have happened. *Damnable.*

Round and round whirled Boyd's thoughts ... fastening on this fact and that. Always they came back to the outstanding disaster of Veronica's remarriage and their child.

'Veronica isn't married to me at all ... do you realise that?' Boyd suddenly spoke aloud, looking at his mother and sister with stricken gaze. 'Oh, my God!'

Gilly swallowed.

'It ... it will be all right, old boy. Poor Charles is a dying man ... one oughtn't to want it ... but in the circumstances ... oh dear!' she broke off, not knowing what to say; what to do to bring the light of hope back into her cherished brother's eyes.

Boyd was thinking:

'Veronica adored Charles ... nearly went out of her mind when she thought he was dead. How will this affect her? She's been so happy with me ... with the kid. She's still his mother – whatever happens...'

Mrs Mansell interposed:

'Lady Lowring says the doctor told her after examining Charles Hallard that he can't last more than a few weeks, or even days, Boyd dear. He is a desperately sick man. He seems to have been through a dreadful time.'

'Poor chap,' said Boyd with a sudden, mirthless laugh. 'What must *he* feel ... finding Veronica married to me and with a child? What a grim situation!'

'Veronica must go at once, dear,' said his mother, eyeing him anxiously.

'Yes, I suppose she must,' said Boyd in a slow heavy tone.

But in that moment he experienced a reversion to the old deep jealousy that he had always had of Charles Hallard. Charles whom Veronica had loved so madly ... for whom she had broken her heart. That he should have come back ... perhaps to break that gentle heart again ... to disturb her newly-found peace ... was a terrible thing, a cruel whim of Fate. They had been so happy, he, Boyd and Veronica, with their son.

Boyd Mansell bowed his head. Then he spoke again.

'I must go up to Veronica,' he said. 'I must tell her. It's got to be got over ... the sooner the better ... and if this chap is really dying... She'll have to leave the boy with Audrey and you, Mother, and I'll take her to Monk's Rest at once.'

'Oh, dear, poor Mummy's dinner-party,' said Gilly in a forlorn voice.

'My party doesn't matter now, dear,' said Mrs Mansell with a sigh.

And indeed, it did not. Mrs Mansell sat silently weeping not for herself but for her son as he turned and walked out of the library and upstairs.

Veronica had just finished 'doing her face' when Boyd walked into their room. She had put on one of Boyd's favourite dresses; a long black skirt with a crisp white piqué blouse which had wide shoulders and lapels. In it she looked slender and sophisticated. The girls were all wearing long frocks tonight in honour of the *Madre's* birthday party. Veronica's hair, glossy, rich dark brown, weaved back from her small, heart-shaped face, and was caught with a small diamond star at one side. A tanned, gay face with grey eyes full of happiness as she turned to smile at Boyd. She unclipped the little transparent rubber cape she had been wearing while she finished making-up and flung it on the bed.

'All complete save for my lipstick. How about a lovely kiss for Veronica before she puts on the rouge?' she said gaily and lifted her glowing face to his.

Something in Boyd Mansell's heart seemed to break at that moment. Of all the difficult tasks allotted to him in life this was the most difficult and painful. To have to break that shattering news to her ... to wipe the radiance from those sweet grey eyes ... to plunge her into the old cauldron of suffering, and this time so much worse because of the endless complications.

Helplessly he stood looking down at her, not even daring to kiss that upturned mouth. She said:

'Hurry up, darling! Where's my kiss? Then you must peep at the Chip. He's been divine and gone straight to sleep. I told him if he was very good tonight it would make Granny happy on her birthday and I do believe he understood...'

Veronica's voice trailed away. She noticed suddenly the strange look on Boyd's face, the despair in his eyes. She jumped to her feet, her sensitive face changing colour.

'Darling, what's happened?' she asked quickly.

He said:

'Veronica, my darling, something very terrible. Something which is going to shock you beyond words and make a terrible difference ... to both of us. Darling, you *must* be brave...'

She stared at him, frightened. His expression, his grave words, alarmed her inexpressibly. It was so unlike Boyd to panic, to take a grave view of anything. He was such an incurable optimist. What on earth could have happened?

He pushed her gently into her chair. Then he drew a chair up beside her. He felt in that moment a hot and biter resentment against the destiny which had brought this calamity into their lives. She was so sweet, so gentle, so *good*. No man had ever had a better wife, nor any child a better mother, than Veronica. It was *criminal* that she must be hurt all over again; criminal that their son should have to suffer, too. Of himself and his own position now that Charles had come back to life he dared not begin to think. But already he was an 'outsider', he reflected bitterly... Veronica was no longer his wife. She was once again Mrs Charles Hallard.

He put an arm round Veronica. With all the tenderness in his nature, he held and kissed her anxious face. Then he told her the facts. Somehow he managed to get out the difficult words. He told her all that he knew ... which was not much ... of the remarkable story of her first husband's disappearance ... his amazing experiences.

She listened in stupefied silence. For a moment Veronica found it hard to grasp it all – to believe that Charles had come back. *Charles* whom she had mourned as dead for so long, whom she had loved so passionately. Then she thought of the baby boy who was her most precious possession and she went white and gasped a little. Her heart began to pound. The palms of her hands felt suddenly damp. She clung to Boyd's arm, pressing her cheek against his shoulder.

'Boyd,' she said in a breathless voice. 'Oh, Boyd, how *awful!*'

He set his teeth.

'Yes, I know, darling,' he said. 'I know.'

'I can't believe it,' she said. 'I *can't*...'

'It's true, darling.'

She looked dazedly at him.

'Charles *alive* ... after all these years. Tell me ... everything again ... for heaven's sake.'

He told her, patiently. She listened, hanging on every word, her face gradually flushing to a deep crimson, her breath quickening. He could feel her whole body shaking. Then she said:

'My poor Charles ... oh, my *poor* Charles!'

That shook the man curiously. The possessive 'my' made him wince as though Veronica had hit him. He could not get used to the thought that she was no longer *his*. But wild horses would not have dragged from Boyd Mansell one word about his own misery in this hour. His first thought was for her. He had never quite forgotten that awful time in London when Veronica's reason had been on the verge of breaking; when she had in truth been a little crazy for a few hours,

405

and lain in his arms in that strange hotel, mistaking him for Charles Hallard. Did she still love her first husband? Were all these years between her and *him,* Boyd, to be wiped out by Hallard's dramatic return? Boyd sat dumb, bruised in spirit, waiting ... watching Veronica ... leaving her to make the next move. Slowly she disengaged herself from his supporting arm and stood up. She said:

'I must go ... to Monks Rest ... at once.'

'I'll take you down, darling,' he said quietly, and looked at his watch. 'We can catch a train up to London in about an hour. I'll get Gilly to phone up for a taxi and Audrey must make us a few sandwiches. We'll miss poor Mother's dinner party.'

Veronica moved towards her wardrobe and started to unhook her skirt. Her fingers trembled so that she could scarcely manage the task. Her mind was seething. Charles was alive and at Monks Rest with Mummy ... Charles ... *Charles* ... oh, it couldn't be true! She had thought of him as dead, lost to her for ever, for so long. She could not begin to think what the repercussions of this astounding resurrection would be. She only knew that Charles was alive and that she was going to see him again.

She said:

'Is ... was Mummy sure that Charles is ... dying?'

'I believe so … but honestly, darling,' said Boyd, 'I have no idea what is really fact and what isn't. It's all come to me third-hand. You'll have to wait until … until you see *him* … to find out the real truth.'

She dragged off the white piqué evening blouse and looked for a suit. Boyd took off his dressing-gown and hurried into his uniform.

Veronica's teeth were chattering. She was wild with excitement. It was as though the last four years had never been .She was back in 1940 … in the old days when she had been waiting so feverishly for Charles to get back from Lagos. How madly she had loved and wanted him then. Would she find him very changed? Did he love *her* as much as ever? Oh, he couldn't be dying. He could not have come through all that awfulness and reached England safely … only to die.

The sweat broke out on her forehead. She glanced at herself in her mirror and saw that her eyes looked huge and wild. Suddenly she took a grip on herself. Steady, she thought … steady, Veronica … don't get in a state. Charles is very ill and has been through hell. He will want you to help him. Keep calm now.

And then her gaze met Boyd's. He was looking at her with an expression of such intense sadness that it made her realise suddenly what this must mean to him. And

407

simultaneously her thoughts flew to the little boy who was blissfully sleeping in his cot next door. She was dragged back to a hopeless confusion of thought and emotion. Charles had come back. It was a miracle. But there was Boyd. She had been his wife for two years and she was the mother of his son.

She dropped the mirror. It fell on to the thick carpet without breaking. White and stricken, she ran across the room, half-dressed, threw herself into Boyd's arms and burst into a flood of tears.

## 6

Much later that night Veronica, scarcely knowing what name she should now bear – Hallard or Mansell – stood at the foot of the polished oak staircase in Monks Rest, with her mother. She was just about to go upstairs and see Charles for the first time. And now that it had actually come about ... this startling, unbelievable thing ... this moment which she had once wanted so madly ... this reunion which she had thought impossible on this earth ... she hesitated; a fit of sheer nerves threatened to destroy her. She trembled violently, clinging to the banisters for support, and looked at her mother with large scared eyes.

'Oh, Mummy,' she gasped. 'I can't get up those stairs. I know I can't.'

Lady Lowring put a firm hand on Veronica's shoulder.

'Now, darling,' she said. 'Don't give way. Charles is very ill and he will want all the help and comfort you can give him. I know this has been a dreadful shock for you, but steady, Veronica, there's my dear, brave girl.'

Veronica nodded dumbly. She looked upstairs with eyes that saw nothing. Her ears were strained as though to catch the first sound of Charles's voice.

Boyd had just left her here. Dear Boyd, who, as always in a critical hour, had been a source of strength and support. During the journey from Horsham he had refused to allow her to worry or fret unduly. He had held her hand firmly and kept telling her that things were going to be 'all right'.

She wished he were still here. Her kind, sensible husband. (No, he wasn't her husband now; she must remember that ... she conquered the desire to laugh, hysterically.)

But Boyd's position in this house with Charles here, too, was impossible. Veronica and Lady Lowring had both realised what he must be feeling, and respected his wish to get away as soon as he had handed Veronica over to her mother. He would stay at the 'Buckingham Arms' for the night, then take the first train up to London in the morning. He was due back at Woolwich tomorrow afternoon, anyhow. If Veronica wanted him she could get him at the flat. She had nothing to worry about, he assured her. Audrey and his mother had promised to take good care of the Chip. She must stay here now and see what she could do for the man who had just come back ... and later they would all meet and talk things over; see what was best to be done.

So now Veronica had bidden Boyd good night. They had kissed with deep affection, like a long-married couple. And he had driven away in the taxi that had brought them here.

It was dark and raining. The last day of June had ended in heavy cloud and a drizzle which had settled into this steady downfall. Monks Rest was quiet and peaceful and full of soft lamplight, but without its customary flowers. Lady Lowring had had no time to get into the garden. She had been much too busy looking after Charles, who seemed to have collapsed since his arrival. She had scrambled him two eggs and taken him up a tray. He had just finished his supper.

'He knows you are coming. He will have heard the car, so do go up, dear,' said Lady Lowring.

Veronica looked at her mother piteously and put a hand to her fast-throbbing heart.

'Mummy ... will I ... find him very

410

changed?' she asked in a whisper.

'Yes, very, dear. His hair is quite white. He has suffered terribly.'

Veronica licked lips that were dry and feverish.

'I ... this doesn't seem real. He's been ... dead to us ... for so long.'

'I know, darling. It is unbelievable. One of those things which do not happen often, thank God. I mean ... well, one is glad poor Charles did not die ... but it is all so *awkward* ... and now he is so desperately ill Dr Morgan says he hasn't a chance ... what with his heart and this internal trouble ... poor Charles.'

Veronica shook her head, still staring up the little curved staircase.

'I ... can't go up...' she whispered.

Then Lady Lowring made an error of judgement.

'Of course I'm sure it must be very difficult and even disagreeable for you, my dear child, when you are so devoted to dear Boyd...' she began.

But Veronica broke in, breathlessly.

'Oh, you don't understand, Mummy. It couldn't be disagreeable to me to know Charles is alive ... that he is upstairs ... waiting for me. It's terrible ... and wonderful. But I still love him, Mummy, I always did. I always will.'

'Oh, dear,' said Lady Lowring, who was

tired out mentally and physically. 'Then I don't know *what* is going to happen. But you *must* remember your little boy.'

Veronica did not answer. And now, for the first time since Giles had been born, the thought of her son did not particularly affect her. And the thought of Boyd, driving away from the cottage alone to the hotel, faded from her mind, too. Body, heart and soul were concentrated on the thought of the man whom she had once loved with a more than ordinary love. The man whose 'death' had broken her heart. She had recovered from that blow ... she had loved again ... married again. But what she felt for Boyd was not comparable with that other love. She knew, in this revealing moment, that *it would not stand comparison*. With Charles Hallard she had been one in spirit as well as flesh. He was her first love, her best love, beyond compare. Boyd had never really taken his place. He had a place of his own ... she had been able to give him passion and deepest respect and companionship. But with no other man on earth could things be as they had been *with Charles*. She had always known that deep down in her deepest heart.

Suddenly it was as though the years between them were dissolved. Like a miracle, Charles was being given back to her. She began to climb the stairs slowly, one by one, clinging to the oaken rail for support, her cheeks crimson, her eyes enormous and shining.

She opened the door of the spare room ... slowly and gently ... and entered.

For a moment she stood on the threshold transfixed, staring at the figure in the bed. A single lamp burned by the table and shed a soft glow on the man who lay languidly against the pillows, a book in his hands. Like one who sees a ghost, Veronica stared at her first husband and her dearest love.

Charles Hallard turned his head and looked at her. The book fell from his fingers. He gave a low cry.

'Nic...,' he said huskily. 'Nic, my love...'

It was almost more than she could bear .. the sound of that *name* which only *he* had ever used. It brought the past back more poignantly than anything else he could have done or said. It brought her to his side with a rush ... she fell down on to her knees by the bed and clutched at his hands, clinging to them frenziedly With tears pouring down her cheeks, she said:

'Charles ... Charles ... *Charles!*'

Her frantic gaze searched his face. Searched for the Charles she had known ... the familiar, beloved features ... and found him tragically altered. For this was no longer the face of the handsome boy she had left in Lagos four years ago. It was a mask of pain and weariness. The lamplight showed up the deep lines that had been carved by much suffering. Only the dark, brilliant eyes were the same, she thought ... but the faun's lips no longer smiled. They were pinched and morose. He was incredibly thin. But what struck at her heart most deeply was the changed hair ... snow-white ... the hair that had been so beautifully black. How crisply it used to spring back from his forehead; and now it was without life. This man in the bed was a shadow of that other Charles ... a sick, tragic shadow.

Veronica cried out aloud in an agony of spirit.

'My darling, my darling, what have they done to you: Oh, *Charles,* my dear, darling Charles...'

'Nic,' he said feebly, and threading his thin fingers through her hair looked wonderingly at the fresh beauty of her. How young she looked; how unutterably lovely ... like the radiant girl he had first met and married. She had not changed at all from that Veronica.

'Oh, my dear,' he said and sighed and could say no more. For ever since he had recovered his memory ... after that bombing incident in Russia ... he had dreamed of her like this ... dreamed of this hour when he could see her, hear her, touch her again.

She went on kneeling beside him, weeping

passionately, drenching his hands with her tears, kissing them.

'Charles … Charles…' She kept sobbing his name.

He felt a deep happiness well up in him because he knew, now, that whatever had happened to her during these years that she had been lost to him and he to her, she still loved him. And he knew bitterness too, because of the waste of it all; the futility of either their sorrow or their joy. He had come back here to die. He was well aware of the fact. It was hard … hard to find his lovely, adorable Veronica and then have to leave her again; this time knowing that he would never come back.

He whispered:

'My darling … darling little wife…'

She sobbed wildly:

'Why did this happen? Why didn't you come before, Charles? It has been so long, *too* long. I nearly died when I first heard you were dead. I couldn't bear it. Now it's too late. Charles, *Charles*, why did this happen?'

'I don't know,' he said. 'God only knows. It was a cruel thing. I lost my memory, darling … forgot that I was Charles … forgot you … everything that had ever happened to us. I've been living in another world, under another name.'

She checked her sobs and keeping his thin hand close to her breast, looked at him

415

through swollen lids.

'Charles, it is all very difficult to understand. I know no details.'

'I can't give you many, Nic,' he said with a faint smile. 'The whole damn thing is still very hazy. But it appears that I forgot completely that I was Charles Hallard and lived again as this fellow George Smith. They gave me that name when I was first taken to a hospital in Norway. I was wearing the uniform of some chap who was originally torpedoed with me and they took it for granted that I was he – an officer, a First Lieutenant. They could find no other identification. Nobody connected me with the sinking of the ship off the West Coast. I had travelled hundreds of miles in that U-boat with this German fellow, Egon Mühler, who was in Dresden with me. Then he and I were machine-gunned by the R.A.F...' Charles smiled again, wryly. 'They didn't realise they were aiming at one of their own countrymen. How could they? Well, from that point onward I was a prisoner in German hands. I was ill for months, then I escaped...'

He paused. Veronica saw that his forehead was wet. She began to realise how very ill he was. Stricken, she looked down at the transparent skin stretched over the fine bones of his face; the deeply sunken eyes. She said:

'Darling ... don't tell me any more ... forget about it. It must upset you ... to try and work it all out. It's such a fantastic tangle.'

'Yes, and what a lot of misery would have been spared us all if I'd had some kind of identity disc or letter on me. But I had nothing. There was no time to dress ... to do anything but swim for one's life once our ship was hit,' he said somberly.

'You must have had a dreadful time, my poor Charles.'

He passed a hand over his forehead.

'It was ... grim ... once I tried to escape. I was sent to a camp ... under a fiendish commandant. Some prison camps are good, but not *that* one. The food there was awful. I had no parcels. I developed this trouble while I was there...' he tapped his ribs, trying to grin at her. 'Not too good now, I'm afraid, my darling.'

She could only look at him dumbly. To hear that familiar voice calling her 'my darling' in that old, familiar way ... was incredible after these long years believing him to be dead. It was all unreal. She said:

'The main thing is that you did eventually recover your memory, Charles.'

'Funny thing,' he said reflectively. 'I passed through so many strange experiences first of all ... served with the Soviet Army ... a half-starved, sick fellow I was in those days

417

… without kith or kin … but they were good to me, and glad to let me join them. Then … in that convalescent home … the Nazis got a bomb close enough to blow us up. And I was hit for the third time, Veronica … in the head again.' He touched the back of his head gingerly. She saw, suddenly, a bare ugly criss-cross patch in the white hair. 'It's a wonder I've a head left,' he added. 'But it brought back the past. It was extraordinary. I woke up and asked for you. They said the first thing I called out was your name. *"Veronica"*. After that … I knew I was Charles Hallard. It all came back to me. I realised that I had been away from you for four years.'

She drew his hand up to lips that were quivering, salt with tears.

'My poor love … my poor darling … what have you suffered!'

He closed his eyes for a moment. Then he whispered:

'It's almost unbearable … seeing you again … and knowing about this other fellow.'

She said:

'Oh, Charles … Charles, don't think I forgot you. Or stopped loving you. Charles, my darling, I married Boyd Mansell two years ago … because I was so lonely and he had loved me so long and I grew fond of him. Charles, it wasn't horrible of me, was it? Oh, my God, if I'd ever *dreamed* you were still living, no other man would ever have taken me in his arms. You know that ... *say* that you know it, Charles.'

He opened his eyes and smiled at her.

'Yes, I know it, Veronica. I'm not holding it against you, darling. You couldn't remain a widow for the rest of your life. Why should you? You've much too young and lovely. You look so very young and beautiful to me, darling. You haven't altered as I have...'

'I haven't been through such hell, Charles.'

'So now,' he said under his breath, 'you are someone else's wife and ... you have a baby?'

She bowed her head. She felt almost ashamed of her motherhood: of the poor little Chip.

'Yes. He ... was born eleven months ago.'

He looked at her wonderingly.

'You ... with a son. Little Nic, it doesn't seem possible.'

'None of this seems possible,' she said in a shaking voice.

'The son I ought to have had,' he added.

She was near to bursting into bitter tears again. She flung both arms round his wasted form and buried her face against his neck.

'Charles, my darling, *don't* ... I can't bear it. It's too much for me. It's too awful ... *all*

419

of it ... for all of us.'

He folded her close, his lips against her hair. In Russia ... lying in the summer heat of the hospital ward to which he had been taken after the bombing, he had so often thought of her like this. In his imagination he had inhaled the remembered perfume of that dark, cloudy hair ... and felt the satin-smoothness of her exquisite skin. He had remembered every detail of their tremendous love for each other. He had wanted nothing but to get well ... to get back to her. He had waited with mad hope and joy for this home-coming. It had all been a tragic, futile waste of time; living as George Smith ... unknown ... unloved ... without hope. But he had to face up to the searing truth, now, that he had found Veronica again too late. She had gone from him. By virtue of the fact that she had lived with another man as his wife and borne his child, she had gone from him a very long way ... and could never really return.

She lay weeping, desolate in his arms. He kissed her hair and her throat and her long, wet lashes; as so often in the past he had tried to kiss away her grief and her tears. But it was a sorrowful embrace without passion. It was utterly sad.

'Charles, Charles...' she kept sobbing his name.

'It's all right, darling,' he said. 'Don't cry

any more. Don't cry for me, little Nic. I've seen you again, which is what I wanted. And if you are fond of Mansell ... and your child ... I am terribly glad, darling. You can settle down with them and be happy once I've gone. It won't be long, Nic...'

'Charles, I don't *want* you to die.'

'My love ... if I don't, there'll be the devil of a muddle,' he said with an attempt at a laugh, and ruffled her hair. 'Look up, darling. Smile at me. It's really damned funny, isn't it?'

She shook her head, inconsolable. She was crying not for herself or for Boyd and her son ... but for *him* ... whose once lithe, graceful body was now such a skeleton. His damp forehead and laboured breathing terrified her. He was dying ... she knew that he was.

'Oh, Charles, my darling,' she said in an agonized voice. 'Are you in much pain?'

'Just a bit ... but the doc's giving me some dope. You don't have to worry about me, Nic. I'm going to get up in the morning.'

'Oh, you *mustn't*...' she lifted her head and looked at him, aghast.

'Yes. I want to ... even if it's the last time I'm on my feet, Nic. I want to ... play a piano again ... play for you ... and hear you sing ... I want that more than anything in the world. Lady L. says there is a piano stored in Whitelands Hall. We'll go there ...

for an hour. We can ... can't we?'

Veronica ceased to argue or protest. She felt too exhausted.

'Of course we can. You shall do what you want, my darling,' she said.

He pushed the hair back from her tear-wet face.

'It's lovely to see you ... looking so well, my little Nic.'

'Charles, I've wanted you,' she said brokenly. 'You won't think because I married again that I didn't love you with all my heart and soul, will you, Charles? I almost died ... when you didn't come back.

'I believe you, darling.'

'I wrote a diary ... for you. You shall see it,' she said in a choked voice. 'I'm glad I kept it. It's locked away here in the cottage. You shall read it ... and see how much I wanted you.'

'I'd love to read it ... but I don't need any proof of your love, my little Nic.'

She drew the back of her hand across her hot eyes.

'I'm so ... muzzy about everything. Charles, whose wife *am* I?'

He gave a wry smile and drew her back into his arms.

'Still mine, my darling ... still mine...'

She could not think of Boyd. It was as though he had faded out of her mind and heart in this poignant hour and she was giving her whole soul to Charles Hallard. She kissed his face repeatedly.

'Charles ... don't leave me again,' she said with a voice of passionate pain.

But he said again:

'It would be the devil of a muddle if I lived, darling. But there isn't a hope for me.'

She could not speak any more but lay in his arms breathless and worn out with emotion. She closed her eyes. Her tears gradually dried up. This thing became a grief too deep for tears. She felt his well-remembered, sensitive touch upon her hair. She heard him whisper:

'Still mine ... for a little while longer, Nic...' And then... 'Talk to me, darling. Tell me ... everything ... about all our friends. How are Iris and Mervyn? What happened to Chaddy and Letty? Where are they? This will be a bit of a shock to everyone... I've played a dirty trick on you all, haven't I? I hope you didn't go into black or wear a little widow's veil – did you, sweet?'

He was trying to be gay. She knew it. She knew, too, that his grief was as deep and hopeless as hers. And after a few moments he stopped speaking and they lay silent in their tragic embrace.

When Lady Lowring stole in to see if either of them wanted anything, she saw Veronica put a finger to her lips and dis- engage herself gently from Charles's arms.

He had fallen sound asleep.

She went with her mother out of the room. Once outside she collapsed once more into heart-broken weeping. Lady Lowring, her own eyes full of tears, took the girl along to her own room.'

'Poor darling, this is too much for you...' she said. 'But you must try not to let it upset you too much. Dr Morgan says there is very little time left for poor Charles. Just let us make him as happy as we can. After all, you have Boyd to live for and your dear sweet little Giles.'

Veronica nodded mutely. The mention of her son did much to restore the balance of mind and emotion. She found herself thinking, suddenly, about the Chip; wondering if he had taken his milk from Audrey without giving her any trouble, and if, as usual, he had gone to sleep with his shabby lamb in his arms. Or if he would miss her.

Poor little Chip. Her poor baby. She had had no right to have him. No right to marry Boyd. (Poor Boyd, he must be feeling so wretched and lonely this evening at the 'Buckingham Arms'.)

But when she tried to unravel the tangle a little and asked herself what ought to be done next ... it all seemed an insoluble problem. She collapsed weakly on her mother's bed, too stupefied to think any further tonight.

*Letter from Veronica to Iris Williams, written from Monks Rest on June 24th, 1944*

'Iris darling,

'First of all my best thanks for the wonderful letter you wrote me and for dear Mervyn's kind messages. I knew it would be a shock to you both to hear about Charles. As you say, one thinks of it all with such mixed feelings. Here I am with *two husbands* ... both alive and both loving me. And I love them both. Oh, Iris, I feel so bottled up inside me I must write and tell you a little of all that has been happening these last few days.

'Charles has now been at Monks Rest for a week.

'Iris, he got up for a few days after he first arrived. He insisted on it although he looked dreadful and Mummy and I both tried to persuade him to stay in bed. Then Dr Morgan had a long talk with us and more or less said that it didn't matter whether Charles got up or not. He has so little time to live. This dreadful internal trouble which started in the prison camp in Germany is incurable. Dr Morgan says they can't operate. He is too far gone and his heart is affected. He has come back to me only to die, Iris. Isn't it tragic! My poor sweet Charles who used to be so gay, so swift on his feet, so full of brilliance. You wouldn't know him, Iris. Mummy didn't when she first saw him get out of that car, and although I was prepared for a change in him, it gave me a dreadful shock to see his white hair and poor cadaverous face. He is just skin and bone, Iris. He keeps saying he ought never to have come back and that it would have been best had he died in Russia, and I know Mummy agrees. She's like that. But I shall always thank God for letting me have my Charles with me again even for this little while.

'Iris, I loved Boyd when I married him two years ago and still do. I'm dreadfully mixed up inside me, darling. I love Boyd still. He has been absolutely magnificent over this affair – just as one would expect. All the Mansells have been divine to me. They have written such wonderful, comforting letters. Audrey is being my little son's mother for the time being. Mrs M. is her angelic self and wrote not only to me but to Charles to say that she is praying for him, and you know, I've told you, what a really religious woman she is. Prayer really means something to her. She told me not to worry or feel awful about Charles because nobody is to blame for anything that has happened. I told her what Dr Morgan said about Charles; that his chances of living this month out are very slender, so none of us, Iris, need worry about the *future* really. It is the *present* which is so grim.

'Yet I don't feel grim when I am with Charles. Iris, you know how much I always adored him. I haven't changed. My love for him was just laid aside – buried, so I thought – with him. Now it has resurrected with him – it is as fresh, as deep, as ever. I feel the old thrill of happiness when I sit beside him and hold his hand and we look at each other. We aren't melancholy. We laugh together over silly things just as we used to out in Lagos. We talk of our old "boy" Nicholas, of our bungalow; our parties; our wonderful musical evenings; our complete unity. We have slipped right back into the past. The thought of Boyd and the Chip doesn't hurt or distress either of us. I know it upset Charles dreadfully at first to think that I had married again and had a son. But now he asks all kinds of sweet questions about my Chip. He has seen all his photographs and takes the greatest interest in any anecdotes about him and his funny adorable ways, or about our Winston, the dachshund; and the life I've led since I've been Mrs Boyd Mansell. Charles laps it all up. He said last night:

'"I'm a ghost, darling, and like all ghosts,

will eventually vanish. Yes, you'll be able to banish me completely this time and I'll promise never to come back and haunt you again. But Mansell is the real thing, the husband who will love and look after you when I'm gone. He's the chap who really matters. If he hadn't been worthy of you I'd be dying a miserable man. But as I know how grand he is, I'm quite resigned. In fact, I'd like to meet him before I quit this mortal life … if he and you care to arrange it…"

'Well, Boyd's quite willing to see Charles. But I'll tell you about that later. Now I want to describe to you the day following Charles's return home. The telephone never stopped ringing. Mummy and I were almost demented. The newspapers had got hold of the news that there was an English survivor from the ship sunk four years ago, who had lost his memory and been in Germany as a prisoner, and fought with the Russians, and so on. A thrilling story, of course, for the Press. Especially as I had married again. Mummy tried so hard to stop it all. You know how she loathes publicity unless there's something to boast about, and she thinks there is a degree of shamefulness in my having two *living* husbands. Poor Mummy, she was agonised by the idea of the public knowing about this. Well, neither Charles nor I wanted it, either. Certainly Boyd in his capacity as a "Regular" didn't.

But you can't stop the Press. They are like ravening wolves when there is a "spicy story". That is why all those wretched pictorial papers had photographs of Charles and me and Boyd and those awful melodramatic stories and headlines. I expect you saw them the day before yesterday. It made us all shudder.

'"*Husband Returns After Four Years' Loss of Memory.*"

'"*Widow Who Has Married Again Meets Husband She Believed to be Dead.*"

'"*Brigadier's Wife Hears Her First Husband is Still Living.*"

'"*Modern Version of Enoch Arden.*"

'And so on.

'We couldn't stop them And, of course, old friends of Charles and mine rang us up. The Chaddons wired. Officials from Whitehall telephoned – wanting information from Charles about his experiences in Norway, Germany and Russia. But we had to put an end to it all and forbid them to trouble us any further by telling them frankly that poor Charles has not long to live, and that he *must* be left to die in peace.

'Well, that morning he got up, Iris darling, and using his stick, and leaning on my arm, walked with me to Whitelands. It was a warm, golden morning. The garden was lovely. The little lane looked cool and restful under its green boughs of the trees. The

429

church and the old graveyard had never looked more attractive. Charles drank it all in and said:

'"It's good to be alive still, Nic, my precious..."'

'I felt so dreadfully sad. I longed to cry. I've been wanting to cry ever since he came. But I have vowed not to do so. I *want* to be brave and to smile for him ... until the end.

'But oh, how ill he looked in the strong morning light, Iris. Such a bad colour; so thin and stooping. He walked so slowly. But we managed to get to the Hall. As we went in, he reminded me of all the happy days we had known there when Daddy was alive; our lovely wedding party; so many memories that are unforgettable for us both. (The one thing he hasn't asked me about and we haven't discussed is my actual wedding with Boyd.)

'Well, we found the Hall very deserted except for the caretaker and his wife. You know the Jacobses left a lot of their valuable furniture and pictures stored there after their son was killed. The Steinway was there, too, in the old drawing-room. The caretaker opened the shutters, let in the sunlight and drew the covers off the piano. Charles's eyes were shining. He looked almost young and well again.

'"I haven't touched a piano for all these years, Nic," he said.

'He sat down on the stool eagerly. I dusted the keys and smiled at him.

'"Go on, then, darling," I said. "It's like old times to see you at a piano."

'But his forehead was wet and his breath laboured and his poor thin fingers had little strength. I dreaded his being up and here, but anxious he should have whatever he wanted.

'He began to play.

'Oh … Iris … it was incredible … for me to stand there listening to that familiar touch which had lost nothing of its beauty and expression, although he was sadly out of practice. He started off with an old favourite of his … I honestly forget the name … but it is something rather slow and plaintive by César Franck. He always played it well. He played it beautifully then. His face was quite radiant and his eyes never left mine. I listened. I was drawn back to the days when he used to play for me on my old piano in this very room. Oh, Iris, then it was not a sad forlorn room with dust-sheets over piles of furniture in every corner, paintings swathed in covers, and floors bare of rugs, thick with dust in the revealing sunlight. It was warm and bright and full of Mummy's lovely things and the flowers she used to do so well. And Charles's hair was not white and thin. It was black and thick and he was strong and well and we were newly engaged, and I had never known such grief, such bitter pain, as I have suffered since those days. Can it be only five years ago? To me, it is five centuries.

'Charles went on playing ... drifting from one thing to another. I knew everything, of course .. and each piece he played held a particular memory ... brought back a particular time or place. I covered my face with my hands, trying not to give way to my emotions. I thought of my *other* love ... my poor Boyd, who was now in London at his job. There were flying bombs up there taking a toll of human life. I was afraid for him. I thought ... *how awful if God were to take both these two darling men from me.* I felt utterly depressed.

'Charles said:

'"Oh, damn ... that's wrong ... I keep playing wrong notes. It must jar on you, my love. I never used to do it. I ... just haven't any strength in these damned fingers. Nic, darling ... sing for me."

'I uncovered my face and looked at him.

'"Oh, Charles darling ... I can't..." I said.

'"Please, sweet," he pleaded. "I've so longed to hear your voice ... it was always like a chorister's ... so high and sweet and pure."

'"Darling," I said. "I haven't sung since ... since you left me. I ... can't."

'"Yes, you can," he smiled, and started to

432

play the old favourite: the opening bars of Bach's inimitable song, *"Jesu, Joy of Man's Desiring…"*

'I just could not help it then. I began to sing. The acoustics were queer in that room empty of curtains or carpets. My voice sounded queer to me. But Charles said:

'"Beautiful … so beautiful, darling … carry on…"

'I sang it through to the end because he asked it. But it was an awful effort. I felt hot and nervy and shaking from head to foot when I finished. I said:

'"Shall we go home now, darling?"

'But he had suddenly withdrawn his gaze from mine and, looking down at the keyboard, ran his fingers up and down with something of the old vigorous touch and broke into the main theme of "Veronica's Concerto". It is a difficult thing to play … but oh, such an exquisitely lovely theme. I always believed it to be Charles's greatest work, and had he finished it I am sure it would have brought him into great repute as a composer. But it is destined never to be finished, Iris. Charles will never work again. He did not get far with my Concerto. He flopped suddenly … over the keyboard.

'I ran to him, my heart in my mouth, and took him in my arms.

'"Darling, *darling*…" I said in anguish.

'I thought he was dead, Iris. Really I did.

But he was only "done in" … had half lost consciousness. He rallied and put an arm about me. He looked ghastly but he smiled at me. He whispered:

"'I'm … all right. But, maybe … all too much for me. Better go home. I … did so love … making music with you again…'"

'I called the caretaker. Between us we got him back to the cottage and up to bed. Iris, I don't think he will ever leave it again. Dr Morgan has just been and has said he is much weaker. We had a specialist, a Dr Saunderson from Harley Street, this morning, and he says it is only a question of days. My poor Charles is just petering out. They are not letting him suffer. They are giving him drugs. But it's pathetic to see him.

'Iris, my heart is being broken all over again. Yet I would not have missed being with him at the end for anything in the world. You know it always used to hurt me so to think of Charles drowning alone … in that dreadful way when he was torpedoed. But now he is with me. He won't be lonely. He'll go … knowing how much I still love him. He seems curiously happy and content when he wakes up and finds me beside him. Once or twice he has apologised for being a nuisance and keeping me away from my little boy. But I tell him how absurd that is. Please God I shall have Chip with me for many long years. For my lifetime. But I only have Charles for a little while.

'I had the most divine letter from Boyd last night. You can't believe what an understanding person he is, how unselfish. He says he is working so hard, he hasn't too much time to think, which is as well, but that he misses me dreadfully. He knows my rightful place is with poor Charles till the end. He said:

*"I don't want you to worry about me ... about us ... at all, darling. It will all be all right. One day you will be mine again. Meanwhile Mother and Audrey are watching over our boy. Just be as happy as you can, my darling, and do what you can for that poor fellow."*

'Could anybody be sweeter than Boyd? And oh, Iris, I wrote and told *him* not to be unhappy either, nor to imagine I am forgetting him, because I am not. I never could. I shall always love him and, as he says, one day I will be all his again. But these few days belong to Charles.

'Boyd is coming to see Charles. It is his wish as well as C.'s. How strange it will be ... my two husbands meeting. Both I have loved ... so differently. Iris, my mind and heart are in a bit of a turmoil. But I'm standing up to it pretty well. Mummy says she is agreeably surprised that I'm so composed.

You know, after the awfulness I went through when Charles was reported dead, I am much calmer now altogether. Those days of trial gave me some sort of spiritual strength I have never lost.

'Do you remember on the morning that I married Boyd, I had that queer presentiment and told you how awful it would be if Charles came back? You laughed at me at the time. I learned to laugh at myself. But there was something in it, after all. Subconsciously, I must always have known he would come back.

'Iris, I miss my baby. You know, I've looked after him since he was born. But I'm sort of *numb* about the Chip. Just as I am about Boyd. I can't think of anything much but Charles. Perhaps it is as well.

'Last night, some time after twelve, I got up because I couldn't sleep. I went into Charles's room. He had his lamp burning and was reading. He reads a lot. He sleeps only when he is drugged, poor angel. He ought really to go to a nursing home or have a hospital nurse, but when Mummy and I mentioned it, he begged us to let him stay here if he wasn't too much trouble, poor darling. He said he couldn't bear a home or strange faces. So we are nursing him between us. He's no trouble. There's nothing much to be done. And the few unattractive jobs that have to be performed we both do so willingly. We both want his last days to be as happy as possible. You wouldn't believe how sweet Mummy is to him, despite all I know she really feels about Boyd and me. She has turned up trumps. Mummy always does in moments of crisis.

'I found Charles reading my diary. I had unpacked it and given it to him. You remember that diary I was keeping after I first got back from Lagos, and which I finished the day before I married Boyd.

'Charles looked at me as I stole into his room and held out a hand.

'"How lovely to see you, darling," he said. "But you ought to be resting."

'I sat down on the edge of his bed and took those cold thin fingers and held them close to my breast. Terribly wan and pinched his face was in the lamplight, Iris. He said:

'"I couldn't sleep so I've been reading your diary again. I think I must have read it a dozen times already. It is the most wonderful expression of your sweet gentle self, my Veronica. And I am humble before it. I do not deserve that you should have loved me so much or been so hurt by my supposed death."

'I leant down and kissed his forehead.

'"You deserve all the love I could ever give you. It was never enough. Look what *you* gave to me, my darling," I said.

'He put up a hand and touched my hair.

'"Yes, I always worshipped you, Nic. Remember that."

'The tears I had tried so hard to check were welling in my eyes now. I blinked them back. I laid my head on the pillow beside his poor white scarred one. I whispered:

'"I'll never forget. Oh, darling, *darling* Charles…"

'He put an arm round me. We lay like that for a little while without speaking. I was happy and yet unspeakably sad. He seemed to find it so hard to breathe. It frightened me.

'I told him I wished to go down and make some tea for him but he said he did not want it. He only wanted me to stay like this with him for a while.

'"Holding you like this, in the depths of the night … in a quiet room where there are lovely things and flowers … that was the vision splendid for me when I lay ill in Russia, once my memory returned," he said.

'I put my cheek against his. He felt the tears and turned and kissed my lashes.

'"You mustn't cry for me, Nic. I'm so tired, darling. I don't want anything now but to sleep and forget … and that's what I'm going to do. Don't grieve, my love. You'll have your kind husband and your little boy. I'm quite happy about you."

'I nodded but could not speak, trying so

438

hard not to cry. But I felt tired and weak. I have been through a very gruelling time, Iris. You can imagine it.

'Charles, with difficulty, lifted my diary up and flicked a page or two of it over, then quoted from it:

'"*I will keep faith with you ... even while I lie in another man's arms...*' I love that, Nic. It's a heart-stirring thing for me to know that you feel that way. That even while you are with – the other fellow – you keep faith with me."

'I pressed my wet eyes against his cheek.

'"Darling..." was all I could say.

'He smiled and flicked over another page.

'"All that part ... about you and Mansell. I don't mind it. I sort of like to know you can be so happy with him."

'"Dear, *dear* Charles..." I said.

'Charles quoted:

'"*I always wanted you two to be friends. You will never meet on earth.*' But we shall, Nic. I'm glad about that. He went through a packet ... at Dunkirk, that chap."

'"Yes," I whispered.

'"And how hard you worked ... with your mobile canteen and in your W.V.S. show. My little Nic..."

'I said nothing, only mutely pressed my lips to his face.

'He read again from the diary:

'"*I descended with you for a time into the*

shadows…' Did you, my poor darling? Was it as bad as that?"

"'Yes, yes … it was terrible," I told him.

"'You said you *loved me beyond all people and all things'.*"

"'Yes," I said. "Yes, my darling … it is true."

'He closed the diary and sighed long and deeply. I raised myself on one elbow and looked at him. His eyelids had closed. So still he lay, so white and frail… I wondered how long before that gallant spirit would die out. Like a flame blown by the wind it was wavering, flickering … flickering, Iris…

'The diary slid from his hands. He was asleep.

'Iris, I'll finish this letter later on. It is so long as it is, it may as well be longer. Boyd is coming down to Monks Rest to stay tonight at the "Buck Arms". He is going to meet Charles tonight…'

*Veronica's letter to Iris, continued later that same day.*

'After all, my dear, Boyd and Charles will never meet on earth. There is little more to tell you. My poor Charles died this afternoon in his sleep. It was the most merciful thing that could have happened. I know it. He just passed from sleep into the final oblivion. He looks quite young again and so beautiful. He died with my diary clasped in his hands. It shall stay there with him. I think, right up to the end, he loved reading all that I had recorded for him.

'I am not going to grieve, Iris. One could never go through the agony of mind that I suffered four years ago over Charles twice. All I know is that I loved him devotedly until the end and that I'm glad he came back. Now he ... and all of us ... can rest in peace. It was what he wanted.

'Mummy is magnificent – taking everything on her shoulders. I am terribly tired. Good-bye for now,

'Your loving Veronica.'

8

*Letter from Boyd Mansell to his sister Gilly. Written from Lowndes Square.*

'Gilly dear,

'I phoned you this evening and John answered and told me he had sent you down to Chidding again because one of those wretched flying bombs got your windows and doors and that it was a bit too draughty for you in the home! Well, just as well you are back with Mother and all of them, and that you will be there to welcome my poor little Veronica when we go down this weekend. You know how she has always leant on you in hours of stress.

'You will have heard the news of poor Hallard's death. I would be a hypocrite not to admit that I personally heard it with a feeling of relief. For all our sakes it was the best solution to what at first seemed to me the devil of a problem. It has all been pretty tragic, Gilly. But at least it has had no lasting bad results. Veronica has taken it more calmly than I dreamed she would. She has astonished us all. There is a surprising lot of strength in that gentle spirit and small fragile body of hers. And I thank God that her life with me these last two years has helped in some curious way to strengthen her, for you know how badly she went to pieces, poor child, when Hallard was first presumed dead.

'Well, Gilly, I went down to Monks Rest as soon as I got the phone call from Lady Lowring. Rather sad, you know, I had meant to meet and chat with poor Hallard that night. I saw his dead body. He looked very tranquil and, as Veronica said, like a figure chiselled from marble, with his white hair and young face. Wonderfully handsome he must have been, poor fellow.

'Veronica was in bed. I saw her only for a moment. Lady L. thought it best for me not to stay. But V. put her arms about my neck like a kid and kissed me and said:

'"Thank you for everything you've ever done, my darling Boyd. Soon we'll be together again and all this will fade away."

'That heartened me a lot. To tell you the truth, Gillo, I've had several bad moments, wondering whether Hallard's return would alter the relationship between V. and myself, and spoil things for good and all. But now I know they won't. Once Hallard is buried – apparently he left a request that he should be cremated and that nobody should mourn or wear black or anything – it is Veronica's wish that we should be married again immediately. So at the end of this week we are going quietly, without another soul, to the Registrar's at High Wycombe. We will be married there. Strange but necessary, as Hallard's return automatically annulled our previous marriage. There are one or two legal formalities to be gone through but I've put it all in the hands of Lady Lowring's solicitors who are in High Wycombe, which will make everything run smoothly.

'On Sunday I'll bring Veronica down to Chidding. She says she is frantic to see the Chip again. Kiss him for his father. He never need know how his young fate hung in the balance for a few days, bless his heart.

'Somehow I feel that now the ghost of poor Hallard has finally been "laid" ... Veronica will be happier in every way.

'Meanwhile our troops in Normandy are

443

moving towards Victory. We have much to be thankful for. Life seems much sweeter tonight than it did yesterday – to me, at least!

'Good night, Gillo. All is well again with your brother,

'Boyd.'

The publishers hope that this book has given you enjoyable reading. Large Print Books are especially designed to be as easy to see and hold as possible. If you wish a complete list of our books please ask at your local library or write directly to:

**Dales Large Print Books**
Magna House, Long Preston,
Skipton, North Yorkshire.
BD23 4ND

This Large Print Book, for people
who cannot read normal print,
is published under the auspices of

# THE ULVERSCROFT FOUNDATION

... we hope you have enjoyed this book.
Please think for a moment about those
who have worse eyesight than you ...
and are unable to even read or enjoy
Large Print without great difficulty.

You can help them by sending a
donation, large or small, to:

**The Ulverscroft Foundation,
1, The Green, Bradgate Road,
Anstey, Leicestershire, LE7 7FU,
England.**
or request a copy of our brochure for
more details.

The Foundation will use all donations
to assist those people who are visually
impaired and need special attention
with medical research, diagnosis
and treatment.

Thank you very much for your help.